STEAM WHISTLE ALLEY

AN ADVENTURE IN AUGMENTED REALITY

BOOK ONE OF THE STEAM WHISTLE ALLEY SERIES

ISBN 978-1-7321892-0-1

Library of Congress Control Number: 2018939616

Bebuka Books

Seattle, WA

This is a work of fiction. Names, characters, businesses, places, events, locales, and incidents are either the products of the author's imagination or used in a fictitious manner. Any resemblance to actual persons, living or dead, or actual events is purely coincidental.

Cover Illustration © 2018 Book Covers Art

Editing by N.P. Browning and Dominion Editorial

www.joshuamason.net

www.steamwhistlealley.com

*For Mom and Dad. Making you proud
has always been my greatest motivation.*

Bebuka, udah baca belum?

Acknowledgements

I'd like to thank the online communities that provided invaluable support during the writing process. Paul Bellow and the litrpgforum.com crew really know how to make a guy feel welcome. Blaise Corvin and the good folks at the Gamelit Workshop always answer questions with brutal honesty, which I appreciate immensely. Zachariah Dracoulis and his group are always a welcome reprieve. All these folks are excellent authors. Check them out if you haven't.

A big thank you to Jeff Hays, Danny Katz and the crew at Soundbooth Theater. Every time I write Banjo I hear your take on him now. I think it's affecting his personality. Shout outs to Taj El, a great guy who went down the same royal road I did, to great success. Charles Dean, the bearded Bathroom Knight, font of knowledge and advice. Paul Campbell, king of the action scenes. Madmax, the greatest MUD wizard of all time. Thank you to the good folks at Royal Road, who make it possible for unknowns to start writing and get a following. And a big *terima kasih* to Mr. Russell, who read it with me from the beginning.

STEAM WHISTLE ALLEY

1. Steam Whistle Manor House
2. Archaeologists' Guild
3. Werewolves' Den
4. Summoner's Guild
5. Engineer's Guild
6. Brawler's Arena
7. Tower of the Thaumaturge
8. Alchemist's Guild
9. Gargoyles' Cathedral
10. Arborbound Glade
11. Airship Landing
12. Food Stalls
13. Beastmaster's Arena
14. The Uncommon Market
15. Wonkel's Hotel and Eatery
16. Thom's Machines
17. Dwebble's Potions

CHAPTER ONE: THE NUTJOB

I was sitting outside a small coffee shop by my apartment when across the street from me, I first saw the lunatic that would ultimately change my life.

He wore canvas pants, a white long-sleeved shirt, a leather vest and black gloves, but the oddest part of his attire was the pair of brass and leather goggles strapped around his head. Attire like that in a city like Seattle didn't strike me as being too unexpected; my city was known for being just a little outside of ordinary as far as fashion and attitudes went. What really threw me was how he shouted, "Get back here, you bastard!" as he ran down the street, leaping over a bench at a bus stop while holding his gloved right hand over his head. As he landed, he brought his hand around, slashing at the air as if with an invisible sword.

I gulped the last of my coffee and picked my phone up off the table, tapping the camera icon to record this nutjob. He moved toward the far end of the street, so I stood up and jogged along the side of the road, keeping pace as I recorded him through the throng of pedestrians, road vehicles and hovercars that passed by.

He continued to slash, thrust and parry his way down the sidewalk with his invisible sword against his likewise unseen foe, much to the amusement of the window shoppers and other passers-by. Occasionally he shouted more profanities or laughed boisterously.

This recording was for sure going to score me some serious views on the vidfeeds.

I picked up my pace to keep up as he turned a corner onto Fifth Avenue, continuing his brisk shuffle as he switched in and out of what looked like a sword fighter's stance.

I had personally taken part in a great deal of swordplay in a few of the VR games I'd played, so while I wasn't an expert, I did recognize the stylized form and movement and judged that this man wasn't randomly swinging away willy-nilly.

As I continued to record, he kept up his onslaught, not even pausing as he reached into his vest pocket and took out a handful of change. He dropped the coins into the cup of a homeless man who sat sprawled on the sidewalk leaning against a tree, staring up open-mouthed at this one-man melee before him.

Then, one wide horizontal slash turned into a downward thrust, and the man erupted with a triumphant cheer. I looked on, not even trying to suppress my grin as the man sheathed his 'sword' then knelt on the sidewalk. His hands reached out before him as if he were searching through leaves, or, as the gamer in me thought, the corpse of his opponent. He stood up, slipped something into his pocket, and adjusted his goggles as he crossed the street to the honks of autonomous cars and taxis.

The man paused in front of the twin rotating doors of a skyscraper and appeared to speak with a nonexistent person. After a few seconds, the man looked back to the street, then disappeared through the doors.

I stopped recording and put my phone in the front pocket of my jeans as I waited for a gap in the traffic. This man, while eccentric, did not appear to be one of the typical crazies that inhabited my city. Although his clothing was odd, he was well dressed, and he didn't exude that aura of danger that made the hair on the back of my neck stand up whenever I encountered one of the more undesirable types downtown. My interest was piqued, and as an opening appeared in the traffic, I crossed the street and found myself in front of the rotating doors he had just walked through.

As I entered, I saw a large reception desk in the middle of the spacious, marble-floored entrance. I could still make out the people and cars outside through the smoky glass walls, which dimmed the bright daylight into a comfortable, warm glow. To the right, a pair of escalators led up to and down from a second-floor veranda with lounge areas and coffee shops, although the entrance lobby stretched up otherwise unobstructed for at least four stories. To the left of the reception desk, a short hallway held banks of elevators and a directory of businesses. The swashbuckler, however, was nowhere to be seen.

I approached an overweight, grey-haired security

guard at the reception desk as he was making notes in a logbook. "Hey... um... did you see a guy wearing goggles and a leather vest come through here?"

The man looked up from his book and gave me an annoyed glare, before looking down at my hand resting on the counter. Thick burn scars covered it nearly to the elbow. As was often the case upon seeing my disfigured hand, the guard's expression softened.

"Sorry, I didn't see anyone like that. Whaddya mean, like ski goggles?" the guard asked as he leaned forward and looked around the lobby.

"No, like... never mind," I replied. "Thanks for your time."

I left the reception desk and approached the business directory boards over by the elevators. I took out my phone and snapped a few pictures of them; the building had eighty-eight stories, and while some floors had fifteen or twenty small businesses and practices listed, others were taken up in their entirety by one or two larger ones.

While the sword fighter might very well turn out to be a cosplay aficionado, something nagged at me about him. The more I thought about it, the more it seemed like he was playing a game, his motions calculated and purposeful. I had made many of the same moves in my gaming career. The most probable scenario was that Mr. Nutjob had spent a little too much time in his immersion rig, and the lines between the real and the virtual had started to blur, or more likely, had been destroyed.

Giving one last glance to the directory, I decided to

head home and look over the video and pictures I had recorded.

As I walked to my apartment, I replayed the events of the hour in my mind. I had entered the coffee shop I'd been going to for the last year-and-a-half to get my morning fix. My favorite barista's name was Jeni, and she wore her purple hair in a pixie cut. Whenever I came in, she always had a warm smile for me and liked to replace the 'O' in Jacob with a little heart when she wrote my name on the cup. I know, they smile at everybody, but the ones she gave me felt genuine. I kept promising myself I'd ask her out one of these days, but I had just wrapped up a beta-test on a full-immersion VR game, Galaxy's Edge, and up until now had almost zero free time.

Not only had this multiplayer space opera paid the rent and kept me in the latest gaming gear, but access to the adult areas of the simulation also let me fulfill some of my more...pressing desires. Still, I don't care what the technology forums say—virtual nookie is no substitute for the real thing.

All thoughts of romantic interludes had disappeared when I saw the strange man flailing down the street.

My apartment was five blocks down the hill, near the picturesque Seattle waterfront. I never utilized the hover shoes or other methods of self-propulsion that pedestrians seemed to favor these days, preferring instead the exercise that came with good old trudging up and down the hills of downtown Seattle. If I had to go further, I'd hail a Lyft or a Hovercab, using the time alone to work on projects or catch up on the news.

I entered the vintage brick building, reinforced against earthquakes and erosion with modern architectural supports, and greeted Lenny the Doorbot.

"How's it going, Lenny?" I inquired as I approached the elevators.

"Good evening, sir," Lenny responded in a droll British voice. He looked every inch the stereotypical butler, in a pressed tuxedo and perfectly tied bowtie. The only thing that gave his lack of humanity away was the missing feet—the cuffs of his slacks truncated in a black platform with two black wheels the size of dinner plates on either side, a blue ring glowing in the center of each. He rolled over to me. "While you were out, my crew and I cleaned and sanitized your room, watered your plants, and fed your monkey. If you should need anything else, please do not hesitate to contact me."

"What would I do without you, Lenny?" I asked with a smile as I entered the elevator.

As the doors closed, I heard Lenny reply, "I do not know, sir."

I pressed the button for the 14th floor, and the doors opened about two seconds later. I walked down the hall to my apartment and lay my hand on the door, which opened with a beep when it recognized me. The lights came on, and as usual, Banjo screeched a greeting at me before running up my leg and throwing his arms around my neck.

Banjo was a squirrel monkey, a biosynth with short tan fur and bright, beady eyes. Biosynths weren't made of meat, but they replicated most biological functions, including breathing and eating—although they were tweaked a bit to make care easier in domestic situations. Banjo didn't exhibit true monkey-like behavior—he wasn't territorial or prone to streaks of scat-throwing wildness, but instead, he displayed the general monkeyness that humans wanted from a pet primate. That, and he knew how to use the toilet.

He smiled at me and picked at something in my hair, which he promptly put in his mouth, then leaped down to the counter as I entered the kitchen.

I opened a cabinet to grab a glass. "Lexi, do I have any messages?"

A monitor on the kitchen wall turned on, showing a short-haired brunette woman floating through a star field. "Hi, Jacob," she said. "You were outbid on your auction for the antique replica of the Ocarina of Time. I sent a message to your phone—didn't you get it?"

I swore under my breath. I'd been bidding on a seventy-year-old promotional piece for the first Zelda game released on the Nintendo 64. "No, I was...preoccupied."

"Well, I'll keep my eyes open. I'll find you one," Lexi said. "Need anything else?"

"No, I'm good. Thanks."

I filled up an ice water from the dispenser on the front of my fridge and took it into the living room, taking a moment to enjoy the majestic view of the Olympic Mountains that was afforded me by the transparent sliding doors that led to my patio. My apartment cost me a pretty penny, but it was worth it, and the rent only amounted to about a third of my monthly income. I caught a glimpse of my reflection in the glass, noting that my dark hair was getting shaggy, almost down to my shoulders. I needed a trim soon. A shave wouldn't hurt either. I glanced for a moment at the white streak over my right temple, thinking back to the incident that gave it to me. I forced it out of my mind and tucked the streak behind my ear. I had more important things to think about—like the man I'd seen on the street. I sat down in my plush leather office chair to review the footage. Banjo immediately ran over and jumped in my lap.

I slipped on my visual interface—styled after the eye gear worn by Geordi LaForge on Star Trek, The Next Generation—and tapped a spot on the side to wake it up. I loved old science fiction and geeked out on adding nostalgic pieces to my collection whenever I could. If the item was somehow functional, all the better. This one was called a VISOR in the nearly century-old sci-fi show, short for Visual Instrument and Sensory Organ Replacement, so that was how I affectionately referred to mine. Although it didn't replace any of my organs, it did afford me full VR, which I used mostly for browsing the web as well as viewing and manipulating any images I might have gathered.

The video I'd taken earlier had become available on my home computer as soon as I recorded it. I made a few hand gestures to bring up the file and began to watch.

I let the video play through in its entirety, watching with amusement as the man danced across the sidewalk with singular intent, fighting his imaginary foe. The visor utilized top-of-the-line retinal projection technology, which along with bone conduction audio made watching the video nearly indistinguishable from when it occurred. The only thing that broke the immersion was the fact I was currently sitting comfortably and petting a monkey.

On the second play-through, I noticed something I hadn't before. Near the hotel's glass doors, the man had turned around and looked directly at me. He even smirked slightly before disappearing inside the building. With a wave of my hand I rewound the footage and paused it, so he was smirking at me again, and with another couple of gestures, I zoomed in for a closer look. My footage had captured every angle of the man at some point, so I was able to manipulate the still, three-dimensional image to examine him from all sides in incredible detail. As I rotated the image, I saw his rusty brown hair was tied back in a leather strap. He wore a single, tiny silver gear on his left earlobe, and his upper lip and chin sported a thin handlebar mustache and goatee that fit his swordsman persona nicely. But it wasn't his face I was interested in.

I zoomed in further until his goggles took up most of the field of view. The resolution was still impeccable; I could make out reflections of people walking down the street in the lenses. These goggles were no prop, and while designed to look old and rustic, they were quite technologically advanced. The lenses were clear, so I could see the man's brown eyes behind them. The thick brass cylinders that held the lenses were adorned with tiny knobs, gears, levers and dials, and the wide, dark leather strap that held them in place looked worn but sturdy, fastening in a buckle behind his head. Surrounding the outside of either eyepiece were three tinier lenses, which I supposed were cameras.

Whatever they were, I needed those goggles.

Zooming back out until his whole face was again visible, I snapped an image, and then brought up my browser with a crook of my finger.

"Facebase," I said, and the browser complied. Facebase was a popular site that let you identify pretty much anyone from just an image, telling the user everything there was to know about that person, including address, place of employment, hobbies, family members, sexual orientation—everything. In its early days it was frowned upon by most of the population, but over the decades, as society became increasingly interconnected, privacy became much less of a concern.

I pasted his image into the search bar, and the computer thought for a whole ten seconds as it searched through the four billion, give or take, profiles it had in its databases.

No match.

Hmm. Interesting.

It wasn't unheard of to have one's profile removed from Facebase and similar sites, although it cost a good chunk of netcoin. I had mine removed soon after I began working as a freelance beta tester—powerful scripts existed which could scour the web and look for any image or likeness of a person and remove them permanently. Personally, I liked to keep my roguish good looks when I played in character. Unfortunately, it was common for opponents in-game to try and find the real-life users behind the avatars to harass them if the user rubbed them the wrong way. Facebase not returning a match meant that Slashy McSwordsman here, or the people he worked for, could afford to have his likeness wiped from the web.

Tapping my visor off, I raised it to my forehead and took a drink of water

So maybe he's not a nutjob. But what is he then?

Banjo squeaked at me from his nest in my lap, and I gave him a quick scratch under his chin.

I put the glass of water back on my desk and lowered my visor again, bringing up the directory board for the building he'd entered, Allen Tower, which at eighty-eight stories was the fourth tallest in Seattle. The directory listed hundreds of businesses, corporations and practices, from janitorial services and taxidermists to VR lounges and massage parlors. A firm called ARGO Enterprises took the top three floors. I had never heard of them.

I opened my browser and with a voice command brought up my search engine to find the company. The first link that came up was ARGO's home page. I opened it, and a large clock materialized in front of me, the hands pointing at five minutes to twelve. The inner clockwork was visible through the center of the device, and I could see the gears turning, some rapidly and others so slowly I wasn't really sure that they moved at all.

But it was the writing floating above the clock that sent my heart racing and a smile across my face. In neon green letters were the words *ARGO Enterprises*, and underneath that, *Augmented Reality Gaming Online*. On the bottom in the same garish font—*Steam Whistle Alley, New Seattle. Welcome to Panmachina AR.*

This info hit me like a sledgehammer.

Augmented Reality Gaming Online.

This was my forte! This was what I did for a living. Well, three of those four words anyway. I'd been gaming online since I was six, and beta testing VR games for the past five years. It paid the bills, and all the contracts I'd signed, in addition to my salary, allowed me to put any items I'd accumulated in-game on the auction sites once the game hit the open market. The gig paid decently and was notoriously hard to get into. But a few lucky breaks, and here I was.

Augmented Reality had been around since the turn of the century, and despite all the advances in VR, had never lived up to its potential as a gaming platform. The first big breakout utilizing the technology had been *Pokemon Go,* which allowed players to capture an array of monsters that appeared against a backdrop of whatever the player happened to be facing. Certain monsters existed in certain geographic areas, and the game was widely lauded for bringing video games outside and getting the players up and moving.

But in the decades that followed, the industry focused on virtual reality, to the point that most VR games nowadays were indistinguishable from the real world—if the real world included orcs, aliens, and impossibly proportioned characters. Augmented reality games still came out once in a while, but they mostly involved a cheap set of AR goggles and a plastic blaster that let schoolchildren shoot imps on the playground. All serious gaming took place in VR.

I spent the next hour searching for anything else I could find about the company but came up almost empty. It had incorporated a week ago and just moved into the offices in Allen Tower over the past five days. The only name attached to the company was I.M. Montebalt.

Further searching in Facebase and elsewhere brought up nothing else attached to this name. I was pretty sure it was a pseudonym—either that or the dude was a ghost. Sighing, I tapped off my visor and set it on my glass desktop, before rising to my feet. Banjo scampered up my chest and perched on my right shoulder.

"What do you think, Banjo?"

He cocked his head and chittered at me as I walked over to the sliding glass doors, opened them, and stepped out onto my balcony. Banjo lowered himself down and propped on the corner of the railing like a fuzzy little gargoyle. We stared at the snow-capped Olympics for a while, stark against the blue summer sky.

I had to find this guy.

STEAM WHISTLE ALLEY

CHAPTER TWO: THE INVITATION

I awoke early the next day and started my morning routine. While showering, I decided my best course of action was to do a bit of espionage—which in this case meant more coffee and another visit with Jeni. After I finished primping, I put on some of my nicer clothes, said goodbye to Banjo, shut down my apartment and headed out. With a spring in my step, I took the elevator down and waved to Lenny as I walked through the lobby.

"How do I look, Lenny?" I smiled at him.

He pivoted to face me and rolled closer, face expressionless. "You look smashing, sir. Does sir have a date?"

"Nope," I replied, "I just have a feeling it's going to be a good day. You ever get that feeling?"

"I can honestly say I have never had that feeling," he replied dourly. "But if I ever do, I shall inform you posthaste."

I shook my head and smiled, then headed out into the street. It was July, the sun was out, and it was pleasantly warm, with a cooling breeze coming off Puget Sound. I started thinking of Jeni as I worked my way up the hill towards the coffee shop. Her eyes forming little crescent moons whenever she smiled. The way she filled out her apron.

It's been way too long.

I reached the coffee shop with a slight rush of anticipation, and after opening the door, sauntered up to the counter.

Where I was greeted by a skinny, bearded man.

"What can I get you?" he asked, revealing crooked teeth.

My smile trickled from my face. "Um... iced mocha, four shots. Tall one if you could." I tapped my thumb on the sensor built into the counter to pay, took my drink, and headed towards a seat at one of the patio tables.

As I sipped my coffee and watched the other customers going about their day, I replayed the swordsman's antics in my mind—the leaping, slashing, ducking and parrying. Granted, I was more of a blaster man than swordsman, but after all I had seen in VR, it wasn't hard for me to mentally insert enemies into yesterday's skirmish.

This must be the next step up in augmented reality, but the logistics alone must be a nightmare.

I had so many questions if I was right. Apparently, the swordsman could see the world around him—couldn't he? He dodged pedestrians, leapt over obstacles. Were these visible to him or recreated virtually? How did he interact with other people in the real world? What did they look like? Was this a quest-based MMORPG, or was this merely running around looking like an idiot in the public's eye while playing some first-person hack and slash? I had a hundred more questions, but I wasn't going to find out anything lounging on a coffee shop patio. The swordsman might never make another appearance here.

Time to go knock on their front door.

I hustled back to Allen Tower and entered the spacious lobby, which appeared especially enormous with all the groups of people mingling about and the sunlight streaming through the plate windows.

I walked across the marble floor and into an empty elevator, selecting the 86th floor. ARGO took up the 86th, 87th, and 88th floors, so I decided to start at the bottom.

The doors opened a minute later to a long, darkened hallway running straight ahead of me. LED lights ran on either side of a dark grey carpet, and they lit up the walls in a deep purple hue. Silvery light cascaded down from more LED lamps set into the ceiling, giving an almost haunted feel to the corridor. The walls were featureless aside from pools and ripples created by the floor lights, with no doors or artwork on either side. When I stepped into the hallway, the doors closed behind me.

A plain, light grey door waited at the end of the hall. Mounted to its right was a hand print sensor with a muted display the size of an envelope. The hallway seemed like it was way longer than it should have been for having just one door—maybe they were going for effect.

I walked towards the door, feeling a bit nervous. As I reached it, the small monitor woke up and projected a half-sized, three-dimensional head of a bald man directly in front of it. The utterly hairless head looked up at me, and I took an involuntary step back. He, too, wore goggles—silver frames with a black strap.

"Can I help you?" the head asked, a hint of amusement in its voice. "What's your name?"

I realized I hadn't planned what to do or say when I got up here, so the fact there was a head asking me questions put me at ease in an odd sort of way, although I was still nervous.

"J-Jacob Tutor," I replied. I don't know what I expected, coming up here, but this wasn't it.

"Ah, Jacob Tutor," the head repeated. "Please place your hand on the sensor below me." He gestured downward with his nose.

I took a step forward and complied. A vertical blue beam swiped from left to right under my hand and made two short beeps. I took my hand back.

"So, Jacob, why are you here?" the head asked.

"Well, I... yesterday I saw a guy dressed in some strange, vintage-looking clothes, wearing goggles. He was fighting off an invisible monster of some sort, I think. I followed him here."

"Ah," replied the head. "I see. So, what is it that you think you saw?"

"I'm pretty sure he was playing a game in augmented reality," I answered. "I've been around the block a few times in the VR world, so I recognized what he was doing. Even saw him collect his loot."

The head chuckled. "I guess our little lure worked."

I quirked an eyebrow.

"Jacob Tutor, you've been involved in the testing of eight different VR games, utilizing everything from VR goggles and haptic setups to total immersion rigs."

Great. Guess all that money I'd spent erasing myself from the web hadn't done much good. These guys obviously had the money to dig deep enough, but he'd just learned my name two minutes ago.

"Seven years ago, you were approached by Eyecandy Entertainment, who you found out had been scouting you during your entire high school career," the head continued. "They invited you to beta-test Arousia Online, even bought you a basic VR rig. You, a hormonal teenager fresh from graduation, were more than happy to accept a healthy college-grad level salary to playtest a virtual reality massively multiplayer online role-playing game chock full of adventure, treasure, and scantily clad women. In the eight months you worked on it before release, you found more bugs and glitches than anyone else in the department, and potentially saved the company millions of dollars."

I blinked, in a mild state of shock. How in the world...

"The money you made from Arousia Online allowed you to upgrade your rig, and you were soon offered your second job, this time with Bytemark Interactive, playtesting that wonderful Gothic nightmare, Deathworld. Your success rate in your first job gave you a major bargaining chip, and in addition to your salary, you demanded permission to sell any gear you acquired from beta on the online auction sites once the game fully released. This income dwarfed your salary, so you could afford to live alone in a mid-range downtown apartment with a gorgeous view and a cheeky monkey."

"How the hell do you know all of this?" I shouted at the floating head. Truthfully, I was more amazed than angry.

The head ignored my little outburst as it continued its speech "Your success continued over the next three years. You are currently working on the sci-fi MMORPG Galaxy's Edge, although things are now wrapping up and you spend the greater part of your days bonding with Banjo. You enjoy your life as a loner but are trying to work up the courage to ask Jeni on a date." The head grinned wide enough to take up half the display. "How did I do?"

"Pretty darn well," I acquiesced, a little spooked.

"Listen," he said, perhaps sensing my discomfort, "the reason we know so much about you is because we like you. We think you are the best at what you do, and we'd like you on the team."

"What team is that?" Jacob asked.

"We'll talk about it more tomorrow if you are interested," the head replied with another smile. "Tomorrow morning at, say, eleven-ish. Just come up to the 88th floor, and we'll talk details. Oh, and bring your monkey."

And with that, the holographic head winked out of existence, and I was alone in the quiet hallway.

I thought about his offer as I walked back down the hallway. Strapping into a VR rig was one thing, but all that crazy running around was quite another. Although the games did an admirable job at making it *feel* like the player was getting in a good workout, in reality, they were just lying in plastic tubes with electrodes strapped to their muscles, flexing them at regular intervals so the body wouldn't atrophy. This was different. If I played this, I would have to ration my energy, replenish it with real food and drink. I found myself looking forward to the change.

I entered the elevator, and the doors closed. My reflection in the polished metal stared back at me, and my eyes went to the white streak over my temple. The memory came crashing back.

I still lived with my parents when I graduated high school and got my first job with Eyecandy Entertainment. They had no idea what the game was about. I told them it was a typical RPG, filled with dragons and quests and whatnot. It *was* an RPG, but if they'd known some of the depravity I embraced in there, they probably would have kicked me out of the house.

Sometimes I wish they had.

My little sister, Holly, was eight at the time. My parents left on a business trip and tasked me with watching her. I told them I'd only enter my rig after she went to bed, and for a couple of days, I kept my promise. On the third day though, I plopped her in front of the television in her room with a sandwich and a glass of juice and jacked into the rig to continue a...session...from the night before. I lost track of time. Three naked alien women and the raging hormones of a teenager will do that.

When I smelled the smoke, I thought it was something

in the simulation. Even when I felt the heat, that too was easily explained by the obscene activities I was involved in. Soon, though, the heat became too much to bear, and I knew something was wrong.

I logged out and threw open the lid to my unit and was instantly choked by the thick smoke blanketing my room. I climbed out and ran to my door, searing my palm on the doorknob as I opened it. The hallway was an inferno. White-hot walls of flame separated me from the door to Holly's room, ten meters down the hall. Staying low, I crawled through the hellfire to her door where a flaming piece of the ceiling had fallen, blocking my path. Using my forearm, I heaved against it, numbed to the pain from adrenaline and the *need* to get to Holly.

I crawled inside, but the smoke made it impossible to see anything. White spots swam frantically in front of my eyes. Then I heard Holly cough. She was under the bed. I crawled to her and reached under the flaming mattress, yanking her out by her arm. Her pajamas were on fire, as was my shirt, but I blocked out the pain and scooped her up, then ran across the room to her broken bedroom window. With the little remaining strength I had, I hurled her limp form through it into the yard, and then tumbled out after her.

It was raining, and the wet grass felt like heaven against my scorched skin. I climbed on top of Holly, smothering the remaining flames on her pajamas, and then passed out.

A day later I woke up in the hospital, hazily opening my eyes to the tear-streaked face of my mother. She wanted to embrace me, but my left arm and a good portion of my side and right leg were wrapped in bandages. She settled for a kiss on my forehead, her tears dripping onto my face as sobs wracked her body.

My father was in the ICU with Holly, I learned. Third-degree burns covered eighty percent of her body. The doctors said she was in a coma.

They never learned of my negligence that day, and I had never been able to bring myself to tell them. They thought of me as a hero, and it's something I still hated myself for. My parents haven't been the same since, and Holly...

Holly's still in the coma.

The elevator doors opened.

I spent the rest of the day at a waterfront park by my apartment, thinking about the offer, my future, and my past. I called my mother—she was doing well, she said, and informed me that Holly's brain continued to show signs of activity. I had been wiring my parents money, so they could keep Holly at home. It also helped cover the cost of the reconstructive surgery. Her face and most of her torso had healed as much as they were going to, and Mom said now she barely looked as if there'd been an accident.

The doctors had healed most of the burns on my body, but I refused to let them treat my forearm and hand. My parents didn't understand why, and neither did I, to be honest.

I pushed the thoughts of the incident way down inside, where they had been hiding for the last couple of years. I would make it right someday. For now, I had to concentrate on my work. Ever since the incident, VR had been more of an escape from reality than a game. It wasn't fun, exactly. More of a medicine, a coping mechanism.

As the sun set over the Olympics, turning the sky brilliant shades of orange and red, I promised myself I would have fun again. Holly would want me to.

CHAPTER THREE: THE 88TH FLOOR

I went home, made a cup of tea, slipped on my VISOR and spent the rest of the day checking my online auctions for the gear I'd acquired while testing Galaxy's Edge. The crown jewel of my current auction listings was a Dartera class Battleskiff, a highly maneuverable starship built for a crew of five or six, with state-of-the-art shielding and armaments. It was currently going for about 54,000 netcoin, but I expected it to finish for at least twice that— enough to pay for my place for the entire next year. It currently had 822 watchers with 23 hours and 57 minutes left to go. Hell yes.

Banjo crawled into my lap, curled into a croissant shape and chittered contentedly as I scratched his head until he fell asleep. I browsed through the remaining items I had yet to list on the auction sites. Probably another 50,000 in netcoin there, too.

For once in my life, I had more money than I knew what to do with. I could afford a bigger place, perhaps get my own vehicle, maybe even a summer timeshare in the Cascades.

Raised modestly, I'd never really seen myself living a flashy lifestyle; Mom and Dad never had much money and were now living simple retiree lives on the east coast.

It was only four hours by tube to travel across the country, but I still hadn't been out to see them in nearly a year. I'd have to go soon. For now, I wired them another 5,000 netcoin, and dropped 5,000 into the account I reserved for my collections.

I kept my treasures in a heated storage unit in the industrial district on the south side of the city. The unit was furnished and very comfortable, and I often fell asleep there on one of the oversized sofas while playing the same games my grandfather had played decades ago. The cavernous room held display rack after display rack of every video game I could get my hands on. Up until about fifty years ago, video games were still available on cartridges, CDs, and DVDs. The oldest of these were nearly a century old—I tried to find games in their original packaging wherever possible, and now had over 3,400 pieces. They weren't just for display; I enjoyed playing the old classics, mostly the pixelated RPGs that would give rise to current games. The Dragon Quest and Phantasy Star series were my favorites— I studied Japanese in school and was able to play the original versions before they got ported to the states. I tried to play them on period-accurate televisions when possible and had about eight different televisions and monitors in the unit.

With a flick of my finger, I closed out of my auction listings and opened a new field to browse for new pieces to add to my collection. I placed a bid for a copy of Earthbound in the original packaging for the Super Nintendo. I had a copy already, but the box was damaged and didn't include the full-sized player's guide and original scratch-and-sniff stickers, so this was well worth the nearly 20,000 netcoin price. I browsed a few more listings before logging off and placing my VISOR on the desk.

"Get up, Banjo," I said.

He complied sleepily, and I got to my feet and stretched. He scurried to the bedroom to resume his slumber, and I walked out to the patio to take in the nighttime air and have a good think. Leaning on the railing, I pulled my e-cig from my pocket and took a puff of berry-flavored vapor while staring at the Seattle waterfront. Shades of blue and green lit up the Ferris wheel tonight, and the waterfront buildings' lights cast rippling reflections on the surface of Puget Sound.

One thing was for sure—that bald head sure knew a lot about me. Where there's a will, there's a way, I guess.

He said he wanted me on the team, so I guessed the upcoming meeting was more of an orientation than anything else. But this was unfamiliar territory for me. Up until now all my testing involved jacking into my rig and immersing myself in the game. This time, I'd probably have to flail around like a weirdo in public. Sure, I never hid my nerdiness, but I was never the type to draw attention to myself in public. What kind of game was it anyway, if it even was a game as I knew it? Maybe the whole purpose was to gild the proverbial lily, put a spit shine on the real world to make it less depressing. Lord knows it could use it. Speculating was getting me nowhere, so I put it out of my mind and wandered to my bedroom to go to sleep.

The next morning, I made myself a cup of coffee and went back out to the patio. Another beautiful morning. Seattle summers are glorious, not cloyingly hot like in the rest of the country, and the salt-scented breezes coming off Puget Sound always helped wake me up. I spent a lot of time out there when I wasn't working— the view was peaceful and helped me do my best thinking. The familiar outline of the Olympic Mountains had seared itself into my mind, and just seeing it centered me in a way, made me feel alert. So, it had become my morning ritual to come out here and recline in my deck chair, enjoy my coffee and a vape, and bounce ideas off Banjo.

As if sensing my thoughts, the monkey chittered and joined me on the patio, jumping up to his usual perch on the railing to enjoy the view with me.

"Morning, buddy," I said. "Sleep well?"

Banjo gave me another friendly chitter and proceeded to groom his crotch. No modesty, this one.

"So whaddya think, Banjo, this sound like a good job?"

"Chk-chk-chrrruuuk," he answered.

"Yeah, it does, doesn't it? But I'm not sure how I feel about the whole AR thing. Feels like they're asking me to switch from flying helicopters to airplanes. It's a whole new system," I mused.

Banjo stayed silent.

I took a puff on my e-cig. "I mean, I know where I am in VR. In the back of my head, I know I'm not really in the bottom of a lava-filled cavern fighting spider-apes or whatever. I'm safe and sound in my rig. But this... this looks like it's going to be in the real world. In front of real people. On real streets. Will people even play something like that? I love the idea, but a lot of gamers I know wouldn't make it to level three if they actually had to *walk* while playing."

Banjo hopped from the railing onto my lap, where he proceeded to groom me. Some primal part of me liked this particular habit of his. There was something soothing about having a monkey check your hair for nits. I know; I'm odd.

Banjo promptly put a fleck of something from my hair into his mouth.

"Still, I should at least hear him out. And he wants you there too. Don't ask me why. Maybe you can carry my gear for me," I quipped.

Banjo followed me inside as I got up and stretched, then proceeded to shower and get ready for the day. At 10:30 I made my way out the door with Banjo on my shoulder and worked my way towards the Allen Building.

I entered the elevators, this time pushing the button for the 88th floor. As I did, a small panel slid open to the left of the bank of buttons, and a female voice asked for another handprint identification. As I pressed my hand to the cool glass, the voice said, "Thank you, Mr. Tutor," and the elevator began its ascent.

A minute later, the doors slid open to reveal another hallway and the same grey and purple motif as the 86th floor, leading to another door at the end. For a second, I thought I had entered the same floor as before, but this one had framed prints spaced evenly along the sides. The first picture on my left was printed on old yellowed parchment, the dark amber lines depicting an abstract array of gears and pulleys. On my right, a man in a black top hat with a robust black mustache piloted a hot-air balloon over what looked like a 19th-century city. London maybe.

I reached the door, which opened for me as I approached, revealing the bald man from the day before, standing upright with hand outstretched—this time in the flesh. He looked like he had in the hologram, although now his goggles were perched on his head, revealing a pair of bright and unnaturally blue eyes.

"Jacob! Welcome to ARGO Enterprises. Man, I'm glad you made it. I'm Ignacius M. Montebalt, but please, call me Iggy." He turned his attention to my monkey. "And hello to you, Banjo."

Banjo smiled and waved a fuzzy hand in greeting. I shook Iggy's hand, not quite sure what to say.

"Thanks for the invitation," I finally decided on.

"Please, come on in. We have a lot to talk about, and I'm sure you have a load of questions," he said, stepping aside so I could enter the room.

The floor wasn't your typical techie office. Instead of cubicles, a gorgeous panoramic view spanned the full field of vision. We were high up—you could see the snow-capped mountains to the west behind the Ferris wheel on the waterfront, which appeared diminutive from this height. To the north and south, Seattle sprawled out pretty much to the limits of my vision, with brief patches of green visible between the bases of distant buildings. Simply beautiful.

Inside the spacious office were maybe two-dozen employees scattered about. Almost everyone wore various styles of goggles, although none of the eyewear could be described as modern. Most were comprised of leather and brass, some of silver, while one man's appeared to be carved from wood. Iggy's were made from black leather straps and highly polished silver eyepieces. Like the ones I'd seen on the guy in the street, these had various levers and dials, and the right eyepiece appeared to have two additional clear lenses he could flip down.

"My office is this way," Iggy said, motioning with his hand. "Follow me; we'll get you something to drink, and I'll fill you in on the key details."

I followed, finally speaking when a cute young woman, also begoggled, wheeled up to me on a vintage, gyro-balanced hoverboard. She offered me a drink, and I requested a cup of black coffee.

I watched her roll away and nearly ran into Iggy's back when he stopped in front of a glass door, barely noticeable in the glass wall. Iggy's office. He opened the door for me and asked me to take a seat in a chair facing a U-shaped black desk, which I did.

"I'll be right back," he said, "Make yourself at home."

I tried to relax a little, taking in the view from his office. Banjo hopped off my shoulder and sat on the armrest, a little bit put off by his surroundings. The girl on the hoverboard rolled back in, dropped off my coffee, gave me a quick smile, and then scooted off.

A couple of minutes later, Iggy came back in, holding

up some papers, and took a seat in a high leather chair on the opposite side of the glass-topped desk.

"So, Jacob, feel like going on a trip?" he asked with a smile.

CHAPTER FOUR: THE DETAILS

My heart sped up a bit at the question. "A trip?" I asked. "Where to?"

"Sign these non-disclosure agreements, and I'll show you," Iggy replied, handing me the papers. I looked through the stack, about ten pages in total, all filled with the usual legalese. "Nothing in there you haven't signed before. This isn't the contract, just something to cover our backsides."

I glanced over them—I never read these things—then signed on the indicated lines. Iggy voiced his approval, but then made a strange request. He wanted to borrow Banjo.

"What for?" I asked.

"The game contains pets and familiars, created by the AI," Iggy explained to me. "I want to let Quirk do a bit of reprogramming, so Banjo can serve those same functions. The code is fully reversible, and out of game I guarantee you won't even notice the difference."

I was a little bit apprehensive, but Banjo didn't seem too put off by the idea, so I agreed, and Iggy summoned the assistant that brought me the coffee. She took Banjo by the paw and led him out of the office.

Iggy opened a drawer on his desk and removed a pair of goggles. These weren't the stylized goggles like Iggy or the swordfighter wore. These were plastic prototypes, unrefined and clunky looking. He handed them over to me.

"These goggles aren't actual game goggles," he explained. "These will just let you observe, but not interact. I'll be doing the playing. You can put them on your head, but don't activate them yet. Anyway, let's get going. Daylight's wasting."

Iggy led me back to the elevators, and he pushed the button for the roof. The computer requested a code, which he keyed in, and the doors silently slid shut. Most skyscrapers had landing bays on the upper floors for people coming and going from the work in hovercars. Roof access, however, was usually restricted to the higher-ups.

The cars on the roof were all high-end, and Iggy's was no exception. I followed him to a cherry-red convertible in a covered parking bay. As he approached, the vehicle came to life. The running lights came on, the side doors opened, and the vehicle rose about ten centimeters off the ground. A female voice welcomed us both by name. We got into the car, and Iggy programmed in his destination on the screen on the front panel. The car pulled forward out of the parking bay and rose into the blue Seattle sky.

Once the car hit its cruising altitude, it banked to the southwest and started forward at a brisk clip. Iggy swiveled his seat to face me.

"Okay, so about the game. Our world, and the game, is called *Panmachina*. You might have picked up some clues that we are going with a very vintage vibe here. A lot of our visuals borrow from the steampunk movement, which in turn borrows a lot from a romanticized version of Victorian England." He leaned back in his chair before continuing. "Ours is a world of fantastic technologies, powerful magic and breathtaking visuals."

Steampunk culture was still pretty strong. To this day, many cosplayed the style and created crafts and clothing that fit the genre, but did it have enough mass-market appeal to support a game like this? He seemed to sense my apprehension.

"We aren't going to use the word "steampunk" in our marketing or anything," he explained. "It's a personal style choice. We're hoping once word of mouth gets around about what we've created here this game will transcend normal genre boundaries, and the players will come pouring in. You with me so far?"

"I'm with you," I answered, trying to remain expressionless.

"There will be no subscription fees. Instead, the cost of admission will be," he tapped the goggles resting on his shaved head, "this." He removed the goggles and leaned over to hand them to me.

I accepted them and studied them for a few moments. They weren't overly heavy and appeared very well made. The lenses were clear, and the buttons and switches on the lens casing all seemed to be functional, although their purpose was a mystery to me at this point. The black material which the straps were made from felt like soft leather, with little silvery rivets holding the buckles and lens mechanisms in place.

"What do you call them?" I asked.

"Um... goggles, in general conversation," he replied. "We're working on a few names for the public rollout, although we're leaning to just print *Panmachina A.R.* on the packaging—the goggles are the game, if you will."

I held them up to my eyes for a second, saw nothing but Iggy and the room around me, and handed them back. He slid them on again, resting them on his forehead.

"Goggles can't be borrowed, although they can be sold and reset to interface with a new user," he said. "The goggles are more than just visual input. They are a complete multisensory neural interface, providing not only audio and visuals but neurologically generated haptic feedback, much like your VR rig. There are no implants, just low to mid-level precision stimulation of various parts of the brain."

Again, I nodded. Same as my rig. Signals sent from my VR rig to my brain could convince me I was holding the sword I looked at in my hand, that the metal felt cool, sharp. It could also convince me that I had just been pierced with an arrow or hit with a bolt from a blaster. Impressive, that they could miniaturize the technology enough to include it in the goggles.

"Each pair is custom-created by the player upon purchase. While they all perform the same function, you can select the material, shape, fasteners—the whole shebang.

Your first step will be creating a pair for yourself.

"*Panmachina* is an A.R. game which will encompass the entire United States, for now," he explained, "although most of the gaming action will be centered around the major metropolitan areas. Picture the game as overlapping what you already know, a shell that sits over the city and includes all aspects of the game. You'll see more of what I'm talking about once you jump in."

I bit back about thirty questions and let him continue.

"We've purchased real estate in many of the industrial parts of metropolises across the country, as well as more than a few rural locations, where we have set up quests and other gameplay related objects," he went on, "and these will be integral to the experience. The game isn't confined to our properties, though. No matter where a player is in the country, there will be much to do within just a few minutes' travel, and with the Hyperloop system, a player can physically be anywhere in the country within a few hours."

Iggy checked the center console, and I stole a glance as well. Unless I missed my guess, we were headed to Vashon, an island in Puget Sound. It was just ten minutes away from downtown Seattle and offered seclusion and a beautiful rural setting to those who could afford it.

"There are many distinct aspects to the gameplay mechanics. Much of the real estate we purchased will house traditional quests— enter, kill the boss, find the item, that sort of thing, although this is just a tiny part of the *Panmachina* experience." He steepled his fingers and continued. "The truly amazing part of the gameplay is what you'll experience just wearing the goggles in every-day life, on the streets. We've developed not only traditional quests but plots of intrigue, occurrences in normal life which will teach you to adapt to new situations and to expect the unexpected. I really should be getting better at explaining this, but *Panmachina* is a game in which you truly have to live it first-hand to understand."

I considered this. "So, what's your system like?" I asked. "I'm guessing you have some proprietary AI."

Iggy smiled. "That we do. Quirk is the brains behind the gameplay. Quantum integrated reality... erm... computer. With a *K*," he said. "Say hello, Quirk."

A voice came from seemingly everywhere in the car at once. "Hi, Jacob," it said in a soothing female voice—the same one that greeted us when we got in. "I think you're going to like what we've accomplished here."

"Um... hi, Quirk," I said. "Thanks for having me."

"The pleasure is ours," the voice said. "Anything I can do for you, just ask."

"Quirk is our pride and joy," Iggy said, patting the dashboard. "She's insanely powerful, capable of generating a stupid amount of calculations per millisecond. You won't hear from her in game, but she controls all aspects of the gameplay, from stats to NPC creation by imbuing all sentient beings in the game with a little spark of herself—so she's not directly in control of the characters. She is our real accomplishment, and the game is her accomplishment, although she's not big on taking credit for anything."

This was all a lot to take in. Almost too much. Before

bombarding Iggy with a bunch of questions, I needed to jump in and see the game for myself.

I stood up and peered down over the edge of the vehicle. I was right; we were beginning our descent to Vashon. We seemed to be heading to a sprawling mansion on the north shore of the island, with a wooded grassland stretching off to the south of it.

"Wow," I said.

"Yeah, that's what I said when I first saw it, too. Welcome to my humble abode."

The car landed on a pad designed for the purpose a couple hundred meters south of the house. It powered down, and the doors opened. "You two have fun out there," Quirk said.

Iggy patted the dashboard affectionately. "Thanks, Quirk, we will be back in an hour or so."

Instead of heading toward the mansion, I followed Iggy down a spiral wrought-iron staircase attached to the pad that led to the sparsely-wooded grassland below. When we got to the bottom, Iggy took a few steps into the field, then turned back to me. He slipped the goggles over his eyes and pushed a button on the left eyepiece. He motioned for me to do the same and told me how to activate them.

I powered them on.

The land itself didn't change, but Iggy did. He was now dressed in a cream-colored, sleeveless tunic that laced up the front with leather cord. Over this was a dark-brown leather vest, its pockets and straps holding an array of small tools, instruments and vials containing colored liquids. He wore khaki pants, tucked into high leather boots that ended just below his knees. Completing the look was an oversized pipe wrench hanging in a holster on his belt. A large canvas sack was slung over his shoulder.

"I'm digging the outfit," I said.

"Thanks," he said. "My character's an engineer. We're the crafters of *Panmachina,* although the archaeologists can do their fair share, too." He reached into his pack and pulled out a gauntlet. He pulled it on his right hand and flexed his fingers a few times. It extended nearly to his elbow. A long copper cylinder running the length of his forearm was affixed to the back, and I could see a blue liquid sloshing around inside through small glass ovals set into the copper at regular intervals. Thin flexible tubes led out of the cylinder and ran down each finger, ending in sharpened metal points on each tip.

He proceeded south, and the already sparse trees thinned out even more, opening to a sunny grassland with wildflowers growing in broad patches, and butterflies dancing from blossom to blossom. A copse of trees stood maybe fifty meters in front of us, and Iggy headed towards it.

As we got closer to the stand of pines, I started to hear a low mechanical humming. The sound was coming from tiny speakers mounted on the straps to either side of my goggles, but it gave the impression that it came from the trees ahead of us. Iggy held out his arm, motioning for me to stop.

I caught the glint of three metallic objects emerging

from the tops of the trees. The objects grew as they headed towards us, and I could make them out for what they were.

Bees. Bees made of polished chrome, and about the size of chickens.

They fanned out as they approached us, and Iggy wasted no time in engaging the first. He held out his gloved hand, fingers extended, and sent bolts of neon-green electricity arcing out towards the lead bee. The bee let out a loud robotic-sounding shriek and crashed to the ground at Iggy's feet.

The second bee took the opportunity to swoop in at Iggy, its abdomen curled underneath it, brandishing a barbed metal stinger the length of my hand. Iggy unhooked the pipe wrench from his belt and swung it two-handed, knocking the bee out of the air with a *clang*. It landed next to the first bee, which was still limping in slow, lame circles. With two swings of the wrench, he caved in both of their heads.

The third bee darted toward Iggy angrily, but he caught the insect in mid-dive with his gauntleted hand. The bee struggled in his grip, wildly thrusting at Iggy's chest with its stinger, but always coming up just short. Iggy's hand began to glow green, and the bee began vibrating, its buzzing whine becoming more high-pitched as the glove glowed brighter. Finally, with a crackle of electricity and a loud pop, the bee exploded, sending jagged chunks of chrome shrapnel flying in all directions.

One of the chunks flew toward my chest, but it passed right through me. I relaxed, remembering that the goggles I wore were for observation only.

"So, what did you think?" Iggy asked.

I was impressed, and I let him know as much. The bees blended seamlessly into the environment and hadn't looked like computer projections in the least. I kicked at the remains of one of the bees on the ground, but my foot went right through it, of course. Smiling, Iggy kicked the corpse as well, sending it a couple meters across the grass.

We proceeded south toward the far tree line that surrounded the borders of Iggy's property.

"Iggy," I said, "I was under the impression that the augmentation actually changed the world around us as well. The whole 'insert enemy into the world around you and blast it' thing has been done in AR before, and it never takes off."

"Oh, you're not seeing a tenth of it. I just wanted to give you an idea of what to expect with the gameplay mechanics. The grand reveal will come later."

I tried to keep my poker face but was sure I failed miserably. "Well, let's say I'm interested," I said. "What is it you want me to do, and what's my cut?"

Iggy grinned. "We want you to play," he said. "Before we roll out nationwide, we want to conduct the alpha right here in Seattle. Quirk has already done a great job working out most of the glitches and bugs, so you won't be debugging anything in the traditional sense, although you will be taking note of anything that seems unnatural, as far as interactions and general gameplay go. I wouldn't be surprised, however, if you didn't find anything. Quirk's gotten good at this. Your purpose is just to play, as a normal consumer would, while we observe." Iggy looked at me with an unreadable expression.

"The alpha will encompass the greater Seattle-Tacoma-Everett metroplex." He continued, "West to the Pacific and east to the Cascades, so there's a rather broad area in play. You'll know if you've gone too far."

"And my remuneration?" I asked.

"Just for agreeing to take part in the alpha, I'm going to offer you 150,000 netcoin per month," he replied.

I stopped in my tracks, and Iggy took a couple more steps before turning to face me. That was a lot more than I'd ever been offered as base pay. Most gave me a decent guarantee and let me make a more substantial income from the auctions. He knew this, of course.

"And items," I asked, pushing my luck. "Do I get to keep the proceeds?"

"Well, yes and no. What we have in mind is a much more lucrative proposition," he said with a grin. His voice took on the flair of a game show host as he continued towards the far tree line. "The alpha will feature three hundred players from around the country, who we've hired to take part in the alpha." All around me, a subtle drumroll began building. "All of you will also be taking part in a grand quest, an undertaking with rewards that defy imagination."

The drumroll got louder, matching the excitement in Iggy's voice.

"The pair who complete the quest first will be awarded the title of Auction Master and be granted the management of," the drumroll stopped, and he paused to tremendous effect, "Steam Whistle Alley."

A fanfare of invisible trumpets filled the field. I chuckled, appreciating the effect.

Steam Whistle Alley, New Seattle—the name from the website.

Iggy must have guessed the upcoming onslaught of questions, so he pressed on before I could ask them, in his normal voice.

"Notice I said 'pair.' You will be teamed up with another player for the course of this alpha, but we will get to that later," he said. "Steam Whistle Alley will be the central trading hub for the Cascadia region of the game—the area that comprises the Pacific Northwest. It's located in the SoDo, or south downtown, area—a few kilometers south of the stadiums. We purchased a couple of abandoned warehouses and an area comprising about six city blocks for the project."

Iggy halted again, as the tree line was now only a few meters away. He reached into his sack again and pulled out a golden orb about the size of a softball. With his free hand, he pointed to the line of trees. I didn't see anything at first, but then I noticed movement—a figure slowly emerging from the underbrush. As it came out into the open and began padding slowly towards us, I recognized it as a cougar. It halted, sniffing the air, then began pacing back and forth, as if guarding the trees behind it. I could now see that it wasn't an ordinary animal. It was missing half the fur on its head, exposing a metallic skeleton underneath. I was too far away to make out any other details, but the cougar remedied that quickly, charging toward us.

Iggy pushed a button on the golden orb, then rolled it at the sprinting animal, and it began increasing its velocity under its own power. Iggy withdrew a second orb from the bag, sending it after the first one. They both stopped in front of the beast, who had halted its charge to sniff the two new objects.

Without warning, long golden tendrils emerged from each of the spheres with a series of high-pitched whipping sounds. They flailed around wildly, before latching onto the beast, wrapping around its neck and ankles. The beast reared up on its hind legs, exposing its underbelly. I could see a metal ribcage peeking through more missing patches of fur. The beast roared, struggling at the tentacles that wrapped around it, but they held fast, even tightening. The angry roar quickly became yelps of pain, as more of the tendrils wrapped around the beast's neck. The tendrils constricted, and the yelping came to an abrupt stop as beast's head flew off with a pop.

Laughing, I gave Iggy a brief round of applause, to which he gave a little bow. The two spheres had retracted their tentacles and rolled back to Iggy, who scooped them up and put them back in his sack. With that, he powered off his goggles, resting them back on his head, and I did the same. The corpse of the cat disappeared, and Iggy reverted to his jeans and black polo shirt, his equipment and sack now gone. He started back the way we had come.

"Where was I?" he asked. "Oh, the alley. Steam Whistle Alley will house shops, hotels, entertainment venues, and

53

the main auction house for the Cascadia region. There will be several other branch auction houses of course, but all revenue generated will pass through the main hub at Steam Whistle Alley. A few companies have already purchased retail spots in the alley. None of the retail locations are exclusive to players—even non-players can go to them, although they will find that without the embellishments afforded by augmented reality, the places themselves won't be as exhilarating. We do expect a small number of the general public to show up just to see what all the fuss is about, perhaps to watch the players. The Auction Masters— the pair that first completes the quest, will share a ten percent tithe on all proceeds generated by Steam Whistle Alley. Ten percent of every auction, ten percent of every potion, every gear, every bolt of cloth, every shot of whiskey, for as long as you remain under our employ. Of course, ARGO Enterprises gets our ten percent as well. Helps to keep the lights on," he said cheekily.

I chuckled—everyone knew that electricity was free.

My head swam as it tried to estimate the numbers involved, and finally, I just gave up and asked him. "How much are we talking here, once the game is released?"

Iggy grinned at me. "Our projections are looking like around 150 to 200 million netcoin a month spent in retail establishments and the auction house once the game is released." He paused to let me do the math.

And boy did I do the math. I found myself getting dizzy for a second, almost forgetting to breathe.

Even if I didn't finish the quest first, I was at least

guaranteed the base pay, which by itself would be more than enough.

I think Iggy could sense I had already made my decision.

"So, Mr. Tutor," he said quietly, "are you ready to become an Argonaut?"

CHAPTER FIVE: THE UNBOXING

When we returned to his headquarters, Iggy led me back to his office. His assistant was already waiting outside the office doors, holding Banjo's hand as he jumped around excitedly as I approached. She handed him off to me, and he scampered up to my shoulder. He didn't seem any worse for wear.

Iggy led me into his office and walked me through the forms I would be required to fill out and sign. As I got to work on them, a chime sounded from the goggles parked on his head.

"Excuse me," he said, "I have to take this." He stepped outside and flipped a lever on his right eyepiece, and a three-dimensional head appeared, floating about a meter in front of him. It was a head I recognized.

It was the swordsman from the street.

I could only make out snippets of the conversation as Iggy paced the carpet on the other side of the glass wall. The conversation was heated, and I saw a different side of the happy, care-free Iggy I had gotten used to over the past couple hours.

"Jameson, I don't care what he thinks. You can't take part in the competition, just observe. You helped create..."

"Quirk can run circles around Quark, and the glitch...

"Screw Chuck! Tell that lying bastard if he even changes one line of code, my lawyers will..."

Iggy finally walked stormed down the hallway out of earshot, and then out of sight. I looked at Banjo.

"What do you think that was all about?"

Banjo chittered in response, so I shrugged it off and dove into the stack of paperwork.

Iggy came back a half hour later showing no signs of stress from his conversation in the hallway.   After examining all the documents, he gave me a link to the website where I would create and customize my goggles, which, he explained, would be shipped via drone about three hours after completion.

We shook hands, and Iggy started to show me out, but my curiosity got the better of me. "Hey, Iggy," I began, "who was that guy I saw on the street—the one that lured me in here? Does he work for you?" I decided not to mention seeing the projection of his head during the recent call.

Iggy grimaced. "Yes, and no," he said. "He was in charge of bringing in recruits, like yourself. Jameson is an old friend of mine, but he's had some... issues recently. I'm not really at liberty to say what."

I raised my eyebrows.

"As a concession to him," Iggy continued, "I'm allowing him to observe the alpha, so you might see him around the alley. But officially, he's no longer part of ARGO."

I had more questions but dropped the subject.

On the way home, I stopped at my coffee shop, hoping to catch Jeni. I wanted to celebrate and had finally summoned the courage to see if she wanted to go out to dinner. Peeking inside, I could see she wasn't working, so passed up the shop and half-skipped down the hill to my apartment. My first month's salary had cleared as soon as I left Iggy's office, and I had mentally picked out a couple high-ticket items I could now afford to add to my collection.

Once in my apartment, I fed Banjo before changing into sweats and a vintage black t-shirt showing an antique cassette tape with two crossed bones underneath, stylized to look like an old pirate flag. Above, in white block letters were the words 'HOME TAPING IS KILLING MUSIC,' and underneath, 'AND IT'S ILLEGAL.'

I settled into my chair and slipped on my VISOR, bringing up the site to create my goggles.

Most modern optical equipment had biosensors that allowed the device to verify that the person using it was authorized to do so, and this let me bypass entering login information for most sites. Iggy had scanned my bioinfo when I signed up, so bringing up the website took me directly to the welcome area, a featureless purple space where I was greeted by an attractive woman in a grey leather corset cinched impossibly tight. A long silvery dress accompanied it, slit up one side to her thigh. She had long, curly white hair, ice blue eyes and wore a pouty smile. The look was finished with a pair of fingerless grey gloves that extended to her elbows, grey leather boots that stretched halfway to her knees, and a pair of black metal and white leather goggles resting on her forehead. She stood there with one hand on her hip, shifting her weight slightly from foot to foot.

"Welcome, Jacob," she said warmly. I brought my gaze up to meet hers. "My name is Carrie. Are you ready to create your goggles?"

I nodded, and she brought up the goggle design interface to the right of where she stood. A 3D representation of my head appeared—a touch unsettling— and with a few subtle hand gestures, I tried on a variety of shapes, sizes, and configurations.

Eventually, I settled on a pair with a black head strap as wide as duct tape, and dark, smoky metal for the buckles and lenses. I made the left eyepiece a smidge larger than the right one, and for no functional reason added a ten-millimeter antenna to the left side as well. Carrie recommended I add three extra lenses to the right eyepiece, which could rotate up or down to provide various sight-enhancing benefits. On the right temple, I added a couple purely decorative interlocking gears to finish my masterpiece.

Carrie voiced her approval, and I chose the option to create and ship my order. "See you soon!" she said with a smile.

She waved goodbye and disappeared, and I closed out

of the site and proceeded to browse the web for a while.

Still no mention of ARGO Enterprises, Steam Whistle Alley, or anything else I searched for in relation to recent events, except for that original landing page. This wasn't a surprise. Part of the litany of forms I had to sign prohibited me from mentioning anything about the project online or anywhere else. Everyone connected with the program certainly got the same treatment.

I checked my email. Mostly notifications of auctions closing. But I *had* won the *Earthbound* auction and let out a triumphant whoop when I saw it only cost me 14,000 netcoins. Two months' rent, sure, but money well spent. I had oodles now anyway. With that thought, I sent another 20,000 to my parents. They never mentioned my donations, but never rejected them either, and it felt good to help them out when I could.

I flipped over to the auction site and placed a couple more bids. One was for a sealed version of Maniac Mansion for the Commodore 64. I already owned copies for the PC and NES, but this one was much rarer. I brought up the NES version of the game to play and kill time before the goggles arrived. My virtual emulator deposited me in front of an antique television and Nintendo in a late 20th-century living room. Not enough can be said for realism.

I pressed start on the controller and sunk into the game.

A few hours later, I heard the chime from the front door, and a text box popped up in my display letting me know my goggles had arrived. Both my storage unit and apartment had delivery doors installed to securely accept packages even if I wasn't home. I went to the front door, opened a hatch by the wall and retrieved my parcel, then took it over to the kitchen counter.

Banjo hopped up and scrutinized it. Whenever I got anything sent to the house, he always ran in to see what was new. Must have been trained by all the pizza deliveries, and just continued out of force of habit, although he did seem genuinely interested no matter what the package, and now was no exception.

I pressed two indentations on the side of the box, and the top opened, revealing foam packing and a single sheet of paper, giving some basic system specs. After removing the foam cube, I pulled the two halves apart to reveal the goggles.

I had to admit—they were cool looking. Exactly how I'd designed them. The goggles, like pretty much everything these days, charged wirelessly using the ubiquitous Tesla charging stations found across the country. In the event I was way out in B.F.E. I had a couple portable chargers that could last a few days. The goggles hooked into the National Internet System, and ARGO hadn't skipped on paying for bandwidth, as apparently, this thing sported a hefty 3.3 petabyte download speed with 1.5 upload. My full immersion rig was a 4-petabyte system— currently, the best a civilian could get. The only other piece of information, aside from some unimportant jargon at the bottom, was the location of the power button: a small depression in the left eyepiece, near the temple.

Banjo reached for the goggles, and I snatched them

away, smiling at him.

"Not for you," I admonished, and he looked up at me with the sad monkey face he used when he didn't get his way. I grabbed a soda from the fridge, sat down at my desk, and slipped the goggles over my eyes.

Banjo jumped into my lap, and I pressed the power button.

The lenses went opaque. In the blackness, three words appeared about a meter in front of me:

Calibrating, please wait.

So, I waited excitedly, sipping my soda.

About thirty seconds later, the goggles became translucent again.

"Hello, Jacob," a female voice said from behind me.

I jumped out of my seat and spun around, a hand clutched to my thumping chest. This earned a screech from Banjo, who bounded into the bedroom, knocking over a lamp in the process.

"Frakking hell, you can't do that to people!" I wailed.

Carrie was sitting on my loveseat with her hands folded in her lap. She wore the same outfit as earlier, but seeing her in it now, sitting on my sofa, seemed much... more real than it had in VR. Maybe because this was the first time there'd been a woman in my apartment. Well, *kind of* a woman. Sitting as she was, her dress did absolutely nothing to hide her legs, and I could display my action figures on that shelf of cleavage created by her corset. Without thinking, I took three steps over to her and poked her leg. Perfectly fleshy.

"Hey, now," she admonished with a pout, "I'm not that kind of character creation subroutine." Her pout turned into a smile.

"Er... I... I'm sorry about that."

My heart decided this was not the time to slow down and continued its drum solo in my chest.

"What... um..." *Words, Jacob, use your words.* "What can I do for you?" I asked, regretting it within about two seconds. She giggled. "Well, I'm here to help you create your character for Panmachina A.R. I promise it will be mostly painless," she said. "Have you thought of a name yet?"

"A name?" I repeated. "Just... give me a sec, will you?"

I walked back to my chair, turned it to face her, and sat back down. "Usually I create my character and name it after, and nine times out of ten I use a variation on my name." My eyes involuntarily wandered down in the time it took to say that sentence. I forced them back up again.

"That's OK with me." Noticing my shift in gaze, she smiled and gave me a wink.

At that point, Banjo ventured back in and hopped on the loveseat next to Carrie. Startled, she let out a squeak before relaxing and giving him a stroke on the head. It took me a second to register Banjo was now wearing a maroon button-up vest with tails on either side of his...tail, and a brass monocle on a chain that disappeared into his breast pocket.

"Banjo! Leave her..." I started, before it dawned on me. Banjo could see her. How in the hell?

She saw my reaction and gave me a reassuring look.

"When you were at our headquarters, we added a couple of subroutines to allow Banjo here to function as your familiar. It was kind of an experiment, but biosynths aren't too hard to work with when it comes to coding."

I blinked. This was already more than I was expecting, and I hadn't even created my character yet. I mean, I was in my living room, for Chrissake. When it came to gaming, I was used to having a whole new world sprung on me, inside the rig. It allowed me to mentally assure myself that I was in a game. Now, I was in my sweatpants in my messy living room watching my monkey, dressed in a fancy vest and sporting an eyepiece, sitting next to a sultry, white-haired, Victorian-era bombshell.

Okay, I'm game.

"So what functions will my familiar perform?" I asked. "Will he carry my stuff for me?" I took another sip of my soda, attempting to appear at ease.

Banjo looked up at me. "I'm not going to be a part of this madness only to be your personal valet," he scolded in a high-pitched, but crisp, Brooklyn accent.

Now I always thought spit-takes never actually happened and were just put into movies and books for effect. Turns out, they're a real biological anomaly, something I became certain of when a carbonated fountain erupted from my lips.

Carrie laughed musically. "I was so looking forward to seeing your reaction to that," she said through a fit of giggling. "Your face, I swear—"

"This is going to take me a second." My attempts at

brushing the soda off my sweatpants were not yielding great results. "So Banjo can..." I paused and then looked at Banjo before continuing. "You can talk now?"

"Just in game. The intelligence provided me by the subroutines they installed comes from the game servers, and from Quirk," he explained. "When you log out of the game, I will be happy, and more than a little relieved, to go back to being my normal simian self."

"So, you won't carry things for me, so you're what... emotional support?" I chuckled. I was talking to my monkey. Well, I did that a lot. Only now, he was talking back.

"I'd love to carry things for you, but in case you hadn't noticed, I'm a monkey," he said as he peered at me through his monocle. "From what I understand, objects you find in the game have authentic weight. As your strength goes up, they become a little easier to lug around. If you can carry it, good for you. But don't expect to carry 500 pounds of gear in your backpack and plan on moving anywhere. If you have a key or a coin or two that need lugging around, though, I'm your monkey."

I looked up at Carrie. "Is this true?"

She nodded. "Things are weighted as they would be in the real world," she said. "Some of the items you acquire might even be actual items if your quest leads you to one of our properties. We like to keep things interesting like that. Mind you, there will be means and methods you might chance upon that will assist in moving gear from point A to point B."

"Good to know," I said. *What have I gotten myself into?*

Banjo spoke up again. "I am also your in-game information system. I will inform you whenever you gain a level, acquire any inflictions, *etcetera, etcetera.* Anything you would normally access a menu for, or any time you would normally see a system message or status update, it will come from me. I will also give you regular health point updates should you get into a battle, but unless you instruct me to, I'm not going to waste breath telling you the damage from every hit you give or receive. I can also help you with the wisdom of attacking a creature—whether you could do it with your eyes closed or would end up a bloody smear on the ground."

Carrie nodded. "We use familiars for this, so we don't have to break the game's realism with messages or text boxes," she explained. "We've really dialed it in; I think you will find it pretty intuitive."

Break the realism? I thought. *My monkey is going to be giving me status updates.*

But I could see her point. Every VR game I'd played had something in my field of vision that wouldn't be there in real life, either HP bars or system messages. A little distracting, but they did help me remember I was playing a game.

"If you have any more questions," Carrie said, "I will be happy to answer them while I'm here. But first, can we create your character? I suggest we do so on your balcony. It's a beautiful night."

I agreed and walked over to pull open the curtains that hung by the balcony doors. I slid the doors open and stepped outside.

And I gasped.

The night waterfront I was used to had changed entirely. Well... not completely, now that I looked closer.

The buildings were all in their same places, but instead of the blocky waterfront restaurants and gift shops I'd seen every night for a few years, I now looked at a row of fine and intricate Victorian architecture. Nearly every building had at least one spire, and the plate glass windows of the storefronts had been replaced with glimmering archways and facades. A tower rose at the far southern end, with a huge clock face adorning the steepled top. A steamboat with a dark copper-colored paddlewheel floated lazily by out on the water, tufts of steam rising from its chimneys.

High above this tableau, I saw a blimp... zeppelin... airship? A *something* I'd never seen before. A series of chains connected a football-shaped white canvas balloon to a wooden cabin with large, circular windows, while a pair of propellers moved it northwards through the sky. But the *pièce de résistance* of the view was the Ferris wheel. Instead of the usual wheels on either side of the axel, two giant, shining copper gears rotated slowly in the night air. The fiberglass cars had been replaced with round, wooden baskets suspended by cables from crossbars, set into every other gear tooth. Giant floodlights on either side lit the contraption up exquisitely as it turned.

I took a couple of seconds to catch my breath. Everything looked so incredibly *real*. I breathed the outdoor air, feeling the breeze on my face. I had felt realism before in VR, from the feel of grass under my feet to the wind in my hair, but this... this was something you couldn't recreate.

Banjo had followed me out and leaped up to his perch on the corner of the railing. His mouth hung open as he jerked his head quickly from sight to sight in this fantastic landscape. I suppressed a laugh—the vest and eyepiece were too cute. I promised myself at the first opportunity I'd find him a monkey-sized bowler hat.

"You like the view?" I asked him.

"Indeed," he said. "I can't wait to get out there and explore a bit. Is the whole world different now?"

Carrie joined us on the patio. Her chest expanded as she took a deep breath of the night air, the sight of which brought a blush to my cheeks.

"Most of the major metropolitan areas will be augmented when the game is in full release, yes," she explained. "For right now it's just the Seattle area. Quirk has done an amazing job, hasn't she? We fed her aesthetic themes and styles of architecture, and she produced what you see before you. We've spent the past two years making minor changes where she took too many liberties, or things that just didn't look right, but this is her creation. You'll appreciate it more once you get out there."

She turned to face me and gave me a scowl. A pretty scowl, but still a scowl. "Which you can't do until you create your character."

"OK," I said. "Let's do this."

CHAPTER SIX: CREATION

arrie snapped her fingers, and an oval mirror half-again as tall as me appeared at the end of the balcony. It was very ornate—the rim was constructed of dark wrought iron attached to a base with four feet shaped like lion paws. Two attachments at the midpoint of the mirror allowed it to swivel to face slightly up or down.

I looked in the mirror and saw my goggles perched on my forehead. I instinctively raised my hands to my face and found my goggles still over my eyes, even though I could clearly see my eyes in the reflection.

Carrie noticed my confusion. "The goggles must be worn to play the game," she explained. "Although they don't actually have to appear on the eyes of your in-game character. We found it a little unsettling if you had to do everything with goggles covering the eyes, so we've given the players the ability to remove them as needed. Put the goggles on in game, and you'll be granted extra abilities, depending on how you customized them. Right now, by flipping down the extra lenses you installed, you'll have the ability to zoom in on objects and also to see enemies' stats. By improving your goggles later, you will be granted other abilities and enhancements, but I will let you discover those on your own."

I thought I understood and nodded, albeit a bit apprehensively.

"Remember," she continued, "that you are, in real life, actually wearing the goggles. To leave the game, you must hold down the power switch on the left temple for three seconds. Otherwise, the game will count any movement you make to remove the goggles as a move in the game and prevent you from coming in contact with the real pair." She smiled. "Confused yet?"

"Very much so," I said, "but I think I get the gist of it."

"Smart boy." She smiled, and in the mirror, she gave me a look over my shoulder that sent my blood pumping.

This still felt so real. I was tempted to power down the goggles just to ground myself in reality for a moment but decided against it. I was getting tired, but I wanted to get the creation aspect over, and then get some sleep, so I could begin the adventure in the morning.

"So... this looks a little funny, wearing the goggles with sweats and a T-shirt," I said. "When do I get some new duds?"

"Your 'duds,'" she replied, "will depend on your path. Which I guess I had better explain now. You ready?"

"Lay it on me," I said, as I turned to look at her.

"Panmachina currently has ten playable character paths. A few more are in the works but aren't set to be released until future expansions." She tousled my hair, pretended to dust off my goggles. "We've taken a simplistic approach to character creation with the intent of bringing in people who might not normally play these types of games. Instead of going the route of many RPGs, *Panmachina AR* instead offers character paths, which will determine your skill set. Some of these paths are races, some of them would be considered classes, while others, professions. This might eventually be upgraded when enough people are comfortable playing the game, but for now, we want people to focus on gameplay and not worry so much about the stats. With me so far?"

"So far, so good."

"Your options are as follows. Please face the mirror."

I turned around and looked at myself again.

"The first path is the Brawler," she said. My reflection shifted to that of a muscle-bound fighter type. I now wore a thick, chestnut brown leather vest barely able to contain ripped pectoral and abdominal muscles. I looked down at two brass instruments strapped across the knuckles of each hand and noticed the palm sides each had a row of buttons. I pressed one, and tiny brass blades rotated out of hidden bases on each knuckle to form spikes. Another push and they retracted. The goggles on my forehead were now attached to a black bandana covering my scalp, although my shaggy hair sprung out wildly from the bottom. I had played muscly types before, but this was *my* head attached to the body, except for a much squarer jaw.

Who needs the gym? I thought. Banjo hopped off the

railing and onto my arm, climbing up to my shoulder.

"It's like climbing a tree now," he said. He admired his reflection in the mirror for a second. "Hey, I look good on you."

I snorted. I never expected to hear that from a monkey. Hard to get used to hearing him speak.

"The brawler is your basic melee character," Carrie said. "They can take damage and give it right back as well as pick up various styles of martial arts, including swordplay, along the way. Not the most intelligent of classes, of course. I'm sure you're familiar with the type." She reached out a hand, squeezed one of my biceps. "The neural interface contained in the goggles will actually help make you a better fighter by interfacing with your primary motor cortex, imparting expertise to your movements and skill to your tactics, even if you've never fought before. This will increase as your level does, and is true for several classes, to varying degrees."

"I know *Kung Fu*," I said in my best Keanu Reeves voice.

"Temporarily." she corrected. "This effect will not last outside of the game as the goggles create a buffer between your motor cortex and your limbic system, so you will have no memory of the techniques, just the ability, and only while you are logged in. You'll also have no magical abilities as a brawler and may the Lords of Kobol help you if you ever even think of trying to make a potion."

I chuckled, surprised at her *Battlestar* reference. Did they program her specifically to appeal to my tastes or was she just an attractive, nerdy, character creation facilitator? Probably a little bit of both.

"I do want to point out that while we can give you the knowledge to perform certain maneuvers, the game cannot affect your physical speed or stamina," Carrie continued. "A lot of the players who've been strapped into full immersion rigs for the last ten years without the benefit of muscular and cardiovascular stimulation aren't going to have an enjoyable time playing melee paths." She paused and then smiled before continuing. "After full release, expect to see a lot of fat casters.

"Early testing, however, has shown that sticking with melee classes will help improve speed, endurance, and flexibility out of game," she said. "But, if you can't kick a guy in the head or run for an hour straight now, don't expect to in-game."

This made sense. I was relatively fit—I walked everywhere, and my immersion rig had muscle stimulators for long stretches of gaming. Without them, a whole slew of health problems could arise.

"Moving on," Carrie began.

"One second," I interrupted. I performed a couple flexes in the mirror, then gave a half-turn to check out my butt. Not too shabby. "OK, keep going."

She rolled her eyes but said, "That *is* a nice butt. Moving on—the next path is the thaumaturge."

I held up my hand. "Do I have to go through these descriptions for every player type in the game?" I asked. "I'm used to just going through a menu, seeing all the stats, and choosing the one that suits me."

"Well, as an employee of ARGO Enterprises, we want

you to have detailed information on all the options available," she stated. "Regular users after release will have a more expedited version of character creation. For you, though, knowledge is power. So, cool your jets and enjoy the ride. You won't be able to begin playing until tomorrow anyway, when we introduce you to your partner."

I had put the whole partner situation out of my mind. I was used to playing solo in my VR games, occasionally teaming up with groups for more challenging quests, but I preferred the difficulty of going it alone. A partner... if they teamed me up with some kid who still thought leet-speak was cool, with a penchant for making 'your mom' jokes and teabagging corpses, this was going to be a rough ride.

I had a thought. "Carrie, what if my class and my partner's aren't compatible? I mean, we'd have a tough go of it if we both ended up clerics or something."

Carrie nodded. "We thought of that. If, after you meet your partner, one or both of you wants to switch paths, we'll allow it. Just summon me, and we'll go from there."

She went on to explain more of the available paths, my body and reflection transforming with each one. After the thaumaturge came the alchemist; my eyes took on a blue glow, and my hands and part of my face were covered with the scars of old burns. Not the most attractive, but according to Carrie they were the potion-makers of the game, highly sought after for their abilities and compensated very well by other players for their goods.

Then there were the werewolves—adventurers by day, raging beasts by night with incredible strength and stamina when transformed. I watched in amazement as my clothes disappeared and were replaced by a tattered loincloth. My face and body sprouted thick brown hair, and my fingernails curved into wicked claws. It was like watching a time-lapse video of an evil chia pet.

Banjo had a ball with that one. "Jakey, Jakey, you do look fierce," he said of my werewolf form. "Pick that one, yeah? Two ferocious beasts prowling the streets looking for unsuspecting victims."

"I think you shed enough hair for the both of us," I replied.

Carrie proceeded to tell me about the arborbound, a race of elf-like healers and archers who made their home in the forests. My reflection became slender, and my face took on elfin features, the tops of my ears extending into points. My outfit changed into simple woodland garb, in hues of brown and green, and a mechanical compound bow appeared on my back, gears and pulleys on either end for providing a smoother draw and more strength to the arrow, I assumed.

The descriptions continued. Beastmasters, summoners, and gargoyles were all interesting to an extent, but not paths I thought I would enjoy playing.

"We've saved the two we think you'll like the most for last," said Carrie. "Wanted to give a fair shot to the rest of the options."

The night had turned chilly, and I yawned in spite of, or maybe because of, the excitement of the evening. "OK," I said, "whatcha got for me?

"The ninth path is the archaeologist," she said.

My body reverted to its natural state, although my face looked a bit more rugged, with a hint of a beard on my chin. A bowler hat with two gears sown into the side sat on my head, my goggles around the brim. I wore a leather vest over a long-sleeve, white shirt, tan pants and dark leather boots. A weapon hung coiled at my waist, which I unhooked to examine. It appeared to be a series of brass-colored rods, each about ten centimeters long, riveted to the one before it so it could bend like a rope. If it were uncoiled and laid out flat, I estimated the whole length to be about four meters. The brass handle was about the size of my forearm and wrapped tightly in leather straps for a sure grip. The last four links of the weapon on the business end were sharpened on either side to a razor's edge. I barely touched one of these edges, then yelped in pain as blood welled from the cut and began to drip on the floor.

"Wait a sec," I said through gritted teeth, holding out my injured hand in the other one, "did I just cut myself on a virtual object?"

"No, you didn't," replied Carrie. She took my finger in her hand and squeezed it, her hand radiating a soft white light. A numb, tingly sensation washed over my finger, and when she let go of the cut, the pain vanished. "The cut, the blood, and the pain were all part of the simulation. It seems more real than what you're used to because you are, for the most part, still in the real world. As your brain can have a hard time deciphering simulated injury from the real thing, the game has been programmed to log you out should you ever get an actual, serious injury."

"I see," I mumbled, a little put off by the experience. I had taken loads of damage in game before, but this cut—it was different. Again, it seemed more... real. But I didn't want to spoil the fun, so I tried to put it out of my mind. "Tell me more about archaeologists."

"I'd love to!" she obliged. "The beauty you just cut yourself on is the chain blade, one of the coolest weapons in the game, in my humble opinion. Archeologist's perception skills are off the charts, and in this game, perception is one of the most important stats, helping you to notice things that others pass over. Yours will not only be a quest for treasure, but a quest seeking answers to questions you haven't even asked. There is much hidden in the world we have created, and the archaeologist is by far the best equipped to uncover these mysteries."

Banjo seemed to be losing interest. "This has been truly enlightening," he said, and bowed to Carrie, "but I must retire for the evening." Carrie bent down to offer him a hand, on which Banjo planted a small kiss. I rolled my eyes. "Until we meet again," he said. And with that he disappeared inside, heading towards my bedroom.

"He's adorable, isn't he?" Carrie gushed. "It seems the subroutines are performing perfectly."

I shrugged my shoulders. "Yeah, he's alright," I agreed. "Anyway... about the archaeologist. The perceptive trait sounds pretty handy, but what else can you tell me?"

"Well," she said, taking a step closer to me and leaning on the railing. "On you, it's a very attractive look." She giggled and booped the brim of my bowler with a finger.

I blushed, smiling more bashfully than I should have. I kept having to tell myself there wasn't a voluptuous woman standing with me on my balcony. "No, really. Any other abilities or stats I should know about?"

She turned around and leaned her back to the railing, supporting herself with her elbows. "Above average in dexterity and intelligence," she said, "and average in most other stats. You'll do double damage in caves and underground areas. Archies are a creative sort and can design helpful devices at their guild. Not nearly as well as the engineers, though. Which brings us to the final path."

My reflection pretty much remained unchanged, except that a bandana replaced my bowler and my chain blade was replaced with a large, lethal-looking pipe wrench tucked into my belt. Spots of grease covered my shirt, pants, and vest, and my hint of a beard had flourished into a facial phenomenon worthy of dwarven kings.

I cringed. "Do I have to use this facial hair?"

"The previews you see are just the starting point," she replied. "After you decide on a path, we can customize the character to your liking, changing the physique, outfit, face—what have you."

"That's a relief," I said, stroking my beard while looking into the mirror.

"I'm with you on this one," she offered. "You look much more handsome clean-shaven."

"Anyway, the engineers are some of the most important players in the game," she said. "They create nearly everything—guns, clothes, grenades, swords, drones, you name it. Some of what they create, like armor and clothes, for instance, can be distributed immediately, while others require the use of a fabricator—a machine located in the Engineer's Guild at Steam Whistle Alley. What this machine does is allow us to ship the real-world item to the alley after fabrication, meaning it is a real item in the real world, but also useful in game. We might modify the appearance in game, but it will be a physical item you can see even after you take off the goggles. An example of these would be spring boots— footwear with pistons built into the soles allowing one to jump farther."

I sighed, picturing VR games with avatars jumping wherever they went. Some things never changed; I'd seen footage of this annoying habit spanning way back to the beginning of the century.

Carrie didn't seem to notice my dismay. "Engineers are probably some of the most well-paid players in the game," she said, "even more so than the alchemists. As you acquire new schematics, which can be done both through general leveling and other means, you can fabricate that item and sell it in the market. You must buy the items you produce in the fabricator from us. But seeing as you are the only one that can produce them, you can sell them for a profit. Engineers gain experience through fabricating items as well as more traditional means, just as alchemists gain XP through creating their concoctions and archaeologists gain XP through exploring. We've spent a lot of resources on balance so that no one group can outgain the other."

I nodded, then yawned again. This had been a long day, and it was well after midnight. After weighing the pros and cons of each option she had presented over the course of the evening, I had made a decision.

"Carrie," I said, smiling, "I would like to be an archaeologist."

CHAPTER SEVEN: THE TRIP

Carrie smiled. "Hah! I knew it. I just won one-hundred netcoin. Thank you very much," she said as she smiled warmly at me. "You're going to love it."

"Wait...you're an NPC, aren't you? How can you have money?" I asked, confused.

"Oh, I'm a player," she replied with a mischievous grin. "Just not a human one. Okay, let's wrap this up, you're looking pretty tired."

I was, but I was still excited. I couldn't remember ever feeling this anxious to get into a game before.

"First things first," she started. "Do you want to change the way you look?"

I looked at myself in the mirror. I had my same, shaggy dark hair, although I swore I was just a little more handsome and rugged looking than usual. I felt my shoulders, then my arms, and noticed more tone and better mass than I'd ever had. I opened my vest, lifted my shirt and looked at my abs.

Abs! Woohoo! I have abs!

Part of me knew as I felt myself up I was running my hands over my un-athletic gamer's body, but seeing is believing, so they say. Whoever they were, they were right.

I took one last look at myself. I still had the white streak over my temple and the scars on my hand. If they had removed them, I would have requested they put them back. "You know, I think I'm good." I thought for a second. "Yeah, I'm good."

Carrie winked at me. "I wouldn't change anything either. You're a handsome man."

"I bet you say that to all the noobs," I replied jokingly, but felt myself blushing anyway. "So, do I get to roll for stats or anything?"

"Nope, your stats are set during player creation," she answered. "Otherwise we'd never get anything done. Banjo can fill you in in the morning. All we have left to do," she continued, as she patted my cheek affectionately, "is give you a name."

"I've been thinking about that. This character, more than any game I've played, feels like me," I said. "I think I'm going to stick with Jacob if that's allowed."

Carrie laughed. "You'd be surprised how many of our testers have said nearly the same thing, including your partner," she said as she walked to the other end of the balcony, and then turned to face me. "Jacob, it's been a pleasure. If you ever need me for anything aesthetic, just summon me. If you get some time, maybe we can spruce this place up a bit," she said, looking around the apartment and cringing as if it pained her. "Meet your companion tomorrow, at Steam Whistle Alley."

"But how do I get there? Where will they be?" I asked, but her outline was already starting to shimmer.

She blew me a kiss, then slowly faded from sight.

It was well after one in the morning, but I couldn't help taking one last look at the waterfront. I could make out the tiny figures of people on the sidewalks and streets, but not many at this time of night.

Who was real? Who was an NPC? Would I be able to tell the difference? Maybe Banjo would know and could tell me. *He's real... she's fake... they're real... he's fake.* That would get old quickly.

A silent boat drifted by on the water, belching steam. How long had it been since the world had seen a steam engine? It was very convincing. I felt like if I swam out there, I could climb aboard. Shades of purple and silver now lit up the giant gears of the Ferris wheel, not moving at this time of night. Spires from the buildings gracing the water's edge formed darkened silhouettes against the backdrop of the water.

This was amazing.

More reluctantly than I'd like to admit, I reached up to my temple and powered down my goggles. Instantly, the world reverted to normal. It felt plain in comparison.

I rested my goggles on my forehead and took in the Ferris wheel in its usual, less dramatic state. All the spires had gone, and the magnificent buildings had returned to their squat, blocky selves. The boat on the water was just the hover ferry, taking its last load of passengers to

Bremerton. Everything was as I had always known it, the view I loved so much. But now, it just seemed... drab.

I couldn't wait to get my goggles back on.

When I woke up the next morning, I stared at the ceiling, piecing together everything that had happened the day before. Banjo was sitting on my chest and poking my face, his way of signaling me it was time for breakfast.

Outside, the sunny morning view had regained some of its splendor, but still felt somehow lacking.

I had to get to Steam Whistle Alley.

Playing as an archaeologist still seemed like a good idea. Secrets, she mentioned. I liked secrets. Secrets were good. They usually meant treasure.

I finished a mug of coffee and hit the shower in preparation for the day. Once done, I wrapped a towel around me and went over to my wardrobe. I could wear my usual jeans and T-shirt, but that felt out of place with the goggles. I knew they projected my clothing for me, so it didn't matter what I wore, but still...

I opted for some khaki pants and a long sleeve, white button-up shirt. Nobody would see it anyway, right? Banjo came into the room and chittered at me with a strange expression on his little monkey face. He seemed naked now without his vest and monocle. As if reading my mind, he bounded over to the side of the bed and swiped my goggles off the nightstand. He jumped onto the mattress, scampered to the edge, and held the goggles up to me in his tiny outstretched arms.

"*BAAAAAAAAAAAH SOWENYAAAAAH, MAMA*

BEESABAH," I sang, laughing. Even this far into the 21st century, *The Lion King* was still a classic.

Still chuckling, I took the goggles and set them on my forehead. I wasn't quite ready to jump back into AR, yet. Besides, from what I remembered of the day before, my apartment hadn't changed. Just everything else. Banjo probably just wanted the ability to speak again. Who could blame him?

"Soon, buddy," I reassured him.

He wasn't placated. He hopped off the bed and sat down, crossing his arms in a little monkey pout.

I went to the kitchen and fixed a bowl of oatmeal with sliced banana. "Lexi," I called, activating my computer. "Do I have any communications?"

Her face appeared on my kitchen screen. "Hi, Jacob. Nope, nothing important. Just the usual assortment of forum replies and auction updates."

Okay, then. I was ready to start the adventure.

"Banjo, you ready?" I called. He flew out of the bedroom and up my arm, perching on my shoulder, chittering excitedly. I didn't remember him being this enthusiastic when he wore the vest. Maybe the subroutines replaced his general sense of wonder with an ability to speak and a smart-ass attitude. *Great.*

We stepped out of the apartment, walked down the hall and into the elevator. I paused before pushing the button for the lobby.

"This is it," I told Banjo. I slid the goggles over my eyes and powered them on.

The interior of the elevator changed into... well, the interior of an elevator, just a much more stylish one. The doors had turned into a sliding brass grating that I could see through into the hallway, and the readout on the panel to the right turned into a pair of nixie tubes—glass bulbs containing filaments that glowed neon orange in the shape of the numbers corresponding to our current floor. Underneath was a series of actual buttons, each with a number or letter in an elegant serif font. The floor was made from planks of dark mahogany. A single Edison-style light bulb hung from the ceiling, casting the elevator in a warm glow.

"It's about time," came a high-pitched voice from my shoulder, making me jump in surprise. I might never get used to that. "Do you think it's funny, depriving me of my ability to speak?"

"What? I'm sorry, bud," I replied. "This is new to me too, you know. Wait. If I remember correctly, you said you'd be happy 'going back to my normal simian self,'" I said, mocking his Brooklyn accent.

"Yes, I know," he said. "I forgive you this time. Just think of the little guy once in a while, wouldn't you?"

I agreed, and grasping on to my collar for support, he stretched out his other arm and pressed the button for the lobby. Tiny puffs of steam came down from the crack between the polished hardwood ceiling and the front grates, and the elevator began its descent. A few seconds later, the doors opened, and we stepped into the lobby.

"Good morning, sir," greeted the droll butler voice of

Lenny the doorman. "Anything you will need today?"

I ignored him—the lobby was breathtaking.

Wrought iron and stained-glass masterpieces had replaced the front windows, depicting landscapes, cityscapes, portraits and more. Wooden beams, carved in intricate vines and flowers, supported the ceiling at regular intervals, connecting to each other in archways crisscrossing the white ceiling. The floor was a checkerboard of light and dark woods polished to an immaculate shine. Looking down, I could see my face, goggles perched on my forehead, and Banjo looking back at me. I also noticed the chain whip at my hip, my vest, my snazzy bowler hat, and everything else I had forgotten was there. It took me a second to get my bearings.

"Sir?" Lenny said, snapping me out of my trance.

If the lobby of my apartment was this amazing, what would the rest of the city be like?

Lenny looked the same, except he now sported a top hat, and his blue, glowing wheels and platform were now one wide, metal-spoked wheel attached between the truncations of his legs. Interesting.

"Sir, are you okay?" he asked again, seemingly worried.

"We're fine, Lenny," I assured him. "Sorry, I was daydreaming. Just the usual today, please. Banjo's almost out of food as well."

"Ah, we will get the place in tip-top shape for your return, sir, and we'll make sure Banjo's comestibles are well stocked," the doorman assured us enthusiastically.

"And don't get the cheap stuff this time. The cheap stuff

gives me gas," Banjo added. If Lenny heard him, he didn't show it.

Stepping from the lobby into the street was a moment I don't think I'll ever forget. The first thing I noticed, even with all the sights trying to assail my senses, was that the air *smelled* differently. Not foul, but not entirely pleasant. For about forty years now, air purification programs had been ridding the air of pollutants left by a century of internal combustion engines running unchecked. The air in Seattle these days was nearly as pure as before Europeans had come in and fouled it all up. Now, it smelled dirty, organic. I breathed in smoke, sweat, and other acrid odors I wasn't prepared for. Was this what it was like in days of yore?

While these new smells fascinated me, the surrounding sights and sounds bombarded me at the same time, forcing my consciousness into overtime just to keep up with it all.

My familiar street wasn't so familiar anymore. At least the nearby buildings were all roughly the same height as before, and the roads the same orientation, so I used those details to ground me as I attempted to take it all in. Up the hill towards the downtown area, I saw the skyscrapers I'd grown accustomed to had turned into towers and spires of brick, mortar, and wood, jutting into an ink-colored cloudy sky.

Cloudy? I thought. *Isn't it another sunny summer's day?*

In the spaces between the buildings where the hover cars, cabs, and buses usually operated, I saw various flying machines of wood, leather, and metal. Some had propellers facing downward like the drones from a few decades ago, while others were supported by large balloons or pieces of canvas connected to ropes and chains. One vehicle seemed to be flapping cumbersome wings comprised of canvas, stretched taut between rods that broke up the fabric at set intervals down the length of each. The buses had turned into grand airships, soaring majestically through the forest of buildings overhead. In the cabin suspended from one of the enormous oval balloons, I could barely make out people through the round porthole windows.

"Do you see this?" Banjo asked in an awed tone.

"Yeah, Crazy, isn't it?"

A thought occurred to me. Carrie said these goggles had a zoom function.

I reached up to the goggles and pulled them over my eyes. A strange sensation, as I knew I already wore them, but tactilely, it didn't feel odd in any way. I flipped down one of the lenses at random. Nothing in my field of vision got larger, but little orange dots appeared over people's heads. I focused on the dot of one man standing under the street under an iron lamppost, reading a newspaper. Three letters popped up next to the dot.

'NPC'

Interesting. I'd have to play around more with that later.

I flipped the lens back up and chose the second one. This time my vision blurred, and I was hit by a wave of vertigo. I blinked repeatedly, before realizing my right eye was zooming in while the left was not. I closed my left eye.

Everything became clear, and greatly magnified. Things darted past quicker than I was used to, and the vertigo returned for a moment. I sought out the man under the lamppost and focused on him again. This time, I could make out the smallest details of his face, even read the words on the newspaper he held. The headline read, "STILL NO HEIR TO STEAM WHISTLE ALLEY."

I flipped the lens back up, and then focused my attention on the action at street level. The street itself was grey cobblestone, and the wheeled vehicles and electric bicycles I was used to were replaced with vehicles powered in ways I couldn't even begin to guess. One woman in a long green dress propelled a bicycle-like vehicle by repeatedly pumping her butt up and down on the seat. Another car had a glowing orb held between two glass rods at the rear of his vehicle, propelling it down the street while emitting a high-pitched whistling. The Tesla poles, generally placed at every intersection throughout the city to wirelessly transmit power, had been replaced with actual Tesla coils. The donut-shaped objects stood on poles about five stories tall, sending bolts of electricity at random intervals to receptors placed on the sides of the buildings at the same level. Every time a bolt flashed, I heard a musical *zzzap* echo down the street, only to be answered by a pole at the far intersection giving the same performance.

Banjo sat on my shoulder wordlessly, sharing in my sense of wonder.

After such a sensory overload, I needed a quick break. I put my finger to the side of my head and powered down the headset.

The sunlight flooded into my eyes, blinding me. It took a good ten seconds before I could start to make out the outline of things around me. When things finally came back into focus, I noticed a few passersby giving me odd looks.

I perched the goggles on my forehead and took a deep breath. "Wow," I said to Banjo, "that was..."

I had no words. Neither did he, I remembered after a second.

The world around me now seemed positively mundane, but also somehow comforting. That place was *intense.*

Preparing myself, I took another deep breath and turned the goggles back on. New Seattle came rushing back, along with the cacophony of smells, sounds, and visuals that went with it. Everything got very dark, and it took my eyes a few seconds to adjust again.

Switching into and out of AR isn't as simple as they make it sound.

"This is going to take some getting used to," said Banjo, sounding a bit ill.

I had to get to Steam Whistle Alley. Iggy had said it was south of downtown on a large parcel of purchased land. I'd been playing the game for thirty minutes now, and the only thing I'd to managed to do was stand on the corner, freaking out the locals while gawking at everything around me.

I decided on a SoDo-bound hoverbus that would disembark from the roof of a five-story shopping center a block down. I could see the building from where I stood, although now it was a mansion with towers on each corner.

As I headed towards the hoverbus, I turned my attention to the crowd around me. Everyone I walked by was dressed in the steampunk-inspired fashions of *Panmachina*. The men's styles ranged from ensembles similar to mine, often with puffy sleeved shirts, vests, top hats or bowlers, to more formal and elegant affairs including expensive-looking jackets, pressed slacks and absurdly tall stovepipe hats. Many of the men sported outrageously ornate facial hair, from long curled beards and goatees to full, waxed mustaches.

The women were every bit as elegant. Some of them wore long, flowing gowns with tightly laced bodices and corsets. Others wore clothing similar to the men, but many opted for shorts instead of slacks, and more than a few had three to four buttons on their shirts undone to accent their shapelier attributes.

So much for Victorian-era modesty.

Nobody I saw wore the goggles, which led me to believe I was looking at all NPCs. Most of the player-testers would probably be gathered around Steam Whistle Alley, looking for the first clues to the quest.

Halfway down the block, I noticed something a bit off. While everyone I saw sported the fashion of the genre, some were... well, dimmer than others. Some were just as vibrant in color as Banjo or myself, while others looked dull. Washed out. I also noticed that the dimmer folks outnumbered the vibrant ones by about two to one, and it was the dull ones that occasionally gave me weird looks.

I had a hunch, so I put on my goggles and flipped down

the info-lens.

The orange dots appeared over people's heads again. I looked at one of the more vibrant women across the street from me, and the same information appeared as before.

'NPC'

Then, I focused on an approaching man, one of the slightly washed out ones. He was dressed in a tan shirt with a black vest and had a two-tiered handlebar mustache. He gave me an odd look as I stared at the information over his head.

'NPNC'

The man muttered something as he walked by, but I couldn't quite make it out. It seemed that even the speech of the less vibrant people was muffled.

"NPNC," I said aloud, wondering.

"Non-player, non-character," Banjo whispered in my ear. "It's the designation given to real people who aren't playing the game. You can talk to them and interact with them, but they won't be in character and have no idea that they're dressed like the queen's chambermaid."

I made it to the building that had the bus stop on the roof and entered the lobby. It was magnificently done, but not as ornate as my apartment's. A decorative sign stood by the bank of elevators, which used to read *"Elevators to Bus Stop."*

In a calligraphic script, it now read *"Airship to Steam Whistle Alley, and all points south."*

"Ding!" Banjo shouted. I jumped.

"Ding?" I asked.

"Sorry, Jakey," he replied, "but I just had a quest notification pop in my head, and I had this irresistible urge to shout 'Ding.'"

"Well what's the quest?" I asked with an amused smirk.

"Get to Steam Whistle Alley and meet your companion. Reward unknown," he answered. "That's all I've got."

"Doesn't sound horribly difficult."

We entered the elevator, similar in décor to the one in my apartment, and got out on the roof. There was nobody else up there, so while waiting for the bus I walked to the roof's edge and took in the view. I could now easily discern the NPCs from the non-players by the vividness they displayed. I was also getting used to the scenery, and the mechanical contraptions gliding through the air around me and on the streets below no longer bothered me as much. Everything was actually kind of awesome.

A clock face on a tower two blocks away showed that the blimp-bus should be arriving in about two minutes. Like clockwork, two minutes later a massive airship glided down towards the landing pad. I took a few steps back to make way for its descent.

The alarm tone it usually sounded, a melodic, rhythmic series of beeps, had been replaced by a loud, wailing klaxon as the airship finished its descent. The balloon, made of white canvas with ropes the size of my leg surrounding the circumference at either end, was twice the size of the cabin, and the cabin itself appeared to be the same size as our standard bus. This made sense, as the cabin *needed* to be the same size as the bus, didn't it?

I tried not to think about it. I was a play tester, not a programmer.

The cabin itself was a masterful display of woodwork, with celestial carvings covering its surface and brass portholes running the length. The entrance stood in the same place as usual, at the midpoint of the bus, and it was from there a wooden plank telescoped out and downward, touching the rooftop a meter in front of me.

A tinny voice crackled from a speaker at the front of the airship.

"This is the 10:35 Airship Andromeda, bound for Steam Whistle Alley and all points south!" it shouted. *"ALL ABOOOARD!"*

CHAPTER EIGHT: THE ALLEY

I boarded the airship and looked around the interior. Just like the exterior, the dark woodwork was carved in reliefs of planets, stars, and galaxies. The seats, which had been vinyl in an uncomfortable shade of green last time I was on the bus, were now maroon plush cushions with elegantly crafted backrests and armrests. The conductor at the front of the cabin sported a striped suit jacket and pants, wire-rimmed glasses, and an impeccably kept white beard which tapered to a point halfway down his chest.

"Doors are closing!" he boomed over the loudspeakers. "Time waits for no one. Next stop, the Grand Stadiums!"

There were five other passengers in the cabin, four of which were the washed-out NPNCs. In the back-left seat, however, sat a boy of perhaps seventeen, with gold-colored goggles perched atop a mass of curly red hair. His freckled face smiled as he saw me, and he waved me over.

My first impression was that he seemed the type who was always smiling, always enthusiastic. He was a pudgy boy wearing robes of silver and green, and a glove with a single emerald on the forefinger knuckle of his right hand told me the kid was a summoner.

I walked over and took the seat across from him. Banjo hopped down into my lap. The airship lifted off the platform and began meandering its way through the skies of New Seattle.

"Heading to the alley?" he asked, but before I could answer he continued excitedly. "I'm heading there myself. Gotta meet my companion, but I have no idea what they look like. I was told when I got to the alley, my third lens will act as a tracker to help lead me to them."

Interesting. I didn't get that piece of information.

"Nice monkey!" the kid said. "I thought we didn't receive our familiars until level five. Are you level five?"

"No, he's level one," Banjo replied, and the kid gasped happily.

"You talk! They didn't say that the familiars talk."

"Not all of them do, and I'm not a game-generated familiar. I'm a biosynth, but I've been repurposed to make sure Jakey here doesn't die."

"Jakey, is it?" said the kid. "I'm Trick. Well, the name's Patrick, but everyone calls me Trick. Nice to meet you!" he exclaimed as he extended a hand.

I took his hand and shook it. "You too, Trick," I said. They were the first words I had been able to get out in the conversation. "My name is Jacob—only Banjo here calls me Jakey, or at least he has in the twelve hours he's been talking."

This kid had an annoying kind of energy, but it was

hard not to like him.

"You're an archaeologist," Trick announced. "What are they like? I thought about it, but I'm crap with a whip. What are your stats? Do you have any special skills?"

"I'm not sure," I replied. "I've only been playing for about an hour."

"I just got in from Boise myself yesterday with my mom, got my goggles and started playing yesterday morning. Took the hyperloop out here—you should see what they've done to it. You think this airship is impressive? You just wait!"

"Are you always this excited?"

"I'm sorry," he said, lowering his chin sheepishly. "Not really. It's just that you're the first other player I've met. Can you imagine? Steam Whistle Alley! We'd never have to work again."

"That would be nice," I agreed. "So, you're a summoner?"

"Yep!" he said. "We get one new summon every five levels, and we can use some basic offensive, defensive, and support spells. My first summon's a bobcat. First level summons aren't that great, I found out, but they get better once you hit different level tiers. At ten I'll be able to reanimate corpses if I choose that route, but I think I'll stick to more traditional summoning. I don't really fit the mold of a necromancer."

I had to agree with him.

The speaker crackled overhead. "We have reached the Grand Stadiums."

Trick and I peered out the window. I had seen Largent Field and Niehaus Park many times before, two of the city's most famous landmarks and home to the football and baseball teams. Now, however, they'd transformed into something even more magnificent. Largent Field looked like a gigantic, medieval castle, with soaring, steeple-roofed observation towers jutting into the sky at regular intervals around the circumference. Niehaus Park looked reminiscent of the Roman Colosseum, had it been constructed of grey stone slabs and dark hardwood. Both were lit beautifully in shades of blue and green.

We landed on a lofty platform nestled between the two stadiums. The doors opened, and the conductor began his announcement. "We have reached the Grand Stadiums! Please check to make sure you have all your belongings. This is the 10:35 Airship Andromeda, bound for Steam Whistle Alley and all points south! ALLLLL ABOOOOARD!"

Nobody got off the bus, but a gargoyle got on. He wore nothing but a grey loincloth, the same color as his skin, and grey metal goggles perched on top of his head. Instead of taking a seat he remained by the entrance with his back to us. He stood nearly two meters tall, and his ash-colored wings were probably twice that length unfurled. A white ivory spike topped each wing, which stretched a half meter over his head, and extended down to his ankles.

"Wow, would you look at that," Trick whispered. "Do you think we should say hello?"

"He doesn't appear to be in a very talkative mood," I replied.

Banjo agreed. "Yeah, I'm good."

The arrival of the gargoyle seemed to put a damper on Trick's enthusiasm, and apart from the low conversation of a couple of dimmer people near the front, we made the rest of the journey in silence. I couldn't make out much, but I heard the word 'goggles' a couple of times. Guess I couldn't blame them.

About five minutes later, the speakers crackled again. "Now arriving at Steam Whistle Alley!" I leaned over Trick to peer out the porthole but couldn't make out much.

"Wait a second," I said. "If this is the bus, this is usually the spot I get off when I'm going to my man cave. Yes, there it is!" I smiled.

"Your man cave?" Trick inquired.

"It's the place where Jakey keeps all his toys," answered Banjo from my lap.

"My collections," I corrected him, then turned to Trick. "I collect vintage video games and action figures and display them in a storage area down there. I have it fixed up real nice, with furniture and framed vintage posters and such. Kind of a home away from home."

"I tried playing a few old Nintendo games on an emulator a couple of years ago," offered Trick, "but those things are crazy difficult."

I agreed with him. "Imagine if that was all there was to play," I said. Trick chuckled in response.

The airship banked to the right, and a wondrous sight slid into view through the porthole windows. Below us, spanning an area of about three city blocks long and two wide, was an amalgamation of buildings, wires, and lights roughly in the shape of a 'U'. It was hard to pick out individual buildings; they all seemed to haphazardly bump into each other. Running down the middle of the 'U' was a wide avenue, with airships and other flying contraptions landing and taking off incessantly.

As the airship descended, I could make out one sign which read, in bright red filaments encased in a thick glass tube, 'Wonkel's Hotel and Eatery.' The ship dipped lower, and I took in flashing arrows directing people down darkened side alleys. Other filament tubes displayed words like 'Apothecary' and 'Respite.' The airship flew lower still, dodging other smaller vehicles on its way down.

A high wall surrounded the entire region, carved with details I couldn't make out from so high up. A massive gate the width of the central thoroughfare sat in the north end of the wall, with a jumble of gears and pulleys to either side.

At the end of the alley, at the base of the 'U' about three blocks away, stood an impressive mansion, with symmetrical towers rising on either side. Every window in it stood dark, however, and I couldn't make out any finer details. It appeared to be the only area down the whole three-block stretch that wasn't illuminated in some fashion.

The airship touched down softly on a platform near the avenue attached to the third floor of an ornate building. The speakers crackled once again, and the conductor shouted, "We have arrived at Steam Whistle Alley! Everyone out who's getting out! We will have a fifteen-minute layover while we wait for passengers."

The door opened, and the gargoyle got out first, walking onto the platform and down the wooden steps leading to the station. Banjo climbed onto my shoulder, and I walked to the exit with Trick following me. We left the cabin and walked by a line of people waiting to board, most wearing goggles, and stepped down the wide, curving stairs into the grand station. The gargoyle was nowhere to be seen, although I did see a female one on the far side of the room, waiting in line to buy tickets.

The station was impressive. The ceiling was three stories above our heads and decorated with frescoes of airships and maps of lands I didn't recognize. Three massive chandeliers hung from the ceiling, each one a series of concentric gears dangling from chains. Clear globes with incandescent coiling filaments provided the light, spaced at intervals around the largest gear. The station was crowded, and as I finished descending the stairs, I thought I saw at least one representative of all the player paths Carrie had mentioned, except werewolves. There might have been a couple, but it would be difficult to pinpoint them during the day. We crossed the marble floor to one of the archways that led to the street and then stepped outside.

I looked around to get my bearings and take it all in. I imagined how I must look, standing slack-jawed, head slightly tilted back as I looked from one wonder to another. I had a feeling this reaction was commonplace around here.

Alley was a misnomer for this place. The main thoroughfare was about twenty meters wide, crammed with people, mostly players and NPCs but a few dimmer folks mixed in as well. Vendors' carts lined the side of the street, and the smell of cooking meats and spices mingled with the odors of smoke and sweat. Shops, hotels, bars, restaurants, and other places of trade and entertainment stretched down either side of the road all the way to the darkened mansion, broken only by the occasional side alley. I glanced down the closest one and saw two hooded figures lurking in the darkness. Probably should avoid those for the time being.

The smell of cooking meat got to me once again. Was the sensation caused by the game, or was this a real aroma I was drooling over?

Trick had closed his eyes, and inhaled deeply, apparently thinking the same thing.

"Do you think the food is real?" I asked. I was starving.

"Oh yeah," he said. "ARGO's subcontracted all sorts of vendors to take part in the game. Here in the alley, if you can smell it, you can eat it." He scowled and seemed to re-think the statement. "You know what I mean."

I chuckled and walked up to a cart. A man standing behind it was cooking skewered chicken over coals. His cart had a spoked wheel on either side, with a single support post by the handles providing the third point of balance. A metal awning covered the whole cart, and the vendor smiled as I approached.

He was a dark-skinned, balding man with a thin mustache and wire-rimmed lenses balanced on his nose, attached to a chain that led to his vest pocket. "What'll it be, boss?" he asked as I approached, not lifting his gaze from his methodical rotating of the chicken.

I ordered a portion, and the vendor put four skewers on a disposable plate, covering it with a sweet-smelling peanut sauce. I took the plate, and the vendor swiveled a thumbprint sensor towards me, framed by a brass gear. "Twenty net, please."

Well, this would make things easy, if netcoin was the coin of the realm. It also meant the game would be very stingy with the coinage awarded for quests and battles.

I pressed my thumb to the sensor, and it made a *clinking* sound. "*Terima kasih!*" said the vendor in a language I was unfamiliar with.

I offered a skewer to Trick, who snatched one from my hands almost before the words left my mouth. "So, where to now?" I asked between mouthfuls of chicken. I offered a piece to Banjo as well, who thanked me and proceeded to nibble away happily.

"Well," Trick replied, gnawing at his skewer. He paused to swallow before answering. "We should go find our companions." He finished his snack and slipped the skewer into his pocket, frowning when he noticed my questioning look. "What? You never know when you'll need a skewer."

Trick pulled his goggles down and adjusted one of the extra lenses over his right eye. "Ah, there they are," he said, turning to the southeast. "So, I'll see you later then?"

"Um... how do we friend each other here?"

"I'm not sure," said Trick, twisting his face.

Banjo piped up from my shoulder. "Touch the power button on each other's goggles at the same time," he explained. "But don't press it."

We did as instructed and a tiny chime rang in my ear.

"Now all you have to do is say, 'Call Trick,' and you can talk to him wherever you are."

Trick waved goodbye and wandered down the street towards the darkened mansion in the distance. *Nice kid*, I thought.

I pulled on my goggles, slid down the third lens in front of my right eyepiece, and a tiny green asterisk appeared in my vision, with '521 M' in minuscule green letters next to it.

"What am I looking at?" I asked Banjo.

"That is your current quest objective," he answered. "You'll only get exact directions like this when you've received the exact location of something. For the first quest, though, I guess they wanted to ease the players in. Otherwise, the first few days would just be hundreds of players wandering around in a fog, asking, 'Are you my companion?'"

I started down the street in generally the same direction Trick had gone, although my target appeared to be on the opposite side of the cobblestone road. The number in my vision decreased as I got closer. Around me drifted the conversations of players and NPCs on the street, some of which appeared to be getting to know their companions for the first time. One such couple, both women, appeared to be a brawler and a thaumaturge. They'll make a good team, I thought as I walked past them.

An NPC with long white hair erupting from the sides of his top-hat beckoned me over as I passed by the building just to the south of the station.

"Ah yes, hello!" he greeted me. His voice was almost annoyingly sing-songy. A horde of odd contraptions zooming around on wheeled platforms surrounded him. Made me think of Lenny. A brass post was attached to each platform, and an ancient-looking monochrome monitor connected to each pole, green text flashing across their screens.

"Hi. Erm...what am I looking at?" I asked.

"Lieutenant Jiggy's Portable Status Screens!" he announced proudly. "Ever wondered exactly what your strength was, or precisely how charismatic you are? Well, wonder no more! With one of Jiggy's Portable Status Screens following you around, we take the guesswork out of life!"

Banjo and I exchanged glances, then looked back at the odd man. He took our continued presence as interest and clapped his hands twice. "Chipper!" he exclaimed, and one of the monitors-on-a-stick rolled up to his side.

"Show this man here... I'm sorry, what was your name?" he asked.

"Jacob."

"Show Jacob his stats," he finished. The monitor rolled over to me and leaned backward, and my stats appeared before me, flickering across its screen in green pixelated text on a black background.

```
NAME:JACOB       LEVEL:1      HP:180/180
PATH:ARCHAEOLOGIST            MP:25/25

STRENGTH:        3
CONSTITUTION:    3
INTELLIGENTS:    6
DEXTERITY:       5
CHARISMA:        3
LUCK:            4

WEAPON PROFICIENCIES:WHIP, DAGGER
SKILLS:PERCEPTION, WHIP CRACK, DECIPHER
GUILD SKILLS:NONE
GUILD POINTS:0
```

"Um...you know you misspelled 'intelligence,' right?" I tried to bite back my grin at the irony but failed.

The white-haired man whipped the monitor around to look at the screen, opening and closing his mouth a few times. Then he looked at me, the toothy grin returning. "That's a local spelling, from the dialect of—"

"I think we'll be fine, but thanks anyway," I cut him off. Banjo and I started towards our destination again, the cries of the monitor salesman fading behind us. A few seconds later, and we heard him greet another mark, extolling the virtues of his wares.

"Why would anyone want a rolling display of their stats following them around everywhere? What's the point?" asked Banjo from my shoulder.

"I don't know. I suppose some people just need to

reassure themselves constantly," I said. Sure, I glanced at stat boxes in games, but didn't feel the need to every five minutes. It was the experience that was my whole reason for gaming, the escape—not the stats.

I stopped for a second in front of the storefront I noticed from the air, 'Wonkel's Hotel and Eatery.' It appeared to be one of the more popular places on the strip, with players, NPCs and even NPNCs entering and exiting at regular intervals. A percussive-stringed instrument sent an upbeat tune through the open doors, and the aroma of stew and ale wafted towards me. The place appeared to have four stories, with some of the illuminated upper windows displaying people's silhouettes against the curtains.

I kept walking until the number in my display read '20M.' I found myself outside of a wood-paneled building the size of a convenience store, with a sign reading 'Thom's Munchies' over the patio awning, behind and a little to the west of the hotel. The two patio tables stood empty, so I walked up the front steps, opened the door and entered the establishment.

An older gentleman greeted me from behind the bar, dapper in a starched white shirt and full-length apron. His long grey mustache rose upward as he gave me a broad smile.

"Welcome to my humble establishment!" he said. "Let me know if there is anything you need. Name's Thom."

A couple of NPCs stood at the bar. High-backed booths around the perimeter afforded their patrons some privacy. The three tables in the middle of the floor stood empty.

The glowing asterisk led me to the booth in the back corner of the room, and I felt a rush in anticipation of meeting my partner in crime.

When I saw who sat there, I almost stumbled face-first into the table. There, smiling up at me, goggles resting on her beautiful purple hair, was Jeni from the coffee shop.

CHAPTER NINE: THE BEGINNING

"*D*ING!" shouted Banjo about two centimeters from my ear. "Dammit," he swore. "That reaction is one hundred percent involuntary. It's almost like a sneeze, just sneaks up out of nowhere. Anyway, quest complete. You got 150 XP for finding your companion. 350 XP until level 2, Jakey."

My ear was ringing but I didn't process the words. Instead, I just stared down at sweet, sweet Jeni, a dorky smile stuck on my face.

Jeni glanced at Banjo before turning her attention back to me. "I know you," she said. "From the coffee shop. Wanna sit down?"

I nodded and took a seat across from her in the booth. Banjo jumped onto the backrest and perched on the corner.

Jeni smiled up at the monkey. "Hey there, cutie," she smiled. "I've seen you around, too. What's your name?"

"Jacob," I answered. I couldn't seem to stop smiling.

"I think she was talking to me, Cassanova," Banjo whispered.

I finally managed to force down the smile. "Thanks," I whispered out of the corner of my mouth.

"My name's Banjo," he said, adjusting his monocle. "It's a pleasure to meet you."

"Likewise," she said. She turned that glowing smile my direction, and my heart leaped into my throat.

"Well, what are the odds?" she asked.

"Yeah," I agreed. My brain function was trickling back. Slowly. "How'd you end up here?"

"Do you know Iggy?" she asked, and I nodded. "Well, he always comes in for a double espresso on his lunch break. One day, he up and asked me if I wanted to playtest a game his company was working on. Originally, I turned him down. But then he mentioned the money, and..." she trailed off, staring at her hands.

"And you couldn't say no," I finished for her.

"No, it's not that. Well not just that," she replied. The blush deepened in her cheeks. It looked good on her. "Nevermind." An awkward silence descended over the table.

I opened and closed my mouth a couple of times, unsure of what to say. Luckily, I was saved by the bartender coming over to take our order. I hadn't even seen a menu, but she ordered us a slice of apple pie and a couple of cups of coffee.

"Hope that's okay," she said after he'd left. "I'm pretty sure you like coffee." Her smile returned, sending my mind back to oblivion.

I wish she would stop doing that, I thought. *Wait. No, I don't.*

"I like coffee," I agreed. *She's going to think I'm a moron.*

She made an amused sound in the back of her throat. "You have quite the way with words."

"Sorry. The past few hours have been a little overwhelming."

"I threw up when I first put on the goggles and went outside this morning," she offered, patting my hand. "I know how you feel."

That simple contact made me lose all semblance of rational thought once again, but thankfully the pie and coffee arrived quickly. I took a bigger gulp than I intended, then tried not to let her see the pain on my face as my tongue caught fire.

She laughed again, and I smiled after forcing down the burning brew.

"So," she said, after taking a bite of pie. "Your character's name is Jakey? That's cute."

I looked over at Banjo and sighed. "No, I kept my real name. Banjo just calls me Jakey."

"Shame," she replied. "I wanted to call you Jakey."

"Well, um..." I stammered. "I really don't mind it that much." She smiled at me again. "What about you? Are you still Jeni?"

She nodded. "Figured it'd be easier. I almost don't feel like I'm playing a character."

I understood the feeling.

"Wait," I said as the thought struck. "What path are you?"

"Can't you tell?" she asked me, grinning now.

She was dressed in a white, long-sleeve shirt with a wide collar, and if I remembered correctly, she was wearing brown shorts and shoes—I decided against peeking under the table to check. I also remembered seeing no whip, or wrench, or anything else that would give away her path.

She cocked her head at me and lifted one eyebrow, waiting for me to figure it out.

"Got it!" I snapped. "You're a brawler!"

She opened her mouth excitedly as if to agree, but then said, "Nope."

Behind me, Banjo let out a soft, "*Oooooooo.*"

I examined her again, and she looked back inquisitively, smirking. The eye contact was nice but made it hard to think. Banjo continued making the '*oooo*' sound.

"You're not an engineer, are you?"

She shook her head.

"An archaeologist?"

"Nope, that's you," she said. "See, I'm actually good at this."

Banjo leaned closer to my ear, and a little bit louder, said, "*Awooooooooooo!*"

"You're a thaumaturge! What, not a fan of robes?"

Banjo slapped me in the back of the head. "She's a werewolf, you moron!"

The bartender looked up from polishing a glass. Jeni burst into fits of laughter.

I rubbed the back of my head and glared at Banjo for a moment. "I knew that!" I scolded the monkey. "I was just playing along."

How could I have forgotten about werewolves?

"So," she said, changing the subject. "Banjo gives you status updates. That's cool."

"Yeah, it's definitely something," I agreed. "How do you get yours? I heard you don't get familiars until level five."

"Well, I've only gotten two updates—one for the companion quest and one at its completion, just now," she explained, "and they've both come as voices in my ear. There's a small speaker in the strap of my goggles. It reads me my stats and gives me other information, if I command it to."

I looked at her goggles, made of a highly polished metal that had kind of a mint green tint to it. "What, you didn't want a stat screen on a stick?" I asked.

"I saw those too," she said. "Not sure how, but I managed to resist the urge to buy one."

Another silence. *Come on, Jacob.*

"So, what did you get for the quest? 150 XP?" I asked.

"Yep," she said. "I decided the best way to complete this quest was to sit in one place and let my companion come to me. Looks like it worked."

I sipped my coffee and took a bite of pie.

"By the way," she said. "What's with the ding?"

Banjo piped up from behind my shoulder. "I wish I didn't have to say it. It comes on like the world's biggest hiccup," he sighed. "But it is what it is. I'm going to try to fight it next time. The status updates, the HP reporting, I'm happy to do that. But the damned ding..." Banjo's sentence trailed off into a low growl.

The conversation continued this way for a while, filling each other in on what we'd found out so far, which, all in all, wasn't much. The more we talked, the more comfortable we became with each other's company, and the conversation became an order of magnitude more enjoyable.

"Jeni," I said, "I want to win this thing. I have no idea what the quest involves, or even where to begin, but I'd like to be on top, at the end."

She raised her eyebrows and looked at me with that pair of soul-snatching blue-grey eyes. It took me a second. "I didn't mean..."

"I know, just joshing you," she said. "Hey...whatever the quest involves, I bet you it involves that mansion at the end of the main drag. People have been crawling over it all morning, but I think they've given up on it. On my way here, I didn't see anyone near it. Want to go check it out?"

I nodded, we finished off the pie, and then we walked to the counter to pay.

When the bartender presented the thumb pad, Jeni quickly snuck her thumb in and gave me a wink. The machine gave a click, and the bartender thanked us for our patronage. We walked out of the restaurant and into the street, Banjo scurrying along behind, all knuckles and feet, trying to catch up.

Back outside, most players we saw ran about frantically, either looking for their partners or tackling some other task. Jeni and I, on the other hand, strolled side by side, not in any particular hurry.

"So, tell me about werewolves," I said.

"Not much to say, yet. I think you know about as much as I do from character creation," she replied. "Which reminds me, what did you think of Duke?"

"Duke?" I asked, confused.

"Duke, the Demon of Creation?" She must have noticed my blank expression. "You didn't get Duke?"

I shook my head. "I had a woman named Carrie. She was super helpful."

"You missed out, he was a very..." she paused, apparently thinking of the word, "manly demon," she finished.

I raised my eyebrows, but she didn't say anything else, just smirked. It was a mischievous look, made her appear almost elfish. Or wolfish. Probably more fitting.

"Well, mine was a very womanly... woman," I replied playfully.

She shrugged. "Anyway, I haven't seen my werewolf form yet, aside from the creation mirror, but I wanted to keep my hair color." she said, brushing a purple lock from her forehead.

Purple was my favorite color.

Then it dawned on me.

"Wait... are you telling me my questing partner is a... purple werewolf?"

She chortled. "You'll have to wait and see."

"Until the sun goes down?"

She nodded. "Tonight, it sets at about half-past eight."

"So, what will you do during the day?"

"Well, I'm not *entirely* useless." She pulled out two sets of brass gauntlets from the pouch hanging at her waist. They looked fierce and well-made, the geared hinges at the knuckles made from dark metal. This metal also extended from each finger, forming sleek claws. She handed me one of the gloves.

"Not bad," I said, turning it over in my hand before handing it back. "So, what time is it now?"

"No clue," she said, looking around.

Now that I thought about it, I hadn't seen any clocks either. Odd, for a place with so much clockwork.

Banjo ran up the back of my leg and sat on my shoulder. He pulled a tiny pocket watch from inside his vest. "Two thirty-eight," he said, then ran back down and fell behind us once again. Smart monkey. *Thanks, Banjo.*

She smiled. "I can't wait for my familiar."

"So, should we wait for nightfall before we go exploring?" I asked.

"We don't have to," she said. "As I said, I have a lot to offer in my human form." She looked at me and gave a slightly naughty wink.

I blushed, and a smile came to my lips.

"There's a fairly low-level quest we could go on. It's almost required for us wolves," she said. "I'm not sure where it is, or what's involved, but the reward at the end is the Lupine Amulet. It allows me to transform at will, regardless of the time of day. I don't think anyone's figured out the quest yet, as I haven't seen a single wolf since I've been here."

A woman wearing a green leather bodice and flowing black skirts walked by us with what might have been her young son, in the washed-out colors of non-characters. The woman wore a huge wire-framed 'bum' under her skirts that accentuated her backside. Accentuated might be inaccurate. It exploded her butt out to gigantic portions and made her sort of waddle when she walked. She ignored us, fanning her face. The kid took a phone out of his pocket and took a picture of us before hurrying to rejoin his mom.

"Nipnicks," Jeni complained, rolling her eyes at me.

I gave her a questioning look.

"Nipnicks are what players are calling the NPNCs," she explained, "at least according to the only other player I've talked to since I've been here."

I nodded. Sounded a bit derogatory, but this was a game, wasn't it? We needed some way of referring to them, and saying 'NPNC,' or, 'that dim, washed-out looking bugger' seemed like too much work.

We reached the final block of Steam Whistle Alley, essentially a courtyard for the dark mansion that took up the entire end of the street. One of the gargoyle characters a couple hundred meters in front of us jumped a good fifteen meters into the sky and flapped his wings once, which let him hover for about three seconds, before falling back to the ground and landing in a squat, both feet and a fist on the ground to give him balance. He must have had an eight-meter wingspan. I wondered if it was the gargoyle from the airship earlier.

"Well that was pretty impressive," said Jeni, but she

twisted her face. "How do you think that works, flying in AR?"

"I think it's more of a hover move," I said. "The AR lets us see the gargoyle shoot into the sky, but I'm betting he never left the ground. Essentially, it's a surveillance move. I'm betting the engineers can produce a device that can give other players the same effect if they're worth their wrenches."

The gargoyle had left, and there were no nearby storefronts, leaving us the only ones around as we reached the gates leading to the mansion's courtyard. Jeni and I shared a nervous look, then I pushed the gates open, cringing as their hinges squeaked. We walked through, following the flagstone path that led to the steps up to the porch, and the enormous double doors beyond. They featured mirror images of relief carvings, depicting a forest scene. I could make out horses and foxes interwoven amongst the carved trees.

I tried the doorknob, but it wouldn't turn. Pushing or pulling yielded the same result.

"Any ideas?" I asked.

She answered by walking to one end of the porch and then the other, trying windows, and looking at the floorboards and siding for clues.

A glimmer in the corner of my vision caught my eye as she approached the front steps again, just to the left of the double doors. I moved in closer to examine it.

"Look at this," I said.

About two meters to the left of the door frame, painted

the same rich deep-brown as the siding and nearly invisible, I noticed a tiny recessed button. Maybe my archaeologist's perception at work. I glanced at Jeni, then back at the button, and pressed it.

Nothing happened.

Jeni moved to the right side of the door. "Hey there's one over here too," she said, but nothing happened when she pressed hers either.

"On the count of three?" I suggested, and she nodded agreement.

"One... two... three."

We both pressed our buttons and a tiny nook opened to the left of the door frame with a *thunk*. Then, one on the right opened as well, followed by another above the door. I looked in the one closest to me.

Inside was a mechanism of interlocking gears, except it looked like one was missing. A stubby, silver-colored post projected out about two centimeters where the cogwheel should have been. I walked over to look in Jeni's box and saw the same thing. Just to be thorough, I jumped and grabbed the top of the door frame, pulling myself up to have a look in the third. Same. I lowered myself back down.

"You see this?" I asked, pointing at the left nook. "It looks like each mechanism is missing a gear."

"Well," Jeni offered brightly, "it's a start."

It was at that. Unless I missed my guess, we needed to find three gears that fit those posts.

Banjo piped up from his seat on the railing. "Well, you're in the right place if you're looking for gears," he said, not entirely helpfully.

At that moment a commotion broke out at the far end of the courtyard, just outside the gates to the mansion. We watched a wide, rectangular platform roll up and stop in the middle of the square, the narrow ends facing either side of the street. On both sides of the platform were two large bellows, pumping up and down rhythmically—when the left was up, the right was down, and vice versa. Between them stood a large machine, where I could see clockwork motors and gears turning in jerky time with the bellows. Above the whole thing hung a brass spotlight, suspended by three short ropes from a balloon adorned with a pair of propellers on both sides. It shined down on whatever was on the platform on the other side of the machine.

An amplified voice cleared its throat from the platform. "*Hear ye, hear ye!*" the voice boomed, in a rumbling baritone that could probably be heard from three blocks away. "*My name is Arnie Drubbins, esquire. Mayor and caretaker of Steam Whistle Alley. In fifteen minutes, I will have an announcement to make to the general public. Please be at the southern courtyard in fifteen minutes. Hear ye, Hear ye!*"

CHAPTER TEN: THE ANNOUNCEMENT

We stepped off the porch and descended the staircase, intrigued by the sudden interruption.

"Arnie Drubbins? Ever heard of him?" I asked Jeni, as we approached the rear of the platform.

She shook her head. "I don't think any of us got a lot in the way of backstory when we signed up."

Banjo cleared his throat. "Arnie Drubbins, Esquire," he explained, "is, as he says, the mayor of Steam Whistle Alley. He's the NPC responsible for collecting the taxes on all the trade that occurs here, as well as protecting the denizens of the alley. He has also acted as caretaker ever since Dramia DeMune went missing three years ago. That was her mansion we were poking around the outside of."

"Really?" I asked.

"Indeed," replied the monkey, "but unfortunately, that's about all I know about the matter."

I turned to Jeni, who just shrugged.

We walked around the side of the platform and took a position towards the front, as more players started to crowd in around us. From here, the platform looked more like a stage, with a framework of braided iron, supporting heavy, black-frilled curtains. There was no trace of the person who had made the announcement.

Scanning the crowd, however, I saw a familiar face.

"Hey, Trick!" I called. "Over here!"

From the far end of the platform, Trick turned his head. When he saw me, he greeted me with a big wave and a smile. He turned to a winged statue standing next to him, and a moment later the two of them made their way over to us, pushing through the crowd.

"Hi, Jacob!" the curly haired boy said with his infectious grin. "I'd like you to meet my companion, Honeybucket. Honey, this is Jacob."

I craned my neck back to look up at the gargoyle, who smiled at me. I use the word smile here loosely, as her face looked like she had run nose first into a stone wall, and the resulting damage exposed the cracked brown eggshells she collected inside.

The woman was hideous.

I wouldn't have even known she was female if it weren't for her chest, despite the fact she wore only a loincloth and her goggles. Her breasts were proportionate to her body, which meant they were huge, and had the same stony grey texture as the skin that covered the rest of her. Also, they were devoid of nipples.

She extended a gnarled, clawed hand down to me.

I took it, wincing from her crushing grip.

I introduced them both to Jeni, and after the

pleasantries, Trick asked if I knew anything about the announcement we were all waiting around for. I shook my head.

It was at this point that Honeybucket screamed in terror, nearly piercing my eardrum, and launched herself straight up into the air. The people standing nearby backed up in alarm, myself included. My hand went to my chain whip—I'd been building a steady itch to use it. After playing for five hours I'd accomplished nothing except finding my partner.

The gargoyle crashed back down to earth, and her arm straightened, pointing to the ground.

Right at Banjo.

"You..." she growled, "have a monkey?" Impressively, she tried to make herself small, and hid behind Trick, which was too humorous an image not to laugh at.

"That's Banjo," Trick said. "He's not a danger, just Jacob's familiar."

"I don't care if he's the president. I don't like monkeys. Or gorillas. Or lemurs," she said, trembling.

"I'm sorry to have startled you, ma'am," Banjo said, giving her a bow. "For the record, you're quite frightening yourself."

Honey kept her distance, and Banjo didn't provoke her, although part of me expected him to leap up and shout, *"BOOGA BOOGA BOOGA!"* The commotion died down as quickly as it started, although Honeybucket didn't take her eyes off Banjo for more than a couple of seconds at a time.

"So, have you managed to find out anything useful?"

Trick asked.

"Not really," I lied, kicking Jeni on the heel with my toe. I wasn't ready to tell anybody else about the three hidden doors around the entrance to the dark mansion. The alpha test phase was, after all, a contest, and I needed to maintain whatever advantage I could. I liked the kid and all, but I liked the prospect of winning better.

"What about you?" I asked.

He shook his head. "Nah, I just found Honey here a couple of hours ago, and we hadn't even left the hotel until the announcement."

I smirked and raised an eyebrow at him.

"Not like that!" he protested. "I mean, we sat in the restaurant *attached* to the hotel... and chatted about the game and stuff."

"I see," I said, but kept smiling, and gave them both an obvious wink.

Trick turned as red as his hair but didn't continue his denials. Even Honey's cheeks appeared to blush a darker shade of grey.

"Quit teasing them," Jeni said. "If they want to keep their beautiful blossoming relationship a secret, that's their business."

"I'm sorry, what was your name again?" Trick said, obviously annoyed.

Jeni just grinned. "I'm sorry. I only tease people I like. And my name's Jeni. One 'N,' one 'I.'"

The crowd continued to grow and pressed in around us, excited to hear the announcement to which we had front row seats. Two spotlights attached to the platform lit up and turned inwards, signaling that our wait was over. Fog machines in the back kicked on, flooding the stage with thick clouds of vapor.

A circular aperture in the platform dilated open like the lens of an antique camera, and a platform below the stage rose from the space beneath. On it stood an obese man—or at least, I thought he was a man. He wore dark red pants with a matching overcoat, a yellow vest with a white shirt underneath, and a comically large red bowtie decorated with yellow stars. His right hand was not a hand at all, but in fact, a claw made out of two plates of brass connected to a series of pistons and gears. In it, he held an old microphone. He raised it, signaling for silence, and the crowd complied.

"Ladies and gentlemen," he began, in a strong but squeaky voice. "I would like to thank you for attending my announcement. What I have to tell you will set you all on your way to attain the ultimate goal: custodianship of one of the most wonderful places on earth..." A pause for dramatic effect. "Steam Whistle Alley."

The crowd erupted in cheers, and I turned to look at everyone who had gathered. Iggy had said there were three hundred players in the alpha, and it looked like most of them had found their way here already. Also present were more than a handful of NPCs, cheering along with the players. Out of curiosity, I flipped down the info-lens on my goggles. The air above the heads of the crowd lit up with green asterisks.

I leaned over so Banjo could hear me. "Hey, Banjo... how can I see just one type of person with this info-lens?" I asked. "I mean, if I just wanted to see NPCs."

He scampered up my leg to sit on my shoulder. "Right here, attached to the base of the info-lens is a tiny dial," he said. "Four positions, left to right. One is for all characters, position two is for players only, three is for NPCs and four NPNCs."

"Thanks, bud," I replied.

On the stage, Arnie Drubbins was going on about his history with the alley. How he started off as a newsboy, *yadda, yadda, yadda.* Nothing of any importance. Still looking at the crowd, I flipped the dial to its second position, and a few of the asterisks winked out, showing only the players. I flipped it again, and the ones that had winked out turned back on, while all the others disappeared.

"Then they bestowed upon me the honor of town clerk, in charge of all the accounts and all the comings and goings in the alley..." Arnie went on from the stage.

I turned the dial to position four, and only three asterisks remained. Two were over the heads of the dim woman and boy I'd seen earlier. Apparently, even though they couldn't see the stage or hear the speech, the crowd was enough to keep them interested. A third asterisk, towards the rear of the group, floated over another nipnick.

But this one was wearing a pair of goggles. And apparently, watching the speech along with everyone else. This struck me as very strange, although I didn't understand what it meant. How could he be a nipnick if he had goggles?

Even more bizarre, immediately to his right I saw a face I recognized, although it took me a second to realize from where. He had eyes that just *looked* like he was up to something, and the pencil-thin handlebar mustache and pointed goatee that made him resemble a villain from a black-and-white movie only furthered the persona. It was... what was his name? Jameson. The man I saw on the sidewalk when I first got sucked into this madness. The man Iggy had been arguing with.

I stared at the two for a few more seconds, then turned my attention back to the stage, as it seemed Arnie was finally getting to the point.

"So, without further ado, I would like to give you all the first little tidbit of a clue that might lead you to untold riches and the fulfillment of your wildest dreams," Arnie announced. The crowd went deadly silent. With his good hand, Arnie pulled a piece of parchment from his breast pocket, looked down his long nose at it, and began to read.

"There's a place in the city that's no more to be seen, but still to this day remains covered in green. This place, though evolved, a beast it still harbors, so seek, if you will, the place of the arbors."

He put the piece of paper back in his pocket.

"In fairness to those who have yet to join us, this quest will open in a little more than two days' time, at the stroke of midnight. This will give you time to learn your skills, get geared up, and maybe gain a level or two. I wish you luck!" he exclaimed, replacing the microphone. As he waved to the crowd with both his hand and his claw, the platform began moving left, sliding silently across the courtyard and into an adjacent alleyway. He turned a corner and was soon out of sight.

The crowd watched his exit, then broke into a murmur of conversation. Some started to run off in different directions, wanting to get a jump on the competition. I scanned the crowd but saw no trace of Jameson or his nipnick companion.

"Ding!" Banjo yelled, followed by an array of creative profanity, and then a sigh. "You've received a new quest, the Quest for Steam Whistle Alley." He grumbled, folding his arms. "You and everyone on this damned street."

It was by now late afternoon, and I wanted to wait until nightfall to test out the combat system, so I could see Jeni rage in all her glory. We had about two-and-a-half hours to kill. I pulled Jeni aside.

"Jeni, Trick's a decent kid, and his gar-girl seems nice, but I'd like to keep all the big quest stuff just between us for now," I said. "But, if it's all okay with you, I was going to invite them along for some low-level grinding after the sun goes down and you wolf out. The gargoyle will be an excellent tank. Sound good to you?"

She nodded. "I was thinking the same thing."

I smiled at her, then turned back to Trick and Honeybucket. "Hey, you two, we were wondering if you wanted to get together and do some level grinding after sunset," I said. "Jeni here's going to go full wolfie for the first time, and we want to take advantage of it."

"We were going to ask you the same thing," Trick said. "We're going to hit a few of the local pubs and restaurants, see if we can get any intel on some good noob zones."

"All right, then," I nodded, "Call me if you hear anything."

They wandered off, as had most of the crowd, leaving me alone with Jeni and Banjo.

"I need a cup of coffee," I said, "and we need to discuss something."

"Lead on," she said.

Banjo hopped on my shoulder, and we wandered in the direction of the markets. It wasn't long before my nose detected the scent of fresh-roasted coffee. We followed the aroma to a roadside coffee vendor, pushing a wooden cart that carried a complicated-looking brass contraption, which hissed and spurted jets of steam. We ordered two and sat at one of the tables as he pulled levers and turned dials to prepare our brew. Banjo curled up on a stool and shut his eyes, sneaking in a nap, and we sat in silence for a minute, waiting for the coffee and watching the odd assortment of people pass by.

One man in a top hat and tails, wearing large wire-frame spectacles, hopped furiously down the road on a steam-powered pogo stick that appeared to be malfunctioning. I chuckled.

The coffee arrived, light and sweet as we had ordered, and I filled Jeni in on what I had seen in the crowd earlier.

"So, you're sure you saw a nipnick with goggles, watching the announcement?" she asked. "It's a bug! It's what Iggy's paying us to report, isn't it?"

"Yeah, but he was with Jameson. He's the one that I followed when I was sitting outside the coffee shop that morning. The one that led me to where I am now," I explained. "Iggy was a bit sketchy on the details, and it seemed like a sore subject, so I didn't want to press. Made it sound like he and Jameson went way back, and that's why he was allowing him to be an observer in the alpha. But apparently Jameson wanted to compete."

"Maybe Jameson knew too much, and it was more dangerous for Iggy if he cut Jameson out altogether," Jeni offered.

"Maybe," I agreed, "but I'm not sure if I want to report this just yet. Might be worthwhile to see what else we can find out. By the way," I said, changing the subject, "any ideas on Arnie's clue? The whole beasts and arbors thing?"

"None, but I'm guessing somewhere woodsy. I wish I'd written it down."

"I'm sure Banjo's memorized it," I said. "He's good at that kind of thing."

"Yep, I am," confirmed Banjo, without opening his eyes.

I sipped my coffee. "Well, Trick and Honeybucket are searching for some low-level mob areas for us to hunt later. Maybe we should go dive into the market, see what we can find?"

She nodded in agreement. "I heard someone talking about a salve they make for werewolves to apply to their claws, in the apothecary," she said. "Gives +2 to damage, but only works on keratin. In theory, you could use it on your hair, but I don't know if headbutting everything is the best combat tactic."

The market was adjacent to the food court, so we didn't have far to go. Banjo got up and stretched and followed us as we weaved towards it. A large banner was strung between two poles across the entrance, the words written on it were in elegant serif lettering.

"The Uncommon Market," Banjo read. "Sounds like my kind of place." He skittered off ahead of us.

The Uncommon Market was the busiest place in the alley. Set just off the road, it spanned a two-block stretch of the main thoroughfare and looked like one of the Sunday flea markets my mother used to take me to as a kid, only stranger by far. The north and south sides bordered actual storefronts and seemed to organically blend in with the stalls and tables that made up the rest of the market. One of these storefronts had a flashing nixie sign out front, the filament in the shape of the word 'Apothecary.' This would blink out before another filament in the same tube lit up, spelling out the words 'Herbs & Potions'. We walked towards it, picking up a couple of large canvas backpacks from a vendor that had set up shop outside the apothecary doors.

We managed to find the potion Jeni had wanted, and picked up ten vials of minor healing potion, as well as five minor mana potions for Trick, as he would probably be our healer for the night. The glass vials had brass plungers, and looked much like a syringe, although they didn't have needles.

We exited the shop and proceeded to browse the market, looking for anything else that caught our eye. I picked up a pair of leather gloves that offered +2 to defense. I had already forgotten what my actual stats were—I knew my intelligence and dexterity were decent—but found in this simulation I didn't care as much. Maybe Iggy was right. Continually bombarding the player with stats and numbers and updates wasn't the way to go. It was all about immersion, and this game had it in droves.

Jeni stopped at a booth selling hats and bought me a new purple feather for my bowler, that, probably not coincidentally, matched her hair. *Does she actually like me?*

The booths got progressively stranger as we proceeded farther into the market depths. One vendor sold nothing but bones. Skulls, along with every other imaginable type of bone, spread across his table and hung from strings attached to the canvas ceiling. Another seller sold books, all of which were written in languages neither one of us recognized. Some even gave off eerie humming sounds.

The next vendor had an array of mystical looking jewelry. Display cases on the table held gemstones of every color and cut, and rings of silver, gold, brass, and obsidian. Jeni picked up an amulet and ran a finger over what looked like a small button on one side. Out of curiosity, she pressed the button, but nothing happened.

A raspy voice, full of gravel and spite, spoke up from behind us.

"Give me the amulet, bitch."

My hand went to my whip.

CHAPTER ELEVEN: THE PARTY

e're screwed, I thought.

I spun around and yanked my whip off my belt, an action which felt woefully unfamiliar. Jeni turned to face our attacker as well, while Banjo ducked under the counter supporting the display cases.

The man that faced us was skinny, with a blonde buzzcut and a perpetual sneer. His left eye had been replaced with... some sort of glowing red lens, ringed with a series of stacked gears, which rotated with a metallic *rizzt* as he appeared to focus on me. His arms were bare, and a series of horizontal black leather straps cinched tightly around his torso, held on with odd-looking clasps that ran down his sternum. His featureless, dark-green pants looked five sizes too big for him.

"What do you want?" I asked, my voice squeaking. Having your voice take a giant leap back into the beginnings of puberty is not conducive to intimidation.

"I want the bitch," he paused for effect, "to give me my amulet."

Jeni, who looked as terrified as I felt, complied, tossing the amulet at the man's feet before pulling her arms close to her sides, protectively. She moved closer to me, and I put an arm around her shoulder—an uncharacteristic display of gallantry on my part.

"That's better," said the man as he retrieved the amulet. "Relax. I ain't gonna hurt ya." His voice had an almost stereotypical Irish accent. The gears around his eyepiece rotated again, and the lens shifted color to seafoam green.

"You called me a bitch!" Jeni blurted, pulling from under my arm and taking a step toward the man, fear apparently forgotten. "Twice!"

"I just calls 'em as I sees 'em."

"Apologize to the woman," I demanded, emboldened by the man's sudden shift in demeanor.

The man held up his hands, palms toward us. "Sorry if ya took offense, ma'am," he said. "There's been a good deal of thievin' around these parts since we opened up the market to your lot, an' it's barely been a week!"

I relaxed a bit but kept up the stern tone. "Well that might be the case," I said, "but you can't call her a bitch."

"Well she is one, isn't she?" the man asked, seeming confused. "I could smell her comin'!"

What was this guy's deal? My anger rose again, and I took a step forward, fist clenched.

Jeni put a hand on my shoulder to restrain me but didn't put much effort behind it.

"What, ya wanna hit me, boy?" the man taunted. "You won't stand a chance." The gears around his eyepiece rotated again, and the lens returned to a deep, fiery crimson.

"I can verify that," said Banjo, peeking out from under the table. "You'd get torn to ribbons."

The man threw his arms out to the side and seemed to flex every muscle in his body at once. His shoulders and arms bulked up before my eyes, and his chest began to expand. The straps around his torso snapped open along the front buckles, and hung behind him, attached to something I couldn't see.

My balled fist wilted like the last dandelion of summer, and I stopped in my tracks.

The man's face began to contort grotesquely. His eyes—well, his one eye and his eyepiece—shifted towards the side of his head, and the front of his face elongated, from nose to chin. He opened his mouth, and his teeth grew into fierce-looking fangs, actually dripping with saliva.

Jeni and I took a couple involuntary steps back, neither of us able to tear our eyes away from the spectacle before us.

Hair erupted from every inch of his skin, like the videos of grass growing I'd seen in the nature-feeds back in school. The rich blond hair covered him from head-to-toe, save for the palms of his hands, which faced us from the ends of splayed, muscular arms. He threw back his head... and emitted what can only be described as a long hoot.

Jeni and I looked at each other, perplexed, a hint of a smile forming on both our mouths.

The man's eyepiece turned a light golden color. "I'm sorry," he sighed. "I can't howl. I dunno why. I keep hoping one of these times I'll try, and it'll erupt out of me like the finest of wolfen specimens, perched atop a windswept cliff, silhouetted against the full moon on a snowy night."

We just stared.

"They keep telling me you lot don' like to be called bitches, but I keep forgetting," he said, apologetically. "Bitches been bitches since I was a pup. You're a wolf too, ain't ya?" he asked, looking at Jeni.

Jeni nodded.

"Well, you're new, and unless I miss my guess you haven't had your first change yet," he said, eyeing her appraisingly. "But you'll be a fine one, you will. I'll do my best not to call you a b..." he paused. "That word. And they also tell me I shouldn't sniff your arse. That true?"

"Yes, please don't," Jeni responded, not bothering to hide her disgust.

"Well, what should I call you then?"

The adrenaline in my system retreated to wherever it came from, leaving only an elevated heart rate, a couple of sweaty palms and a light fog in my mind as evidence it had ever arrived. Banjo gingerly made his way out from under the table to the back of my leg and watched the beast warily from behind it.

"My name's Jeni," she said, her expression relaxing. "And this is Jacob."

"Name's Bartley," said the werewolf, extending a paw. I shook it tentatively, followed by Jeni. The skin around his pointed teeth pulled back in what I thought was a snarl, making me tense again, until I realized it was Bartley's version of a friendly grin.

"So, let's see your fur then," he said to Jeni.

Her shoulders relaxed. Seemed to be getting used to Bartley's abruptness. "From what I understand, I can only transform after the sun goes down. And you're right, I haven't done it yet."

"Right, right," he nodded, his muzzle bobbing. "Your lot need the amulet, I forgot."

"The Lupine Amulet!" exclaimed Jeni, turning to me. "That's the one I was telling you about. I get that, and I'll be able to transform whenever I want." She turned back to Bartley, excitement brightening her features. "Do you know where I can find one?"

"Aye, that I do," said the werewolf. "But it won't be easy."

Bartley's eyepiece rotated, and the lens turned a dark purple. "Head to the Alkira Coast, southwest of the city proper. Once you find it, follow it south. It will end at a steep hillside, and you'll be able to walk the beach no further."

Jeni smiled excitedly at me, then turned back to Bartley.

"You'll see a gate in the hillside, which leads into a series of tunnels under the hill. It's in there you'll find your amulet," he said.

I heard a grunt from the area near my feet and looked down to see Banjo's monkey face contorted in what looked like a painful spasm.

"Mnrrrrghhhh," Banjo groaned.

Banjo continued spasming. Jeni looked worried, and Bartley like he had no idea what was going on.

"DING!" the monkey shouted, followed by a series of profanities.

Jeni and I both laughed, relieved. Bartley looked even more confused.

"You've received a new quest," Banjo said with a sigh, seemingly resigned to his fate. "It's called, surprisingly enough, the Quest for the Lupine Amulet. Plus one for originality there," he grunted. "Anyway, I recommend a party of three to four people, all around level three."

"Hey, you know you've got a talking monkey?" asked the werewolf, wide-eyed. Well, wide-eye.

"Yeah, kind of hard to forget," I said. "His name's Banjo."

We thanked Bartley, and he nodded. "Don' mention it," he said, then tossed something to Jeni, which she snatched out of the air.

She opened her hand and smiled. It was the amulet she'd been looking at earlier.

"That'll help you out, I should think," Bartley said. "Press the little button there three times, and it'll light the area around you a good thirty paces. You'll need it where you're going."

"Thanks again, Bartley," Jeni said, and I echoed the sentiment.

His muzzle twisted once again into his version of a smile. "It's not every day a bi—" he began, "beautiful girl turns into a werewolf for the first time."

Nice recovery.

We made our way out of the market and back to the main street, Banjo once again on my shoulder.

"The sun will be down in about an hour," said Jeni.

"Should we call Trick and Honey?"

"Yeah, probably should," I said, "although I don't think we'll be able to do the quest tonight. We could spend a few hours leveling though if they've found us a good spot." I scratched my eyes. It dawned on me that I'd been wearing my goggles for nearly nine hours now. My eyes were starting to itch regularly, and although I'd rubbed them repeatedly, it didn't help much. I must've been rubbing my augmented eyes—my real ones were still under the goggles.

"Call Trick," I said, and a soft beep emitted from a spot behind my right ear. A few seconds later, Trick's head, completely lifelike, floated in front of me.

"Heya, Jacob," he said. "Whatcha find?"

"We got a quest while we were in the market. The reward is an amulet that Jeni can use to turn into a wolf whenever she wants," I explained. "What about you?"

"Useful!" Trick said. "We found a map in the library showing the low-level places around New Seattle. There's a ton of them. Honey's up for some nighttime grinding if you guys are."

Jeni laughed, and Trick's head turned to face her. "Get your mind out of the gutter."

"You can see him?" I asked her.

"Yep," she said. "Companions can see calls that their partners make, from what I understand. There's a way to bring more people in too, and set calls to private, but I'm not sure how."

"ARGO really needs to work on their manual," I said.

"So anyway, you want to meet at the café by the airship

station?" Trick asked.

"Sure thing," I agreed.

"Okay, be there in five," Trick said, and his head winked out of sight.

We were only a block from the café and the dock, so we strolled over and got a table. A few other tables were occupied, the closest by a group of engineers poring over a pile of schematics spread on the table top, the corners weighted down by coffee mugs. At one of the far tables, a gargoyle and what looked like another archaeologist talked in hushed tones.

A couple minutes later, they arrived, Trick displaying his ever-present grin.

"Hello!" he greeted us. He pulled out a chair for Honeybucket, who sat down, but not before giving Banjo a wary look.

"Listen, I'm sorry you don't like my kind, but I'm not that bad, really," Banjo said from my shoulder. "But if it makes you more comfortable, I'll hide down in his lap."

"No, you're okay," said Honey. "The fact you can talk makes you a little bit more bearable, I suppose."

Banjo seemed to accept this and began to groom my hair. Trick sat down between Jeni and Honey and pulled out a large, rolled parchment, aged a yellowish-brown.

"So, where are we going for our first real grinding spree?" asked Jeni.

Trick moved some of the coffees aside and rolled the parchment out. I recognized the map of Seattle. Seeing it like that made me think of something one of the first

European settlers of the area had drawn over two hundred years ago. On closer inspection, I took in schematics of various geared mechanisms on the corners of the paper, and what looked like a large dragon inked out in Puget Sound, labeled as The Pugeot Channel on the map.

"Most of the beaches are good newbie zones," he explained. He pointed to an area on the west side of the landmass. "This is Golden Gardens, but in the game," he squinted at the map, "oh... it's still Golden Gardens. Don't mess with a good thing, I guess. This area's infested with slimes—they give minimal XP but present us with hardly any danger. Green ones mostly, but a few blues and purples mixed in. Head north on the beach and you start to run into a few sand diggers. They're a bit tougher defensively but if you stay clear of their claws and don't let them gang up on you, you should be okay. This area, like most of them, will be crawling with nipnicks, and I don't know how that'll affect XP grinding."

"They'll probably just stare, maybe take a couple of pictures," Honey said.

Trick ran a hand through his mop of red hair, knocking his goggles slightly askew on his forehead. "This area over here," he said, pointing at the area I knew as Ravenna, renamed Gaslight Gulch, "has also been designated as a newbie area. Again, a ton of nipnicks, but we'll be able to hunt tanglebells, a kind of mobile plant-looking thing which spits a weak venom, as well as a few slimes there, too."

I nodded, intrigued. Ravenna was by the university, and I had spent a lot of time there in my youth.

"Or," offered Trick, "we could head to Alki." He pointed to a spot on the southern side of the map.

"The Alkira Coast!" said Jeni, reading the map's label. "That's the spot Bartley mentioned, where I can find my amulet. He mentioned a cave at the south end."

"Well, we should head there, then. It's a long beach, with a magnificent view of the city," I said. "I wish there were a noob area not infested with nipnicks, but I'm not too worried about it. What's there for us to hunt?"

"Let me guess... slimes?" asked Jeni.

Trick nodded. "And the sapphire crabs. High defense, decent offense, more of a level two or three beast but with the four of us we'll be okay. According to what I read, they drop some good loot, including sapphires every once in a blue moon."

"Well, should we head out then? The sun'll be down in a few minutes," I said.

We finished our coffees and entered the station to board the next airship into the city. We could already see it to the north, floating through the twilight, growing steadily larger as it approached. We would have to transfer at the stadiums to get to Alki... the Alkira Coast.

The airship touched down, and the conductor called for passengers to board after a couple of players disembarked. We got on and found a pair of plush bench seats facing each other. Banjo plopped into my lap and promptly fell asleep. I sat across from Jeni, who sat next to Honey. I rubbed my eyes again.

The airship doors closed, and we lifted into the air. A

single Edison bulb hung on the wall between us over the porthole windows.

"Guys, I need to stretch my eyeballs for a second," Jeni said. She put a finger to her temple, then, her whole body dimmed.

What a fantastic idea, I thought, then followed suit.

My earlier experience had taught me to close my eyes when logging out, so I could adjust gradually. I raised the real goggles to my forehead and slowly opened my eyes, blinking a few times. Jeni was smiling back at me. She was now dressed in jeans and a green T-shirt, but little else had changed.

Next to Jeni sat a tall woman, about eighteen or nineteen, with long, dyed black hair, and black eyeshadow and eyeliner framing her eyes. She stared out the window, expressionless, her goggles perched on her head. I looked from her, to Jeni, then to my left to see that Trick had taken off his goggles as well.

The airship had turned into its usual, sanitary self, the same hoverbus I'd ridden for years with its plain beige walls, and rows of advertising screens above square windows that ran the length of the cabin. Outside the windows, the city of airships and Victorian towers had reverted to the jungle of glass and concrete monoliths, flying cars, and building-sized advertisements. It felt good to be back, but at the same time so very bland.

We all looked at each other, blinking, then Jeni started to giggle. The laugh proved infectious, and Trick and I both caught it, laughing at the odd feeling of having one reality

STEAM WHISTLE ALLEY

completely replacing another in an instant, but not in the way that stepping out of a VR unit changed your perspective. This was more like having the world's most glorious coat of paint stripped off the world in front of your eyes. I think our brains weren't prepared for the change.

The laughter continued, drawing a couple of stares from the other two people on the bus, and a glance in the rear-view mirror from the driver. Even Honeybucket caught it, albeit reluctantly, and her low, throaty chuckle made Trick completely lose it.

"Honeybucket!" he guffawed. Banjo opened his eyes to look at the commotion but didn't say anything. *Well, he can't say anything now.* It was amazing how quickly I became used to having a talking monkey.

When Trick caught his breath, he said, "I'm sorry," and gasped for air. "I just... didn't know what to call you, and Honeybucket just popped in my head and it just seemed so..." The laughter died down to a round of winded sighs between the four of us.

"It's okay," said the former gargoyle. "I get it. My name's Shauni, with an 'I.' You guys can still call me Honey in real life if you want. Honeybucket was a name my little brother gave me when we were kids."

"Well it's nice to meet you," said Trick. Jeni and I made some awkward introductions, as Shauni already knew our names.

We got off at the stadium and waited on the platform for the bus to take us to Alki. All four of us still wore the goggles on our foreheads but were now in our usual attire.

Trick's green robes were now a baggy green shirt and grey jeans that hung loose on his portly frame. Banjo had woken from his nap and now chirped from my shoulder. If he was missing his ability to talk, he didn't show it. Shauni gave him an uneasy look.

The sun was now just a tiny sliver over the Olympics, and we paused for a second to take it in. I wasn't sure about them, but it was an odd, reassuring sort of feeling for me. Spending the day in the aesthetically mind-blowing AR had made the real world seem flat and dull, but the sunset was a reminder that real life had its wonders too.

This feeling was reinforced as I watched the last rays of the sunset reflect off Jeni's face. My pulse quickened, then the sun sank completely behind the mountains. Jeni tilted her head back and howled softly, then turned and smiled at us.

The moment was interrupted by the arrival of the Alki Bus. The doors slid open, and we all got on.

"Next stop, the Alkira Coast!" Trick exclaimed with a wide grin.

CHAPTER TWELVE: BLACK AND WHITE

The hoverbus pulled up to the platform floating above the Alki strip, and we all disembarked.

The area had long been one of the most popular places in Seattle. The waterfront afforded a panoramic view of the city skyline, from the Space Needles on the north end all the way to the stadiums in the south. The east side of the strip was packed with shops, restaurants, and residential buildings. The west side bordered Puget Sound, with a wide sidewalk for joggers, bikers, and hoverfooters. A broad, sandy beach stretched below the path, where people threw Frisbees and kicked balls, or just combed the shoreline looking for odd bits of flotsam and jetsam. From our vantage on the bus platform, we could see bonfires popping up, creating halos of flickering light on the sand. Music emanated from circles of people sitting around the fires playing drums and guitars, and also from speakers hanging over restaurant patios. The beach activity centered around the area most densely populated with storefronts, while to the north and south the glows of fires became fewer and farther between.

Trick pointed down the beach to the south. "That's where we'll be going," he said, and then turned to Jeni. "And that's where your cave is, as well."

We took the lift down to street level, and crossed the road, joining the people enjoying the warm night air. We walked south on the jogging path, getting passed by joggers getting in their after-work exercise. I for one wasn't in a hurry to put the goggles back on; Alki provided enough sensory stimulation already. Besides, it felt good just to have the air hit my eyes. The itch in my sockets had just gone away, which reminded me to pick up some eye drops. The rest of the group didn't seem to be in a big rush, either.

Trick and Shauni took the lead, while Jeni, Banjo and I brought up the rear. We continued south until the storefronts gave way to a residential area, mostly expensive condos and apartments constructed to take advantage of the waterfront view. After negotiating a set of stairs down to the beach, I brought our group together in a loose huddle.

"Ready to go back?" I asked, and in response everyone lowered their goggles and powered them on.

The transition was almost instant. Shauni was Honeybucket once again, already spreading her wings to give them a flap. Trick was back in his robes, but when I looked at Jeni, I took a couple involuntary steps back.

She had an adorably short muzzle and two impressive canine fangs, protruding from either side of her snout to extend below her jaw. Her goggles still rested on her head, just in front of two pointed ears. Despite her newfound ferocious appearance, her body was still quite feminine, covered by nothing but a loincloth. Modesty, however, didn't seem to be a problem, as thick purple fur covered every inch of her, from the tips of her ears down to her clawed feet. Her natural resting stance had become hunched, very tense, almost like one of my He-Man figures.

I couldn't help but stare, a goofy grin plastered to my face. Trick and Honey seemed to be enjoying the transformation as well.

"How do I look?" she asked, a wolfish smile on her face as she turned from one side to the other, striking model poses.

"I'd do you," said the gargoyle. Trick appeared to choke on his tongue.

"You look great," I said. My mind inadvertently wandered to thoughts of stuff I'd seen on furry fetish sites during late night browsing sessions. *Bad brain.* "Yeah, um... great." I could feel my cheeks burning red and was certain she noticed.

"Where are your clothes?" asked Trick.

That was a good question. Bartley had that strange leather strappy outfit that seemed to accommodate his transformation. We didn't get to witness Jeni's.

"Well, the real me is still wearing them, I'm pretty sure, or I'd be getting a lot more stares," she said, her speaking ability apparently unaffected by the fact her mouth was now a snout. "I'm hoping when I change back my clothes will mystically reappear, although I don't plan on still being up at sunrise to find out."

Banjo cleared his throat from the sand near my feet. It was easy to forget him when he wasn't on my shoulder. "She is, more or less, correct. For the sake of modesty, the AI has created an expedited transformation sequence," explained Banjo. "ARGO didn't want a bunch of pervs following people around waiting for them to wolf out, so the effect can be best described as a slow fade from one form into the other."

"So how do we group?" I asked.

"You know the dial that lets you see the stats on NPCs and such? In the center of that is a little indentation. That's your function button," Banjo said. "You press it and give voice commands. You'll mainly use it for forming parties, unlocking skills and distributing stat points. Just press it once and say 'form party,' followed by the names of the characters you want to join. The person forming the party becomes the leader. Experience is distributed evenly if you take part, so stay active in the battles, and you'll get your fair share."

"Got it," I said, smiling. Nice to have my own furry instruction manual.

I tore my eyes away from Jeni and looked around at our surroundings for the first time. Unlike the trip to Steam Whistle Alley, not too much had changed here. An airship negotiated the skies in the distance, and a ferry traveled out on the Sound, far enough away that all I could make out was a paddlewheel and belching smokestacks, and the reflection of its lights off the water. The occasional nipnick who passed us seemed even dimmer at night, and the sky was still...

My breath caught as I looked up at a gap in the clouds. There, hugging the half-moon was a second, smaller half-moon, pale silver and slightly brighter.

"Okay, that's cool," I said, and the rest of the group followed my gaze, uttering soft sounds of wonder.

I took in the two moons a minute longer, and then turned my attention to the group. "All right, who's gonna lead this shindig?" I asked. "Honey? You're our tank. Want to do the honors?"

"Despite my appearances," she said, "I'm more the submissive type."

I snorted. Not the best trait for the tank. "Trick?" I asked.

"I plan on hiding in the back. It's what I'm good at," he said, a grin splitting his freckled face. I could almost swear his freckles were casting their own shadows in the moonlight.

"I nominate Jacob," said Jeni.

"Seconded!" Trick chimed in.

Secretly, that's what I'd been hoping for, so I didn't bother protesting. "All right, then," I said, and pressed the button on the lens dial. "Form party," I stated, "Jacob, Jeni, Honeybucket, Trick." Then as an afterthought, "Pizza, disco music."

"Your party's been formed, minus the food and tunes," confirmed Banjo.

"Banjo," I said, fiddling with my goggles, "this dial can show me who's an NPC, a NPNC, and a player, right? What about mobs?"

"Mob stats are on the third lens, the one you haven't used yet," he said. "In its base state it will show you the mob's name, level and HP only. Upgrade your goggles with an engineer, and you can show other stats, like mana points, weaknesses and status effects."

I nodded and swiveled the third lens down, leaving the other two upright.

"Is there any way to track my own health?" I asked.

"I can give you blow-by-blow damage reports if you want, or I can just tell you when you fall below a certain percentage," said Banjo. "In the markets you can buy a wrist screen that you can glance at to let you know where your stats currently stand, as well as check on skill progression and such."

"Yeah, they're pretty useful," said Trick. He extended his arm so his hand emerged from his sleeve, and showed me his device. It looked like a wide brass bracelet, a thin screen on the surface, with four dials to the right, green and blue crystals to the left, and a series of buttons underneath.

"Well, I wish you would have told us that earlier," I said. Now that I was about to get into battle, I found myself rethinking my earlier sentiments regarding stat screens. I still didn't feel the urge to pore over numbers, but a way to monitor my health without having to rely on Banjo would be useful.

"So, what about our skills?" I asked. "Do any of you have any idea what you can do yet?"

"I do!" chirped Trick, looking at his wrist. "I have a level one summon, as well as a level one slow spell. Jeni," he said, concentrating on the screen as he turned a dial, "you have level one slash and howl skills. Slash is your basic attack, and howl makes the enemy cower." He turned another dial. "For a one-point reduction in damage. It has a ten-minute cooldown."

I needed one of those wristbands.

"Honey," he said, pressing a button, "you're level one in glide, which gives you a fifteen-meter hover, and," he turned a dial, "you have a level one pound."

Honeybucket snickered. "I'll take it."

"Jacob," Trick said, "at level one, you have whip crack, perception, and the decipher ability—that last one uses MP, lets you read things the rest of us can't, although at level one I'm betting you'll just get snippets."

"Oooh, exciting!" Honey teased, then turned on a voice suited for movie trailers. "Thrilling translation action!"

"You can get these read to you, through your goggles, too," Trick explained. "Or by your familiar when you get one. I opted for the wrist screen as soon as I saw it. I feel naked without my stats."

Well, it was a start. I checked my pouch to make sure the potions I'd purchased were readily available, then looked at the group. "Are we ready to do this?"

I received a chorus of enthusiastic affirmations in return, so I set off south down the beach, Jeni to my right, Honey to my left, and Trick bringing up the rear. Banjo scampered up my back and onto my shoulder.

We'd walked maybe five minutes when I noticed a

glimmer along the beach maybe a quarter-mile ahead—a flicker to get my attention, my perception skill in action. As we got closer, and I saw the creature's name and level, superimposed over a short red bar.

'Sand slime, Level 1'

The creature looked like someone had dumped an entire bucket of purple snot on the beach and tried to bury it in sand. It contracted and pulsated rhythmically, but other than that exhibited no signs of free will, intelligence, or aggression. It simply sat there in all its blobby glory.

Without warning, Honey rushed at the creature and thrust downward with a clenched fist in the middle of the amorphous blob. Fat drops of purple goo splattered everywhere, and the creature's health bar dropped by about a quarter. As Honey tried to right herself, a tendril of sand-covered ooze emerged from the slime's central mass and wrapped around her forearm. Without thinking, I grabbed my whip and cracked it at the slimy tentacle. The razor tip found its mark, severing the appendage in two. Honey fell backward and landed ungracefully on her butt.

Trick shouted, "Come to me, Shorty!" and a small bobcat appeared by his side in a cloud of white vapor. "Attack!" Trick commanded, and the bobcat leaped nimbly on the pulsating ooze, scratching twice before darting away, shaking its paws. At the same time, Jeni rushed in, a purple blur, and swiped once with each clawed hand. The remaining health in the slime's health bar shrank away. The ooze *blurped* out a sad bubble and stopped pulsating.

An elderly couple, out for a romantic moonlit stroll,

witnessed the entire glorious ordeal. I imagined what they saw: a group of four people in street clothes wearing crazy goggles, rigorously attacking a spot on the beach, while a monkey watched silently.

My cheeks burned as the couple stared, not knowing what to make of us.

I pointed at the sand. "Slime," I explained, then bent over to examine the motionless blob.

The couple went on their way, the man mumbling something about drugs.

I found nothing of value in the corpse, but Banjo informed me we each got five XP from the fight and had 345 to go until the next level.

Two things became immediately clear to me. First, this wasn't VR. Fighting here expended real energy, required real muscles. AR was actual exercise, a realization that stirred mixed feelings as I leaned over, already a little out of breath. A quick look around the group told me that the girls were having similar thoughts, as they panted from the exertion of fighting one weak slime. Trick seemed fine. Maybe he had this all planned out ahead of time.

I did some quick calculations and informed the group we'd have to kill sixty-nine more slimes before leveling up, and that was if we all stayed active in each battle. With the four of us, we could split the energy expenditure four ways, and it occurred to us we didn't have to pretend to be battle masters to dispatch these slimes.

We blasted through about ten of them before we took a break, winded. Trick, thinking ahead once again, pulled a canteen from under his robes and we all took a big drink.

"Forget health potions," Jeni said, "next time, let's bring more water."

Our first sapphire crab proved to be a bit more of a challenge. It appeared after we moved farther south, the lights of the strip now far behind us. Its shell glinted blue in the moonlight, about the size of a manhole cover. It skittered sideways across the beach at a remarkable pace for a crab, claws extended out in front of it threateningly. The beast's stats hung over its shell.

'Sapphire Crab, Level 3'

The crab's health bar was over three times as long as the slime's.

"*Sloven!*" Trick shouted and pointed at the crab. The air between Trick's finger and the crab rippled, and a thin line of distorted space corkscrewed out of Trick's hand, impacting the crab. Its movement slowed to a crawl, and the girls rushed in to attack with claws and fists.

Even slowed, the crab's claw managed to nip Jeni on the arm as she struck its shell. Honey hammered a fist down on the crab's back, and together the two attacks drained the crab's health by maybe a quarter. I struck with my whip, aiming for one of its eye stalks. The point of impact erupted with bright blue sparks, a critical hit, and his remaining health dropped to just over half. The eye I struck hung limply on the stalk, and blue ichor dripped onto the sand. Trick's bobcat leaped in and swiped at the other eyestalk, and the crab, now blind and with only a sliver of health remaining, made a beeline towards the surf. But Jeni rushed in, and with another swipe of her claws, finished it off before it could get there.

She bent down and removed a blue gem from the shell of the corpse. "Sapphire!" she exclaimed. "To the deathblow goes the spoils?"

"For now, that's fine," I said, "but I saw some dice at the market. Tomorrow we roll for loot?"

The group agreed.

"And twenty XP apiece. Now we're getting somewhere!" said Banjo.

"Nice. Everyone okay?" I asked, panting.

"Yeah, just let me..." Jeni plopped down on the sand next to me, "sit for a second."

I collapsed next to her, and the other two joined us, while Banjo flipped over rocks looking for real crabs, and the bobcat took a catnap.

"Well, 275 XP to go, at least for me," I said. "Do all paths level at the same rate?"

"It would appear so," replied Trick, examining his wrist screen. "Which means fourteen more crabs. They seem plentiful down here—I can see three more south of us. You guys up for it? It's not even midnight yet."

I was exhausted, and my muscles were aching in ways I wasn't used to, but I didn't want to seem the weakest link, especially in front of Jeni. "I'm up for it if you guys are."

We fought our way south, dispatching eight more crabs before the beach ended at the base of a steep hill jutting into the water. We'd taken minor cuts from the melees, but our regen rates appeared high enough that we healed back up before it ever became a problem. It was nearing one A.M. now, but I wanted to level before logging off, and that meant two more crabs.

Jeni looked around. "This is the spot Bartley told us about! Spread out and look for a drainage gate in the hillside somewhere."

We did as we were told, picking through the underbrush growing from the hill, looking for any openings. As I worked my way along the hill's edge away from the surf, pulling back vines and creepers, I saw a cement tunnel extending out about a meter from the hillside, with a rusted metal grate set about two meters in. I was about to call out when I noticed a pair of glowing yellow eyes focusing on me. I barely had time to make out a humanoid body with green, leathery skin, a forked chin, and pointed ears, before the thing lashed out with a short, rusty blade, and slashed me across my neck.

My vision went bright white and a heavy ringing filled my ears. I felt myself fall on my back, then hands on my shoulders, pulling me frantically through the sand.

After a minute, the dragging stopped, and I lay silent. I don't know how long I stayed like that, mostly paralyzed, but my vision slowly returned, and the ringing decreased to a dull whine. I propped myself up on an elbow, my right hand immediately going to my neck. Pulling it away, I didn't see the blood that I was expecting. I felt my neck again to make sure.

The first thing I noticed was a counter in the upper right of my field of vision, counting down in green numbers.

5:00:00, 4:59:59, 4:59:58...

Five hours, I thought. *Five hours until what?*

I looked around but saw no sign of the yellow-eyed beast that had hit me. Everything I could see, aside from the timer, had lost all color—everything was black and white, like the old movies they made us watch in high school.

I was relieved to see, however, that the rest of my group was here, forming a circle around me. Jeni took my head in her hands, her purple hair now a shade of grey, and that's when I realized.

"Jeni... you're not a wolf," I said woozily.

"I am," she said, her voice sounding distant. "You just can't see me."

My eyes returned to the clock, which continued ticking down.

"Whrrr.... What do you mean?" I asked.

She gave me a sympathetic smile.

"You died, Jakey."

CHAPTER THIRTEEN: THE GLITCH

I sat upright in the sand. There was no sign of the thing that attacked me, nor any other mobs on the beach.

"There's a counter," I said, still in a daze. "Counting down from five hours. I'm guessing that's the time before I'll be able to play again."

I looked at Banjo for confirmation, but he just looked at me and gave me a soft "*Ook.*"

"I can't see players, I can't see mobs, and I can't hear Banjo," I said, frustrated. I powered down my goggles and slipped them off my forehead. The color returned to the real world, which gave me a sudden sense of relief. Odd, earlier, the transition from game to world was disappointing, as I had to go from a technicolor wonderland to the humdrum of mundane living. Now, the world seemed vivid and bright, even at night.

"We should probably call it a night, anyway. I'm exhausted," said Trick.

I could relate. I couldn't remember the last time I felt this sore.

"Should we meet back here tomorrow then, say noon?" suggested Jeni.

Everyone voiced agreement, and the others powered down their goggles. We began the long slog through the sand back to the bus platform. I was pissed off at myself for dying. After a beach full of slimes and crabs, something so vicious had caught me completely off guard.

Aside from Trick suggesting new tactics and strategies a couple times, the ride home was spent in relative silence. Jeni told us we'd collected four sapphires and asked us to remind her to split them up tomorrow.

We disembarked at the stadium shop. Trick and Shauni headed south, while Jeni and I were going into the downtown area. When our hoverbus arrived, we said our goodbyes, with Trick reminding us to bring water, snacks, and the dice I'd mentioned for loot rolling.

My stop was two before Jeni's. She gave me a brief hug, as well as her phone number—*hell yeah*—and asked me to call her when I woke up.

I got off the bus, took the lift to ground level and began trudging to my apartment. The usual two A.M. riff-raff was emptying out of the bars, and I tried to ignore them as I shuffled past. Too bad I wasn't in game, so their appearances and sounds would be somewhat muted. It didn't seem to bother Banjo, who draped around my neck producing a series of soft monkey snores.

When I got to my apartment, I went into my room and set Banjo carefully on his sleeping pillow at the end of the bed. Not even bothering to remove my shoes, I flopped on top of the mattress, and let my exhaustion overtake me.

I woke up at the crack of eleven, finding I hadn't even shifted from the position I collapsed in nine hours earlier. My head pounded worse than from a hangover, and my mouth tasted like someone had washed their socks in it while I slept. Banjo sat on my pillow, looking at me. I resolved that the next trick I taught him would be how to make coffee.

I got up and stretched the stiffness from my body, feeling a couple satisfying pops from my back and shoulders. Feeling slightly better, I checked my phone and saw a text from Jeni.

Good morning, sleepyhead, it said, and the time stamp showed it to be ninety minutes old.

Hey there, I replied. *Just got up. Will call you once I finish the morning routine.*

I made a delightful pot of coffee and poured myself a mug with double cream and sugar so I could drink it faster. I took the cup to the balcony and sat down, sipping and enjoying a morning vape. Clouds were rolling in off the mountains to the west. *Looks like rain.*

My thoughts drifted to the night before, to the yellow-eyed thing which had slashed my throat. It had *hurt*. Most games I had played let you choose your pain threshold, but Iggy had never mentioned it. *Thanks for the heads-up.*

There had to have been blood, but the insta-death booted me out of the game before I had a chance to see it. The creature had been guarding the cave entrance where Jeni's amulet was hidden, and I'd stumbled right into it.

That thing had to die. It had almost ruined my entire night, embarrassed me in front of my companions. I wanted to whip that monstrous grin off his face. If I was getting one-shot like that, Honeybucket would have to step up and tank.

So much had happened yesterday, but meeting Jeni at Steam Whistle Alley was unquestionably the highlight. She was the first girl I'd been interested in since junior high, and I didn't want to mess it up. After the incident with my sister, my disfigured hand had deterred me from attempting any meaningful relationships. It's hard to feel confident when constantly wondering if one's body is grossing out one's date. There'd been a couple of girls, but those flings were purely physical. I *liked* liked Jeni.

Play it cool, Jacob, I thought. *Remember the quest. Win this thing, then worry about her.*

I took a shower, cleaned my teeth, and opted for a shave, as I was beginning to look like a hobo. Just when I was about ready to head out, the door chimed, and the screen to its right came to life. I wasn't expecting any deliveries.

The man squinting into the screen looked familiar, recently familiar, but I couldn't remember from where. His gut hung over his belt, and a double chin hugged his shirt collar. He wore a flat-topped, brimmed hat, and a pair of wire-framed glasses. Didn't see many people wearing actual glasses anymore.

I hit the talk button but kept my face hidden. "Can I help you?"

"Jacob Tutor?" he asked.

"Who are you?"

"I was wondering if I might have a moment of your time." For some reason, those glassy eyes staring into the camera gave me the unsettling impression he was looking right at me.

It suddenly hit me where I remembered this guy from—he was the nipnick with the goggles, standing with Jameson in the courtyard at the announcement the day before.

What is he doing at my apartment?

"Sorry, can't right now," I said, "There's somewhere I've gotta be."

"I have a very, *very* lucrative proposition for you," the man said, still looking at me. Gave me the creeps. "I'll tell you what," he continued, "I'll be at your coffee shop. Come get a cup of joe on me and hear me out."

Before he could turn around, I took a screenshot of his face and with a swipe, sent it over to my computer.

"I'll think about it," I said.

The man gave me a thin-lipped grin, then turned and left. The monitor went black.

"Lexi," I said, and a blue light lit on the station at my desk. "Run the picture I just sent you through Facebase and any other image identification sites you know of."

Her face appeared on the kitchen monitor. "Hi, Jacob. I'm looking." She paused. About thirty seconds later she spoke up. "Nope, I'm not seeing anything. Who the hell still wears glasses?"

"Yeah, I thought that too. Thanks, Lexi," I said.

I grabbed my phone and called Jeni, swiping the image up onto my living room display. When she answered I saw

STEAM WHISTLE ALLEY

Alki beach behind her.

"Hey there, where you at?" she asked. "We got here about ten minutes ago."

Banjo bounded up my leg and stood on my shoulder, raising a paw in greeting.

"Hello, Banjo," she said. "Tell your lazy roommate to get a move on."

"I just had a strange visitor," I said, ignoring her barb. "Remember that nipnick from the announcement yesterday? The one wearing the goggles? He just showed up at my apartment."

"What did he want?" she asked, concern etching her face.

"Something about a proposition. He's waiting for me at your coffee shop."

"I say you hear him out, at least," she replied. "Something's not right with him and Jameson, and I'd like to find out what. Me and the group'll grab a bite or something while we wait for you, so we don't level ahead. Call us when you're in the area."

I said goodbye and closed the connection. Strapping my goggles on, I went to the kitchen to fill a canvas backpack with bottled water, fruit, and some dried meat. Then, backpack on one shoulder and Banjo on the other, I headed out.

When I got to the café, the man was sitting at a corner table inside, sipping an espresso with his pinky raised.

"Ah, Jacob," he said, standing as I approached the table. "Would you like a coffee?"

"I'm not staying," I said, sliding in across from him. "Who are you?"

He sat back down. "My name is not important," he replied, his demeanor turning businesslike, looking me in the eye. "What is important is my offer." His gaze shifted to the goggles on my forehead, then back down again.

"Which is?" I asked, trying to sound uninterested. Banjo eyed the man warily.

"The people I represent want to give you fifteen-million netcoin," he said, and nonchalantly took another sip of his drink.

Good thing I hadn't taken him up on the drink, or he would have been wearing it. To my credit, however, I managed to play it cool.

"And what do these people you represent want from me for such an enormous payday?"

"All they want," he replied, setting his espresso back on its saucer, "is to make a tiny modification to your goggles, one you will not even know is there."

"Why *my* goggles?" I asked. "There's a couple hundred other people playing, and who knows how many when it's released. So why mine? Why not your buddy Jameson's?"

He frowned, and his eyes narrowed for a second, but he recovered quickly. "My motives and those of the people I represent will remain our own," he said, sternly. "Our offer to you is only good up until the first gear is found. Think about it." He handed me a business card made of thick, cream-colored paper, on which was printed only a telephone number. Then he stood up, placed his hat on his head, and walked out of the café.

I left a couple minutes later, replaying the short conversation in my mind. I didn't really care about the money. That the man had misjudged my motives so severely told me he didn't know as much about me as he thought. I walked a block south and boarded the bus to the stadiums.

I should talk to Iggy about the unsavory man, but I wanted to see what Jeni and the crew had to say about it first. Still, something about the conversation nagged at me.

Why did he come to me? If he wanted to upload something or record something, any other player would've jumped at the chance with such a fortune involved.

There must be something different about my goggles. Or about me.

Then something else hit me.

He knew about the gears! Which meant Jameson probably did, too.

I shelved this line of thought as the bus reached the stadiums and I got out to transfer to Alki. The ride there was uneventful, and after a quick phone call, I met up with Jeni and the group, who sat on a bench on the main strip, eating ice cream.

"Hey, guys, sorry you had to wait so long," I said.

"It's no problem," Trick replied. "There was ice cream. So, how'd the mysterious meeting go?" he asked, grinning.

"He offered me fifteen million netcoin to make a modification to my goggles."

Trick's ice cream hit the floor with a splat. "No way! Really? Did you take the offer?"

Jeni and Shauni looked just as surprised.

Shauni wrinkled her brow in thought. "He could have asked anybody else in the game, and they'd be multimillionaires by now," she said. "I know I would have taken it in a heartbeat."

"What did Iggy have to say about it?" Jeni asked.

"I don't know, I haven't called him yet," I answered. "Wanted to get your reactions first."

"You're not thinking of taking the money, are you?" Jeni asked, looking at me with an expression I couldn't place. Disappointed, maybe?

"No, I'm not taking the money," I said. "There seems to be more at play here than just the game. It makes sense, considering how amazingly valuable the *Panmachina* property is going to be once this releases to the public. I just want to know what we've gotten in to. And honestly, how much do we even know about Iggy? He seemed like a decent guy the *one* time I met him."

The crew was silent for a second, then Trick spoke up. "I've only met him the one time, too, but he seems like a better option than a mysterious visitor arriving on your doorstep with stacks of shady cash."

"Plus, he is our employer," added Jeni. "We need to at least let him know that this guy is poking around. Call him. At the minimum he'll probably know why you were singled out."

She had a point. I sat down on the bench next to her and dialed Iggy. He picked up on the first ring.

"Hello, Jacob!" he said, smiling on my screen. Behind

him, I could see a starfield, and he seemed to be wearing a reflective material—at least from the shoulders up. A stereotypical greenish-grey alien walked by in the background and waved at us before walking out of view.

"Um... Iggy? Where are you?" Jeni asked, peeking over my shoulder.

"Jeni! How goes it? I'm currently working on a VR simulation, a little pet project if you will," he said with a smile. "This isn't really me you are looking at, but my virtual projection. But then again," he shrugged, "scientists say we're all virtual projections, so who knows? How's the game going, Jacob?"

"It really is a work of art, Iggy," I said, "but I'm calling about something else." I told him about the visit and the bribe laid at my feet by the illicit man.

Iggy's expression turned serious, and he sighed. "We call him 'the Glitch,'" he said. "He's another ex-employee of mine. Name's Chuck Blatman." Iggy must've seen me smirk. "Yeah, we all made jokes too. I'm sure he's heard them all his life. Back when he worked for us, we caught him a few times slipping backdoors and other nefarious bits of code into programs. You can see why he's an ex-employee. Rumor has it that now he's working for Tardigrade Technologies, another startup that has some AR and VR games in the works. You said he just wanted to modify your goggles?"

I nodded. "Yeah, said I wouldn't even notice."

Iggy looked down, and steepled his fingers under his nose. "We chose the people for this alpha based on a very precise set of circumstances," he explained. "Everyone we invited has had extensive VR experience, which has led to a fascinating and exquisite set of data—namely, from your brain waves. Not unlike DNA, brain waves are unique to the individual, showing reliably repeatable firings of synapses. But DNA, ever since the Floston Accord of 2028, has been deemed the sole nontransferable property of its owner. In other words, you can't sell it, and any cloned organ or organism produced by that DNA belongs solely to you. You follow me?"

Not really. "Sure," I said. The rest of my group was now huddled around my shoulders, following the conversation.

"Brainwaves, however," he went on, "as far as the law is concerned, are all in the public domain. You can't produce anything with them, but VR companies have been recording them for years, especially with the advent of total immersion. In AR, we need these brainwaves to tailor the interface to the user. No two sets of goggles are alike. They're imprinted with your specific brain patterns."

"So, what does that have to do with me?" I asked, my mind in a whirl from all the technobabble.

"Unbeknownst to us until just recently, Blatman chose your brainwave patterns to construct a program around, probably because of your wealth of VR experience and skill. You see, your brain has a specific receptor that we haven't found in any of the other players we've tested yet. I'm not sure of the actual science of it all, to be honest, but it allowed the Glitch to make a particularly evil bit of code, uniquely tailored to you. From what my techs have told me, if he were to make this 'modification' he would be able to jack into a VR immersion rig and make a connection with your AR goggles."

"So, he could see what I see, feel what I feel, if I'm understanding this correctly?" I asked, furrowing my brow.

"No, Jacob," Iggy replied. "If he were to get that code into your goggles, he could take control of the forced feedback emitters, the part of the goggles that controls your muscles when they come in contact with an object that doesn't really exist. It takes a lot of energy to convince your muscles to generate an equal and opposite force, if you were to say, punch a virtual wall or something, and make it seem realistic. The goggles, in essence, can control your muscles."

The realization hit me like a bucket of ice water. "If he gained control of my goggles..."

Iggy nodded. "He could gain control of your body."

CHAPTER FOURTEEN: THE FEAR

y body could be controlled by another person? While playing, the Glitch's program could rob me of my free will. Part of me wanted to immediately power off the goggles and wash my hands of the whole thing. He couldn't control me if I didn't play.

No, I realized, he can't hijack my will. Only my ability to act on it.

The distinction seemed a trivial one.

But what's the purpose of controlling me in the first place?

The rest of the crew scrutinized me as I sat on the end of the bench, stunned, replaying the call in my mind. A program was tailored with the sole purpose of taking over my body. Not anyone else's, just mine. Not an easy thought to put out of my mind.

Ever since I was a kid, I'd been visited by horrors at night. I'd wake up to a giant weight pressing down on my entire body, smothering me. To my mind, it felt as if a being was in the room with me, lying on top of me, pinning me to the bed. It had presence. Except for my eyes, frantically searching for the intruder, and screams tearing from my throat, I couldn't move a muscle while this happened. Not my arms, my legs, despite my brain sending them frantic signals to kick, thrash—do anything. The sensation would pass after a few minutes, usually right after my mother would rush in to comfort me.

This phenomenon would occur irregularly, sometimes visiting me a few times a month, while other times months would pass with no disturbances.

Thankfully, it hadn't happened since I reached adulthood, although on some quiet nights the memories and the fear still haunted me. A little online research had found that other people, from cultures across the world, had also experienced this strange, sentient heaviness in the dead of night, describing sensations eerily similar to mine. My mother, though, was always the one there to pull me through.

I found myself missing her and vowed to take the hyperloop to visit once this alpha was over.

"Who's up for some crab meat?" Trick asked, pulling me out of my haze of memories. He stood, and the girls got to their feet with him.

"Yeah, let's get going," I said.

We all pulled on our goggles, and the world transformed. In the daytime it was easier to see how much had changed. All the road-based vehicles parked along the strip had turned into machines of pistons, pulleys and levers, in a wide array of shapes and materials. The lampposts had gone from the typical sleek, curved design to a dark, wrought iron motif with large Edison bulbs in cages at their tops. The storefronts behind us now looked like something straight out of the 19th century, with ornamental facades built from expertly carved wood and worked metals. Instead of the standard signs over the doors, they hung from awnings suspended by chains, like old medieval taverns, or were lit up in the nixies I'd been seeing everywhere. Those things were starting to grow on me.

A jogger ran by and gave us a disapproving look, effectively shattering the sense of wonder.

What're you looking at? We're just a few guys and girls, sitting on a bench wearing fashionable goggles. Oh, and one of us has a monkey.

"Nipnicks," hissed Honey. I looked over at the gargoyle, who was sneering disgustedly. Although I couldn't be certain—she may have been smiling.

Sometimes, it looked as if Quirk had a tough time adapting certain things to his world. Before we'd put on the goggles, a group of teenagers in front of us had been playing volleyball in the sand. They still played in the AR world, but were now dressed in clothing Quirk had judged as more suitable for the simulation. The men wore dark velvet vests and flared, cotton shorts or slacks, with the random buckle thrown in for effect. The women either emulated the men or wore velvet tube tops, with wide linen leggings. The white ball had simply morphed into one of dark maroon. Made me think of a gang of pirates and their harem—playing volleyball. Overall, it fit into the simulation as best as it could, but I assumed Quirk didn't have a lot to go on when creating athletic steampunk beachwear.

We retraced our path from the day before, skipping the slimes and heading straight to the south end of the beach. It was nearing high-tide now, and the water lapped at the stone retaining wall. Gears taller than me were embedded into it at even intervals and buried far enough within the wall that only about twenty centimeters protruded. Old barnacles clung to the wall's bottom half, with algae and hanging seaweed filling in the gaps between them.

We marched through the wet sand, timing our passage with the waves so our shoes wouldn't get soaked. Nothing worse than soggy feet.

Jeni pulled on the clawed gauntlets she'd shown me the day before then made a fist, so the four dark claws attached to the knuckles protruded over her hands. "I'm a lot squishier in my human form," she said, "so, I'm going to be doing a lot of swiping and ducking. Honey, you'll be taking the brunt of the damage today, at least until the sun goes down."

"Alright," said Honeybucket. "But keep an eye on me. That thing that obliterated Jakey seemed to pack quite a punch."

"Caught me by surprise," I grumbled.

"I'll keep an eye on you," said Trick. "I don't have a cure spell yet, but I picked up a pouch full of 'Dwebble's Healing Squirt Potions' at the alley earlier this morning."

"You picked up what?" Honey asked.

"They call it 'Dwebble's Squirt,' ten netcoin apiece." He

pulled out a brass syringe from a pouch inside his robes, the same ones that I'd picked up the day before. "They're accurate to seven meters although I could probably hit you from ten. You'll get thirty HP per squirt, according to the guy at the shop."

Honey turned around to look at him. "So, let me get this right. You have to stand within seven meters of me and squirt goo at me with that thing," she asked incredulously.

"Um, yeah," he said, before looking at the ground. "I thought... err... cold out here today, looks like rain," he mumbled, and pulled up his hood.

"I think I'll take my chances, but thank you, Trick." She started forward again, then paused, contemplating, and turned back once more, fixing him with the grimace of someone experiencing severe gastric distress. Or it might have been her smile. "Last resort only."

The beach gradually became wider and rose in elevation as we continued walking. The retaining wall ended, replaced with woody brambles and a gently sloping hillside. The first crab appeared in the distance. We gathered in a rough circle to prepare ourselves, pulling the augmented goggles to where our real ones actually were. I unclipped my chain whip from my belt and held it by my side.

"I almost forgot," said Trick, rummaging in his robes. "I picked you all up some wristbands to monitor your own HP." He pulled them out one by one and handed them out.

I thanked him and snapped mine on. It was longer than I'd assumed, stretching halfway up my forearm. The dark purple metal felt cold against my skin and was decorated around the edges with etched knotwork entwined with vines and leaves. The two rounded stones glittered green and blue, and appeared to be filled with glowing liquid, which would drain as my HP and MP did. A small screen took up the middle of the armband, and below it was a four-way directional control made of a green-hued wood, along with a series of matching round buttons.

"They say ARGO's talking about giving them to everyone when they first join the game, instead of making players buy one," Trick informed us. "At least that's the scuttlebutt. Making it the reward for an early quest. Apparently, there's been a lot of guff about not having a visual display of our stats built in, so this is their compromise. Makes sense, if you ask me."

"Well, I'll just go then," said Banjo, affecting a hurt expression. He tugged on his vest and pouted.

"Aw, Banjo. You're still my number one source for news and information," I said in my best newscaster's voice. Jeni chuckled.

"Ready?" Honeybucket asked, and she began marching towards the nearest crab before we could reply, her tail swinging menacingly.

She punched her fist down on the crab's shell, eliciting an ineffective pinch at her ankle. Trick summoned his bobcat and sent it charging in but didn't bother slowing the crab; with the four of us we didn't need it. Jeni rushed in next and pinned one of the crab's claws with her right gauntlet, while driving her left into the thing's face. At the same time, the bobcat tugged at one of the crab's legs until it gave, then returned to Trick and deposited the segmented leg at his feet.

The three of them had sapped nearly ninety percent of the crab's health before I finally got a lash in, a killing crack right between the eyes. The blow flipped the crab on its back, where it twitched once before going still.

I saw a second crab about twenty meters up, by where the brambles met the sand. "There's another," I pointed, and adjusted my bowler as I started towards it. I was in whip range before Honey could get close enough to attack. I lashed out with a metallic crack that caught it on the seafoam blue shell, and the beast skittered towards me.

"Why you pulling aggro?" Honey asked.

Trick's bobcat sprinted past me and clamped onto one of the crab's rear legs. It barely slowed the meter-wide crab, and it continued at me, dragging the bobcat behind it. I lashed out again as I retreated a few steps, catching the beast in its eye. The crab's health was still at about seventy percent when I stepped back again and stumbled. It closed in and lunged with its claw, catching me in the thigh.

I let out a loud groan. It hurt like hell, and as the crab backed up for another lunge, my blood glistened on the ends of its claw. I tried to scurry away, but my lower limbs were too numb to move. When I put my hand on the wound, it came up red.

The crab started at me again, and as I reflexively raised my arm, I saw that the little nip had cost me about forty percent of my HP. Maybe because of the critical failure from stumbling over my own feet.

The girls finally decided to help and attacked the crab from both sides, Honeybucket unleashing a powerful double-fisted smash as Jeni delivered a trio of shell-piercing thrusts. The crab's HP dropped to about five percent, but it remained intent on me, lashing out again and slicing my calf. I swore loudly.

"Your HP's at about twenty percent, Jakey," said Banjo worriedly, hopping from foot to foot. But Honey slammed her rock-like elbow into the crab's back, cracking open its jeweled shell and killing it. She stood up and extended her wings triumphantly.

I sat up on the sand, wincing from the pain, although at least augmented pain faded faster than the genuine article. My whole leg still throbbed, even as the gashes in my thigh and calf started to close. I looked at my new wrist monitor again and saw the red gem nearly drained.

"Jeez, Iggy really needs to let us dial back on the pain. This isn't pleasant," I said, wincing.

"Don't worry, I got ya," said Trick helpfully, and unload the contents of Dwebble's Squirt on my leg.

It was thick, dark green, and smelled like an ogre's armpit. I had to hand it to Dwebble, though: The stuff did the trick, closing the wound and easing the pain. The red gem on my wrist filled to roughly seventy percent. The girls each extended a hand and helped me to my feet.

"Ding!" Banjo exclaimed and did a backflip.

"I thought you hated the ding?" I asked him.

"I've decided that my best option is to embrace it," he

said, tugging on his vest and looking dignified. "Congratulations! You are now level two. All of you, unless I'm mistaken. Which I never am."

A heavy sprinkle had started falling from the sky, but there was nothing to do for it. My goggle lenses, the actual ones, had a superhydrophobic coating that the drops and humidity couldn't stick to, and the GPU edited out the distortions caused by the drops bumping off. Unfortunately, I was still getting wet.

"Jakey," said Banjo. "Your whip crack has reached level two. You've gained thirty max HP, bringing you to two-hundred-ten. You've also gained two stamina, so maybe next time you won't bleed all over everything as much. One each to strength, dex, and intelligence. You've also got one skill point to spend at the guild."

I didn't even realize I had a guild. I knew the engineers did, but I hadn't heard of an archaeologist's guild. Something to think about for later.

Everyone else used their wristbands to check their stats, although I kind of preferred Banjo's updates. Trick informed us he received a heal spell called Dimony's Whisper, a single phrase whispered into the ear of the target which would restore forty to fifty hit points.

Honey's gargoyle ears pricked up. "So now my choices are having you splooge all over me with a tube of goo, or having you whisper in my ear?" she asked incredulously. "What's the phrase?"

Trick looked at his wrist screen. "Can you…" He paused, squinting. "Feel it."

I laughed out loud, and Jeni went into one of her fits of giggles.

Both Jeni and Honey's main attacks and a few stats had gone up as well, although neither of them gained any new skills or abilities.

Jeni turned her attention to the corpses. The first one we'd killed left nothing behind, but the second shell held a large blue sapphire, lustrously reflecting the grey of the sky. Drops of rain glittered on its surface as Jeni held it up.

"Our first roll," I said, and got the four twenty-sided dice from my backpack.

I handed one to everyone, and we squatted, rolling them on the hard sand. Trick's seventeen won the gem, so he took it from Jeni and slipped it into his robes as I collected the dice.

"So, what's the plan now?" Jeni asked.

"We kill that frakking imp," I said. "If we go forewarned, with Honey tanking, we should be fine."

They nodded agreement. Seemed we all wanted more than just slimes and crabs.

We took a moment to drink some water and eat the snacks we brought. It seemed odd: I was used to eating and drinking on adventures before, but this was real food, needed to keep my actual strength up.

We packed up and headed south, where the sand of the beach turned rocky, and tidepools had formed from the retreating surf. They'd always fascinated me as a kid, the green anemones flowering to life inside them, as well as tiny crabs that would scamper from underneath rocks just to hide beneath another.

It was in one such tidepool I saw something shiny glitter in the periphery of my vision. I walked closer, found the glimmer again and kicked over a half-submerged rock, revealing a silver dagger beneath, untarnished despite lying in the water. I picked it up, noting that it wasn't overly ornate but still held an impressive edge, although the leather wrapping the handle was old and weathered. I slipped it into my belt, glad to have a short-range weapon after the crab fiasco.

"Nice find," Jeni said, looking impressed.

I gave her a thumbs-up and flashed a grin.

Before long, the grate entrance came into view about a hundred meters in front of us. I flipped down my zoom lens and closed my other eye, and the circular entrance jumped into focus. The little bastard who'd KO'ed me the night before still guarded it, resting against the slimy gate that barred access to the tunnel. A strange looking creature, its face looked vaguely wolf-like, while its body appeared more reptilian, save for thin hair growing between what might have been scales. I flipped my lens up.

"He's there, that imp-thing" I said.

"I think he's probably more of a kobold," Trick corrected. "Imps are smaller, plus he's got a muzzle, see? And the three-toed feet are a dead giveaway. And he is guarding a cave."

I flipped down my info-lens.

'Lupine Kobold, Level 5'

"Kobold it is, then," I said. The thing had a health bar

so long it extended into a second line.

The creature hadn't attacked until we were right on top of it last time, but to be safe, Honey took the lead. As we drew closer, it became clear the surrounding terrain favored the beast, leaving us no option to get the drop on it.

We decided on the tried and true tank and spank; just had to send in Honey to collect a little aggro while the rest of us did what we could.

When we were about ten meters away, Honey turned and gave us a nod, and we nodded back. She barreled in, fists raised. The kobold backed against its grate, into the shade formed by the tunnel entrance. Honey landed a blow on the creature's jaw, while Trick cast his slow spell, and the kobold charged at Honey as if running through syrup. I lashed out twice with the whip, cracking it in the shoulder and side, leaving large gashes of dark-orange blood.

Ignoring the damage, the kobold pulled two long daggers from either side of his waist and continued towards Honey. Mid-lunge, Trick's slow spell appeared to dissipate, and the kobold sped up, piercing Honey twice in the stomach. Jeni threw back her head and howled wickedly, then ran in behind and slashed twice across the back of the beast's neck, spilling more of the foul-looking blood. The kobold spun around, turning his attention on Jeni, and I lashed out with the whip again, this time nearly severing the thing's ear.

The kobold was too fast, and caught Jeni twice, once on each forearm, She countered with a devastating swipe across its face. The kobold swung once more, slicing Jeni on her right cheek, but another crack from my whip hit the back of its hand, causing it to drop one of its weapons. Honeybucket brought both meaty fists down on the back of its head, and the little bastard fell to the ground.

Jeni retreated from the fracas. "I'm at about twenty percent, here," she panted, grimacing from the pain and exertion.

Trick was already on it. As she ran toward him, he pulled a metal tube from his robes and unleashed a torrent of Dwebble's Squirt at her. Jeni stopped in her tracks, wiping the thick green liquid off her face and out of her eyes.

"Trick!" she shouted, furious. "Don't ever squirt me with anything without warning me first!" She flicked a glob of green goo towards him and gave up on cleaning the sludge still running down her neck and into her shirt.

I chuckled. Only in games would you ever hear a sentence like that. Or maybe certain massage parlors.

The kobold was now back on its feet, and Honey had managed to draw the its attention once again. She began pummeling it with both fists. The kobold, now below twenty percent and down to one weapon, sliced at the gargoyle. Both of them suffered from numerous cuts, but true to tank form, Honey was still holding at just over fifty percent health. The bobcat clawed and bit at the kobold's bloody calves. I caught it with two more lashes to the torso, followed by a near perfect swipe across its neck, leaving a crevasse that spurted blood in long arcs.

The kobold collapsed to the beach, choking, its HP drained.

I approached the thing and bent down to examine it. I noticed a band of alternating copper gears and what appeared to be teeth circling its wrist, and as I began to slip it off him, his dying breaths offered a few raspy words.

"The spiders... they're coming... click, click, click," the thing gasped. It gave one last bloody gurgle, then went limp.

I wasn't a fan of spiders, but they weren't any worse than kobolds.

"Everyone okay?" I asked.

"Fine," said Honey. I gave her a tube of Dwebble's, and she began rubbing it into her cuts, sighing with relief. "I do agree with you, though. Iggy needs to let us dial back the pain."

Jeni dug inside her shirt, scraping more of the goo from between her breasts while Trick mumbled apologies. She caught me looking and met my eyes, smirking, before turning away.

"That thing gave you 225 XP each, reported Banjo. "1,275 XP until level three." He flipped over a rock in a puddle of seawater by his feet and found a tiny crab, scooped it out, and popped it in his mouth.

We rolled for the bracelet, which Jeni won and slipped into her pouch. The two rust-pitted daggers the mob dropped looked worthless, and none of us had the ability to identify items yet, so nobody protested when Trick asked if he could have them.

Once everyone was healed and rested, I approached the grate. The air turned cooler at the mouth of the tunnel, making me shiver in my damp clothes. Grabbing the slimy metal bars, I pulled, and it screeched outward on rusty hinges.

I peered into the darkness beyond but couldn't see anything. Barely audible, however, behind the sound of the surf echoing down the tunnel, were hundreds of tiny clicking sounds.

Trick slid in beside me, staring into the void.

"You hear that?" I asked.

"That clicking?" he replied. "Yeah, I hear it. And it's getting louder."

CHAPTER FIFTEEN: THE AMULET

The four of us hunched over to fit into the tunnel and took a few tentative steps inside before it became too dark to see much of anything. Jeni took out the amulet Bartley had given her and turned back towards the entrance for a little extra light. I looked over her shoulder and could barely make out the small picture of a sun engraved on one side. As instructed, she pressed the tiny recessed button three times, and the tunnel lit up with a warm, golden glow, emanating from the amulet.

"Not bad," I said, as she put the amulet around her neck.

Like the retaining wall on the beach, the base of the tunnel was covered in barnacles and seaweed, shining black in the artificial light and making the footing slippery and treacherous. Small gears sticking out from the walls rotated and clanked at regular intervals, driving some unknown mechanism. The ceiling was only about half a meter above our heads, and about every two meters a head-sized hole was cut into it, ostensibly for ventilation.

Those clicking sounds we'd heard at the entrance now

came from all around us. Trick suggested it sounded like a room full of people typing—I thought it sounded more like thousands of tiny legs skittering against the stone, inside the walls and ceiling. I tried to put that picture out of my mind.

The tunnel continued onward and we advanced warily, expecting some sort of beast to jump out at any moment. I tried to breathe through my mouth, not relishing the scent of rotting seaweed and fish.

Banjo paced behind us, alongside Shorty the bobcat. "Remember," he said, "the recommended level for this place is three. You all just made two."

None of us relished the thought of spending an entire day grinding crabs in the rain. "We'll be okay," I said. "We've got Trick the Mystical Squirter to protect us." Honey chortled, and Jeni rolled her eyes. The remnants of the green goop had dried into a crust on her hair and skin. "As long as Honey takes the lead, we'll be fine."

The tunnel had been curving steadily to the left, and we'd gone far enough that the entrance could no longer be seen behind us. I would've felt more secure with Jeni in her wolf form—a second mini-tank bringing up the rear. Instead, I shouldered that burden in our single-file trek, as I'd need the space to swing the whip should anything hop out of the darkness.

The clicking continued growing louder. Jeni said something I couldn't make it out over the din. A few seconds later, I had no problem hearing her scream, as something about the size of a saucer dropped out of one of the holes in the ceiling and fell on her shoulder. Jeni screamed again as the thing sank fangs into her neck, just before Honey grabbed the creature and crushed it in her stony fist.

We gathered around Honey and she opened her hand, revealing a spider-like corpse, with eight mechanical legs sprouting from its center. The legs were made from white and yellow metals, a three-hinged series of pistons and gears on each disappearing into the furry, organic thorax, which now leaked guts onto Honey's hand. The creature's bulbous abdomen, however, was metallic grey, and the markings etched into the surface looked just like the head of a wolf.

I flipped down my info-lens.

'*Araneae Lupus, Level 1*'

Its health bar was tiny, barely passing the 'r' in the spider's name.

The bite on Jeni's neck had already healed, and she'd regained the two percent of health lost from the wound.

"Well that wasn't too bad," Trick said. An instant later, he let out a scream that made Jeni's sound manly.

A steady trickle of the mechanized wolf-spiders began dropping from multiple holes in the ceiling, increasing in frequency until it became a deluge. The clatter was loud enough to make my ears ring and made thinking difficult. The group, myself included, launched into an impressive lexicon of profanities. We began pulling spiders off ourselves, throwing them to the ground, and then stomping on them.

Two had fallen on my shoulders, and another latched

on to the brim of my bowler, snapping at my eyes with its fangs. Two more had skittered up my legs, sinking teeth into the flesh of my calves and knees. I ripped the one from my hat and smashed it against the wall, but three more dropped down to replace it, tearing at my ears now. I felt thin rivulets of blood running down my neck.

Honey had the worst of it, veritably covered in them—her arms and back were a mass of tiny red lacerations. She shoved her back into the tunnel wall, smashing five of them in the process. I couldn't help but wince at the ensuing *thunk*.

I looked at my wrist and saw that these things had already drained thirty percent of my health. Banjo confirmed it for me. "Jakey, at this rate you can't take more than another two minutes of this," he said, crouching against the wall. The spiders appeared to be ignoring Banjo, but the bobcat was having a ball, pouncing from spider to spider and crushing them in its jaws.

"Trick! Squirt me!" Jeni shouted. Ah, such sweet poetry.

Trick complied, covering her back and shoulders in viscid green gunk. Then, for good measure, he doused Honey and me with a vial as well. The stuff stank, but it did the trick, bringing my HP back up to about eighty percent. We continued the dance of snatching and stomping until the metal corpses of the spider-wolves littered the floor around us, crunching under our feet. I took out my new dagger and began piercing the spiders clinging to the walls. At least they'd stopped pouring from the ceiling, but there were still at least fifty attached to both us and the walls.

Eventually, I managed to make myself spider-free, although even after my dousing I was below fifty percent health. Free to help my companions, I grabbed one off Jeni's back and threw it to the floor, stomping on it with a satisfying *crack*.

Before too long, the bobcat had found the last moving arachnid, batting it back and forth between its paws before tossing it into the air and chomping down on the soft, furry center. The spider's legs went rigid, sticking straight out from the cat's mouth, then grew limp.

I slid down the wall to sit on the floor, ignoring the spider corpses and wet seaweed. I rested my arms on my knees. "Well, that was fun," I said, panting.

The girls sat down also and took water from their bags, drinking deeply. Jeni used some of hers to wipe the goop from her face.

Interesting, I thought. *Real water washing away virtual goo.*

Trick squatted next to me, moved his mouth close to my ear, and whispered, "Can you feel it?"

I could. My whole body tingled, a chill breeze washing over me, and my wristband showed most of my HP had returned. He knelt down and whispered to each of the girls in turn, which got a grimace from each of them, although Honey might have been smiling. After he'd taken care of everyone, Trick sat down and drank a potion, and we all caught our breath.

Absent of the incessant clicking, a breeze whistled through the tunnel, and the pounding surf was a whisper in the distance. Aside from that, it was silent, save for our panting breaths.

"The party killed two hundred, forty-eight spiders in that melee," Banjo informed us. He pulled out a tiny calculator from his vest pocket and stared down his nose at it, typing away frantically. *Cute.* "Five XP per, that's 1240, divided by four, that's 310 XP for each of you. 1,065 until level three."

"Thanks, Banjo," I said, my breath coming back. I was starting to worry we might have entered this area a level too early. I didn't voice my concerns, however. No one likes being the person who suggests turning back.

We began kicking through the corpses, looking for anything useful. Our search turned up a handful of gears and mechanisms, as well as a couple of tiny crystals. After splitting the mechanical items up evenly, we rolled for the crystals, with both Trick and I taking one.

We continued forward, and before long the tunnel opened into a chamber. A chest sat on a raised platform in the room's center, and behind it, two more pitch-black tunnels branched to the left and right.

The four of us made a beeline for the chest, but something on it caught my eye, and I threw out my arms, holding them back. Runes covered its entire surface in no discernable pattern.

"There's something written here, give me a sec," I said. I knelt down in front of the chest, and before I could do anything, the runes began to swirl on its dark wooden surface. They came to rest a few moments later, spelling out a message in perfect English across the center of the lid.

"The left path leads to the end of your quest," I read. "The right path to eternal rest. Before the end, expect one more test. The perceptive will be able to open this chest."

Trick had started beatboxing about halfway through my reading. *Funny kid.*

"Well, you're the perceptive one, mister archaeologist," Jeni said with a grin. "Get us our loot!"

I glared at her playfully from the corner of my eye then returned my attention to the chest. Aside from the runes, the edges of the box were decorated with a score of tiny reliefs of wolf heads and spiders. They all looked the same to me, so I ran my fingers along them, feeling for any incongruities. I found none, but upon a second examination I noticed one of the tiny raised spiders was a little more worn than the others, and slightly shiny. I put a finger to it and exerted a little pressure, and heard a mechanism click. The chest sprang open.

Inside, I found a handful of squirt potions, which I handed to Trick. I also found two obsidian rings, which none of us had the means to identify. A piece of fabric concealed something circular at the bottom of the chest.,. I removed the cloth, revealing a coiled length of thin metal chain attached to an intricately woven leather handle at one end, and three vicious looking black blades at the other.

"Need!" I called out, perhaps a little overzealously. Nobody objected.

I pulled out the whip, admiring the craftsmanship. Again, I had no way to identify its properties yet, but it just *looked* more lethal. Besides, usually any weapon found in a game is better than the one they give you from the beginning. I put the old whip in my backpack, replacing it with my newfound treasure.

"Nice haul," said Jeni.

Trick held one of the new squirt potions in his hand, squeezing a blob of a white gel onto his finger rather than the green. Looked almost like toothpaste.

"You are *not* squirting me with that!" exclaimed Jeni, prompting a bout of laughter from Honeybucket that sounded like someone had put a bucket of rocks into a washing machine.

Trick handed the tube to Banjo, who took a taste. "Ah yes, Jerry's Gel. Plus ten to stamina and all resistances, plus five to strength, duration of thirty minutes," he said, before handing the tube back.

"You can squirt me, Trick," Honey said in a sultry voice. Now Jeni was the one laughing. "No seriously," said Honey. "Dose me before whatever's down that left tunnel. I have a feeling I'll need it."

"There's got to be a better way to get buffs than having goo squirted all over us," I said. "We're a mess!" I reached over to Jeni's ear and wiped away a glop of the green stuff from earlier.

"Thanks," she said quietly, giving me an affectionate look.

"Well this one's a pre-fight buff," Banjo said. "You can just empty a tube into your palm and rub it into your hands and arms."

"Oh," said Trick, trying hard not to look disappointed.

"Pervert!" Honeybucket teased.

Trick handed each of us one of the new potions and we emptied the contents into our palms, rubbing it into our hands and arms. Our skin absorbed it in no time, and I had to admit, I did feel stronger, although I couldn't quite explain exactly how.

We took the left path as the chest had instructed, Honey leading and the rest of us in the same order as before. Banjo perched on my shoulder once again. We ambled into the darkness surrounded by a nimbus of orange from Jeni's amulet, hearing nothing but our footsteps and the gentle *whoosh* of the breeze.

The passageway curved to the left and went gradually downhill, and the walls now displayed hieroglyphics of unknown origin. My decipher ability apparently couldn't read these yet, but I did notice a definite spider and wolf motif going on. We continued onward until the path wound down into a gigantic chamber. We stepped inside and stood shoulder to shoulder, taking in the surroundings.

There wasn't much to take in aside from a mosaic floor of red and grey tiles. The light cast by Jeni's amulet illuminated a good twenty meters in every direction, yet we saw no walls—just more blackness

Honey stepped forward tentatively, and we followed.

The entrance eventually disappeared behind us. The four of us huddled together under the sphere of golden light, surrounded by pitch-black on all sides. Jeni took my hand, squeezing it tightly. I tried not to smile.

In the darkness ahead of us, a group of tiny red lights came into sight, growing brighter as we approached. "You see that?" I asked.

Honey jerked her head from side to side and the bones in her neck popped. Jeni let go of my hand and stretched her arms, flexing her gauntlets.

We continued towards the tiny lights, and finally the far wall of the cavern revealed itself. A stone throne sat in its middle, and in it sat a clockwork monstrosity. The glowing lights revealed themselves to be the creature's eyes, inlaid into polished bronze above a metal muzzle twice the size of a bear's, filled with rows of sharp, red metal teeth. Its arms and legs were comprised of a series of pistons, gears, and hinges, and the beast's chest was a thick cage of metal. At the center of the cage, a globe about the size of a basketball pulsated with an angry red light. *Nice of 'em to give me a target.*

The girls swiveled their info-lenses in front of their eyes, and I did the same.

'Clockwork Wolflord, Level 6'

Its health bar was purple instead of red and took up two full lines. *We're in trouble.*

"Banjo, do we have a chance with this thing?" I asked, not taking my eyes off the Wolflord.

"There's always a chance," he replied, backing to the edge of our halo of light, "but in this case, at your level, it's not a very good one. Minuscule, even."

With a whirring of gears and hydraulics, the thing stood up, and walked a couple of steps toward us, its feet clanking loudly against the tile.

"I have five tubes of Dwebble's left," said Trick, "so holler if you need one."

The beast stared down at each of us in turn, a good two heads taller than even Honey, then threw back its head and spread its metal arms wide. Two sword-like claws sprang from the back of each fist with a *clang!* A whining of machinery followed, and eight segmented appendages unfolded from the wolflord's back, dagger-tipped and swaying threateningly.

With a bestial scream, Honey charged in, swinging both fists at the cage surrounding the glowing orb. She connected, leaving a small dent in its chest.

But the attack left her exposed and the beast grabbed her by her shoulders, immobilizing her as four of the legs on its back stabbed her in the shoulders and chest. Honey howled in pain.

"*Sloven!*" Trick screamed, pointing at the Wolflord. Once again, a line of air between them rippled, and the beast's movements slowed noticeably.

I lashed out with my new whip at the Wolflord's arm, connecting with its elbow in a shower of sparks that left some of the mechanisms dangling uselessly. The thing reeled back, releasing Honey, and she retreated, bleeding and already at about fifty percent health.

"Squirt!" she cried, and Trick shot a jet of Dwebble's at her from about ten meters away.

At the same time Trick's bobcat rushed in and fearlessly tore at the beast's heels, but it ignored the cat and advanced on Honey again. Jeni threw back her head and emitted a piercing howl. The monster stopped its advance, and Jeni took advantage of the opening. She rushed in behind it, severing one of its spider legs appendages at the base with a powerful swing of her claws. The limb fell to the ground, twitching, as Jeni retreated and hid behind the throne.

It wasn't enough to pull aggro, however, and the Wolflord lunged at Honey once more. She tucked and rolled to the left, narrowly avoiding its clawing arms. She sprang up behind him and smashed both fists onto its back, rendering an opening in its chest cage. The Wolflord turned to confront her, presenting its back to me.

Time to shine. I unleashed a series of lashes and managed to sever four more of its back-legs, bringing the beast under fifty percent health. *High offense, low defense.* But my attacks pulled the creature's attention, and it turned and rushed me. It was then that I saw my opening. The bars of the creature's chest cage now hung bowed open slightly in the front, perhaps from Honey's pounding on it while I sliced apart its back. I jumped backward, lashing out at the opening with my new three-bladed whip and caught the beast with a critical hit on its glowing heart. The Wolflord's HP dropped to about fifteen percent.

The bobcat continued to rip at the Wolflord's ankles, littering the floor with bits and pieces of metal. The thing was markedly slowed, and its three remaining back-legs twitched and spasmed. It advanced on me in great, lurching lunges, furious at the damage I had done to its now sputtering and flickering heart.

So intent was the boss on me that it missed Honey and Jeni flying in from the sides. The gargoyle's granite fist crushed into the base of its muzzle with a loud snapping as metal broke and the ruined hydraulics hissed. Jeni drove the claws of her gauntlet right through the side of the Wolflord's neck. Its head shot backwards and came to rest on its upper back like a Pez dispenser, held on only by a few pneumatic tubes. The monster collapsed to its knees. The light in its chest flickered, then winked out.

The Wolflord fell over with a crash.

I *whooped* loudly, adrenaline coursing through me. The group echoed me, and Jeni ran over and threw her arms around my neck in a celebratory embrace.

I hadn't expected it, and we broke the hug awkwardly before turning our attention to the corpse.

"Everyone okay?" I asked, to a chorus of reassurances.

I used a foot to shove the corpse onto its back. Right away I noticed a small latch on its chest cage. I opened it, and the chest sprang open, startling me backwards—much to my allies' amusement. Grinning sheepishly. I reached in and took out the now lifeless orb, and the group formed a circle around me, so we could examine the sphere together.

"Does it open?" Trick asked.

I couldn't see a catch or a lock of any kind.

"Let me see it," Honey said. I handed her the orb, and she squinted at it a moment, her tongue peeking from between her lips. Then, she threw the globe on the ground, shattering it.

"That works," I said.

I squatted down and pushed away shards of broken glass, revealing what we had come for: a thin silver chain with a silver pendant in the shape of a crescent moon. I picked it off the floor, shaking off tiny shards of glass, and handed it to Jeni.

CHAPTER SIXTEEN: THE GALILEO

Jeni took the amulet from me and turned it over in her hand, running her finger over the surface, a broad smile on her face. "I'm not seeing any buttons on this one," she said, her smile dimming.

With a shrug, she pulled it over her head, the medallion disappearing down her shirt. Her eyebrows shot up. "Oh, I get it now." Two seconds later the purple werewolf stood before me, hunched and ready to strike. Then, just as quickly, the fur disappeared, her clothing returned, and Jeni was herself again.

I took a seat on the floor and watched on in amazement.

"I can do it at will!" she exclaimed, wonder in her voice. "It's the most interesting feeling; sort of like how the headset sends skills directly into our brains but magnified." Grinning, she turned back into the wolf and danced around the room laughing. It was a strange sight, but I laughed with her, and the other two applauded.

Banjo jumped in between us, arms in the air. "Guys, guys, I almost forgot," he said, panting. "Ding! Ding! You have completed the Quest for the Lupine Amulet, and along with the XP from that boss, you've reached level three. Excellent job, Jakey. Decipher went up a point, and Perception went up by two. Your Max HP is at 240, and you also got another skill point for the guild. Also, a nice smattering of points to your base stats."

Everyone went to their wrist, checking their new skills. Honey had received a first level stone spell, which hardened her skin while slowing her movements. Trick and Jeni received only stat and skill boosts. I checked mine and saw my dexterity had jumped three points. I knew this boost didn't make me faster, but it *would* make my whip more accurate and deadly. I could live with that.

We spent the better part of an hour getting out of the tunnels and back up the beach. It was close to low tide, and sapphire crabs and sand slimes had come out in force to cover the new stretches of sand and rocks. The rain had stopped, leaving behind that fresh rain scent, which mingled with the smell of salt water. I kept taking deep breaths through my nose. Way out over the mountains the sky was clearing, and whenever the evening sun shone between cloud cover and the rain-soaked beach, everything would get this otherworldly golden glow, a sight augmented reality didn't try to change.

We passed a beastmaster and an engineer, fighting slimes down by the surf line. The beastmaster, dressed in a leather suit and a felt top-hat, had taken control of a crab and was currently using it to rip a sand slime apart with its claws. The engineer looked familiar. He wore blue overalls and a red shirt, with dark, wavy hair and a thick handlebar mustache completing the look. He held an oversized pipe wrench in both hands, repeatedly bashing the slime-covered ground.

Get 'em, Mario.

We approached the main drag and paused to rest at the first picnic table we came across, seeing a lot more people now.

"Reality break," said Trick. He put his hand to his goggles and went dim.

The rest of us did the same, and I slipped my goggles off my head, blinking my eyes, the air stinging them.

Trick furiously rubbed at his eyes. "They need to install fans in these things or something."

Jeni had sat next to me, and we both looked out towards the setting sun and mountains. The sun's warm orange glow lit up her face and sparkled in her blue-gray eyes. She caught me looking and smiled at me. I took a mental snapshot of her before turning back to the view.

"So, guys," Trick said, interrupting my reverie. "Tomorrow night starts the first quest for the alley, but I haven't even started deciphering the little poem the mayor recited. Hell, I didn't even write it down. Something, something, something, find the place of the arbors."

I turned around and gave him a smug grin. "Oh, you haven't figured it out yet?" I asked him. "Well, best of luck to you."

"You know where it's at? Tell us!" Trick exclaimed, sitting up excitedly. Jeni eyed me expectantly as well.

"Well, not really. I have a couple of ideas, though," I said.

Honey chimed in. "I heard a bunch of people discussing Lakenhilly Park, what we know as Interlaken," she said. "They held the Seattle's Arbor Day celebration there for over twenty years."

I nodded. "That was my thought, too," I said. *Well, one of my thoughts.*

"Anywhere else you think it might be?" Trick asked.

"The Ravenna Ravine has some of the largest, oldest trees in the city," I said. "It just feels right to me, and so far, I haven't heard any scuttlebutt about it."

"Gaslight Gulch," Trick said, remembering the name from the map.

"How about this," I said. "Trick and Honey will go scout out Lakenhilly tomorrow, and Jeni and I will go to Gaslight Gulch. Report back on our findings in the evening. Then, we'll pick our best option and go from there."

"Works for me," Honey said, and Trick and Jeni voiced their approval as well.

Honey and Trick said their goodbyes and headed off towards the bus platform. Jeni and I sat in silence for a while, taking in the final minutes of the sunset.

"So, you really think it's at Ravenna?" Jeni asked.

"No, I don't. And I don't think it's at Lakenhilly either," I said. I looked at her. I was unsure what kind of reaction I was going to get from her, seeing as I had just lied to our new friends.

"You know something, though. Spill it, Jacob."

Uh-oh. She didn't call me Jakey.

"The Locke Wetlands on the shores of Lake Washington," I said. "Over two square kilometers bordering the lake."

"I've been there," she said. "Beautiful place. What makes you think the quest will start there?"

"Before 2021," I replied, "it was known as the Washington Park Arboretum. It's got to be the place."

We sat in silence for a while after that, watching the sky darken to twilight. I hoped she understood why I had lied to them. This was a contest. I was all for helping them out, but if the Locke Wetlands turned out to be the right place, it was valuable information. I had only known Shauni and Trick for a whole two days now.

I glanced over at Jeni. She didn't seem angry. Then, without warning, she slipped her hand over mine. My scarred hand. Aside from my mother, no woman had ever touched it before. Heart pounding, I turned my hand to interlace my fingers with hers and stroked her thumb gently with my own. She didn't object.

We stayed until the sun finished its descent, then we headed to the transit platform and made our way home. When we reached my stop, I leaned over and gave her a soft kiss on her cheek. She smiled at me, holding eye contact. Wordlessly, she brought her hand to my temple, stroking the swath of white. I felt like my whole body was blushing as I broke away from her and stood up, but I turned to look at her one more time as I disembarked. And ran into a pole in the process.

Smooth, Jacob.

Needless to say, I spent the walk to my apartment thinking about her. I rubbed my fingers through my hair and found myself missing my bowler hat. Weird, to miss something that didn't actually exist, but it looked so nice with the long purple feather she'd given me at the market. Banjo, perched on my shoulder, took that as his cue to search my hair for edible treasures.

She had touched my scarred hand and my streak. That thought brought me back down to earth. One day, she would ask about them. Would I tell her? Would she hate me for it? With great difficulty, I pushed aside all thoughts of her.

I made a quick sandwich when I got home, grabbed a soda, and plopped in my captain's chair. I set my goggles on the desk and put on my VISOR, munching on my sandwich as I logged in. Banjo curled into a ball on the loveseat.

The subject line of my first email almost made me choke—my Battleskiff had sold for 455,000 netcoin. Nearly half a million netcoin, for a virtual spaceship. More accurately, the promise of a spaceship. The game hadn't even been released yet. Some people like to start the game with a bang.

I hurriedly logged into the auction site to transfer the winnings to my account and sign over possession of the ship to *Barfolomew2030*. My bank account now held north of 1.1 million netcoin. Not the richest I'd ever been, but pretty darn close. Almost instinctively, I sent another 100,000 to my parents' account.

I took off the VISOR and danced a happy jig around the

room, picking up the sleeping Banjo and swinging him in circles, earning a screech and a swipe at my face. I let him go, and sat back down again, donning the VISOR once more. There was something I wanted to buy.

The new Airavan was a ten-passenger hover vehicle, with enough headroom to stand up in and a retractable sides and roof. With the roof on, it looked remarkably like a Starfleet shuttlecraft from Star Trek. The geek community had even created paint schemes to emulate the look of the famous runabouts.

I'd always fantasized about having one, and now that I could comfortably afford it, it was time to fulfill that dream.

I brought up their site, and selected the newest model, with all the features I could want: a mini fridge, seats that transformed into beds, unobstructed 360-degree viewing, and an onboard computer that rivaled the one at my house. I selected a third-party paint scheme from Geekskins, then rammed the "Buy Now!" option. A confirmation message appeared on screen, and after a few additional details, the transaction was complete.

"Congratulations on being the proud owner of a Tesla Airavan!" it said. *"Your new vehicle will arrive tomorrow morning at ten A.M."*

I also got a notification that my account had been debited 425,000 netcoin. This made me cringe for a second, until I thought about the situation; I had just traded a virtual ship for a real one.

Even though it was just after nine o'clock, I couldn't go to sleep fast enough, and after the exertion of the day, it wasn't a difficult task.

I got in a solid ten hours—which felt wonderful—and woke up with a spring in my step. I hustled through my morning routine and settled onto my balcony with Banjo, enjoying my coffee and vape, waiting for the delivery. The rain from the previous day had been replaced by a brilliant blue sky once again.

At ten sharp, my door signal chimed, and Lenny the doorman informed me my ship had arrived. I threw my goggles in my backpack, rushed downstairs with Banjo, and bolted out to the parking lot.

And there it was.

The delivery driver had already gone, leaving the vehicle parked in the apartment's guest zone on the ground floor. There was resident parking beneath the building, and another zone between the ninth and tenth floors, where I would be parking my new beauty.

I approached the work of art and whistled appreciatively. The van was about nine meters long, the body a neutral grey color, doming subtly at the roof, and the leading end slightly contoured inward to make it aerodynamically efficient. The smoky, nearly black window stretched all the way around the vehicle, unbroken by any fixtures. This could be transformed to perfect transparency with the mere touch of a button.

I strolled around the vehicle, taking it all in. A double red racing stripe streaked down each side, meeting in the rear and ending in the front with the asymmetrical arrowhead symbol of Starfleet. The van, which was designed to float on water as well, had two pontoons at the base that ran the length of the craft, stylized to look like warp nacelles. On the rear of the vehicle, just above the racing stripe and below the window in black block lettering, was the registry number, NCC 1701-D, and the word *Galileo* written in script. I *squeed* with joy. So help me, I *squeed*.

I pressed my hand to the sensor near the front of the vehicle, and the gullwing style door swung upwards. "Hi, Jacob," said a familiar voice. I looked at the center console screen and saw Lexi smiling at me. The computer in the craft had synced with mine as soon as I waved my hand over the exterior console to unlock the van. I stepped inside and sat in the front-right seat, swiveling it around to face the cabin. Banjo hopped into the seat next to me, *ooking* appreciatively.

"This is a sweet vehicle," Lexi said, glancing around the spacious interior. "I always did want to pilot a shuttlecraft."

The word spacious didn't do it justice. Long bench seats ran along either side of the three-meter wide interior, with two more swivel chairs in the rear. Compartments under the benches provided a ton of storage, and the overhead refrigerator held a week's worth of food. I'd have to investigate all the features later, but for now, I wanted to cruise.

I pressed two fingers of my right hand to the ignition panel, and the instrumentation lit up before me in a soothing display of dim blues and reds. A map appeared on the center console.

"Where to?" asked Lexi.

I thought for a second before speaking. I wanted to go out over the Sound. I wanted some water beneath me.

"Deception Pass," I said.

"Good choice," said Lexi. "Keep your arms and legs inside the vehicle at all times."

The door hummed downward and shut itself securely, and then the van lifted into the air without a sound. It rose straight until it was about fifty meters above my apartment building, then accelerated over the park that lined the Seattle waterfront.

"Yes!" I shouted with joy as I spun around in my seat. I pressed another icon on the console, and the top of the van split down the middle, the roof folding against the windows as they retreated into the vehicle frame. The windscreen in front of me remained, although that could also be retracted if the vehicle wasn't moving. Although I couldn't see it, an invisible safety barrier now surrounded the vehicle, preventing anything from falling out, yet it didn't stop the sunlight and fresh salt air from pouring over me. The forcefield did keep out a lot of the wind, however, which was nice when cruising at the speeds I was. Banjo pranced around in circles on the seat next to me, apparently loving it as well.

In a minute I was over Puget Sound, flying north to the bridge that connected Whidbey Island in the south with Fidalgo Island in the north. The Deception Pass Bridge connected the two islands in a pair of long, graceful arches hundreds of meters above the turbulent waters below.

Nestled in among forests and cliffs, it was one of the most beautiful places in the state, especially after Mount Rainier blew its top.

I brought up my music subscription, selected my favorite late 20th-century alternative station, and cranked it up.

I stood up as a fanfare of trumpets and trombones erupted over the speakers, and the lyrics of *Dr. Worm* filled the cabin. I threw my hands in the air, singing along as I cruised over the blue-green waters of the Sound, islands covered in forests whisking by on both sides.

After the song was over, I called Jeni. Her face took over the wide screen between the seats, while Lexi's moved to a box in the lower left corner.

"Hey, Jakey," she said. "Where are you?

"Cruising over the Sound in my new Airavan," I replied, beaming.

Her eyes went wide as I explained the windfall I received from the auction.

"And you didn't invite me along?" she asked, pouting.

Of course, I broke into a slew of apologies, telling her how I just got it thirty minutes ago and how this was pretty much my test drive. She smiled, and I relaxed, realizing she was playing around, and our conversation turned to work.

"So, what time do you want to meet?" she asked.

We agreed to meet at the alley in the early afternoon and planned to try and gain another level before the quest started at midnight. A nap wouldn't hurt either, if we were to be up until the wee hours of the morning.

The rest of the cruise was just as amazingly glorious as the first half, and I spent it singing along to the radio and getting the feel for my new ride.

About thirty minutes later, the two arches of Deception Pass bridge came into view.

"Lexi," I said. "Circle the bridges a couple of times so I can take some photos, then set me down on the landing bluff on the north end of Whidbey."

She complied, and I pulled out my phone, getting some beautiful aerial panoramas, and sent a couple to Jeni. An island jutted up hundreds of meters in the middle of the pass. The bridge ran over it, forming two bridges, although it had always been referred to as one. I could make out people on the island, taking pictures and enjoying the view.

Lexi set us down on the bluff, as requested, and I put the roof back up before grabbing my bag and hopping out with Banjo. I took in the beautiful vista, the morning sunlight glinting off the water under the 130-year-old bridge. Banjo reached up and grabbed my hand as he stood beside me and gazed outward, just as awed as I. Boats sailed by underneath, ranging in size from small yachts to two-man dinghies.

"Well, Banjo," I said, "let's see what it looks like." I reached into my bag and took out my goggles, putting them on my head and powering them on.

"Jakey, I frickin' *love* your new ride," said Banjo right away, looking up at me. His maroon vest had turned olive green for some reason. Maybe Quirk wanted to spice things up a bit.

"So do I, bud," I said with a grin.

I turned my attention to the view and gasped in astonishment. Eight stone and lumber spires now graced either side of the bridges, one on each corner. Two enormous golden gears grew vertically out of the center island, perpendicular to the roadway. Each one was taller than the surrounding trees and ratcheted slowly in opposite directions. The shaft that ran through the middle of the gears formed the tunnel all the road traffic drove through. The gears cut deep into the island, disappearing into the cliff face, where the mechanism that drove them was likely housed. It was a fantastic sight.

"This is almost more than my monkey brain can handle," Banjo said, his jaw hanging open.

My jaw did the same when I turned around and looked at the Galileo. Where I parked it, a beautiful airship now rested. The cabin exterior had been redone with brass trim and lacquered mahogany, and the windows had turned a translucent blue. I walked around it, admiring the beauty of the design. Four circular brass lamps graced the front of the cabin, a crisscross of brass mesh lying over the glass, and a small brass figurehead of a griffin jutted proudly from the center. About two meters above the top of the cabin, an oblong spheroid floated, crafted from a thick, deep-purple canvas. The balloon pulled at eight sturdy ropes which attached to large brass eyehooks on the sides of the cabin. I whistled in admiration.

Banjo tried to as well, but quickly found out he couldn't whistle.

At the rear of the ship, written in silver filigree calligraphy, was her name, *Galileo*. I finished my circle of the airship, then walked to the front entrance. Sensing my proximity, the paneled glass door gently lifted upward on brass hydraulics.

"Hi, Jacob," said Lexi, and I stopped in my tracks.

She was sitting in the front seat. Her face looked as it always had, but now she wore a leather cap with tarnished silver goggles perched high on her forehead. A baggy white button-up shirt hung on her petite frame, and brown leather gloves covered her hands. Brown knee-length trousers and sturdy leather boots came into view as she swiveled the chair around.

"Where to next?"

CHAPTER SEVENTEEN: THE RABBITS

The ride back was just as enjoyable, the only clouds to be seen were way out over the mountains to the east, the remains of the storm that had passed through yesterday. The interior of the *Galileo* was rendered gorgeously, with the same lacquered mahogany from the exterior trimming the richly upholstered seats and benches, done in plush magenta velvet. Lexi worked the instrument panel, made up of a series of brass knobs, levers and toggle switches. The center console screen was now a brass-rimmed vacuum tube display.

We sailed south over the water, and soon the Space Needles came into view, followed by the downtown skyline and the giant double gears of the waterfront wheel. I told Lexi to set course for the alley, and the *Galileo* drifted southeast, over the stadiums.

Steam Whistle Alley rose up before me, and from the air, I appreciated it in a way I couldn't in my first visits. Long and narrow, the shape reminded me of a giant tuning fork, with the mansion at the base and the opening on the north. From here, the estate appeared enormous, as wide as the central boulevard and both tines of the fork combined. The front gates of the walled district drew closer, and I could just make out the gears of the apparatus tasked with opening and closing the towering gates. It wasn't the only entrance into the place, however.

The *Galileo* descended to a two-block-wide parking lot on the west side of the complex and touched down gently. Banjo jumped to my shoulder and wrapped his arms around my neck as I exited the vehicle.

Jeni had messaged me on the ship's monitor on the way in, asking me to meet her at *Thom's Munchies*, the little café where I'd first met her in the alley. It was on the west side of the alley, and as I approached the wall, I noticed a few narrow passageways and alleys that led to the main thoroughfare. Convenient, as I wouldn't have to walk the two blocks to the main entrance at the north end.

As I approached, I scanned the backs of the buildings visible above the three-meter wall. I'd walked by all their facades before, but from my new vantage behind, it was all wood and windows. A few painted murals on unbroken stretches of wall advertised various products. One of them showed a grey-bearded man in a monocle, holding a potion in his hand. Large ornate lettering to the right declared: '*Dwebble's Potions, Reliable and Affordable.*' Good ol' Dwebble.

I had a fairly good idea on how to get to the café from here, so I headed towards one of the side entrances to the right. Two muscular figures stood on either side of the access to my chosen path, leaning against the walls. Brawlers, maybe.

"It's gotta be Lakenhilly Park," one of them said to the other. "There's more trees there than any other I know about, and from what I hear, anything we fight there will be low level."

"Yeah, it's gotta be one of the noob places, but there's like forty or fifty of them around, at least," replied brawler number two, cleaning his nails with a dagger. "Most of 'em have trees."

They looked at me as I approached with expressions of malice. I tipped the brim of my bowler, but neither one of them returned the gesture.

"Good day, gentleman," I said, with a friendly smile. Banjo played the part and squeaked as he smiled and gave the men a lazy salute.

Brawler number one glanced at the chain whip on my waist before spitting in the dirt by my feet. Brawler two chuckled. I suddenly realized nobody had said a single word to me about PVP, but these fellows' excellent manners had me yearning to find out if it was active here.

"Your girlfriend looks a little bit hairy to me," said brawler number two, and the other gave a dumb-sounding snort. Banjo ignored them. They weren't worth my time either, so I strode by without any further acknowledgement. They didn't try to stop me.

I passed through the passage and found myself in the alley proper, about three doors down from Thom's. I walked into the establishment and found a decent crowd inside this time. Jeni had taken a small round table by the front windows.

"Hi, Jakey." She smiled. "Hungry?"

I sat across from her, watching her scarf down a plate of fish and chips, and my mouth started watering. AR might've not been perfect, but I sure loved the ability to eat real food while in-game. She offered me a piece, and I accepted, dipping it in her tartar sauce before popping it in my mouth. I chewed the fish and swallowed, finding it surprisingly delicate, with a crunchy cornflake coating.

"So, what's the plan for the day?" she asked.

A lot of players were within earshot, including two of the Arborbound at the table next to us, heads lowered in conversation.

A thought struck me. "Banjo, what do you know about the Arborbound?"

"Just what Carrie already told you, for the most part," he said. "According to their backstory, they supposedly came down from the mountains to trade and compare technologies with the city folk."

Hmm. Maybe my Arboretum guess wasn't full-proof after all. If anyone knew where the place of the arbors was, it would be the Arborbound, wouldn't it?

I lowered my head closer to the table and whispered my misgivings to Jeni.

"Well, from what I've heard this morning, none of them are sure where it is either," she said with a shrug. "The majority of the people I've overheard are heading to Interlaken Park—Lakenhilly. I've also heard more than a few talking about the ravine at Ravenna. Haven't heard a peep about..." she looked around, "the other place."

I furrowed my brow, giving it some more thought. "Might be a good idea to talk somewhere a bit more private," I said suspiciously, looking around with narrowed eyes. Then, I smiled and shot her a glance. "Hey, feel like going for a ride?"

She gave me a mischievous look which broke into a wide grin, throwing her napkin on the table as she stood up. "Was wondering when you were gonna ask. Let's get stocked up first, shall we?"

Banjo wrapped his arms around my neck as we stood up and walked back outside the small café. We stopped in Dwebble's and picked up a few more potions, as well as a pair of one-use rings that automatically brought the wearer back to max health when their HP dropped below ten percent. The proprietor warned us that the hit *had* to take us below ten percent for it to activate, but if we went from twelve percent to zero, nothing would happen. I also purchased a belt with slots for tools and utilities.

I put one of the rings on my finger, then handed the other to Jeni. Before taking it, she paused for just a moment, and then placed it on, thanking me. She took a handful of the potions we'd purchased and put them into my belt slots for me. "Looks like you get to be the squirter, now," she said.

The proprietor smirked at us from behind his counter, and I burst into laughter. Two seconds later her eyes went wide, and her face turned beet red. A little slow to the punch. Jeni stammered a few words before throwing her hands up, realizing it was pointless, and I chuckled as I followed her out of the shop. I wasn't going to let her live this one down.

Just outside, the shop owner had an identification station where we could identify items found out in the wild. I pulled out the two rings and the bracelet we'd plundered during our conquests and popped them into the station. The rings were nothing special but could take an enchantment, at least. The geared bracelet, on the other hand, offered plus three to dexterity. I showed it Jeni, who took it, then closed it around my wrist.

"You need all the help you can get," she explained with feigned gravitas.

"Can't say I disagree."

"What about your whip?" Jeni asked.

I had forgotten about the whip. I unhooked it from my waist and laid the coiled weapon on the identification table. The monochromatic amber-on-black screen showed an icon of a grandfather clock for a few seconds before returning its results.

Jeni read them out loud. "Trifecta Chain Whip. Plus 15 to damage, and plus three to dexterity." She whistled. "Your dex is getting a bit crazy, Jakey."

I checked my stats on my wrist screen out of curiosity. Between the two levels and the bonuses from my items, my dexterity was now at 15. *My whip's going to be deadly.*

We left the shop and began to make our way across the main avenue. Players had already started heading out to whichever location they thought housed the first quest, leaving the alley mostly barren. A strange time for the steam whistle blast from the rooftops to the east, heralding Arnie Drubbins' entry into the courtyard in front of the mansion, bellows pumping on his rolling platform. He came to a stop in the middle of the thoroughfare, just meters in front of where it ended, and the courtyard began.

Speakers came to life throughout Steam Whistle Alley, and Arnie's voice filled every corner, but instead of the expected grandiose voice he'd orated at us with before, this time he spoke in a tone far less urgent.

He cleared his throat and squinted at a cue card. "Citizens of Steam Whistle Alley," he began, "now that the first quest for the alley is about to begin, there is something I want to... tell you."

"I'm a citizen now?" Jeni asked with a scowl.

"You have been given ample opportunity to learn the ways of this land," Arnie continued.

I would have bet netcoin that Arnie hadn't written this.

"Therefore, beginning tonight at midnight, the mysterious shroud of protection that envelops this land will be lifted." He squinted again, moved his face closer to the card, as if certain he hadn't read something right. "Choose whether you wish to participate by informing... the one who helped create you. They can provide further details," Arnie finished. Without further comment, the bellows resumed pumping, and Arnie put the note into his breast pocket and left the way he'd come.

"What was that all about?" Jeni asked, scowling. She was cute when she scowled. Well, cute-*er*. "I think I know," I said, prickled by misgivings. "At least part of it, anyway.

I'll tell you once we're airborne."

We made our way out through the same passage I entered by. The brawlers had left, and the remaining airships in the parking lot were dwindling in number. I pointed mine out, and Jeni's face lit up. Banjo jumped off my neck and ran ahead of us.

"Welcome, milady, to the *Galileo*," he said, bowing and extending his hand toward the craft.

I opened the door, and Jeni poked her head inside, marveling at the interior before climbing in and sitting on one of the side benches. Lexi swiveled around in her chair. "Heya, I'm Lexi," she said. Jeni didn't seem surprised, but I still felt the need to explain.

"Lexi here is my computer," I said, "and apparently, in the game, she's my pilot as well."

I climbed inside and moved to one of the bucket seats at the rear of the cabin.

Jeni joined me in the other one and swiveled around in a complete circle. "All the extras?" she asked.

"Oh yeah, both in AR and the real world, apparently," I said.

I pulled a lever between our seats, and the two long benches folded out toward the center of the cabin, and then connected with a click before flattening out, expanding into a thick mattress, Rollers stretched sheets and blankets over the whole bed, and four slots slid open in the backrests, where four plush maroon pillows fell out, two on either end.

Jeni looked over at me, eyebrows raised.

Whoops— thought that was the lever for retracting the

roof. "For camping and stuff," I said lamely. I pulled the lever again, and the bedding retreated, and the bed folded back into seats.

"We should uh...get going," I said. "Lexi, set a course for the Locke Wetlands, 30 KPH."

Lexi swiveled around in her chair, hands swiftly manipulating the levers and dials before her.

Then, with a motion of my arm, "Engage."

Stabilizers compensated for a lot of the movement generated by the vehicle, so when the *Galileo* rose into the air, we didn't feel a thing. Jeni leaned back in her chair, swiveling again to take in the view as we ascended.

I smiled over at her as we reached cruising elevation, and when the *Galileo* got up to speed, I told her what I thought about Arnie's little speech.

"I think either Quirk, or maybe even Iggy wrote that message," I said. "Pretty obvious Arnie didn't. I'm also pretty sure that they're trying to tell us that PVP will be open tonight for those who opt in."

"What makes you so sure?" she asked. "And what do you think he meant by the 'summon your creator' bit? Is there some religion system here that I don't know about?"

"God, I hope not," I said, scowling. "Religion makes everything so complicated. And I'm not sure, but I've played enough alphas and betas to know a veiled message from the engineers when I hear one. Or maybe it's just my archaeologist's perception kicking in." I winked.

Banjo hopped into the spot between our seats. "As to the creator bit, he's referring to the one that helped you choose your character. You can summon them."

I frowned in thought. *Carrie had mentioned that, hadn't she?* "Do you want to enable PVP, Jeni?"

"Hell yeah, I do," she said with a bloodthirsty grin. This girl was more than just a purple werewolf.

"So how do I summon Carrie?" I asked Banjo. "Is there a spell or something? Do I just say, 'I summon Carrie' in a booming voice?"

With a little pop like a bursting cartoon bubble, Carrie materialized in front of us. This time she wore a dark purple dress with long ruffled sleeves, the V of her neck plunging almost to her belly button. Jeni kicked me in the shin. Must've caught me staring.

"Good to see you again, Jacob," Carrie said with a familiar smirk. "You rang?"

"Carrie, I would like to enable PVP when it becomes available tonight," I said.

"Certainly!" she said., and a green, swirling vortex appeared behind her. Her arm disappeared inside, and she felt around for a few seconds, her tongue sticking out between her lips. Then her face broke into a smile, and she withdrew her arm, now holding a rifle. The vortex behind her winked out.

"PVP in Panmachina must be ranged, by necessity," she explained. "The liability is too great if we allow melee player combat, even with the abilities the goggles provide. Too easy to accidentally smack someone."

She handed me the gun. The scope was a series of lenses welded to the barrel, which grew increasingly smaller as they approached the carved wooden stock. I knew a bit about guns but couldn't see anywhere to load the ammunition. In the spot where the bolt and receiver would normally be, two brass cylinders attached on either side, mounted to the stock with screws.

"Your starter rifle," she said. "Those two cylinders are filled with ferrolium. They create BB-sized pellets, which are propelled through a series of miniaturized gravito-electric..." She paused. "It fires little balls of metal very fast. Those two cylinders hold around 300 shots. You can get more in the market. Though feel free to try out other forms of weaponry if you can them." She leaned over, giving me a generous view. "This is just Quirk's suggestion. She's uncannily good at predicting people's desires. Just like me," she said with a hint of mischief.

Jeni kicked me again. That one wasn't my fault.

"Will there be anything else, Jacob?" Carrie asked.

"What about my gir..." I caught myself. That could've been bad. "My friend?" I said with a heroic recovery.

"I did not create her, silly," she said, and then vanished with another pop.

Jeni raised her eyebrows.

"What?" I laughed. "She created me; I didn't create her."

She faced forward, then gave me a sidelong glance. "I summon Duke!" she exclaimed a flourish of an arm.

A very tall, very shirtless bronze-skinned man appeared before us. He gave Jeni a slight bow, affording me a view of tiny horns poking from his raven-black hair.

Jeni gave me a smirk, then told the demon she wished

to activate her PVP.

"As my lady wishes," the Demon said in a smooth bass voice that would make James Earl Jones applaud. A vortex opened behind him, swirling with fire, and the demon reached in, fishing around a moment before pulling out what looked like a single gauntlet that had spent a lot of time in a tube factory. He handed it to Jeni, who turned it over, examining it. Cylinders ran down the back of the fingerless glove, terminating over the first set of knuckles. The cylinders were connected to a series of black hoses, which attached to a small pneumatic piston at the base of the glove. From the other end of the piston, another hose ran around the wrist, attached to a pressure plate in the palm.

After saying his goodbyes to Jeni, Duke glared at me as he disappeared with a hiss. Jeni shrugged at me, then tried on her new toy.

"Aw, man, this thing looks badass," she said with a wide-eyed smile. She put it on her right hand and flexed her fist, pointed it towards the front of the cabin and squeezed the pad in her palm. Four silver darts flew out of the cylinders and sank deep in the woodwork below the windows.

Lexi jumped in her chair, and swung around, glaring.

"Sorry, Lexi," Jeni said. "Just uh... yeah. Sorry."

"I just got this car," I said, staring at the silver darts sticking from the wood. Jeni gave me a second to think about it, and I blushed a bit. "Oh, yeah."

Of course, this wasn't really my car, and those weren't

actually silver darts.

"I think I'll wait until we get there to test mine," I said. I slung my rifle over my shoulder, and Jeni took off her new gauntlet, stuffing it into her pack.

We flew north, the familiar mountains and inlets drifting past us. Jeni moved to the windows, leaning on her knees as she took in the scenery and threw her arms above her head, giving a loud whoop of excitement. I'd had a similar reaction. To our right, the city skyline sparkled in the sun, and after we passed the main bulk of skyscrapers, or more accurately skyspires, the ship banked starboard and made a beeline for the Space Needles.

The first needle, built nearly a century ago, still stood at a majestic 200 meters tall. The new needle, created about twenty years ago and mirroring the design of the original, dwarfed its younger sibling by at least another 100 meters.

This was my first time seeing the Space Needles up close in the AR world as well; from afar they pretty much looked how they always had, but from this distance I could see the usual observation decks on both towers had become a series of concentric gears—reminding me of those old water-wheels, spinning slowly in the summer sun. The supports and pylons that made up most of the structures were encased in burnished copper, adorned with an assortment of clockwork mechanisms and steaming release valves. Two steam stacks atop the larger tower belched billowy clouds that drifted lazily eastward, while a single stack graced the smaller tower.

We drifted between them, the three of us taking in the

artistry that Quirk had created. The minutiae were startling in their complexity. From here I could see that the large gears surrounding the observation decks were, in turn, driving smaller gears, and those turning others the size of bicycle wheels. Some of these powered the cylindrical bronze elevators that rose up and down the center pylons of both needles. Other clockwork mechanisms went all the way to the base, where I could make out movement but not much else.

We drifted northeast. From so high up, I could already see Lake Washington, and after a few more seconds, the Locke Wetlands spread out straight ahead of us. I slowed down to 20 KPH for the last couple kilometers.

When we reached our destination, I ordered Lexi to circle the park.

"So, this is it," I said. "The Arboretum."

"I haven't been here in a couple of years," she said. "I used to come here to read. Spring and summer are amazing—blooming trees from all over the world. Squirrels and geese, and the occasional heron in the rushes by the water."

We landed at the southern end of the park next to a few other vehicles. Most of the cars were now the brass and wood vehicles I'd seen on the roads of the city, but there was one other airship. A few bicycles on a rack were gyrocopters in this world; their blades folded down against the center shaft.

We put on our backpacks and Jeni, Banjo and I stepped out, waving goodbye to Lexi.

On our way through the parking lot, we passed the other airship, which bore the name *Alnitak*.

"It's one of the stars in Orion's belt," said Banjo, "along with *Alnilam* and *Mintaka*."

"Thank you, Wikimonkey." Jeni giggled.

"Just staying useful," Banjo said with a bow.

We reached the end of the parking lot and a field of grass spread out before us. The park was crowded. Couples dressed in fine silk shirts and wide floral dresses sat on blankets.

"They're all nipnicks," Jeni said, squinting in the sunlight.

"Not all of them," I said, pointing. I put on my goggles and zoomed in, not bothering with the info-lens. "Looks like a garg and maybe a brawler? I'm not sure." I scanned the field to the right and saw an engineer and a spellcaster of some sort walking briskly towards the trees as well. I didn't see any mobs though, just the usual rabbits that inhabited the park. People liked to dump them here once they realized what crappy pets they made, and then the rabbits did what rabbits do.

I parked my goggles on the brim of my hat and proceeded into the park, then paused, turning back to Jeni. "Lead on, Tank," I said.

Banjo ran ahead of us, anxious to stretch his legs in the grassy field.

The park was massive. The tree line was a good 200 meters ahead of us. A system of trails ran through the woodsy part, winding their way through to the marshlands that bordered the lake.

The two teams I'd seen earlier were no longer in sight, apparently disappearing into the woods. Nothing but a handful of nipnicks and the rabbits remained. It was strange—this was more rabbits than I'd ever remembered seeing here. A few were a light chocolate color, while a couple of them were white with large black patches, and an inordinate number of albinos. Their pink eyes always creeped me out, but on closer examination, I noticed that not all the white rabbits had pink eyes.

Some were jet black.

The more colorful rabbits contentedly nibbled away at the grass, but the black-eyed fur balls—maybe it was my imagination—seemed to be clustering towards us. Not charging or anything, just leisurely hopping in our general direction, until we were surrounded by a halo of perhaps twenty of the white bunnies, looking up at us with twitching noses and black eyes that didn't even reflect the sun. Demon bunnies.

Jeni inched closer to me involuntarily, and Banjo scampered up my back and disappeared into my pack.

There was maybe five seconds of silence, where none of us moved.

Then, the first rabbit screamed and leaped at my throat.

CHAPTER EIGHTEEN: JAMESON'S GIFT

For the next fifteen minutes, our world was flashes of white fur stained with blood.

The rabbits attacked in an all-out onslaught, leaping at us and sinking their sharp incisors into any exposed flesh they could find. I had my dagger in my hand, and I was slashing and stabbing as frantically as I could. If I was quick enough to catch them, the rabbits went down fairly quickly, but more often than not, they'd leap in, tear at my neck or forearms, then dart away before I could get a swing in. One rabbit was clinging to my left arm, scrambling up it to get at my neck. A quick thrust between its ribs and the rabbit fell away, limp. For a moment I was bunny-free.

Beside me, Jeni was a blur of purple fur, her claws disemboweling bunnies with aplomb. One leaped at her face, and she caught it in mid-air, snapping its neck with a twist of her paw. Another white demon had found purchase in the back of her neck, so I unhooked my chain whip and lashed out, skewering it on the three-bladed tip. I yanked the whip, and the bunny, still impaled by the blades, flew from her neck and left a bloody trail as I dragged it to my feet. I put a foot on its skull and pulled the blades out, wiping them on my pants before lashing out at another.

Soon, the only rabbits left were real ones. I'd never look at the supposedly-cute creatures the same again.

Jeni and I stood back to back, panting. What a sight we must have looked to all the nipnick picnickers. Then again, if they knew of our glorious bunny slaughter, they'd probably be cheering us on.

Banjo peeked out of my bag.

"Is it over?" he asked, looking around nervously.

"For now," I said.

He crawled out of my bag and sat on top of it, peeking over my head like a nosy neighbor behind a picket fence.

Our respite, and Banjo's courage, was short-lived. More of the furry dead-eyed bastards came at us from the tree line—wave after rabbit wave attacked as we approached the forest. They didn't cause much physical damage, and what they did manage we regenerated rapidly, but they hurt like hell, and it took a lot of energy to deal with them. And who knew how long the psychological aspect would torment us. The XP was good enough, at least; Jeni and I each got 30 to 35 XP for each one.

By the time we reached the tree line, we'd plowed through three more waves of the killer rabbits. About midway through the last wave, Banjo popped his head out of the bag and meekly squeaked "Ding!" before retreating back inside. We finished clearing up, and he made another appearance, looking around for leporine invaders before deciding the coast was clear and hopping to the ground between Jeni and me. Jeni also looked around, then reverted to her human form.

I smiled at her. "Is it wrong that I like watching that?"

She opened her mouth and gave a theatric gasp of mock modesty.

We headed down one of the many trails that entered the woodlands. After only about twenty meters into the forest, we came across a small log shelter with a single picnic table sitting on the side of the dirt path. Someone had nailed a large gear, about the size of a dinner plate, to one of the poles.

Jeni and I exchanged a glance, but I just shrugged. "This is as good a place to take a break as any."

We took off our bags and parked ourselves at the table. Banjo scampered up a support beam and ran onto the thatched roof, out of sight.

"Reality check?" she asked, and I agreed. Needed to stretch the old eyeballs.

I powered the goggles down and took them off as Jeni did the same. I blinked, then blinked a few more times. Nothing had changed. Even the gear was still there, nailed to the post. Had I just taken off the virtual goggles? Was I still in the game? A moment of panic rushed through me, and my heart started beating faster as I tried to understand which reality I was in.

Jeni must have seen my expression. "Don't worry, we're out," she said, grabbing my forearm and giving it a comforting squeeze. "I thought the same damn thing, but look, we're in our regular clothes."

Her touch centered me. She was right.

We got some food out of our packs, and I set into a roast beef sandwich while Jeni pulled out some jerky and an apple. A thought occurred to me, and I stopped chewing. "Banjo!" I shouted through a mouth full of beef, earning a wince from Jeni. "Sorry," I mumbled.

A moment later Banjo popped his head over the edge of the roof, then scampered down the support pole and hopped onto the table.

"You dinged us earlier," I said. "What did you want?"

He gave a half-hearted screech and then snatched my goggles off the table, handing them to me. Jeni giggled.

I feel dumb now.

I strapped my goggles back on and powered up. Banjo's vest appeared, as well as Jeni's in-game attire, putting my mind at final rest about the whole 'trapped inside the game' scenario. That kind of thing never happens in real life.

"You summoned, master?" Banjo said in a sarcastic droll.

"Yeah, you dinged during the last bunny slaughter."

"Oh!" he exclaimed. "Level up! Congrats, Jakey, you're now level four." He did a little dance. "Your perception skill went up by two, a couple of other stats went up a point, but nothing important; I don't want you to get a big head. And a third point to spend at the guild, should you ever decide to go there."

Hard to remember everything with so much going on.

"Oh, and you've learned a new skill," Banjo continued.

"The skewer skill lets you... erm... skewer things. You unleashed it on a rabbit back there, useful for retrieving small mobs or items. You actually levelled up before you used it, but I was too... comfortable in your bag. The skewer skill does some decent damage. But fair warning: I wouldn't use it against anything too big and meaty."

"How do I activate it?" I asked.

"Well, from what I understand, you just gotta wish really hard," he replied in all seriousness.

I gave him a looked that asked if I was being screwed with. Jeni snorted, and I shifted the look to her.

"You know I can't understand a thing he's saying, right?" said Jeni, gesturing to her goggles on the table. "It's all just monkey chatter."

"Of course, I know," I lied. I could tell from her face I wasn't fooling her. *Looking dumber by the minute, Jake.* "He told me if I want to activate my new skill, I have to 'wish really hard.'"

Jeni nodded. "Sounds like the same thing I do to change into my werewolf form."

I thanked Banjo and powered down the goggles, but as I did, something caught my eye. A word carved into the table—among countless initials of lovers and poorly rendered phalli—flashed softly. I took off the goggles and ran my finger over the spot, but nothing was there.

"Jeni, put your goggles on for a sec," I said, then did the same. A single carved word appeared amongst all the real carvings. *Score one for perception.*

"*Bruse,*" Jeni said. "Mean anything to you?"

"No, but it's gotta be important," I said, looking up at the real gear nailed to the post. I checked the table a few times, turning my goggles off and on, but saw no other changes, so I removed the goggles again to focus on my sandwich. I closed my eyes for a few seconds, appreciating the break after so much sensory onslaught. When I opened them, I saw Jeni, wearing her goggles and poking at her wrist.

"You alright?" I asked.

"Yeah, we leveled up, just checking stats," she explained.

That made sense. "Anything interesting?"

"A couple of points to stamina and strength, and a point to my slash," she explained. "I also got a skill point. I have three now, but I don't know where to spend them."

"Yeah, I'm in the same boat," I said. "Banjo mentioned the archaeologist's guild. You think there's something similar for wolves?"

"Well I highly doubt there's a guild for what amounts to a genetic mutation," she said with a chuckle. She powered off her goggles and slipped them off. "But, we got seven hours to kill before midnight. Once we're done here, we should head back to the alley and figure out where to spend these points. Might come in handy for whatever goes down tonight."

She took out her phone, typing something into it.

"*Bruse* is a Danish word, meaning either 'roar' or 'fizz,'" she said. "Either of those mean anything to you?"

I shook my head. "Not a thing," I said, but I *would*

investigate later.

After our brief meal, we powered back on and began exploring the woods, searching for anything that might be relevant to the upcoming quest. The trees towered around us on either side of the path, their boughs meeting above us, blocking much of the sunlight. The delightful smell of pine and moss kept me breathing deep through my nose, and an array of birdcalls filled my ears. Every so often tiny level three wood goblins appeared, but always one at a time. They provided no real challenge but did give us some XP, and one of them dropped a strange green potion that neither one of us was keen on testing.

We came across a few more of the picnic shelters, each one with a gear adorning it, and the word *'Bruse'* carved somewhere into the table.

"Well if anything else," Jeni said at one of the shelters, "I think your hunch was right about the location of the quest. Why else would this word be carved everywhere?"

"I was thinking the same thing," I said.

We walked along for another few minutes, dispatching a few more goblins. Eventually, the path widened, and the forest gave way, and we found ourselves at the base of a grassy hill.

The park as a whole formed a giant circle, a woodland donut surrounding a grassy rise in the middle. All the wooded paths that began in the outer fields and parking lots eventually wound up here. At the top of the hill was an ornate gazebo.

I was about to leave the tree cover and start up the hill

when Jeni grabbed me by the shoulder. "Wait," she whispered.

I turned around. "What is it?"

"There's someone up there," she said, flipping down her zoom lens.

She crouched behind a bush growing on the tree line, and I did the same. Banjo scampered out of sight in the undergrowth.

"Well, it is a nice day, and this is a park," I said.

"Picnickers don't wear goggles," she said, adjusting the zoom on her lens, "or have wings."

I flipped down my own zoom lens and scrutinized the gazebo with her.

"That's..." Jeni began.

"Jameson," I finished for her. I adjusted my lens to maximum magnification, then swore under my breath when my gaze landed on the portly man sitting across from him. "And he's talking to the Glitch."

I needed to find out what their game was but had no way of getting close without being seen.

"I don't see the wings you're..." I began, but cut myself off. A gargoyle leaped into the air from behind the gazebo, hovering high above. It turned three-sixty degrees as it scanned the park, pausing in our direction. Seemed familiar... No, it couldn't be.

"Isn't that... Honeybucket?" I asked, bewildered.

The gargoyle fell from the sky and landed behind the gazebo, and I watched her converse with the two men inside. Then Jameson turned his head, looked directly at our hiding spot, and he smiled.

The two men got up from the table, and for a second, I thought all three of them were going to come charging down the hill at us, but that would have been pointless—PVP hadn't started yet. Instead, the three of them walked out of the far side of the gazebo and disappeared.

"What the hell is Honey doing with them?" I asked angrily, slipping my virtual goggles around my neck.

"We don't know enough to risk jumping to any conclusions," Jeni said rationally, removing her goggles as well. "We're not even sure if that was Honeybucket. Sure, she had Honey's... endowments, but all the gargoyles I've seen pretty much look alike, guys *and* girls."

"I can tell them apart," I fumed. "I have good perception, and it's telling me that was Honeybucket, talking with Jameson—the man that got kicked out of Argo for who knows what, and the Glitch—the man who wants to steal my goggles, so he can implant a virus that will allow him to take control of my body whenever he feels like it!" I finished my rant and crouched there for a few seconds, catching my breath. "I'm sorry," I said, "it's just..."

"It's OK, Jacob," Jeni said, putting a hand on my shoulder. "I get it. You want to go up there and look around?"

We climbed the hill in silence. When we got to the top, there was no sign of its three previous occupants. Four picnic tables sat in a diamond pattern inside the gazebo, but we had the place to ourselves. From here, we had an unobstructed view of the whole hill and surrounding forest, but only saw a handful of people. An older couple was out walking with their dog, and on the opposite side of the hill a group of kids threw around a football.

We searched the gazebo for anything that might have told us what the three of them were doing up here, but there were no gears, no carvings—nothing unusual at all. Banjo ran under each of the tables, looking underneath, but his report also came back negative.

"Well, what's next?" Jeni asked, sitting down at the nearest table. "Should we head back toward the alley?"

"I think we should—" I began, but Banjo cut me off.

"Guys...do you hear that?" he asked, a hint of alarm in his voice.

None of us made a peep, our ears straining to pick up what Banjo had heard. All I could make out was the sound of the light breeze and the distant sounds of the city.

Then I heard a faint ticking.

I tilted my head, trying to zero in on the tiny metallic sound. It was definitely coming from above me.

I nudged Jeni as I looked up. A tiny silver sphere hung from one of the rafters by a thin metal chain. It was about the size of a golf ball and had a golden gear around its circumference that rotated in time with the ticking.

"What is that thing?" Jeni asked.

I stood up and reached out to grab it, but the ticking suddenly stopped, and I froze in place. The object opened up like a clam, and a brilliant blue light poured out of it. So bright it obscured the entirety of my vision. I turned my head, stumbling around. I couldn't see anything except that piercing blue light. Jeni and Banjo were both screaming in confusion, but I couldn't help them.

After what felt like an eternity, the blinding blue light faded, replaced by a deep red afterglow that I couldn't see through either. After a minute, that faded as well.

Everything was completely black. I felt around for the table.

A hand gripped my forearm.

"Jacob," Jeni whispered, voice shaking. "I... I'm blind."

CHAPTER NINETEEN: THE GUILD

I took Jeni's hand and sat next to her, using my other hand to feel my way along the table. The blackness was complete, heavy, surrounding me like a suffocating blanket. I powered down my goggles, and the darkness gave way to an intense brightness. I blinked a few times, my eyes slowly acclimating themselves to the daylight.

"Power down, Jeni," I said, squeezing her hand before letting go.

She reached up and shut down her goggles, then ripped them off her face, squinting against the harshness of the daylight. I rubbed her back, and her panicked panting slowly gave way to steady breathing. Banjo seemed to calm down as well—now that we were in normal reality, I assumed his vision had returned as well.

"What the hell was that thing?" Jeni stammered.

"I'm not sure," I replied, "but I think we need to call Iggy. If the Glitch is up to something, I'm sure he'd like to know. So would I for that matter."

Out of curiosity, I put my goggles on and powered them

on again. The daylight once again faded into complete blackness. Swearing, I powered down and removed the goggles.

"Well?" Jeni asked.

"Still black," I said. "I really don't like that guy."

"It has to be temporary, right?" she asked. "They wouldn't put something in the game that would break it for a player."

"No, they wouldn't," I agreed. "But if Jameson's working with the Glitch, nothing would surprise me. I'm gonna ask Iggy."

I pulled my phone from my pants pocket and video called Iggy, who answered on the third ring. He was in his office, his goggles perched on his head.

"Hi, Jacob," he said. "What's up?"

"We just had another run-in with Jameson and the Glitch," I said. "They left some sort of contraption that blinded us when it went off. We can't see anything but blackness when we enter the game." I described the device to him in detail.

Iggy's brow furrowed in what might have been annoyance. "It sounds like a dark bomb," he said. "It's an engineer's recipe, but," he paused, checking something off camera, "it's not available until the engineer hits level twenty. There's nobody in the game above level six yet, so I don't know where he got it."

"Could he have purchased it?" Jeni asked, looking over my shoulder at the phone.

"Hi, Jeni," Iggy said. "No, it has to be created. All the

components are available in the alley, but engineers don't get the schematics until twenty. I have no idea how he got it, but I'm going to look into it."

"It has to be the Glitch, doesn't it?" I asked.

"That's a safe bet," replied Iggy.

"How does he still have access to the game code?" Jeni asked.

"He put in some back doors while he was still here," Iggy said. "I have a team working around the clock whose sole purpose is security. We've closed a lot of them, but new ones keep popping up. I do have a more permanent solution I am working on, but it will take some time. Just watch your backs until then."

"How long do the bomb's effects last for?" I asked.

"By design, ninety minutes," he said. "The one you described sounds like a level one dark bomb. The level two bomb blinds for three hours."

"But blinding other players with a device like that, wouldn't that be considered PVP?" Jeni asked. "I thought that hadn't gone online yet."

"It hasn't," Iggy said, his whole face drooping with his frown. He steepled his fingers and pressed them against his lips. "But if they could have fully accessed PVP, I think they would have done something more...damaging. I will have the security team make this their top priority."

"One other thing," I said. "Do you know a player named Honeybucket?" I asked. "She's a gargoyle. Her real name is Shauni."

His face went cold. "Yes, I know her," he said. "We

were... close. For a long while."

"She was with Jameson," I said. "Seemed to be helping him. But she's Trick's companion, another player we met in the game. Why would she be in league with Jameson?"

"It's a very long, very personal story, Jacob," Iggy said with a sigh. "It is part of the reason I had to force him out of the company, but also why I can't kick him out of the game entirely."

"I don't understand," I asked. "Why can't you just boot him? What does he have on you?"

Iggy's lips twitched, and his eyes kept darting off screen. "I can't say anything more. Please, drop it for now," Iggy pleaded.

I didn't want to drop it, but it sounded personal. "Okay then. Ninety minutes. We can handle that."

Iggy nodded, obviously relieved. "When you get some time, I'd love a report of your experience with the game so far. Until then, good luck, you two." He nodded towards the screen, then closed the connection.

Jeni and I shared a look, and I shrugged.

The sun had dipped below the forest tree line. I checked my phone and saw it was just after six o'clock—it'd be getting dark soon.

We made our way back through the woods toward the parking lot. It was nice, not having to worry about the rabbits, but I couldn't seem to shake the feeling that I was surrounded by them as we crossed the field where the nightmare had taken place. A few of the normal ones hopped around lazily.

Jeni shared my apprehension, looking over her shoulders every few seconds. "I feel like there're invisible bunnies everywhere," she said, voicing my thoughts for me. "It's giving me goosebumps."

"I know, right? It's super creepy."

But we reached the parking lot without incident and approached the shuttlecraft.

Jeni laughed suddenly, startling me. "You're a nerd, you know that?" she said, shaking her wryly.

I felt my face burning. This was the first time she'd seen the van in its true glorious form, and only the second time for me. I couldn't pick which one I liked more—the airship was a work of art, but this, this was my shuttlecraft. I ran a hand along it reverently, tracing word *Galileo* with my fingers.

"So, if I want some attention like that, I should get into some sexy *Trek* cosplay?" she asked with a grin.

"Definitely couldn't hurt," I said, and she punched me in the arm.

The doors opened to my touch, and Lexi welcomed me from the screen as we climbed inside, the door shutting behind us.

"So, we've got about an hour still before the bomb wears off," I said. "When it does, I want to hit the alley and see if I can find my guild."

"Mind dropping me off at my place?" Jeni asked. "I have some stuff I need to take care of."

I agreed, and she entered her address into the computer. The *Galileo* lifted off the ground and headed back to the downtown corridor.

We didn't talk much on the way back, but the silences didn't feel awkward, at least for me. Most of the time we spent enjoying another beautiful sunset, this time from five-hundred meters over the city. Before long, we set down on the top of her building next to a bank of elevators.

We sat there in silence for a minute, enjoying a prolonged period of eye contact. *Enjoyed* might not be the right word. I felt like I had swallowed one of the rabbits and it was trying to claw its way out through my gut. Summoning my courage, I leaned towards her and kissed her on the cheek. For a moment, she looked disappointed, but then she smiled and touched my cheek.

After a couple of uncomfortable instances of us both speaking simultaneously, we agreed to meet at the alley at ten o'clock, which should give us both enough time to do our own thing for a while. She gave me one last smile before exiting the van and disappearing into the elevator.

I sang a happy little tune as I made my way back to the alley. The events at the arboretum had been overpowered by thoughts of Jeni. I couldn't wait for this job to be over—I wanted to say so many things to that woman. But I had promised myself I'd wait for the alpha to finish, and it was a vow I intended to keep. Even so, it was incredibly difficult during moments like that one.

I shook my head, forcing myself to concentrate on the upcoming task. My next stop was the archaeologists' guild, wherever that may be. Since I started playing the game, I'd only seen one other archaeologist, so I had no idea where to even begin.

I was south of the stadiums now, and I could just make out Steam Whistle Alley, although as it came into view, the difference between the actual and the augmented came into stark contrast. Aside from the tuning fork shape of the alley, not much else was recognizable. The buildings were all an undecorated, washed out white that twilight did little to improve upon.

I landed in the same parking lot I'd been using, collected my backpack and my monkey, and set out towards the alley.

I entered the same side street as I had on my previous visit, although this time there were no brawlers guarding the entrance. My mind was mentally filling in all the features from memory as I entered the alley proper. The bus landing pad looked just like any other bus stop, except for all the passengers wearing goggles. Most were dressed in ordinary street clothes, although a couple had opted for outfits more in line with the simulation.

For some people, there was no such thing as too much immersion.

Behind the bus pad, a few people mingled among a wide array of low, nondescript tables, looking at items that didn't exist to my eyes. It did look kind of odd from this perspective, even when I knew what they were up to. Down the main strip, I saw other begoggled people walking in and out of buildings, going about their business. The place looked like any other warehouse district, albeit a popular one.

I checked my phone—only about three minutes until the bomb's effect disappeared. Nice.

I started walking towards the market—it seemed to be where the most activity was happening, and where I would be most likely to get answers about my guild.

By the time I got there, I was certain enough time had passed, so I retrieved my goggles from my bag and put them on, powering them up.

The splendor of the true Steam Whistle Alley filled my vision once again, and I sighed relief. The bare tables around me had been replaced by ones covered with a myriad of wares, and multi-colored awnings covered the whole expanse. The two goggled players standing next to me, before wearing jeans and T-shirts, now wore the long robes of a summoner and a thaumaturge. They must have seen me go from a dim, washed out nipnick to a glorious archaeologist, as they gave me a nod and continued browsing ocular attachments spread across the table in front of them.

"It's gotta be the Locke Wetlands," the thaumaturge said as he turned an eyepiece over in his hands. "I've been there, and it's nothing but trees and fields."

The summoner shook his head. "The people at the guild have it on good authority that it's at Lakenhilly. They won't say on whose authority, but whoever it is—if they trust them, so do I."

The thaumaturge shrugged. "Flip for it?" he suggested. I left the two to hash out their plan.

I passed a booth resembling a miniature hardware

store, stacked with bins and buckets full of gears, bolts, and springs, as well as an assortment of wrenches and tools. A man and a woman perused the items, putting a few choice ones in a pile in front of them, under the watchful gaze of a scrawny shopkeeper wearing a dirty apron over what appeared to be bare skin.

The woman wore a tight white shirt, sleeveless and covered in grease stains that had managed to splash her chest as well. I don't think she could have fully buttoned the shirt even if she wanted to. Red hair hung to her thick belt, the oversized pipe wrench of her trade tucked into it at an angle. Tight green shorts and a matching cabby hat completed the look, along with a pair of white fingerless gloves reinforced with strips of thin metal.

The man with her towered over both of us, his dark-skinned shaved head broader than a battering ram. He was dressed in black shirt, black vest, and black trousers, and at his waist hung the chain whip of our trade, its handle wrapped in black leather.

He was using one of the lenses on his goggles to examine some tiny metal object from the table. The girl looked over his shoulder to examine the item with him, her red locks spilling over his chest and tickling the side of his face. He shifted his gaze to her and smiled warmly, and she returned the gesture.

I cleared my throat, and they both turned to look at me. Tipping my cap in greeting, I walked up to the table, nonchalantly picking up a small golden gear from the table, turning it over in my hand.

"Oh, you don't want that one," said the woman. "Go for one of the dark ones over there. It doesn't look as flashy, but it's not going to lose teeth the first time you use it."

I thanked her and picked up the one she had suggested, examining it.

The woman stood up and extended her gloved hand. I shook it and tried not to wince from a grip which was probably as strong as that of the wrench she carried.

"My name's Alex, and this is my husband, Alex. You can call him Al, for sanity's sake," said the woman warmly.

Now that she was facing me, I couldn't help but notice that this girl was a complete knockout, with a figure you'd normally only see in the more risqué VR games. I was tempted to power off my goggles just to see how close this was to her real appearance but managed to control myself. Gentlemen didn't stare, and appearances were only an illusion these days anyway, whether you were playing a game or not. Even so, it was incredibly difficult to maintain eye contact, and I mentally patted myself on the back for succeeding.

"I'm Jacob, and this is Banjo," I said, gesturing to the ground beside me.

"Oh, you got a familiar! Level five already?" asked Alex.

"Oh, I'm not a familiar," said Banjo, and Alex jumped. "I'm a biosynth. I've been with Jacob since long before we came to the alley. I just follow him around, make sure he doesn't get into too much trouble."

Al put his goggles on his head, seemingly unperturbed by the talking monkey, and extended his hand as well. I shook it. His grip seemed almost bearable compared to hers.

"A fellow archie," said Al. "Nice to meet you."

I nodded in agreement. "So, you guys got a spot picked out for the first quest?" I asked, making small talk.

"We have a hunch," said Alex, "but we're gonna keep it under our hats. Well, my hat anyway." She laughed and gave Al an affectionate rub on his shaved head. "What about you?"

"Yeah, we have a spot in mind," I said.

"Well, best of luck to you guys," said Al. "Maybe I'll see you around the guild, and we can trade tips later or something."

"Sure, man, sounds great," I said, noncommittedly. "Speaking of which, I don't suppose you could point me in the direction of the guild?"

Al looked surprised. "What, you haven't been there yet? You know where the mayor's house is?"

"Yeah, down by the mansion on the southeast end of the alley, right?"

Al nodded. "To the north of the mansion, you'll see an alley between a tavern and a small potion shop. Five nixie lanterns hanging from a rope," he said. "Go down that alley, take your second left. You'll come to a stone archway set into the wall on your right, with a set of stairs leading down."

I thanked them both and put the gear I was holding back into its bucket. The shopkeeper kept giving me dirty looks like I was gonna pocket it. I left the booth and made my way south along the main road.

Despite the beginning of the quest being less than five hours away, many players still roamed the streets making last-minute preparations. Vendors called out their wares in the glow of the omnipresent nixie lighting, and the players were purchasing as much as they could carry and then some. I saw one brawler lugging a huge bag full of who-knows-what over his shoulder, before finally giving in and walking backward, dragging the bag behind him.

As I got closer to the mansion, I saw the side alley Al had mentioned, with five nixies suspended from a rope that stretched between the buildings on either side. I entered the passage, passing what looked like a guard or constable of some sort. He wore a tall bobby helmet that had a silver badge on the front inscribed with the initials 'S.W.A' in ornate lettering, standing out in relief. He wore a navy-blue, double-breasted jacket and trousers, with buttons and cufflinks styled like silver gears. His goggles, which rested on the brim of his helmet, looked almost military grade, and a baton hung at his waist with two copper leads at the end that looked like they could deliver quite a painful shock.

I nodded to the man as I headed into the alley, but he didn't return the gesture, eyeing me warily instead.

Banjo scrambled up to my shoulder as we passed under the lanterns and into the narrow alley. "He's the first guard of any kind I've noticed since we've been here."

"Yeah, I noticed that too."

I followed Al's directions, passing a solitary archaeologist going the other way, along with an assortment of NPCs going about their daily lives. I finally came to the archway Al had described, framed by a nixie-lit staircase that twisted down and out of sight. I followed the curving stairs down, thirty, maybe forty steps, and arrived at a looming oak door imbedded into a stone wall. Two ornate iron bands spanned its width to reinforce its stout frame, connected to two oversized hinges. I tried pulling on the handle, but the door didn't move. So, I knocked.

A peep slit slid open at about eye level, a pair of goggled eyes filling it and looking me over before the little sliding hatch closed again. I shuffled my feet, uncertain if maybe I missed a password or if I should say something.

"Hello? Archaeologist, here," I decided on. About ten seconds passed by, and the door swung open, held by a very short, very round man in a bowler much like my own. He barely came up to my chest, and if he wasn't as wide as he was tall, he was very close.

"Welcome to the Egalitarian Guild of Archaeologists, unit 101," he said, presenting the room to me with a sweep of a wide arm. I entered, and he closed and latched the door behind us. "My name is Jimsworth Dunning. And you are?"

"Jacob," I replied, nodding in greeting. "And this is Banjo." I nodded to my shoulder. Banjo gave the man his best smile, but the man ignored him.

He pulled a sweaty clipboard from under his arm and checked it over, adjusting a lens on his goggles. "Yes, yes, here you are. Let's get you checked in. Follow me, please."

I did as he suggested, trailing him into a large, richly decorated chamber. Lacquered hardwood beams supported the ceiling at regular intervals, framing a gaping stone fireplace on the far side of the room, built into the center of the wall. From here, I could see a selection of masks hanging over the hearth, and a line of colorful antique ceramics graced the mantle. A half-circle of couches and plush armchairs surrounded the fireplace, a few of which were occupied by various NPCs, reading books and smoking pipes. Ancient-looking statues sat in rows of recesses on either side of the room, lit from above by hidden lamps. The entire room was illuminated by a fancy brass clockwork chandelier, which ticked softly as it rotated.

Jimsworth waddled towards the far end of the room, his footfalls absorbed by an ornate rug the color of burgundy wine that stretched the length of the room. "Come along," he said.

I followed until we reached an intricately carved section of wall to the left of the fireplace. He stopped in front of a life-sized nude carving of a woman holding a basket of fruit over her head, causing her chest to jut out prominently. Waggling his eyebrows at me, Jimsworth put both hands on the carving's stone breasts—and pushed.

A section of wall swung inward, revealing a well-appointed office tucked inside. I chuckled at the reference; Iggy was apparently an Indiana Jones fan as well. How many other people would get the reference from a movie nearly a century old? Somehow, it reinforced my trust in Iggy—nobody who was into such cool stuff could be a bad guy.

Jimsworth led the way into the office, where he sat down in a leather-upholstered chair that seemed to swallow him whole, behind a cherrywood desk. He motioned for me to take a seat across from him, and once I complied, he opened a drawer and pulled out an ancient looking scroll fixed to a pair of wood rollers, spreading it out over his desk. He cleared his throat and adjusted a lens on his goggles.

"Now then," Jimsworth began in an official sounding voice, "please raise your right hand."

I raised my right hand, trying to stifle a smirk I could feel building at the corners of my mouth.

"Do you solemnly swear to abide by and spread the best practices of the Egalitarian Guild of Archaeologists, and to conduct yourself in a manner forthwith benefitting the guild and its members?"

"I do," I said.

He proceeded to ask me about twenty more questions, each one more difficult to understand than the one before it. I agreed to it all, of course, and found myself wishing for the nefarious 'I agree' button to appear so I could just press it and get it over with.

"Then I officially welcome you, Jacob, as the newest member of our guild, with all the benefits and provisions thereof," Jimsworth stated proudly. He stood up and extended a sweaty hand, which I reluctantly shook, trying not to wipe it on my pant legs when he let go.

"Now then," he said with a grin, "let's figure out your specialty and get you geared up."

CHAPTER TWENTY: GEARING UP

Jimsworth led me out of the office, talking as he walked. "The guild is divided into two specialties," he said over his shoulder as he led me towards a lamp-lit passageway. "Artificers and collectors. The artificers are, for all intents and purposes, low-level engineers capable of creating an assortment of mechanical contraptions for use in combat. As an artificer, you will never have the expertise of an engineer, but combined with your other skills, it can prove very effective."

We reached the other end of the passageway and stepped into a magnificent library. Banjo walked by my feet, head craned back to take in the room and ancient-looking artifacts, skulls, and globes, interspersed among bookshelves that extended upwards a good fifteen or twenty meters. More NPCs sat around the room on plush chairs and sofas, two of them engaged in a game of chess. Jimsworth guided me towards an archway at the far end of the room.

"The other specialty is the more lucrative of the two,

depending on how you play it," he said. "The collectors are experts at identifying and appraising artifacts. You will be able to look at a table full of junk and pick out the one piece that will bring you the greatest return, whether it be for its special powers, its usefulness to particular people, or just for its general rarity. You will always get the best price when both buying and selling, and as you spend more points in the skill, the effect only grows. You can identify items and their particular properties in the field. Some archaeologists, who are none too popular around here, have become quite adept at...erm...making their own artifacts. We don't recommend this, of course, as folks will not take kindly to it if you are discovered." He stopped, and looked up at me, squinting. "Plus, it gives archaeologists a bad name. More money for you, yes, but you quickly lose friends."

He resumed walking, and we passed beneath the archway into another passage. The stones of the wall appeared to have been taken from an ancient temple or ruin, every square centimeter covered with hieroglyphics and pictograms. At the end of the hall, two intricately carved doors waited.

"Well, here we are," said Jimsworth, holding out an arm like a magician's assistant showing off the doors. "Whichever path you choose, we're behind you one hundred percent—give or take." He turned back to me and spread both arms wide, bidding me to pick a door.

The left door was made of a golden-hued wood and covered in carvings of treasure chests, stacks of gold and unidentifiable artifacts. The door to my right of lighter wood, almost white, and covered with reliefs of archaic machinery, framed by carvings of gears and flywheels.

I'd made my choice as soon as he'd described each class to me. As crazy as it might sound, I had no use for more riches. Sure, I wasn't Nikola Musk or anything, nowhere near the top one percent, but I already had more than I knew what to do with. I'd almost chosen the engineer path—the decision was by no means an easy one—but perception was such an underrated stat in RPGs, and it had always served me well in the past. So, with a tip of my hat to Jimsworth, I walked to the white door and turned the ornate silver doorknob, pushing the door open. I looked back at Jimsworth.

He smiled. "You have chosen... wisely," he said, then turned his bulky frame and walked back down the hallway, leaving me alone.

I entered the room, Banjo at my heels. A giant worktable divided the long, narrow room—almost like a great corridor—lined with stools and covered with notches, burn marks and oil stains. Tall wooden shelves dominated the walls on either side, stacked with barrels, and crates, and stuffed to the brim with various bits of machinery. The far wall was one enormous pegboard, its holes jammed with countless wooden pegs to hold in place the largest assortment of tools I'd ever seen. At the base of the pegboard, an ancient-looking book sat on a stone-blue pedestal. As good a place to start as any.

Banjo hopped on the table and kept pace with me as I walked the length of the workroom, reading some of the labels on the containers. "Number two spiral gears... fourteen-millimeter pinions... miniature peristaltic pumps—maybe I should've gone for door number one."

"Looks like we could have some fun in here," said Banjo, looking around. He walked to the end of the table and sat down, watching me as I approached the book.

It was opened to somewhere near the middle, but both of the brown parchment pages visible were blank. I flipped back a few pages— still empty. I scowled and flipped to the beginning, where I finally saw some ornate writing in faded iron gall ink.

"*Professor Harron's Compendium of Useful Tools and Gadgets for the Successful Archaeologist,*" I read aloud.

"Ooh, that sounds like great bedtime reading," said Banjo enthusiastically. I knew he was being sarcastic, although I couldn't hear a trace of it in his voice. He jumped from the table and climbed up to my shoulder, so he could read along.

I flipped the page and saw the next two were both blank, apart from the top of the left page. In flowing cursive script, it read:

Do you wish to spend a guild point to unlock first level creations?

Underneath that, it had the words '*Yes*' and '*No*' written in the same ornate lettering. "Ah, the information I've been receiving makes sense now," said Banjo. "You spend one guild point to unlock a tier of creation recipes. From there, you can spend further points to either unlock the next level or make a level you already know more effective and durable."

I reread the line, then leaned over the book and said, "Yes." Nothing happened.

"Touch the page, brainlord," said Banjo.

I turned to glare at him—or at least tried to. It's difficult to glare at something sitting on your shoulder.

I reached out and touched the word 'Yes,' and both pages filled with schematics, diagrams, and instructions. The top of the page now read:

Do you wish to upgrade your level one creations? Yes / No.

I flipped forward to see the following pages were still blank, except for a flowing cursive prompt at the top of the first one asking me if I wanted to unlock the second level recipes. Turning back to the first new page of writing, I began to read.

Something called a 'Shrapper' was my first discovery, an item that could be made from any of the basic metals. About the size of a golf ball, it was featureless save for a small button inset into the top, and a seam running around its middle. From what I could gather, it was a shrapnel grenade, and whatever one put inside would explode in all directions. Considering the grenade's size and level, the effect couldn't be *too* devastating.

I focused on the next page, reading over schematics for a potion sprinkler. Its use was just how its name sounded— a brass sprinkler head on top of a glass cylinder that held up to a liter of the potion of your choice. A bent nozzle protruded from the top, attached to a pump which ran down the center of the cylinder. A tripod allowed it to sit firmly on any ground, and it had two small L-shaped lens-capped tubes attached to the sides of the cylinder. One of them was used for tracking the subject, and the other for monitoring whatever it was set to. If the dial was turned to 'health,' it could be filled with a healing potion which would spray whenever the target's HP dipped below a set amount. I could similarly set it up for poison antidotes, mana potions—whatever I needed. It also had a five-meter radius, which I believed would go up if I dumped another point into it. The whole thing was powered by something called a 'condensed steam motor, 21-10'—a device the size of a marble.

I made a judgement call and dumped both my remaining guild points into upgrading my level one creations and watched the effective radius of both devices increase to eight, then eleven meters.

"Banjo, what time is it?" I asked.

"Eight-thirty," he replied. Such a useful monkey.

I had about ninety minutes before I was scheduled to meet back up with Jeni, so I decided to try my hand at putting one or two of these sprinklers together. Looking at the schematics, I saw that each required piece had a series of numbers next to it. The glass cylinder had a line drawn between it and the numbers "14-17" written off to the right—should be able to find those in one of the shelves lining the walls.

I walked down the room until I stood in front of shelf fourteen. About two meters above my head, the third shelf from the top, I found a label reading 'seven cm cylinder, glass.' A sliding ladder of the kind seen in libraries was attached to the shelves, so I dragged it over to the fourteenth shelf, and climbed up, retrieving two of the cylinders from the bin. Materials in hand, I returned to the book, setting them on the table behind me.

"Hey, Banjo, want to help me with this?"

"Sure thing, Jakey," he said. "What you need?"

I proceeded to call out the list of required components, and he set off, jumping from shelf to shelf and bringing the items to the table much quicker than I could have. I retrieved the required tools from the pegboard, and within a couple minutes, Banjo had collected all the necessary items to craft a pair of sprinklers. I got to work.

The first one took me about twenty minutes, as I kept having to check the book to make sure everything was in the right place. I was pretty handy with this hands-on kind of work—I'd modified and upgraded rigs, processors, and VR goggles in the past - but this was more... organic, somehow. A little ironic, how creating a simulated contraption could feel more satisfying than working on a real one. Iggy must have spent a fortune researching the psychological effects of playing AR as in-depth as *Panmachina*.

I got to work on the second one, and found that having built the first, I no longer needed to refer to the book, halving my construction time.

I decided to test one out, so I spread the tripod legs, and placed it on the table. It was smallish, a little larger than an average soda bottle. I pulled a squirt potion from its holster on my belt, emptied the contents of the syringe into the glass canister and sealed it tight. The thick green potion filled maybe a tenth of the reservoir. I turned one of the dials to 'HP,' and the one next to it I cranked to one hundred percent. A third dial had a list of status ailments, in case the device was to be used for curing blindness, poison, and a host of other maladies, but I left this one in the 'Off' position. I took a few steps back.

"Banjo," I said. "Look through that targeting reticle and focus it on me—it's the little bent tube on the left there."

He did as I instructed. "Okay, I see you, now what?"

"Flip the switch labeled 'power-tracking' on the top of the canister," I ordered. Again, he complied, and the machine began to whirr. I took a few steps to my left, and the cylinder rotated, the nozzle following my movement. I walked back to the right, and it tracked me flawlessly. Banjo looked up at me for further instructions.

"Now flip the one next to it labeled 'power-pump,'" I said.

I almost didn't have time to finish my sentence before a jet of Dwebble's Squirt hit me square in the face. I coughed. Banjo went into hysterics. "I'd say it works, Jakey!" he said, before succumbing to another bout of raucous laughter.

I wiped my face off with my sleeve and spat a mouthful of the green goo onto the floor. It tasted as bad as it smelled. I reached into my backpack on the table, and pulled out my water bottle, rinsing out my mouth before taking a few gulps and then putting it back.

I put the tools back, and stowed my new creations in

my backpack, slinging it over my shoulder. I had just enough time for a couple quick errands before meeting Jeni and beginning the night's activities. I also needed to call Trick, but after the events with Honey, I'd been putting it off.

I headed back towards the market, stopping at Dwebble's. I picked up a couple of Dwebble's Night Eye potions, which as the name suggested, augmented one's sight in the dark. I spent a pretty penny on a couple Dwebble's All-Stats, which gave a slight boost to stats across the board. I also picked up a two-liter bottle of Dwebble's Squirt, enough to fill both cylinders without exhausting the ones on my belt. Lastly, I had the ring I'd purchased earlier, which would fix me up automatically should I need it.

As I was walking out of the market, my goggles informed me I was getting a call. I answered, thinking it was Jeni, but instead saw the floating head of Trick pop into my vision.

"Hi, Trick," I said. "Was just about to call you. How you doing?"

Trick smiled at me, but it lacked his trademark exuberance.

"Alright, I guess," he said. "Except that I haven't talked to Honey since yesterday. She's not answering any of my calls, and I don't think I can go it alone without her tanking."

"About that," I began as I took a seat in a chair by a peanut vendor, on the side of the main street. "We saw her earlier." I paused, not sure how to tell him. Best to just come out with it. "She appeared to be helping Jameson and the

Glitch." I proceeded to tell him about the events from earlier, and he looked at me with disbelief.

"You sound like you were far away," he said, annoyed, "and all gargoyles look pretty similar. You sure it was her?"

I told him what Iggy had told me about their past together, and his face contorted into an expression of hurt, then anger, then finally resignation.

"Well, I guess I can go it alone," Trick sighed. "Maybe between my summons and me we'll be okay. I scoped out Lakenhilly earlier—a bunch of other players seem to think it's the right spot, and I was doing alright solo. I'm level four now, and I got a new summon called a Draki—looks like a dragon about the size of Banjo, but she's full grown."

"Give me a second, will you?" I asked. "I'll call you right back."

I had been hesitant about partying with anyone else, sharing any quest info. The thought of Trick going it alone changed my attitude a little bit. I pictured him in the middle of the rabbit tornado we had survived earlier. Poor kid would get squished in a heartbeat.

I used my goggles to call Jeni, and her head popped up in my vision about five seconds later. I told her about Trick's dilemma and asked if it would be okay if he joined us.

"But groups are limited to two members," she said.

"Yeah, I know. He won't be official. But we'll figure out the numbers later," I said. "For now, he can party with us, share in the loot. I just... kinda feel bad for the kid, you know?"

Jeni gave me a look of understanding. "Okay, fine by

me," she said.

I called Trick back and invited him to join us.

"Where are you going?" he asked, and I told him about the Locke Wetlands, how it used to be called the Arboretum, and about the gears we saw nailed to the posts. I also told him the decision to go there had been a split second one. I didn't want him to know I had intentionally deceived him.

"And the gears were there in real life as well?"

I nodded. "Yup." Although I didn't tell him about the word inscribed on the table—I didn't mind having him along, but I wasn't ready to share all my advantages.

"Sounds good, Jacob," Trick said, relieved. "Thanks, man. I owe you one."

I disconnected the call and extended my arm down so Banjo could climb up to my shoulder. "You ready for this, buddy?" I asked him with a grin.

"I would feel more prepared if I could help in some way," he said as he frowned. "As it stands my favorite tactic is to hide in your backpack."

I chuckled. "If we had the time, I'd throw together some of those shrappers for you, but we're already running behind. Next time," I promised, starting towards the side alley that led to the parking lot.

When I got there, Jeni and Trick were already outside my airship, catching up. I wished I would have told Jeni not to mention the word on the picnic table, but she was a smart girl, and as serious about the game as I was. Hopefully she hadn't said anything.

"Hey, team," I greeted the pair of them.

"The *Galileo* is a beast!" exclaimed Trick, admiring the miniature airship.

"You should see it in reality," I said, although he probably wasn't into vintage sci-fi as much as I was.

I opened the doors and we climbed inside. Lexi waved to us in greeting.

Trick practically sprinted up to her, his characteristic jovial smile returned. "Well, hello. My name's Trick," he said to her, extending a hand.

Lexi shook it. "Hi, Trick. You're a cute one," she said, and Trick blushed so hard I expected his freckles to launch off his face.

We still had just under two hours to go, but that would give us time to talk strategy. I closed the hatch and Lexi started the engines. The airship rose silently into the sky, straight up, and soon the whole of Steam Whistle Alley could be seen below. Trick pressed his nose up against the glass, admiring the fantastic view of the nighttime alley.

"Step back," I said, and ordered Lexi to open the ship's top. She complied, and the fresh night air filled the cabin. I activated the climate controls, one of my favorite features—even driving with the top down through a snowstorm, the cabin would stay a comfortable 24 degrees Celsius.

Trick clapped his hands, and Jeni and I smiled at each other over his excitement. Above us the view was obscured by the long elliptical balloon, although we still had an excellent 360-degree view of the rest of the sky. An interesting aspect of the AR, one I hadn't noticed before—the night sky was as bright as if we were 500 kilometers away from civilization. I could see constellations that I recognized, and the stars seemed impossibly bright and more numerous than I had ever seen in the city. I could even make out the hazy cloud of the Milky Way streaming across the blackness.

I set a slow course for the Arboretum, and the *Galileo* drifted lazily to the northeast. Trick looked like a kid in a candy factory.

"The Ferris wheel!" he spouted, "It looks like two giant gears. Man, that is cool."

I rotated my chair and pulled the rifle I'd received out of a cubby built into the frame. I pressed an eye to the scope, and the building I was sighting popped into sharp relief. Out of curiosity, I put on my goggles and popped down my zoom lens, and the building grew even closer—I could make out a robotic janitor cleaning one of the top floors, his head filling the targeting reticle.

"Pyoo," I whispered, mimicking firing the gun.

Jeni took her dart-shooting gauntlet out of her bag, then transformed into the purple werewolf. Trick jumped back a bit, eyes wide. She strapped the gauntlet on over her fur, and flexed her hand a few times, seemingly satisfied with the fit. She checked something on her wrist display on her other arm, and smiled, apparently satisfied.

"Do you think we'll be able to use these on mobs as well, or just other players?" Jeni asked, looking at the gauntlet.

"I learned a little about PVP from the Summoner's Guild, when I reluctantly opted in," said Trick. "I'm more of a PVE kind of guy usually, but from what my creator told me, players not in your party that have opted in will have a slight reddish glow about them. There are no factions yet, so it will be sort of a free for all, from what I understand."

"Good to know," I said. The gun would do me no good in a battle like the one against the rabbits, but I still felt better for having it.

"Speaking of guilds," said Jeni, "did you find yours?"

"Yeah, I did." I proceeded to tell her everything that had just happened. I then opened my bag, took out the two sprinklers and the bottle of Dwebble's squirt. I filled them both, sealed them, then handed one to Jeni. She turned it over in her hand, looking at it.

"We will have to stay close to them," I said, then had a thought. "Banjo, can I put you in charge of the sprinklers? As we advance, you can carry them and set them up behind us. Make sure they're always within eleven meters. Can you do that?"

"Sure thing," Banjo said. "Although if the going gets too rough, I'll be in your backpack."

I chuckled. "Well, keep at it as long as you can." I had no idea how Banjo fit into the battle programming, but he had been fine just keeping out of it so far. A thought occurred to me.

"Banjo, can you even get hurt in the game?"

"From what I can tell, not if I don't participate in the fighting," he replied. "What I don't know is if being your little sprinkler monkey equates to participation."

I nodded. Banjo had become more than a pet to me, and I would hate to see him get hurt on my account, even if it was all just an illusion.

"What about you, Jeni," I asked. "Did you find your..."

"Den," she finished for me. "Yes, I did. In a nutshell, I could either choose to become an assassin or a berserker. I didn't think a purple werewolf would be that great at stealth, so I chose the latter. I have a berserker skill now, and I haven't tried it out yet, so fair warning. It also makes any fear-based talents more effective, so my howl should be pretty kickass, if I can remember to use it."

I had to agree, although the thought of a werewolf assassin definitely intrigued me.

I put the sprinklers back into my backpack and shouldered it on, then slung the rifle over my shoulder. I mimed a few whip cracks to make sure that I still had a decent range of movement. In the end I decided to leave my backpack in the car, and asked Trick if he minded carrying the sprinklers and some snacks and water in his sack, as he would be on the back lines and didn't need to be as agile. He agreed, so I handed the gear off to him.

It was just after eleven o'clock when we touched down in the parking lot of the Locke Wetlands. About fifteen other airships filled the parking lot, and I figured they must belong to players, as the park closed to the public an hour after dusk. I did some quick math in my head, figuring two players per airship, that's thirty, plus perhaps another thirty that got here by other means. It was going to be a crowded night.

As we exited the cabin, I spotted four guards, the kind that I had seen by the alley that led to the guild, standing next to an airship that had '*S.W.A. Constabulary*' written on the sides. A bar of blue and red lamps ran across the top of the ship's cabin. I had a hunch these might be real cops.

Trick seemed to be thinking along the same lines. "I'm guessing Iggy has made quite a few donations to law enforcement agencies, to allow us to take part in events like this," Trick mused. That made sense.

As we walked to the edge of the park, we could see a few other players in the lamps of the parking lot, lining up on the edge of the field. I reached into my pouch and handed one of the night vision potions to Jeni, telling her to drink it once the battle started. The potions would be more effective than her light amulet, in that they wouldn't surround us in a glow, drawing attention to us.

"I wouldn't drink those," Trick said. "You rub those into your eyes. I've got one as well."

Good to know.

We reached the edge of the grass, where I saw a brawler talking in muted tones to an alchemist, judging from the scars on her hands and face, and a pair of engineers.

Trick greeted them, then asked, "Why has nobody entered the park yet?"

"Try it," the brawler suggested with a smirk.

Trick took a step forward onto the grass and swore loudly, and leapt back onto the concrete, patting at his robes frantically.

He looked towards us sheepishly, must have seen our questioning stares. "Everything, the grass, hell even the sky, was on fire," he explained, panting. "God, I hope that's not what we have to fight through. It's freaking hot!"

"It's not, at least I don't think so," said the brawler. "I think it's just to keep us out until midnight. Means we're in the right place."

I nodded my thanks to them. We walked a good fifty meters down the parking lot along the edge of the field. With the PVP launching the same time as the quest, I figured it would be wise to be as far from anyone else as possible when this free-for-all started.

Trick's description of the fire had brought the incident with my sister to the forefront of my mind, maybe the last thing in the world I wanted to be thinking about right now. As we walked, I found myself wondering if there had been any change in her condition, and how my parents were coping. I forced my thoughts to focus on the game and my companions—anything to distract myself from the memories. At least I tried to.

"You guys ready for this?" I asked.

Trick pressed the stones on the back of his summoner's gauntlet, and Shorty the bobcat appeared, twitching her tail, alongside a tiny green creature that looked like a cross between a dragon and a monkey.

Banjo timidly walked up to the drake, who promptly belched a puff of fire onto Banjo's arm, causing his fur to sizzle and smoke. Banjo scurried behind my leg, peeking out at the newly summoned beast.

"Sorry about that, Banjo," said Trick. "That's Dexi. She was just startled is all."

Dexi gave a flap of her leathery bat-like wings and lit

onto Trick's shoulder, and Shorty rubbed against the hem of his robe, appearing a little bigger than I remembered. Trick scanned the field, the usual smile in his eyes replaced with a sort of worried reserve. He adjusted the backpack on his shoulders and gave Dexi an affectionate scratch.

Jeni cracked her neck and limbered up her arms, bouncing from furry foot to furry foot.

I sighted my rifle at the far tree line, making out nothing but dim shadows in the starlit night. I rested my hand on my whip. A feeling of confidence came over me, and I nodded to myself, smirking with one side of my mouth.

We were ready.

CHAPTER TWENTY-ONE: THE MESSAGE

At a minute to midnight, we each rubbed the night vision ointment into our eyes—not the most pleasant sensation. After blinking a few times, the world lit up with an unnatural blue hue, but we could see everything nearly as clear as if it were daylight; details of the far tree line, blurry a moment ago, now stood out in stark focus. I put my goggles down and activated the info-lens, seeking as much information as possible about whatever laid ahead of us. I looked over at Jeni, and then Trick, then checked my wristband for a quick stat update.

Well *that* was interesting. Apparently, we had never disbanded the party, and Trick was still grouped with us. Honeybucket wasn't, however. A quick flick of a dial showed me that Jeni now had an impressive 450 hit points, while Trick was maxed at 180. His MP listed as 350 out of 570. That must've been from summoning his two creatures. Currently, I was at my max of 290 HP, but I hoped we could keep Jeni healthy enough as our tank to where I wouldn't need to worry about my own hit points too much. *Wishful thinking, Jacob.* My stats also still showed my 25 MP, but I had no idea what it was for.

I pulled both my sprinklers out of Trick's bag, setting one to track me and the other to track Jeni, and both to activate the moment we dipped below 25 percent of max health. Banjo had no problem lifting them and moving them around and assured us he would keep them in range. He appeared to be tapping into a new reserve of courage—I just hoped it would last.

At twenty seconds to midnight, Banjo began a slightly overdramatic countdown. At least it started as overdramatic. By the time he got to 'five,' I was hanging on his every word, and the adrenaline coursing in my blood made me feel as if I could take on whatever was to come with just my teeth and fingernails.

Shorty paced back and forth in front of our group as Banjo continued to count. Three... two... one...

A thin white line formed just below the tree line on the far end of the field, glowing blue in the artificial light provided by our potions. As a group, we rushed forward, my whip already in hand. The thin line was getting bigger, closer, and my info-lens was already starting to do its job.

'*Lepus Machina, Level 5*'

More of these lines of text began to appear, and soon became so crowded that they would overlap the text of the creature next to them. Whatever they were, their HP bars were nothing to take lightly. In the formation they were in, their health bar almost looked like one solid line that stretched from one end of the park to the other.

I zoomed in as we ran, able to examine individuals in the line now. Again, with the damn rabbits. As I squinted, though, I noticed a few differences. These were bigger, about the size of a small dog. Their fur was still white, but inconsistent, appearing in random patches on their bodies. The gaps between the fur were filled with gleaming silver-colored framework, encasing a collection of gears and pistons. They reminded me of the cougar I had watched Iggy tackle on his property. Jets of steam appeared to be— there was no way else to say it—jetting out of their asses as they hopped forward. Their eyes glinted red, large and oval in the faint light, and as the distance closed further, I could see they were faceted rubies.

Twenty meters separated us now. I heard battle cries farther away as players met the surging tide, and the constant dull roar of hundreds of mechanical bunny feet thumping towards us.

Suddenly, the eyes of the one closest to me flashed brightly, and I was momentarily blinded. Jeni, who was running about ten paces in front of us, swore loudly. I put my goggles up and blinked as the shadowy spots in my vision started to fade.

"They have frakking laser eyes!" Jeni swore.

I would have chuckled, but more laser bursts streaked around us, the blue tinge of the night potion making them glow an otherworldly purple. One of the streaks caught me in the shoulder, and I swore and checked my wrist to see that the blast had drained about ten percent of my health. I glanced behind me, relieved that Banjo was keeping pace, a sprinkler tucked under each arm. Heroic little monkey. Behind Banjo, Trick brought up the rear.

"Trick, stay back, I'll bring them to you!" I shouted. He gave me a thumbs-up.

The line of rabbits started to break apart, half-circles of them forming around individual advancing groups of players. There was at least fifty meters between us and the nearest party—on our left, the brawler and alchemist we'd seen earlier, apparently grouping with the two engineers. They didn't have the red PVP glow, so I put them out of my mind. I estimated about twenty of the creatures had focused on us, closing in fast, nearly within range of my weapon.

Jeni threw back her head and howled loudly enough to make my ears ring, and the rabbit's advance slowed, apparently second-guessing their intentions. One of them turned, hopping back the way it came, propelled by jets of steam emerging from underneath a puffy white cotton ball tail. Before it got too far, I lashed out with my weapon, its blades skewering the machinery.

"Get over here!" I shouted with a malicious grin as I yanked backward.

The rabbit flew up and over me, and when my whip went taut behind me, flew off the blades and landed neatly at Trick's feet, where Shorty pounced on it, teeth tearing. Dexi hovered over it burning off what remaining fur it had with miniature jets of flame.

Our advance had halted— the rabbits were on us. Banjo had set both sprinklers out, and they followed our every motion, which was comforting.

I looked over at Jeni, and my heart sank. She was crouched into a ball, her head between her knees. Was she hurt? I glanced at my wrist and saw she was nearly at max HP. A second later, she sprang upwards, her wolfen face a mask of rage, and proceeded to tear apart rabbits like nobody's business, a virtual whirlwind of snapping teeth and slashing claws. A nimbus of torn fur and ruined gears surrounded her.

Ah... that must be her berserker ability. I like it.

A couple more strokes of the whip and I'd deposited two more of the creatures at Trick's feet, where his minions again set upon them. Four of the rabbits had attached themselves to Jeni, one of them sinking its silver incisors into the back of her neck, her fur growing dark with blood. She couldn't reach the thing, so I lashed out, catching it in the torso. It fell to the ground, twitching, and a swipe of Jeni's mighty claws finished it off.

Two more of the laser beams caught me, one of them in my shoulder and another in a knee, which promptly collapsed beneath me. I swore as I went down. In an instant, two of the beasts were on me in a blur of fur and machinery. I pulled my dagger from my belt and tried stabbing at one on my shoulder, but in the fracas I ended up piercing my own skin. Blood welled up, a black pool darkening my shirt in the false light. The rabbits continued their onslaught, biting and clawing at any exposed skin they could find. A glance at my wrist showed my health was draining rapidly, less than a third of its maximum.

A few seconds later I felt something cold and wet hit me

in the back of my neck, oozing down the collar of my shirt. I shivered at the sensation but instantly experienced a rush of energy as my wounds began mending. The sprinkler had done its job. Ripping a rabbit from my leg, I raised it over my head with both hands and threw it back towards Trick.

Up ahead, Jeni was a blur of purple fur and claws. Piles of mechanical rabbit parts had begun to rise in a heap behind her as she advanced. I could see that she had been doused in the green goo at least once as well; her fur was matted down and discolored in several spots. With a swipe of her left hand, she dispatched the last remaining attacker

Breathing hard, we regrouped.

To our left, we could no longer see the brawler and alchemist. I was pretty sure we had advanced the farthest, so I assumed they hadn't survived the onslaught. Farther down the field, I could make out a few more groups still locked in combat, and far to the right, I could see more movement, although even with the zoom lens I couldn't tell what it was. Banjo was scouring the remains of our battle, picking up the ruby eyes left behind by the creatures.

"I found 38 rubies," Banjo declared proudly, handing them to Trick to put in his backpack.

"We can divvy up the spoils later," I said. "Everybody okay?"

Jeni and Trick both voiced in the affirmative, and we each gulped down some water, Jeni and I both using a few splashes of it to clear the green goop from our clothes.

"You know, I could keep you guys healed," said Trick. "It's not as effective, but at least you don't have to worry about getting slimed. All I have to do is get close enough to whisper."

"I'd rather keep you on the back line. It seemed to work well," I said.

Trick shrugged. "Okay then."

Plus, I was kind of proud of the little squirters, the first items I had created in the game. I smiled as Banjo picked them up again, one under each arm.

Having regained some energy, we rushed across the last hundred meters or so to the band of trees surrounding the central clearing. As we approached, the blue glow from the potion gave the forest an otherworldly quality that set my teeth on edge. Faint sounds—soft clicks and drawn-out cooing—floated down from the high branches. As we reached the trailhead for one of the paths, Jeni tossed her head back and howled again, and all the noise stopped.

Jeni turned back to us, a wide grin on her muzzle. "See? There's nothing to worry about as long—"

Something fell out of the branches above us, a huge something that crashed onto Jeni, wrapping itself around her. In the blue light, I could make out a ridiculously long, segmented body with alternating bands of copper and silver down its length, reflecting the sparse light. The beast must have been about four meters in length, and a pair of spindly legs sprouted from every segment of its body, digging into Jeni's fur and flesh. Its metal head sported two curved pincers, sunk deep into Jeni's neck. Patches of black fur had already begun to form again where the creature was drawing blood.

My info-lens named it a level six metalpede.

Great.

Jeni was frantically slashing at the beast wrapped around her, her claws doing some damage but not seeming to phase it. She spun around so I faced her side, and I flashed out with my whip, catching the creature with a direct hit where it wrapped around her back. It disengaged its pincers from Jeni's neck and let out a chilling, metallic screech as the tip of my chain whip split it in two. The rear half fell to the ground, but the half with the head still clung to Jeni's waist, and it sank its pincers into her neck again, eliciting a yelp of pain. The sprinkler doused her with another stream of goo.

As her wounds healed, she gained a second burst of strength, wrenching the beast from her neck and slamming it on the ground, the creature screeching each time it hit.

"Jakey? Jakey!" Banjo shrieked, pointing at the ground.

The other half of the metalpede had sprouted a head of its own and skittered through the undergrowth straight at me. I lashed out with my whip as both Shorty and Dexi set upon it. My whip's three blade tips skewered the arthropod directly between its mandibles. I yanked my arm back, and the metal centipede flew over my head and landed in the field behind us. Trick slowed it with his *sloven* spell, and his beasts flew by me, jumping on it and tearing it apart in earnest.

Before long, it was a smoking heap of disfigured metal. Jeni's half of the creature hadn't fared much better from its repeated pounding—it too was left as a twitching heap at her feet.

I giggled at the absurdity of it all. Jeni fell to the ground, laughing and panting, giving the heap of metal parts beside her one last kick for good measure. Her face relaxed as the berserker rage left her. Banjo was already searching the wreckage, picking out an assortment of gears, bolts, and screws and handing them to Trick, who stashed them away in his robes. Once again, we took a minute to hydrate and catch our breath. This whole 'expending energy while playing a game' deal was still a nuance I hadn't gotten used to.

From our left, screams of pain floated through the trees, where we assumed another team was facing a metalpede. Hopefully two. As we continued towards the center hill, we ran into three more of the beasts, although these we were better prepared for.

After the fourth creature died, Jeni and I both leveled up, although Trick was apparently a few XP away. Banjo informed me I could now use cross lash, a whip skill that allowed for a close-range attack employing four crisscrossing strokes. I tried it out once in the air, nailing it on the first attempt, the whip whistling with each lash before ending with a resounding crack.

Jeni had learned eviscerate, a finishing move that could open up an opponent and spill its innards, but only if it was below fifteen percent health.

The three of us shared a look, nodded to each other, and walked the last few meters of the trail, reaching the base of the hill without any further opposition.

The hill wasn't how we'd left it. A square hedge, about a meter taller than me, curved to either side of us as far as we could see, with an opening about five meters to our right. We walked to the opening—weapons at the ready, constantly looking all around us—and peered inside. The opening was outlined in blue, and our visibility limited to about three meters in front of us.

Now I'd been in hedge mazes before, but this one was different. The leaves extended over the top of the hedges, forming a ceiling. I guessed this was implemented so the gargoyles didn't have an unfair advantage. With a final glance at each other, we entered.

Trick, bringing up the rear, pulled a gear from his robe and dropped it on the ground. Jeni and I both nodded in approval, immediately understanding what he was up to. Every five meters or so, he would drop another, and whenever we took a turn down a new path. We frequently had to backtrack, our path constantly blocked by hedges, and the gears served as markers for the paths we'd already tried.

This cautious trial and error continued for a good thirty minutes, and frustration began to creep in. Not only did we feel like we were going in circles, but we spent most of the journey trudging uphill. The blue-tinged darkness began to feel like it was closing in around us, which was why Trick's next announcement didn't surprise us much.

"Guys, these passages are getting narrower," he said, holding his arms out. His fingertips just brushed the leaves on both sides. "Earlier there was a good twenty centimeters clearance each way."

The ceiling appeared to be getting lower too, and I found myself having to duck, while Jeni's head, as well as Trick's, lightly scraped the leaves overhead.

On our umpteenth backtrack, we started down another passageway that became so narrow and so short that before long we had to crawl on hands and knees to proceed, the hedges scraping the backs of our necks.

Hands and knees soon gave way to stomachs, and even Banjo had to duck to proceed. Twice more we had to backtrack, crawling backward as there was no room to turn around.

Finally, when the pressing of the hedge walls nearly became too much to handle, suffocating, squeezing from all sides, Jeni turned her head and whispered excitedly. "I can see the exit!"

Jeni crawled faster, and the rest of us followed, then we all tumbled out into blessed open space. We lay on our backs, gasping, and soon the gasps turned into laughs of sweet relief. We were on the top of the hill, and from here we could see over the top of the hedge, a thick donut of green leaves surrounding us, sloping downwards as it sprawled toward the bottom of the hill.

"Guys, you know that hedge isn't really there," I said, standing up. Confidently, I ran headlong into it but found it as impenetrable as any real hedge would be. The branches poked and scratched as I tried to untangle myself from them, cursing. Jeni and Trick laughed.

"You must be pretty good at pretending then," said Jeni

with a grin. Only a moment later, a scowl replaced it. "Hey, I don't see the exit we came through." She peered at the hedge line.

I walked the length of the hedge, about twenty meters in either direction, not seeing any openings at all.

"Maybe they all closed once the first team got through until we deal with..." I paused. "Whatever's up there." I pointed to the gazebo.

But my curiosity had already been roused. I wanted to see what this place really looked like. I reached for my goggles to power them down. As I pressed the button, however, a voice sounded in my ear.

"Leaving the game at this location will result in forfeiture of your current quest. If you wish to continue, you may power the unit off now."

I removed my hand.

"So? What's it look like?" asked Trick.

"If I leave the game, I forfeit the quest," I explained.

Trick raised his eyebrows and Jeni gave a resigned shrug, and we instead turned our attention to the top of the hill.

We were still a good fifty meters from the gazebo. We walked side by side the rest of the way, on the alert for any more surprises this quest had to offer. But nothing disturbed the remainder of our jaunt up the hill, and soon we were standing in one of the archways that led into the gazebo.

There, in the middle of the picnic tables, was a small grey goat, wearing a collar, illuminated by a shaft of light with no visible source. The goat turned his head towards us as we entered. He made no aggressive movement, just stared at us. Jeni started forward, but I put out my hand, holding her back.

I looked at it through my info-lens.

'*Goat*'

"Goat?" I asked incredulously. "That's all it identifies as. Goat. No HP bar, no level, no nothing."

Jeni twisted her lips. "What the hell?"

The goat bleated at us, then folded its legs under itself and lay down, tucking his head into his shoulder. Within moments it was asleep.

The three of us shared a look.

"We don't have to kill the goat, do we?" Jeni asked, incredulous.

"No, can't be," I said, taking off my bowler and scratching my head.

We heard a rustling sound from behind us, and we turned around, prepared for another skirmish. Instead, we watched as the hedge began to shift, the maze parting to either side so a straight corridor opened before us leading to the base of the hill.

It couldn't be over—something had to be wrong. We searched the gazebo and the surroundings, but found nothing else of interest, and the softly snoring goat wouldn't wake no matter what we tried. I still couldn't log out here without abandoning the quest, either, so I couldn't search the table and gazebo for any more carved clues. What I did read didn't look relevant.

So, not knowing what else to do, we walked down the newly formed path, through the woods and across the field unmolested. Other groups far to our right still battled rabbits, late to the party, a couple with the red glow of PVP about them. I considered taking a pot-shot with my rifle but decided it would be a juvenile move.

We walked to the parking lot and approached the Galileo.

The four constables we had seen earlier appeared from behind the constabulary airship parked a few meters from mine. They each stared fixedly as they approached, vile sneers warping two of their faces.

They split into twos, a pair of them running at Jeni. She tried to fight them off, but her werewolf strength didn't transfer to the real world, and they wrenched her arms behind her back and slipped a bag over her head.

"What are you doi—" Trick shouted, struggling futilely as his hands were tied and his head bagged.

"Leave her alone," I barked, and started toward Jeni, unsure exactly what I was going to do, but certain I had to do something. A voice stopped me.

"Hello, Jacob," it said coldly.

I turned around. There, emerging from behind the Galileo, was Jameson. I reached for my rifle but hesitated when I saw he didn't have the PVP aura about him. Ah, what the hell. I snagged the rifle from my shoulder, aimed at him point-blank, and pulled the trigger.

Click. Nothing. I pulled it again. *Click. Click.*

"So, what did you find up there?" he asked as he

approached.

"Nothing I plan on telling you," I said, lowering the useless rifle to my side.

Jameson glared at me with a hint of a grin twitching the manicured mustache curling above his lip. He stroked his goatee into a fine point as he came within arms' reach, his hands behind his back.

My hand instinctively went to my dagger but stopped—it would be just as useless.

Jameson's baseball bat, however, was very useful, and I never saw it coming. One blow to the side of my head was all it took, and in a flash of brilliant, real pain, everything went black.

CHAPTER TWENTY-TWO: THE UNKNOWN

When I finally came to, I opened my eyes to Banjo's furry face hovering over me as he gently shook my collar, trying to wake me up. My head pounded like the world's angriest timpani, and when I raised a hand to explore the damage, it found a lump the size of an orange on my temple.

I looked around, taking note that I was in one of the front seats of the *Galileo*—the shuttlecraft, not the airship. The clock on the display read 3:48 AM and the sky was still black. The rest of the parking lot was now empty.

I was still wearing my goggles, but apparently, the game does you a favor and logs you out when knocked unconscious. As I stirred in my seat, I heard muffled voices pleading behind me. I spun around, too quickly for my broken head, and I nearly passed out again. I waited for a wave of nausea to subside and saw two forms with bags on their heads in the cabin behind me. I took my goggles off and threw them on the seat next to me.

"How long have I been out?" I asked Banjo. My voice

sounded like I'd swallowed nails.

Banjo just chirped at me sadly. *Right, no goggles. Normal monkey.*

Across the cabin, Trick and Jeni lay sprawled on one of the side benches, arms still tied in addition to the bags. I gingerly made my way over to them, removing the hoods and then gags. Jeni hungrily sucked in mouthfuls of air while Trick stammered his thanks between fits of coughing. I then untied their hands and Jeni threw her arms around me and squeezed hard, nearly making me black out again. Still, I hugged her back tightly.

"You guys okay?" I asked as Jeni pulled away.

"Yeah," Trick said, "I'm fine." He rubbed his hands, restoring circulation.

"Forget us, what about you?" asked Jeni. "What the hell happened?" She raised a hand to touch the lump on the side of my head, but stopped herself, wincing sympathetically.

"Jameson had a baseball bat," I said.

"Well, we have to get you to a hospital," said Jeni worriedly. "You probably have a concussion. They can fix those pretty reliably."

"Right now, we call the police," Trick said, taking out his phone.

Jeni extended her hand, pushing Trick's phone down. "I wouldn't. I think those constables that jumped us were real police officers, hired to help patrol the game. I don't know who to trust anymore."

"I don't know, either," I said, scanning the parking lot, frowning. I didn't know much of anything right then. Hard to think after one's brain was used as a tee-ball. My head throbbed, and I was exhausted.

"I wouldn't use your goggles again," Trick said. "After we got tied up and blindfolded they left us while they dragged you into the van. They could've installed that program Iggy warned us about while you were out. It was a good thirty minutes before they dragged us into the van with you."

"Yeah, I had the same thought," I said. "I'll call Iggy in the morning."

I started up the van and directed the Lexi to take us to the emergency room at the university. We lifted off, and I closed my eyes again. Nobody said anything in the brief time it took us to get there.

Two hours later, I was patched up, and my head no longer hurt, although the ball on the side hadn't completely disappeared. They'd injected me with some good meds—my head felt like a balloon, light, trying to float free as we made our way back to the van. A new day was starting, the sky beginning to show the first hints of blue. Looked like it'd be another sunny day.

"If you guys want, we can crash at my space in SoDo," I said. "There's a couple pull-out couches and beds, plenty of room. We'll call Iggy when we wake up."

They must've been as tired as me, and barely even acknowledged my suggestion, so I set a course for my man cave. It was only a few blocks from Steam Whistle Alley. In the early morning sunlight, stripped of its augmentation, it looked like any other warehouse district.

The van set down on the roof of my facility, and we got out with our gear. Nobody spoke as we rode the elevator down to my floor. We walked down the hallway to my facility, where I opened the large garage-style door with a hand wave in front of the sensor.

On the wall across the room from the door, glaring sunlight flooded the cavernous interior. We all squinted at the glare, shielding our eyes with our hands.

"Lexi," I said. "Can you put the window opacity at 75 percent?"

"Sure thing," she said, from the screen in the kitchenette. As the windows darkened, Jeni and Trick's hands went down, and they looked around the spacious room. My den was about twenty meters wide by forty meters long, with elevated areas on either side that were home to the racks and glass cases displaying my collections. Carpets and runners covered the center strip, which led to the seating area up front by the windows. A semicircle of sofas surrounded a bank of monitors and old-style televisions, where I could play any one of the thousands of games I'd amassed over the years, many of them rarities kept in climate-controlled cases underneath the windows.

"You live here?" Trick asked, wide-eyed.

"Not usually," I said. "But I could." Sometimes I wondered why I didn't; this place was the one luxury I afforded myself. Well that, and an airship-slash-shuttlecraft. "There's beds on either end of that raised bit over to the right there, and that door in the middle leads to the bathroom. Make yourselves at home."

The ceiling had an array of ropes and platforms that I had built for Banjo, and he quickly scampered up a rope to where he had made himself a sleeping nest. Jeni and Trick picked their beds and said their goodnights, even though the sun was still well above the horizon. It had been a busy day.

I walked up to the couches and flopped on my favorite, already equipped with pillows and blankets, and ordered the computer to set the windows at 98 percent opacity. The room darkened to a reasonable semblance of night, and within seconds I was out.

Hard to say whether it was the head injury or the excitement of the past few days, but my dreams were especially vivid that morning. I only remembered snippets, but they were... interesting. In them I explored the hedge maze from the hill again, except this time I was alone, and instead of the pathways getting narrower as I progressed, they got wider. At the end of one corridor was a four-poster bed, on which a nude, hooded female figure sprawled out, her arms bound by the wrists to the two posts at the head of the bed. Jeni's voice called to me softly, seductively, from under the hood. I climbed on the bed, and her legs shifted, her feet wrinkling the white silk sheets as I crawled towards her.

When I lifted up the hood, instead of Jeni's purple-framed face I found Honey's, her black hair flowing over her shoulders and down her chest. She shot her arms forward, snapping the ropes that held her down. Her flesh turned a concrete gray as she threw her head back and cackled. She spat in my face, then spread her grey wings out wide. She seized me by the shoulders, claws digging into my flesh. Still cackling like a witch, she shot straight into the air with me in tow, and I screamed Jeni's name.

"Jeni is dead," she said calmly as the ground spun, falling away below us. She leaned forward, and a forked tongue the color of ink emerged from her cracked, grey lips to lick my cheek. Then she dropped me. The ground rushed towards me, and I screamed—

—and jolted awake, still screaming. Panic set in momentarily as I took in the dim surroundings, unsure where I was. My clothes and blankets were damp with sweat, and the headache I had managed to lose at the hospital was back with a vengeance. *Baseball bat.* The events of the previous night came flooding back, and I ordered the computer to raise the lights.

My friends were nowhere to be seen, but I found a note on the coffee table. It read:

Jacob –
Thanks for letting us crash at your place. Call me when you wake up. – Jeni

I set it back down and went to the bathroom, downing three aspirin with a handful of water. I splashed some on my face, finding momentary relief, so I opted for a full shower. By the time I finished, the headache had eased, and my mind was working again, if not at optimum levels.

I queried Lexi and she informed me it was a quarter-after-five in the evening. I should've been surprised, but it'd been a crazy few days, and concussions made one sleep like there was no tomorrow.

I plopped down on the couch, and Banjo dropped down from the ceiling to crawl into my lap, forcing his head underneath my hand like he always did when he wanted scratches. I obliged. Comforting, having my old, non-vocal Banjo back.

I grabbed my e-cig off the coffee table and took a big draw, then slowly exhaled a thin cloud of vapor. The nicotine levels were low, but it helped relax and center me. I took another puff and picked up my phone, finding a few text messages from Jeni and one from Trick, checking to see how I was doing. I'd also missed three calls from Iggy, and one from an unknown caller.

I called Iggy back, and his face immediately appeared on my screen.

"Jacob!" he exclaimed, sounding relieved. "Jeni filled me in on what happened. Are you okay?"

He sounded genuinely concerned. I entertained the idea it might be a ploy to prevent me from suing his company into oblivion. If I thought about it, I'd been attacked by one of his ex-employees, while playing *his* game. No matter what I had signed, a good lawyer almost certainly could have made me rich and put him out of business. But that wasn't me.

"Yeah, I'm fine," I said. "A little groggy."

"Are you at your place in SoDo?"

"Yeah."

"I'll be right over," he said, then hung up.

I made a pot of coffee in the kitchenette in the corner of the room and poured myself a cup, then returned to the couch and fired up my SNES, resuming a play-through of Chrono Trigger I'd started a few weeks beforehand. Banjo sat next to me and watched, captivated, as he always did when I played these old games. About thirty minutes later, a chime sounded, letting me know there was someone on the roof who wanted to get in.

I paused the game and went to the front door. The screen next to it showed a live picture of Iggy, his identity already verified in the corner. I pressed a button, and he waved at the screen before entering the elevator, and a moment later he was inside my cave.

"Good to see you, Jacob," he said as he shook my hand.

"Coffee?" I offered. He accepted, then I gave him a tour of my place.

It wasn't often I got to show off my gems to someone who'd truly appreciate, so I took advantage of the opportunity, leading him over to my main display case—a temperature and humidity-controlled glass cabinet where the jewels of my collection were on display. On each side stood an arcade cabinet from the nineteen-eighties— Dragon's Lair on the left, and Mortal Kombat on the right.

"A Sega Genesis version of Tetris!" he exclaimed as he looked inside the case. "Really? Here I thought I was offering you a fortune... and you have a Genesis Tetris?"

"Trust me, what you offered made my head spin," I assured him. "I lived on nothing but Nutros for a year to afford this baby."

His enthusiasm was genuine as he gushed over more of my games. A moment's respite from the impending, less enjoyable conversation.

"Jacob, we need to talk about Jameson," he said bluntly, changing the subject. I nodded, and we moved to the sofas and sat down opposite each other, Iggy setting a satchel he'd brought beside him. Banjo went up to greet Iggy and was rewarded with a scratch on the chin.

He took a sip of coffee. "Jameson has been banned from any association with the game, via a restraining order, and a warrant has been issued for his arrest after his assault on you," he said flatly. "I also pressed charges against Blatman, for creating the malware I'm assuming Jameson installed on your goggles after he knocked you out. Legally, that little bit of malicious code constitutes assault as well. You haven't used them since, have you?"

"No, I haven't," I said. "But what good will a restraining order or a warrant do? He has the police on his side. Four of them helped subdue us."

Iggy looked down at his palms for a moment. "The four officers involved in the incident have also had warrants placed on their heads, but I think they're long gone by now, probably spending their riches in Mexico." Raising his head, he said "Blatman, and his new company Tardigrade Technologies, have very deep pockets. Nearly as deep as my own, and they want what I have. I trust the police for the most part, but bribes are bribes. Cops don't make much."

I sighed, then went to the end table to retrieve my

goggles. I handed them to Iggy, and he took a small device from his pocket and hooked it up to a minuscule port on the side of my goggles. Hadn't noticed that before. He then took his phone out of his pocket, more a small tablet really, and began to poke and swipe at the screen.

"Yeah, he jacked them," Iggy said, scowling at his phone. "If you would have logged in, the Glitch would have had control of you in a heartbeat." He reached into the satchel, and pulled out a nearly identical pair of goggles, except that the leather band appeared a bit slimmer, and was a snazzy dark grey instead of the original black. He handed them to me, and I turned them over in my hands

"Same specs," he said. "I've contacted Trick and Jeni and gave them a new pair too, just to be on the safe side. I'm not holding my breath that Blatman and Jameson will be caught any time soon—they're pretty resourceful and know how to beat the facial and DNA recognition systems installed throughout the city. So, in the meantime, I've secured a little extra protection for you. Do you remember Alex and Alex?"

"Sure do," I replied, picturing the bald archaeologist and the supermodel-engineer I'd met in the market.

"They're not actually a part of the 300," Iggy admitted. "They're in the game looking into Jameson's activities, and his association with Blatman."

I raised an eyebrow, and Iggy went on.

"They're investigators from a firm down in Portland who specialize in inserting their agents into VR games to track down those who would exploit bugs, or generally play the game in ways that violate the EULA," Iggy explained. "A lot of their work involves tracking down gold sellers, but they are capable of much, much more— both of them are ex-agents. Alex was in the FBI's virtual crimes division for three years, and Al was CIA. Needless to say, they know what they're doing, and have a much better chance of bringing in Jameson and the Glitch than the authorities do."

"But do they have the authority to?" I asked.

"Absolutely, they do. Both are licensed and bonded for exactly this type of work," Iggy said, scratching his chin, "although this will be the first time they've extended it into augmented reality. For now, though, you'll see quite a bit of them. They're not your bodyguards, per se, as I don't want them to interfere with your gameplay, but they will have an eye on you. I took the liberty of giving them the ability to track you through your goggles."

This didn't bother me much; there were a hundred agencies and businesses that could track an individual no matter where they went. Actually, it made me feel a good deal safer, after last night's incident in the park.

I scratched at my temple, going through all the questions I'd wanted to ask. "What about Quirk? Surely an AI has the power to know what they're up to?"

"Blatman built Quirk," Iggy said bluntly. "Or at least was part of the process. He knows how to hide in her blind spots—he put them there himself. And there's something else," he said, frowning.

I looked up from my coffee.

"Even though we've booted Jameson from the game,

Quirk has informed me that both he and Blatman still have access to it, and for now we can't do anything about it. But we're working on it."

"How so?" I asked.

"Blatman has created ocular implants that allow full augmented immersion, in conjunction with two subcutaneous stimulation units," Iggy explained. "They allow him to observe *Panmachina* without goggles. We also believe he's implanted these in Jameson as well, and these implants will give them access to not only the world of *Panmachina*, but any other augmented world we choose to create. So, although we have banned him from playing the game, we can't stop him from watching."

"Come to think of it," I said, "he wasn't wearing goggles when he attacked me. So nothing has really changed, then. He's still an observer."

"Yes, and no. He can't interact with the game any more than the other NPNCs, and he will appear just like any other nipnick, just one who can see what you're doing. Just watch your back, and you should be fine."

"He seemed to be able to attack players just fine," I said, rubbing the sore spot on my head.

"Physically, yes." Iggy nodded.

"It's the physically bit that worries me," I replied. "Anyway, why even bother? What's his endgame here, if he's not in it for the quest?"

"Oh, he's still in it for the quest. Just because their plan to control your person has failed, don't think they've given up," Iggy said. "The Glitch has a million tricks up his sleeve.

Quirk thinks Jameson and Blatman are recruiting players from within the 300, giving them financial backing in exchange for partial control of the alley should they succeed. We've screened everyone in the 300 thoroughly, but some might have fallen through the cracks, and we don't know who, if anyone. Even if Jameson and the Glitch don't succeed at gaining control of Steam Whistle Alley, as long as they succeed in making my life miserable it's a win for them."

Iggy smiled reassuringly and took a sip of coffee. "That's why we brought in Al and Alex. Let them worry about Jameson and the Glitch. You worry about the quest. If you're still up for it."

"Yeah, I'm not giving up. It's personal now. And speaking of the quest," I said. "We fought our way through hordes of rampaging rabbits and centipedes, expecting some grand reveal, and all we got was a sleeping goat."

"Sorry, Jake, you're on your own, man," he said with a wink. "I'm sure you understand."

"Yeah, I get it," I sighed. "So, let's talk about something else. What happened with Honeybucket?"

Iggy turned away, lip curling in what I assumed was annoyance. "I'm not going to talk about her, Jake," he said. "What I can tell you is this—assume for all intents and purposes that she is part of Jameson's team now. I've sent amended contracts allowing for parties of up to four to compete in the quest. Trick will be able to share in your prize. Should you succeed, that is. Some of the original pairings weren't as balanced as Quirk predicted. If you checked your email once in a while, you would know all of this. Speaking of which, I'm going to need some updates eventually, Jake. It's what I'm paying you for, after all."

"I'll get one to you tomorrow," I promised. "I want to regroup with Jeni and Trick, and then plan our next steps. I'm quite content taking a little break from the game for a day or so anyway," I said, "so I should have the time. I would have sent it this morning, but," and I raised my voice for emphasis, "I was too busy recovering from getting hit in the head with a baseball bat by your disgraced ex-employee!"

Iggy raised his hands. "I get it, I get it," he said. "Just give me something, will you, when you get the chance? I'm anxious to hear some actual player feedback, but all my players have been too busy playing."

"I promise, Iggy. First thing tomorrow," I said.

I really *had* intended to keep that promise.

CHAPTER TWENTY-THREE: THE KNOWN

After Iggy left, I started up a conference call with Jeni and Trick to let them in on the latest news. I threw their faces up on my old television monitors—Jeni on a bulky 33-inch CRT television that still had dials to turn different channels, while Trick was on a turn of the century flat screen.

"So, what do you think, Trick, want to make it official?" I asked him, after telling him about Iggy's reworking of the contract.

"Join you guys? Yeah, sure," he said.

His lack of excitement deflated my sails a little, but I tried not to take it personally. Must've still been a bit sad about losing Honey.

"Won't that give us an unfair advantage, though?" he asked

"Iggy told me he's reworking the contracts to let pairs join up with other pairs, of their own choosing, and split the prize four ways. He said that some groups might be at a disadvantage, so this was his fix. Check your email, he sent out all the details. If anything, with only three, we might be at a bit of a disadvantage, but I'm confident." But I wasn't. Not only was I unsure what to do next, but I was certain I'd missed something back on the hill with the goat.

"Let's meet up in the morning," Jeni suggested. "We'll sign the new contract—plan the next steps and go over what we have so far."

"Sounds like a plan. Ten o'clock, here?" I asked. They agreed, and I disconnected the call.

I looked around my sanctuary and just felt so... at home. Cozy and content. After all I'd been through, the feeling confirmed a decision I'd been putting off for a while—I was going to move into this place. At least while I was playing *Panmachina*. It was just down the street from Steam Whistle Alley, and everything I valued most was here. My own personal fortress of solitude. Besides, the lease was up on my apartment downtown at the end of this month.

I grabbed my bag and threw in the new goggles I'd received from Iggy—these things weren't going out of my sight. I also grabbed a taser I'd purchased a couple years ago after a mugging. I decided I wouldn't let that happen again, but I only carried it around for a month before changing my mind, and it had been sitting in my drawer ever since.

The device still had a full charge—it charged wirelessly—and I fired it to make sure it still worked. A tiny bolt of purple electricity sizzled between the two electrodes. Satisfied, I shoved it into my jacket pocket.

The elevator sped me up to the roof, and I got in the *Galileo,* illuminated by the roof lights that shone in the early night. Clouds had rolled in again, and a brisk wind was blowing from the north.

I set a course for my apartment downtown and parked at street level a couple minutes later—I wanted to talk to Lenny, let him know I was going to be finishing my lease and enlist his help in moving a few things down to the lobby.

I entered the building, and Lenny greeted me from his spot behind the desk. "Ah, Master Jacob, good evening, sir," he said, with his unique blend of drollness and enthusiasm. "How are you this evening?"

"Fine, Lenny, fine," I said. "I think I'm going to be moving out, though. My work keeps me south of downtown, and while I like it here, I just wouldn't be here all that often."

"I was wondering where you have been, sir," Lenny said. "I was worried we hadn't met your needs. Are you sure everything was satisfactory with your stay here?"

"Absolutely," I said. "Once my current gig is over, who knows, I might be back. But for now, I was wondering if you could help me move a few things."

"It would be my pleasure, sir," he said, sounding a bit forlorn. If I didn't know better, I'd think he might genuinely miss me.

He rolled out from behind the counter and followed me to the elevator. I pushed the button for my floor, and he got in behind me.

The door hissed shut, and Lenny's face twisted into a snarl, and his hand clamped around my throat, squeezing with mechanical strength. He lifted me off the ground, wheeled forward and slammed me against the elevator wall.

I could barely breathe, every inhale a choking struggle. "You will not succeed, Jacob," he snarled. "The alley will be ours, one way or the other." His droll British voice had turned gravelly, without a trace of an accent. It dripped with hatred. His hand clenched tighter around my neck, and I started panicking, flailing my arms and kicking my legs, afraid he'd crush my windpipe.

"Why... do you want... me?" I gasped. "Why... me?"

"You're the odds-on favorite, Jakey boy," he said with a sneer. I recognized that voice now—the Glitch. "We can't let you win." His face pressed close to mine. "Whoever wins the alley will be able to shape *Panmachina* into what it was supposed to be. Not Jameson's vision of airships and clockwork. Not that sap Iggy's goal of creating a game that spans the country. This," he hissed the word, "has so much more potential."

The man was insane. "But you can't play, and neither can Jameson or Honey," I coughed.

"We're not the only ones in the game, Jakey boy, who are sympathetic to our cause. They win, we all win. Simple as that."

Spots danced across my vision. I was light-headed, dizzy, and beating on his arm and clawing at his face had no effect whatsoever. My hand slipped into my pocket and closed around the taser. I pulled it out, pressed it underneath the arm he was grasping me with, and fired.

Lenny collapsed to the ground in a twitching heap, and I fell on top of him. The blood rushed back to my head, and I leaned back against the wall in a squat, panting, waiting for my sight to return to normal, rubbing my throat tentatively. Damn, I was glad I packed that taser. I was almost sure he would have killed me.

I began to rethink the confidence I had when I assured Iggy I would continue playing the game. This game was amazing, yes, but it wasn't worth dying for. It wasn't worth losing Jeni for. But I've always been stubborn. There was no chance I was would give up this quest now. I had to trust in Iggy. Quirk. Alex and Al. Jeni and Trick.

I stood up, shook my head, and pressed the button for my floor.

When the doors opened a couple of seconds later, I stepped over the crumpled doorman and entered my apartment. And stopped abruptly in the doorway.

My stuff was everywhere—the sofa torn and flipped over, my living room computer gone. I ran into the room where I kept my immersion rig. Thankfully, it was still there. They would've had a tough time getting that out; I had to bring it in piece by piece and assemble it inside the room.

Everything else I owned had been ransacked. My vintage copies of Nintendo Power lay strewn about my bedroom. My clothes were everywhere.

I went back to my living room and threw my bag on the couch, then plopped down beside it. Good thing I'd left Banjo back at the sanctuary. He would've flipped if he had seen this.

Something on the floor caught my eye, my VISOR sticking out from under my 'home taping' T-shirt. I almost put it on, then realized that without my computer, it had nothing to boot up with. I stuck it in my backpack instead.

Should I call the police?

Truthfully, I didn't want them involved any more than they already were. I hadn't given a statement over the beating I took—I assumed they had all the footage they needed from Iggy, and besides, I didn't trust them. I couldn't know how far the Glitch's influence reached, and until I learned more, I wasn't going to the authorities.

Alex and Al. Iggy had given me their contact information before he'd left and told me to let them know if anything happened. This probably qualified. I called Alex, and her face appeared on my screen after the first ring. She looked exactly as she had in the game.

"Hi, Alex, it's Jacob. Iggy said I should call you if I ran into the Glitch or Jameson," I said.

"What happened?" she asked, her face an expression of professional seriousness. Al appeared over her shoulder. He, too, looked as he had in-game.

I explained the situation, and they said they'd be right over. And they didn't lie. They showed up at my apartment within fifteen minutes.

In person, I could tell that aside from their clothes, neither one of them had been augmented by AR in the slightest. Alex was gorgeous and paired with Al's good looks and dark skin I suddenly felt a little self-conscious.

After I went through everything that had happened in detail, they went to the elevator and dragged Lenny into the apartment. Al handcuffed Lenny's hands behind his back, and Alex reached for a spot in the back of his neck, turning him on. Lenny's face came to life.

The robot looked at me, and a sad, pleading expression poured over his face. "Master Jacob, please accept my sincerest apologies. I can assure you that I had no control over my faculties."

"We know, Lenny, but thank you," I said.

"I maintained complete awareness the whole time, but I was powerless to act," he said.

"Can you tell us anything that might help?" Alex asked him, and Lenny turned to her.

"I'm afraid there's nothing to tell, ma'am," Lenny said. "One minute, I was welcoming Master Jacob into the building, and the next, I had my hands around his throat in the elevator."

Al took a device from his bag that reminded me of a Star Trek tricorder and held it close to Lenny's head. Lines of code started scrolling across the screen.

"Remote access confirmed, but he bounced his location through nearly a thousand other servers. It's going to take a bit of time to track him down," Al said. "I've sent the data back to HQ."

Alex looked at me. "Jacob, you're going to be okay. Was there anything on your computer that you think will help him?"

"No, I haven't really used it much since I started playing. Plus, if it gets removed from this house by anyone but me, the drives get a clean wipe. They might as well have melted for all he'll be able to recover." It did piss me off, though. Lexi was backed up in the cloud, my computer at the cave, and in my van, so she would be fine. While most of my photos, documents, and anything else I valued was stored on the cloud as well, I did have a lot of information stored locally. Nothing I couldn't live without, but just the thought of someone going through my personals, ransacking my home... it made me feel almost dirty. Violated, in a way.

Convinced that Lenny was no longer a threat, they uncuffed him and helped him upright. Once on his wheels, he immediately set about the place, tidying it up with grim determination.

I went into my room, retrieved a few sets of clothes and some of my more personal mementos, packing them into a second bag. The rest I could leave for later.

The Alexes followed me down to my vehicle. Al said he wanted to install a firewall on my onboard systems, assuring me there was no way anyone could get through it unauthorized, and I thanked him.

While he was working on the dashboard computer, Alex said, "We'd also like to follow you to your other unit." She glanced down at her phone, and then looked back up. "We need to make sure nobody gets in there. We've already figured out how they got in here: your apartment security had a back door that should have been patched months ago, but never was."

"Sounds good."

When Al finished, they went to their own vehicle, and I set a course for my sanctuary. The *Galileo* rose into the night air and headed south, and my two new protectors followed not far behind.

"Lexi, you still there?" I said, and her face popped up on the dashboard screen.

"Yeah, I'm here. Your friends installed some new firewalls and security measures, I see. Effective stuff," she said appreciatively.

"What happened to the unit in the apartment?"

"A localized EMP took me offline before they entered, so I don't have footage of the incident," she said. "As soon as I was back online, I instituted a wipe and meltdown of the drives on the actual unit and changed all access to the backups on the cloud. All your data is safe and untampered with. I've been watching."

"Good, good. Thanks, Lexi, you're an angel," I said. "I'll call you if I need you. Let me know if you see anything strange."

I pulled out my phone, and saw I'd missed a call earlier. No message though, so I dialed the number and sent it to my dashboard screen. Two seconds later the green 'ringing' icon was replaced with the face of Shauni.

"What the hell do you want?" I asked, furious at the audacity this girl—this turncoat—had to call me.

"Jacob, thank you for calling me back," she said, her face showing its usual complete lack of emotion. "I need to talk to you."

"Well, I don't want to talk to you," I said and pressed the disconnect button.

"Wait, I—" she said, but the line dropped.

I growled under my breath. What the hell did she want?

It didn't matter. She had a role in all this, but at that moment I was too upset to be interested.

I reached my building and landed on the roof, and Alex and Al landed beside me. Their vehicle was sleek and black, with dark tinted windows and silver trim. The rooftop lamps gleamed off the car body's polished reflection.

They stepped out as I did, and we approached the elevator. Moments later, I stood in front of the door to my space, and when it opened upwards, I was relieved to see everything where I had left it. Banjo ran up to greet me, and I lowered an arm, so he could scamper up to my shoulder. We entered the room, and the thick door slid shut behind us.

Al took out his device and got to work on the door control interface. Alex walked into the room and looked around. "Nice place you have here," she said.

"Thanks," I replied. She went back and stood over Al's shoulder while he worked.

He stood up a few minutes later, dusting off his hands and smiling. "There, you're secure," he said. "Nobody but you is ever getting in here. Well, unless you invite them in, of course. Your cameras and sensors now monitor for any concealed weapons as well as heart rate and perspiration. The computer will inform you if it believes the person at the door has any ill intentions."

I thanked them both, and they made me promise to tell them if anything even remotely strange happened in the future. I told them about my missed call from Shauni.

"We are investigating her, but she currently poses no

threat," Alex said. "Apparently she's on the outs with Jameson as well. Right now, we're going to concentrate on what operatives he has in-game. They're the ones you're going to have to look out for as you move forward. We don't know if they're going to be PVP enabled, so watch your back for another real-life ambush. Don't trust anybody."

Great. It was odd, having to worry about real world threats while playing a game. It made sense, in a twisted sort of way. This game had real world ramifications, but it still wasn't a feeling I'd get used to any time soon.

I showed Alex and Al to the newly digitally reinforced door and thanked them again for their efforts. After the door slid closed behind them, I walked over to the kitchenette to prepare a snack. Banjo hopped from my shoulder onto the counter. I made myself a peanut butter and banana sandwich, which took longer than I intended as Banjo helped himself to every other banana slice.

With sandwich in hand, I plopped down on the couch and picked up the SNES controller, still paused on my current game of Chrono Trigger. Playing these old games helped me concentrate—most of them required very little of my attention after the hundredth play-through.

"What do you think, Banjo, should I give up the quest?" I asked my monkey, who was staring at my sandwich. "A game isn't worth dying for."

Banjo *ooked* at me and walked on all fours over to the end table, where he picked up my new goggles and threw them in my lap. Alex and Alex had taken my old ones, hoping to squeeze some clues out of the malware the Glitch had installed.

I paused my game and looked down at the eyewear.

I liked *Panmachina*. It was the realest game I'd ever played. I liked the characters and loved the outfits. With a little polishing, I could see myself spending a lot of time in it. On top of that, the thought of being auction master just felt so perfect to me.

"Hello," I said to myself. "My name's Jacob. What do I do? Oh, you know, I'm an auction master." I laughed, and Banjo gave me the monkey equivalent.

So maybe a game wasn't worth dying for, but were dreams?

I un-paused my game and continued to play.

About ten minutes later, the first few bars of the Chocobo Theme from Final Fantasy sounded over my room's speaker system. I forgot I'd set that to my door chime, along with a few other choice tracks. I didn't receive a ton of visitors here.

I paused the game again and walked over to the display by the door. Shauni was standing on the roof, looking up at the camera.

"Please, Jacob," she pleaded, "we need to talk. I'm not going to hurt you or anything."

I looked at the information at the bottom of the display.

ID: Shauni Ferro

Threat assessment: negligible.

No hidden armaments or other devices deemed hostile.

Wow, that was some useful software. I scrutinized her through the screen for a couple of seconds. It had begun to rain, and her hair was starting to stick to her forehead. This girl... it had looked like she might turn out to be a friend, but then, out of nowhere, she joined the enemy forces? What was she getting out of it? Why betray us without saying a word? Against my better judgment, I decided to let her in. Curiosity can be a powerful motivator.

She entered my sanctuary a minute later, her hair and clothes damp. I made no show of hospitality, not even offering her a towel.

"What do you want, Shauni?" I asked.

She looked around my place for a second, then focused on me. "I just want a chance to explain myself," she said. "I've been kicked out of the game, I have no contact with Jameson or Iggy anymore, and I... I just want to explain myself," she repeated. "Can I sit down?"

I considered for a moment, then nodded. I led her over to the sofas, and she took a seat. Banjo didn't seem to mind, and he was usually a good judge of character. Shauni, however, backed away. I forgot she hated monkeys.

"Banjo, go play in your nest," I told him, and he obliged.

I studied Shauni as she sat down. She was dressed in black pants and a blue hooded shirt, spotted with raindrops. Her face had always been expressionless, but now looked even more distant. "Say what you came to say," I told her.

She looked down at her hands. "I'm sorry for leaving you guys," she mumbled. "I've known Jameson for a long time. There were moments I'd do anything for him. Other times I wanted him dead. These days it's mostly the latter."

"Is it me you should be saying this to?"

Her mouth twitched as if it wanted to smile but it wasn't something the rest of the face was capable of. "I've tried to contact Trick, to explain to him," she said, "but he won't talk to me."

"We saw you at the Locke Wetlands," I said. "Jameson blinded us. Last night he hit me upside the head with a baseball bat."

"I know," she said. "And that's part of the reason I left him. He's ambitious, and it's a trait I admired him for. But it's also why I despise him. He will stop at nothing when he sets his sights on something."

"What does he want?" I asked.

"He wants Iggy out of the picture. He wants ARGO enterprises out of the picture. He wants to build the company he and Blatman conceived originally. They believe Quirk to be their property, not Iggy's," she explained.

"So why does me achieving my quest stop him from doing that?"

"Once the auction master is seated, Iggy plans on releasing the game. If he stops you from getting it, there's a better chance they can control whoever does. In essence, whoever controls the alley controls the game. Read the fine print. You not only get your ten percent; you get creative control. You can build. You can change. The alley will be yours."

I should've read the contract more carefully. I didn't think I had ever read to the end of the one.

"Iggy didn't mention anything about control, just the ten percent," I said. "Why would he give up control?"

Shauni looked down at her hands again, contemplating. Then she looked up. "Iggy is dying, Jacob."

I hadn't heard her right. "What?"

"He's dying. Brain tumor. One of the few that doctors can't remove yet," she said, looking back at her hands. "He told me soon after I left him. Jameson was handsome, driven. Iggy was just Iggy. You know him." She laughed, one of the few displays of emotion I'd seen since I'd met her, but it quickly turned into a sob, and soon her cheeks were damp with tears.

I went to the kitchenette and came back with a box of tissues.

She took one and wiped her face and nose. "The doctors say he's got a year, maybe a little more," she said. Then she stood up quickly and headed for the door. "I'm sorry, Jacob," she said. "Tell Trick... and Jeni... that I'm sorry for betraying them."

She reached the door and said, "Open." The security system recognized her, and the door slid upwards. She turned around. "Goodbye. I'm sorry," she said again, and then she was gone.

The door swung downward, and a beep signaled the security measures were back in place. I watched her leave on the monitor, then returned to the sofa.

CHAPTER TWENTY-FOUR: THE MENAGERIE

I woke up the next morning on my couch with my SNES controller stuck to my face and my phone ringing incessantly. Banjo was rapping me on the head with his knuckles, as the repeated ringtone—*particle man, particle man, doing the things a particle can*—wasn't doing the trick, and was probably getting on his nerves. I sat up and the controller fell from my face, clattering to the floor as I answered my phone.

"Jacob! I was so worried... are you okay?" asked a frantic-sounding Jeni. "You look like crap."

"Yeah, I don't have the world's best morning face," I said.

"Trick thinks he has figured it out," Jeni said excitedly, worry apparently forgotten.

I yawned and stretched a crick out of my shoulder. "Figured what out?"

"The goat... the clue—the whole thing," she said. "Get up! Can you meet us at the alley in an hour?"

"Sure," I agreed, and said goodbye. I went to the

kitchen to start a pot of coffee and headed towards the bathroom for a shower.

An hour later, Banjo and I were in the *Galileo,* heading towards the alley. I slipped on the new goggles, logged in, and my shuttlecraft turned into the airship—and the world changed with it. Lexi appeared in the driver's seat and gave me a wave.

I had only been gone a day, but I found myself missing the look, the *aura,* of the place. In the real world, the sun had started to burn off the cloud cover in places, but as soon as I powered up my new goggles, everything got a shade darker. Thick clouds replaced the thin, effectively masking the sun, but also using it to light themselves up in shades of burnt amber, giving a surreal glow to the ornate towers and spires around and below me. I passed a Tesla tower, and a bolt of blue lightning jumped from it to a receptor on a nearby building. Another airship, propeller-driven and belching steam, passed by in front of me, and the *Galileo* automatically altered course slightly.

I opened my main dashboard screen and brought up the new contracts Iggy had sent out establishing the new split rewards for completion of the quest by three and four-person teams. I took the time to actually read through the contract—not word for word, of course, but I did give it a very heavy scanning. I paused on the clause I had missed before.

"Those awarded proprietorships of the entity known as Steam Whistle Alley, as specified in section IV clause 3, will also be awarded creative control over the aesthetics

and game mechanics of the area known as Steam Whistle Alley, defined in section I clause 2. All decisions made by the proprietors must be ratified by the lead programming board of ARGO Enterprises for feasibility and implementation purposes and are subject to scrutiny and adaption by a fifty-two percent majority of the current ARGO populace, of those who have chosen to opt in to the implementation protocols described in section VI, paragraph 8."

I stopped reading after that, proud of myself for reading more of a contract than I ever had before. I affixed my electronic signature and sent it off.

Traffic was heavy, the sky thick with airships in an array of colors and designs, adding a couple minutes to my flight. The alley finally came into view, and I entered the landing sequence into the computer.

I got out in the parking lot, slinging my backpack on one shoulder while Banjo clung to the other. We approached the passageway that led into the main street but stopped when we spotted a couple strange new additions to the Alley.

"What the devil are those things?" Banjo asked.

In front of the arched passageway stood two burnished bronze humanoid figures. Each was about a head taller than me and held strange looking weapons in their three-fingered hands.

We took a few tentative steps closer, and they swiveled their heads towards me on narrow, segmented necks, glaring at me with eyes that were black disks with a single red diode in the center of each. They had wide, barrel-shaped chests, which truncated abruptly at the abdomen where another series of brass segments connected the torso to the hips. Their knees, an array of gears and pistons, bent backwards like the satyrs of mythology. Their feet were flat pads of the same polished metal, with three segmented toes protruding out of the front and the rear for gripping.

I took a few more cautious steps forward, and the machine-men lifted what looked like sawed-off shotguns—each had a dark metal barrel attached to a red wooden stock, and a little glass sphere filled with dancing motes of electricity where the firing mechanism should go. A series of progressively smaller rings adorned the business end of the gun, but whether their purpose was functional or decorative, I couldn't tell. Knowing this place, probably the latter, but I wasn't about to find out. I continued forward.

"Halt, citizen," said the robot on the left. It raised a hand, and I stopped about two meters away.

A thin slit opened above its eyes, like a robotic unibrow, and a flat beam of yellow light emerged from it, scanning my face from top to bottom and up again. The slit closed, and the machine nodded.

"Welcome to Steam Whistle Alley," it said, and stood rigid once again, letting us pass. I walked past them, and into the main thoroughfare. Guess Iggy got some security upgrades.

A boy in a cabbie cap and dusty brown vest stood on the corner, hawking newspapers. "Extra! Extra!" he cried. I wasn't sure what it was an 'extra' to as I hadn't seen newspapers sold in the street here before. "Official recognition given for four-companion parties! Extra!"

I took a paper from the kid, and he held out a small disc of glass circled by a copper gear. I pressed my thumb to it, and the boy thanked me, then went back to hawking his papers.

I rubbed the paper between my fingers. Actual newsprint. I had clippings of the stuff, but nobody had sold newspapers in years. I stuffed it in my bag for later reading.

I saw more of the bronze machines inside, patrolling the streets. Their leg motions reminded me of water birds, long and lanky movements that gave them sort of a pompous strut. Once inside, I called Jeni on my goggles, and her head appeared, floating in my vision.

"It's about time," she said, and sent me her location.

I pulled on my virtual goggles, which now seemed by default to rest on my forehead when I logged in, and flipped down the location lens on my right eyepiece. The green asterisk appeared, with '322 M' in green lettering next to it. Following the asterisk led me down a side-alley I hadn't been to before, between Dwebble's potion shop and a clothing store. I looked in the windows of the clothing store as I passed—I could use some new duds; I'd been wearing the same stuff since I arrived in the game.

The asterisk led me down a flight of stairs to a rough-looking wooden door, with a plank hung from a post overhead reading 'Shimmy's Tavern' over a wood-burned image of two tankards of ale. I turned the knob and entered.

The interior was all done in dark, well-worn wood. Only

a dozen or so tables filled the tavern, set between a series of carved pillars supporting the ceiling. No windows, since the place was basement level, but the glowing orange filaments of perhaps twenty transparent glass Edison lights filled the space with a warm glow. One bartender stood behind the horseshoe-shaped wooden bar, wiping it down with a grimy rag. There were few people in the tavern at this time of day, and I saw Jeni and Trick in the corner as soon as I walked in.

I sat next to Jeni, across from Trick, and we exchanged hellos. Banjo hopped on Trick's side of the table, standing on the bench so his hands could rest on the polished wood. He adjusted his monocle.

"You didn't call us yesterday," Jeni said, "or return any messages. We were worried. Everything okay?"

"Yeah, fine," I said, and proceeded to tell them of the events of the previous day, starting at the beginning with the attack in the elevator.

"He took over your doorbot?" Trick asked, wide-eyed. "This isn't good. This isn't good! He could take over anything, couldn't he?"

"I don't know, Trick," I said. "I'm not really up to date on the science of it all. Lenny's been there for a while now, maybe he's older technology. And speaking of bots, what's up with our new robot overlords?"

"They're calling them 'automatons,'" Jeni said. "I'm not sure what they'll do to people who aren't in the game, like if some nipnick came in here looking to cause trouble, but they seem to be keeping the players in line. My guess is they're more for effect than anything."

"Good to know." I told them about the rest of my day, including the security work performed by Alex and Al, then finished with my visit from Shauni. Trick's expression darkened at the mention of her name.

"She says she's sorry, and if you saw her face, you'd believe her," I said. "It sounds... complicated. She also mentioned why Jameson and the Glitch want control of the alley so bad."

They leaned a little closer to me, Jeni looking around conspiratorially.

"Whoever controls the alley not only gets to split the ten percent, but they also get creative control. I'm not sure to what degree, but it's in the contract. I already signed the new one—did you guys get yours?"

"Yeah, sent it in this morning," said Trick.

Jeni nodded. "So did I."

"What did you make of it?" I asked.

"Well, we get to split the tithe, and we can make design changes to the alley, I think," said Trick. "I don't think I'd change too much, though. I like it here." He studied the room as he spoke, smiling.

The bartender came over and hovered near the table. His mustache was so thick that it completely hid his mouth, and a rich baritone voice originated from somewhere inside. "What ya having, sir?"

"Try the birch beer," Jeni suggested, and I followed her advice. He nodded and left.

I finished detailing Shauni's visit, concluding with the

bombshell about Iggy's tumor.

"What?" Jeni exclaimed, her jaw dropping.

Trick's eyes were so wide they looked in danger of popping from his skull.

"Yeah. I know. I have no idea what will happen to the company, but I guess this quest is his way of ensuring that at least part of it falls into capable hands," I said. "But I don't know if it will. When the Glitch attacked me this morning, he said that there were other teams, more... sympathetic to his cause."

Trick stared at the table for a second, then looked at me, his face a mask of concern. "How did Shauni know where you lived?"

I blinked. "What?"

"You're nowhere on the web; I checked," Trick said. "Neither am I. But she showed up on the roof of your storage unit. I mean, not even your apartment, but your hideout."

I hadn't exactly gone to great lengths to keep its location private, but I hadn't advertised it either.

"That's a good question. I don't know, Trick, but I'd like to find out." I pulled out my phone and sent a brief message to Alex and Al, asking them to investigate. "If I had to guess, I'd say the Glitch or Jameson told her, but then I don't know how they found out either. At least now the security's been upgraded, and the walls are thick Permacrete reinforced with an earthquake-resistant titanium alloy, and the windows are unbreakable. Barring a bomb, I don't think there's any way someone could get in there uninvited."

Was there?

The bartender returned with my mug of birch beer. I took a sip—it *was* good—then took a healthy gulp. "So, Trick, what did you find out about the quest?"

"Oh, yeah, the quest. Jeni filled me in on everything... the mansion, the gears, the message on the picnic table," he said.

I gave Jeni a look, but it was the right call. "Well, welcome to the team, Trick. We wanted to tell you, you know."

"I get it, I do. I would have done the same thing," Trick said. "But I think I know where we have to go next. And I think I'm the first one to know. Several teams have made it to the top of the hill at Locke Wetlands... but as far as I know, we're the only ones to have discovered the clue on the table as well."

"*Bruse,*" I said.

"Close. It's pronounced 'bruise-uh,' and it's Norwegian."

"I thought it was Danish," I said. "Jeni translated it, and it means..." I thought for a second, "um... 'roar' or 'fizz,' right?"

Jeni nodded. "But according to Trick here, it also means 'gruff.'"

"Gruff?" I asked.

Banjo cleared his throat. "Rough, brusque, or stern in manner, speech, or aspect," he quoted. Nice to have my own walking dictionary.

I looked at Trick.

"My grandmother's Norwegian," he explained.

"Granddad's Irish."

I smiled. "You don't say. So, what about the goat?"

"The goat is the second part of the clue. Gruff. Goat. Ring any bells?" Trick asked, nearly bouncing in his chair.

I scratched my head. "The first gear is being guarded by a grumpy Norwegian goat?"

Jeni laughed. "Not quite," she said. "Trick?"

Trick looked at Jeni, eyebrows high on his forehead, and then back to me. "When I was a kid, Grams used to read me a Norwegian bedtime story, 'The Three Billy Goats Gruff.' Heard of it?"

I shook my head.

Banjo cleared his throat again. "Once upon a time—" he began.

"Thank you, Banjo, but, uh... do you think you can give me the edited version?" I asked.

He seemed a bit put off by the suggestion but shrugged after a moment's hesitation. "It's about three goats that want to cross a bridge to eat the grass on the other side," Banjo said. "There's a giant troll that lives under the bridge, and every time one of the goats tries to cross, the troll threatens to eat them. Each goat tells the troll to wait for the next one, as they get progressively bigger, but the third goat knocks the troll into the river, where he drowns. The end."

I furrowed my brow. "So, what's the next bit?"

"What do you mean?" asked Trick.

"Well, she said you figured it all out. What's the next bit?"

"All the clues point to this children's story," Trick said,

excited. "The word on the table, the goat. It's all here!"

"Well, *where* does the story point to?" I asked.

"I... uh..." stammered Trick. "I don't know."

I sighed. "Well, it's a solid start. Good job."

We spent the rest of the morning and early afternoon walking around Steam Whistle Alley, restocking supplies and potions. The place was crowded now, the nipnicks more plentiful too, although I still wasn't sure why. The Alley was boring in its natural state, aside from the real food, and I guess eavesdropping on a bunch of weirdos in goggles and watching them buy invisible merchandise could be fun for some people. I'd heard a few talking about the game's release, so maybe these were all prospective players.

People were already grouping in teams of four, it seemed, and often they were followed by an array of animals. One team, comprised of a gargoyle, an alchemist, a werewolf, and what might have been a thaumaturge had a pair of small dogs and another clockwork monkey in tow. A brass owl, reminiscent of Bubo from Clash of the Titans, hovered above them as well.

Jeni's face lit up. "Trick, have you hit level five yet?"

"This morning," he said. "I soloed some slimes down at the beach."

"You want to go pet shopping?" she asked with a grin.

"Oh yeah, we can get familiars now, can't we. I'm game," Trick said.

Apparently, the place to pick up feathered or furry companions was "Binkton's Menagerie," near the entrance to the alley. It was a good three blocks away, so we stopped to get some chicken satay and fried rice from Tole on the way. This stuff was seriously delicious.

Tole had upped his steampunk game as well, dressed in a long-sleeved shirt he'd rolled up to the elbows, with a green leather vest overtop with brass buttons shaped like suns. His slacks matched his vest, and the whole look was finished by a black stovepipe hat trimmed in dark green leather with a pair of serious looking goggles on the rim that put the rest of our eye gear to shame. *"Terima kasih, mister!"* he shouted as we walked away.

Kind of cool, to see the surrounding culture adapt to match our game.

We ate as we walked, finishing our meal by the time we got to the pet store entrance. The place was packed—a bunch of people must've hit level five at nearly the same time. Even outside we had to shout to hear each other over the din of the excited players and animals emanating from the wide double doors.

One couple in particular irked us. The woman was dressed in a flowing dress trimmed in black and red who insisted on carrying her open parasol over her shoulder wherever she went. She displayed a constant disgusted frown, as if appalled she was forced to interact with the common-folk, looking down her nose at people and animals alike. Her goggles rested on her forehead, her hair immaculately styled around them. Her companion, a man in black pants and a maroon jacket adorned with silver chains, pushed his way through the crowd ahead of her, ordering people to make way for 'his lady.' His silver goggles rested on the curved brim of a Cahill hat, trimmed in what looked like beaver skin. These two must've really been into the roleplaying aspect of the game, something I hadn't seen much of until now. Hard to tell what class either of them was—if I had to guess, I would have said an overdressed beastmaster and a thaumaturge that opted for dresses instead of robes—but I had no way to be certain. I had nothing against roleplaying, but this couple's act of superiority and disgust rubbed me the wrong way.

We squeezed inside and found ourselves faced with rows of ornate metal cages. It sounded like every animal in there could talk, their voices mixing with the players' excited chatter to create an overpowering din. If the animals could talk, they were at least moderately intelligent, which made keeping them in cages seem kind of cruel to me. At least the animals didn't seem overly put off by it. They did, however, take every opportunity to tell anyone within earshot why they were obviously the best choice.

"You ain't never gonna see feathers like these," said one parrot, spreading his wings wide. "I come from superior stock. I mean... look at the plumage!"

A decorative terrarium held a small green and yellow iguana, which, for some reason, had a French accent. "You want to take me with you, I know all of ze secrets zis place has to offer," he was saying to an engineer looking through the side of the glass.

One section of the shop held nothing but metal animals. Some had their internal mechanisms showing through their fur or scales, while others looked like they were completely skinned in brass or gold. I was particularly amused by what looked for all the world like a silver, chihuahua-sized rhinoceros.

I shouted over the din to Trick and Jeni. "You guys have fun, I'll meet you outside when you're done."

Trick's revelation about the gruff goat had given me an idea, and I wanted to do a bit of research. Besides, the noise was giving me a headache.

I walked out of the store and found a coffee stand nearby. Steam Whistle Alley had a lot of coffee shops— fifteen, I'd counted so far—which wasn't too surprising. People in Seattle loved their coffee, me included, and the coffee machines in the alley looked extra awesome. I ordered a quad-shot iced mocha and sat at an empty table, pulling out my phone, which the game had augmented as well. I could now see through the back of it, and apparently the whole thing was run by a large torsion spring and an intricate series of gears. I spent the next half hour looking up Seattle history between sips of sweet coffee. Banjo curled up in the chair next to me and fell asleep. How he was able to nap in this racket, I had no idea.

It wasn't long before Trick and Jeni emerged from the pet shop with their newfound companions. I stood up, and Banjo woke up and climbed to my shoulder to greet the new team additions.

Trick's was perched on his shoulder. It was a bird, completely rendered in burnish copper. A formidable bird of prey, down to a wicked hooked beak, scowling emerald eyes, and sharp talons that clung to Trick's robe. Except it was about the size of a robin. It wore a little brass helmet with a crest of red feathers down the middle, and a golden lens extended from the brim, circling its left eye.

"This is Babiji," Trick said. "He's a Sundanese hunting falcon."

"Is he a baby?" I asked.

"I am a masterfully-crafted credit to my species, and a handsome one at that," said the bird. The animal's voice was extremely high-pitched, like it had swallowed helium, and the bird's attempted intimidating tone made it all the more comical. I tried to suppress a laugh but failed.

"Don't make me peck you," he squeaked.

Jeni emerged behind Trick, leading her new companion by the hand. "This is Lizzie," she said. A monkey stepped from behind Jeni's leg, wearing brown shorts and a sleeveless shirt embroidered with flowers.

I took off my bowler and tipped it to the new arrival.

"Hello, it's nice to meet you all," the monkey said. Her voice was light and melodic. She looked to be the same species as Banjo, who scampered down my leg to greet the new arrival.

"Hello, my name is Banjo Tutor. It's a pleasure to meet you," he said. He held out his hand with a smile.

Lizzie ignored him, crawling up Jeni's side to sit on her shoulder. "Lizzie, that wasn't nice. Say hi to Banjo."

"Hello," she said flippantly. "So, what are we up to today?"

"If it's up to Jacob, probably going to go around looking for more animals to insult," chirped Babiji from Trick's shoulder. Trick laughed.

"I'm sorry about that," I said, "you're just..."

"Small? Yeah, thank you, Captain Obvious."

Off to a good start with the new familiars.

"Anyway, guys, I think I have a lead," I said.

"What is it?" Jeni asked.

I looked around at the throng of people surrounding the menagerie, and with a jerk of my head, led them to an alley entrance around the corner from the shop.

I checked again to make sure nobody was within earshot. "I think I know where we have to go next," I said. "I think I found the troll."

CHAPTER TWENTY-FIVE: THE BRIDGE

What? Where?" asked Trick excitedly. The bird on his shoulder took off and perched on a rooftop overlooking the side alley.

"Back before the new Aurora Bridge was built twenty-some years ago, there used to be a large... I guess I'll call it a piece of art... underneath the base of the north end, called the Fremont Troll," I told them. "It was a big, ugly thing holding a Volkswagen Beetle in its hand, even had a hubcap for an eye."

"You say 'used to,'" said Jeni. "Where is it now?"

"Well, I did a little research. There was a movement to get the troll moved before the old bridge was demolished and the new one went up," I said, "but the effort failed. They couldn't raise enough funds in time. So, the troll was destroyed and buried along with the remains of the old bridge, under where the new one stands today."

I saw Banjo out of the corner of my eye, smiling at Lizzie, who was completely ignoring him. Poor guy.

"Well that doesn't do us any good," Trick said. "Does it?"

"There're rumors on the web that the troll wasn't actually destroyed," I said. "There are those who think it's still there. Rumors talk about tunnels and passages, shored up by the remains of the original bridge. It was used as an underground homeless camp for a couple of years before the Homeways Shelter opened its doors fifteen years ago. And for the past year or so, there's been a ton of underground construction in the area."

"Maybe Iggy's been building something there, is that what you're thinking?" Trick asked.

I nodded. "Knowing him, yeah. It would be expensive, but I think he's got the money. The question is, what did he build?"

Babiji glided down from his rooftop perch and returned to Trick's shoulder. The bird lowered its voice, which didn't do anything to reduce the pitch. "I just thought you should know; there's a man around the corner with some contraption pressed to his ear. I think he's eavesdropping. Maroon jacket and silver goggles."

The bird took off again to resume its surveillance, while I ran down the alley to see if I could catch the man. When I got to the end of the alley, he was already a good 50 meters down the main thoroughfare, but I still recognized him. The role player in the Cahill hat from the pet shop. He was holding a curved brass horn, ostensibly a listening device of some sort. The man rounded a corner by the market and disappeared.

I swore. Jeni and Trick pulled up behind me.

"Was that the rude dude from the menagerie earlier?"

Jeni asked.

"Yeah, I think so, and I think he heard us," I said. A hawk screeched above us, and I saw Trick's bird soaring the direction the man had run.

That bird's gonna come in handy.

A minute later, Babiji came back and landed on Trick's shoulder. "He's gone, can't find him anywhere," the bird squawked. "But I'll recognize that hat when I see it."

"We'll have to be more careful moving forward," I said, frustrated that our discovery might have been overheard. Nothing for it, now.

"Thanks, Babiji," Trick said, and offered the bird a peanut, which it happily gulped down.

My mind always struggled with what was possible and what wasn't in AR. Banjo had a digestive system, so could eat pretty much anything I could. This bird was a figment of the game.

Trick must've noticed me scowling at the nuts. "They're not real," he explained. "Virtual nuts. Well, augmented nuts. The funny thing is, our software lets us eat them too. Try one."

I took a nut, popped it into my mouth, and was surprised to find it tasted like a nut, although the texture was a bit off. Trick showed me the other side of the cloth bag, where the words 'Augmented Food—No Nutritional Value' were stenciled. I had eaten food in VR before, but this was something else. The goggles were a fantastic piece of technology.

"Well, should we go see what we can find at the Aurora

Bridge?" Jeni suggested.

"Definitely, but I want to stop by the guild first, spend the point I got from level five on something," I said. We agreed to meet at the airship in an hour, and then we split up. We didn't have a lot of time to waste, especially if the hat man had overheard our plans.

Ten minutes later, I was in the Artificer's Hall in the guild, staring at *Professor Harron's Compendium of Useful Tools and Gadgets for the Successful Archaeologist*. I'd already enhanced my first-level creations by two, and the first page had the option to dump my new point into them as well, if I wished. But my sprinklers were powerful enough, and I hadn't even made any grenades. I flipped over to the next page, blank except for the writing at the top.

Do you wish to spend a guild point to unlock second level creations?

The words 'Yes' and 'No' were once again written underneath. I touched 'Yes,' and an array of schematics and instructions blossomed into view. I turned the page and found the next two were blank, then flipped back to the new diagrams.

An assortment of animals appeared on the two pages, each of them wearing what looked like mounted armaments.

"Boss, look!" Banjo exclaimed. He was pointing to a picture of a monkey on the second page. On its back were two glass spheres encased in copper strapping, attached to shoulder straps the monkey wore like a backpack. Inside of each sphere, a rod supported a disk of metal at its center. Two segmented metal tubes ran from the base of the spheres down the monkey's tail, where they ended in a copper cone capping the tail, held up and over the monkey's head as it crouched on all fours, so it looked like a—

"Scorpion," I said as I read the title underneath the image.

Banjo didn't have to tell me how much he wanted this device. I could see it in his excited money eyes. I wanted it for him too.

I pressed the picture with my finger, and the writing shifted, both pages filling up with details, part lists, and assembly instructions. Right away I began instructing Banjo on what to retrieve from the various cubbies that lined the walls, and soon a small pile began to form on the table behind me. Once again, everything I needed was readily available here, but I had no doubt that would cease to be the case as my artificer level increased and rarer schematics were unlocked.

When all the parts had been assembled, I grabbed some tools from the rack behind the book and got to work, and the contraption came together quickly. A monkey-sized hand grip with a trigger button attached to the pack for firing. The power supply for the device looked like a tiny, glowing green hourglass, which clicked into place inside the rectangular platform supporting the two spheres. I flipped a toggle switch on the right shoulder strap, and the spheres came to life. Minuscule bolts of electricity danced from the middle discs, lancing around the inner surfaces of the spheres. The contraption was finished.

"You ready to try this on?" I asked Banjo.

"Since the moment I first saw it," he breathed in awe.

Banjo strapped the device to his back, and I helped him affix the tubes and the cone tip to his tail. He gave his tail a wave, finding that the device didn't impede its movement. Trigger mechanism in hand, he flipped up the safety cover, then crouched down on all fours with his tail arched over his head, as in the diagram, aiming at the far wall. He looked back at me. I nodded support, and he pushed the trigger button.

A beam of blue-white energy shot out from the cone with a *zzzap* and struck the far wall by the entrance. Chunks of plaster fell away, and a charred black circle remained where the bolt had struck. It wasn't Death Star powerful, but for a second-level creation it was pretty impressive. Plus, it'd give Banjo something to do in battle rather than just lug around sprinklers.

"Hell, yes!" Banjo exclaimed. "Watch out, *Panmachina*. Banjo the Destroyer is coming for you! All shall fear me!"

He began leaping from shelf to shelf in celebration, bouncing around the room like a pinball. All I could do was watch him and chuckle.

After a minute he stood still again, but he hadn't stopped grinning. "Hey, Jakey," he said, sounding thoughtful. "Do you think we could build one more of these?"

That's my smooth little monkey. "Sure thing, bud. Let's do it up."

The second one went quicker than the first, and we found a small box to store it in. Banjo grabbed a length of twine from one of the cubbies and wrapped it twice, finishing it off with a neat bow. Not the typical present, but still romantic, in its own way.

I still had over an hour to kill, so we threw together a few of the shrapper grenades for good measure. I intended to give them to Trick, so his bird could drop them on targets. We were becoming quite the formidable force.

On our way back to the alley, I passed the clothing store I'd spotted across the way from Dwebble's earlier. The wooden sign above the door read 'Sir Marby's Fine Raiment.' I still had a bit of time, so I walked in, and a distinguished older gentleman welcomed me from behind the counter. Several other players browsed the shelves and racks, keeping the place busy. I still wore the clothes given to me during character creation, and truthfully, beige and white was never my favorite combo. Just because I was an archaeologist didn't mean I couldn't *pop* a little bit. Except for the bowler hat, I wasn't really attached to anything else I wore. So, I decided to build around it, and the purple feather which adorned it.

After a good ten minutes browsing the racks I settled on some comfortable looking black cotton pants, a dark purple shirt with three-quarter length sleeves—so I could still see the readouts on my wristband—and finished with a dark-grey cotton vest. Then I went to the changing room to try them on. Signs in the store described everything as 'insta-fit,' so there were no sizes on anything.

The changing room had an ornate mirror and a plush bench upholstered in green velvet. I slipped off my old duds, grimy messes by this point, and set them on the bench. I put on the new outfit, and as advertised, they fit perfectly. I slipped the goggles over my eyes, and put my tool belt back on, fastening the whip to my side. Finally, I put the bowler back on and, smiling, admired the completed look. I was never much for vanity, but *damn* I looked sharp.

I left the changing room, my old clothes in my bag, and went to the front counter to pay. The gentleman behind was dressed impeccably in a black and green suit, and his long, droopy white mustache was groomed and curled up at the tips. He nodded approval at my new outfit, and a press of my thumb later, I was on my way to the parking lot and the *Galileo*.

Jeni and Trick were already waiting. I smiled as I approached, held out my arms and spun around once. Trick clapped and gave me a whistle. Jeni's eyes widened, and she laughed.

"You are one handsome archaeologist," she said, as she adjusted the collar on my vest.

"And you are the prettiest werewolf I've ever met," I replied. "I mean that."

Trick rolled his eyes. "You guys can get a room later, daylight's wasting."

We all climbed into the *Galileo*, which despite three humans, two monkeys, a bird, and an augmented pilot, wasn't crowded in the slightest.

As midday approached, the morning clouds had mostly burnt off, so I retracted the top to let in some sunlight. I had Lexi plot a course towards the Fremont area at the north end of the Aurora Bridge, where the Fremont troll used to be, and where all the recent mysterious construction had been happening.

We got underway, the ship lifting to cruising elevation and heading north, where the stadiums were already coming into view. Babiji had taken off to fly beside the ship, banking back and forth in the midday breeze.

Jeni sat next to me on the bench and surprised me by taking my hand, interlocking her fingers with mine. I said nothing, but gave her hand a little squeeze, and she smiled at me.

"Um... Jacob?" Trick asked. I looked over to see him staring down at Banjo. "What's Banjo wearing?"

I grinned. "I've been busy in the workshop. That's called 'the Scorpion.' Show him, Banjo."

Banjo leaped onto the dashboard and assumed the stance, curling his tail over his head. He fired a bolt behind the ship, the blue-white beam disappearing over the stadiums rapidly falling behind us. Jeni and Trick applauded.

"How much damage does it do?" Trick asked.

"Don't know, haven't shot anything yet," Banjo said. "But I'll let you know."

Nonchalantly, Lizzie hopped up on the dashboard beside Banjo. "I don't suppose you'd let me try it out," she said, examining the electrified spheres on his back.

Banjo feigned annoyance and looked at her askance. "No, you can't try out my new toy." Leaving Lizzie with a disgruntled look on her face, he hopped off the dashboard and went to my bag. He fished out the wrapped box, then set it on the dashboard next to Lizzie and hopped up behind it.

Jeni gave me a questioning look, but I just shrugged and smiled back, inclining my head towards the monkeys.

"What's this?" Lizzie asked, cocking her head at Banjo.

"Open it," he replied.

Lizzie undid the bow and took the lid off the box. When she saw what was inside her eyes lit up, and she pulled out the device and immediately put it on. Banjo helped affix the tubes and cone-shaped tip to her tail.

"How does it work?" she asked.

"It becomes second nature pretty quickly," Banjo said as demonstrated how to power up the device and use the trigger mechanism.

She assumed the scorpion stance and fired a bolt into the air behind the Galileo, laughing with excitement, and Banjo smiled at her.

"Well, what do you think?" he asked.

"It's amazing! Thank you, Banjo," she said. Then, the smile left her face, and her voice got quieter. "I...I'm sorry if I was rude to you earlier. All the monkeys I've known from the pet store weren't the most...polite."

"Aaaah, there's nothing to forgive," he said, and extended a paw. Lizzie took it and shook it, then Banjo got back on all fours and fired another shot out into the air.

"What's the cooldown between shots?" Lizzie asked, firing another bolt of her own.

"About ten seconds, from what I've seen," he answered. They spent the next few minutes laughing and shooting bolts into the air behind the ship. Sort of a crazy sight, all things considered, but I couldn't really blame them.

As I watched their revelry, a troubling idea came to me. "Banjo, if you're going to be on the offense, does that mean you can get hurt now as well?" I asked.

Banjo thought for a second, then shrugged. "I suppose," he said. "But we're not easy targets. I still have your backpack if worst comes to worst."

Ahead the Aurora Bridge came into view, spanning over the waters of Lake Union as it fed into the Fremont Cut, leading into Puget Sound. The bridge was heavy with wheeled midday traffic, and the water beneath us crowded with boats and kayaks enjoying the mild Seattle summer. I could just make out Gasworks Park to the northeast when a sudden pain erupted in my left shoulder. I winced and brought my hand to it, and it came away bloody.

"What the hell?" I swore. Another burst of pain spread across my lower back, and I reflexively crouched onto the floor of the cabin, wincing.

The rest of the crew followed my lead, the monkeys leaping off the dashboard as Jeni and Trick crouched beside me. I glanced at my wristband, noticing that the two hits—whatever they were—had drained over a third of my health. *Damn.*

I peeked over the rear dashboard and saw another airship, like mine, trailing us by about two hundred meters. Flipping down my goggles and zoom lens, I examined a ship similar in design to mine—a large oval canvas balloon supporting a cabin painted dark green.

"Jeni, can you hand me my rifle?" I asked. She retrieved it from the compartment by my chair and handed it to me. I used the scope in conjunction with my zoom lens, then swore.

Details of the ship jumped out now, the word '*Prospero*' visible in silver filigree against the olive-green hull. Above that, two familiar figures; the lady in the black and red dress and the man in the Cahill hat. The pompous role players.

Red flames surrounded the woman's hands, and the man was aiming a rifle similar to mine right at us. A slight red aura highlighted them both. I swore again.

"What is it?" Trick asked.

"The woman with the parasol and the guy we ran into at the menagerie," I said. "He's got a gun, and she looks like she's about to flame us with something."

"What the hell do they want from us?" Jeni asked.

"Apparently, our corpses, but we'll worry about their motives later." I said as I continued peering through the scope. I ordered Lexi to decrease speed by twenty percent, and she complied.

"Trick, summon Dexi and call in Babiji," I ordered, an odd calm settling over me as I began calling out commands. No way were we gonna get bested again. "And grab those eight metal orbs from my bag if you can. Jeni, put on your dart gauntlets. Banjo and Lizzie, be prepared to take stations on the corners. Lexi, hold our course. Wait for my signal."

Everyone did as ordered and the *Prospero* crept closer. Dexi appeared behind us with a pop.

"Trick, send Dexi to flame the ship and have Babiji grab one of those shrappers and follow her," I said.

"The metal balls? What do they do?"

"Shrapnel grenades. When they get there, the rest of us will open fire. Hit them with everything at once."

With a flap of her wings, Dexi took off towards the approaching ship, Babiji right behind her with a shrapper clutched in each of his talons. As soon as Dexi breathed her stream of flame, the monkeys hopped up on the dashboard, and we all opened fire.

The next few seconds were chaos. Babiji dropped his payload, which exploded in a flash of silver light and a piercing metallic *crack*, while Dexi seared the two players with repeated jets of flame. The man took aim at the animals and fired repeatedly, but they were both too nimble for him to get a bead on. The woman launched multiple fireballs at the two creatures but didn't fare any better.

"Fire!" I shouted, and the rest of us let loose.

My first shot hit the man in the arm, and the impact knocked his rifle from his hands. They were close enough to where I didn't need the scope to see the anguished expression on his face. The monkeys fired their beam volleys, the first few missing their marks as they got used to aiming, until their third shots struck the woman with a dual burst of blue light. Even from here, I could hear her scream.

On the bridge below, all those packed cars were oblivious to the firefight going on over their heads.

Babiji returned to grab another two shrappers, and set out to the approaching ship once again, this time dropping them into the ship's cabin right between the man and woman. They exploded just as another bullet from my rifle caught the man in the chest, and a volley of bolts from Jeni's gauntlet hit the woman, sticking in her arms and torso. Both attackers collapsed to the deck. Dexi and Biji returned to our ship, landing next to Trick.

I raised my goggles, the zoom no longer needed, Jeni and Trick following suit. The *Prospero* began to pass us, and as it did, the two attackers rose back into view.

I raised my rifle, preparing to fire, and then lowered it again.

Both the man and the woman were the dull, washed out shades of nipnicks.

Or of players who had died.

The man in the Cahill hat gave us a one-finger salute as the *Prospero* banked right and returned the way it had come.

CHAPTER TWENTY-SIX: GASWORKS AVENUE

We all sat back and caught our breath as the ship disappeared back into the downtown corridor. The battle had been painful, and it had been frightening, but now that it was over, I realized it had also been completely exhilarating. There was something about AR that I still couldn't put my finger on—maybe knowing I was in the real world, in an actual ship and surrounded by real people, fresh air, the outcome of contests determined by real-time decision-making and physical exertion and skill—but that skirmish had excited me in a way that no VR ever had.

"You okay?" Jeni asked, examining my wounds.

Two small holes now adorned my new vest and shirt where the man's bullets had hit. The pain had lessened to a constant throbbing ache, and Jeni lifted my shirt to apply a little Dwebble's to the bullet holes. It felt cool against the hotness of the angry wounds, and the effect was immediate as Jeni gently massaged it in. A glance at my wrist showed my HP filling rapidly, and I flexed the arm and shoulder for good measure.

"Good as new. Thanks," I said as I smiled at her. We held the glance for a moment. This whole waiting game was getting old.

"Who *are* those guys, anyway?" Trick asked, exasperated.

"I don't know. The Glitch said he had others working for him among the 300 in the alpha," I replied. "I'd say we found a couple. Or maybe after eavesdropping in the alley they just want to get to the troll first."

As we approached the north shore of Lake Union, I slowed the *Galileo* to a crawl, so we could get the lay of the land. The north end of the Aurora Bridge, where the troll statue used to sit, was to our left, the silhouette of the ancient Fremont Bridge behind it. Gasworks Park was in clear view just off to our right—the red amalgamation of giant pumps and storage tanks from the early 20th century that was later turned into a public park. It had originally been a coal gasification plant, producing coal gas for the stoves and streetlights in the early days of the city.

Spanning the entirety of the curved stretch of land between the park and the Aurora Bridge was a strip of grass and trees known as Gasworks Avenue. The remnants of the old Aurora Bridge had been buried there, and the park built on top. I could make out people milling about on the grass and paths below, riding bicycles, jogging, walking dogs and enjoying the view of the downtown skyline south across the lake. I couldn't make out clothing from up here, but I did see more top hats than I was used to. The bicycles ranged from old-fashioned penny-farthing models to multi-wheeled contraptions belching steam from tiny pipes extending upwards from the frames.

A row of condos, boutique restaurants, and coffee shops ran parallel to the one-kilometer strip of park, transformed now into a spectacle worthy of Jules Verne himself. Five tall Tesla towers stood evenly spaced behind the row of buildings, the first nearly at the base of the bridge and the last at the entrance to the park on the right. Bolts of blue and purple electricity danced from the huge coils of the towers to receptors on the building tops.

The buildings themselves were incredible to look at. Wide, sloping rooves with multi-hued shingles supported an assortment of spires and towers. Stained-glass windows decorated the fronts of many shops, and even from this distance, I could make out beautiful combinations of carved woodwork and intricate metalwork.

Airships of every color and shape imaginable floated overhead. Some of the airships utilized the sleek, elongated balloons like my own, while colorful, bulbous balloons supported others. I even saw one propelled by a series of bat-like metal and canvas wings that flapped lazily down either side of the cabin.

We touched down in the main parking lot for Gasworks Park proper, intending to walk the length of the strip to perhaps find an entrance to the underground construction area, or at least more information to help determine our next steps. Right now, all we had was a very general idea.

We weren't expecting to battle or be out for too long, so

I took a swig from my water bottle and left my backpack in the *Galileo*. But just in case, I shouldered my rifle, and holstered a couple of squirt potions on my belt. Jeni turned into her wolf and adjusted her spike-shooting gauntlet over her right paw. The monkeys each grabbed a potion sprinkler. Then we left the vehicle and headed towards Gasworks Avenue.

The sun was getting low in the west, partially concealed by a strip of darker clouds moving in from the ocean. Behind us to the east, the two moons were rising over the Cascades, both completely full.

"So, what's our plan, Captain?" Trick asked.

"I'm not entirely sure, but I'm nearly certain we're in the right area.," I said. "My intuition and research tell me the answer is right under our feet. Just gotta find an entrance."

We crossed the street to the row of shops and buildings, the three of us walking side by side while the two monkeys followed behind and Babiji circled lazily overhead. One of the first buildings we passed had a sign hanging over the door that read 'Bastard's Brews.' The smell of coffee drifted out, mingled with scents of cinnamon and nutmeg.

The street was crowded, as it always was in the summer, most of them washed-out nipnicks. While their colors were muted, their outfits certainly weren't. A woman nodded at us as we passed, dressed in a green tunic embroidered with gears and stars in gold thread, tucked into a pair of shorts which ended just a couple centimeters above high leather boots. She pushed something vaguely baby carriage-shaped, although it was constructed of brass and wood and seemed to be powered by a tiny steam engine. A slender smokestack rose from one corner and left a trail of steam behind.

We continued walking west. At one point I saw an NPC sticking out among the nipnicks, in vibrant colors and a top hat decorated with a ring of wooden stakes. He wore a monocle attached to an earring on his left ear, and he sported a thick black mustache, peppered with grey, and a curly black beard that tickled his rotund belly. His shirt was a bright red with puffy sleeves rolled up to his elbows. Instead of pants, he wore a black and red sarong. He stood beside a rolling cart, and I could see jewelry on the flat surface and necklaces dangling from display stands that surrounded it.

"Amulets!" he called as we approached. "Potions! Charms!" The dull nipnicks couldn't hear a thing, however. His eyes locked on us.

"Welcome, welcome!" he greeted us as we stopped by his cart. "You've found Mister Yudi's Travelling Trinket Shop. We have several nice items that can assist you on your journey." His eyes went to the dagger at my belt.

"Good sir, how can you expect to do any damage with that old butter knife?" Mister Yudi asked. He reached into a drawer and pulled out an ornate dagger, then handed it to me. Its hilt was wrapped in purple-dyed leather. At the push of a button, a silver gear at the base of the blade split down the middle, acting as cross-guards. I touched the blade's edge as gently as I could, and still a thin welling of red rose on my finger. The thing was bloody sharp.

"Enchanted, too, you see," said Yudi. "Stab someone with that, and the wound won't heal right away. It's called the Defiant Dagger of Bleeding. For you, good sir, just 1,500 netcoin, and I'll be taking a loss at that price," said Yudi.

Trick made a choking sound.

I haggled with the man for a good five minutes, but we eventually settled on an amount. With a press of my thumb I was 1,050 netcoin poorer, but the proud owner of a snazzy new dagger. I slid it into the sheath on my belt and thanked the man. I handed my old dagger to Trick. If he collected skewers, I was sure he'd appreciate an actual dagger.

"By the way, Yudi, we heard talk of an underground area around here," I said. "There's also rumor of a troll. Heard any gossip?"

"Unfortunately, I trade in merchandise, not rumors," he replied. "But for you, I'll keep my ears open." I thanked him again and we continued walking.

Aside from the merchant there wasn't another non-nipnick to be seen on the strip, and most of them didn't give us a second glance. I had to think for a second to remember what I was really wearing—jeans and a purple t-shirt featuring a cartoon crow downing a bottle of whiskey. Nothing too ostentatious, except for the goggles. No reason to look at us at all.

That was about to change.

A group of five short, hooded figures stepped out from an alley just ten meters ahead of us. They were clothed in brown cloaks, and all I could see peeking out from the hoods were golden-colored goggles on each and thin, pointy snouts jutting out beneath their eyewear. Crooked whiskers sprouted around them, and two curved yellow fangs hung beneath.

The lead creature raised an ornate pistol and leveled it at me. At the base of the barrel, two vials jutted out on either side. One was filled with a translucent blue liquid and the other an opaque milky goo. The other four brandished daggers or short swords.

Trick wasted no time summoning Shorty and Dexi, who gave a growl and a screech, respectively, as they popped into existence. I unfastened my whip and held it at the ready. My goggles were perched on my forehead; I wanted to slip them on, so I at least knew what level we were dealing with, but I had that weird pistol pointed at me. *Worth a try,* I decided, and raised my left hand towards my head.

It never got there.

The lead creature pulled the trigger, and a ball of white energy streaked out and hit me in my left shoulder, and my whole arm turned incredibly cold. The cold helped to numb the initial shock, but a layer of ice and frost inched across my bent arm, preventing me from moving it—anything from the shoulder down just wasn't responding to my commands.

My right hand, however, held the whip.

I struck out, catching the lead creature in its pistol hand and sending the weapon clattering to the ground behind it.

Twin bolts of blue-white energy sizzled from either side behind me and struck the leader in the chest. The scorpion monkeys must've assumed their stances, and a glance beside me showed both sprinklers deployed and tracking our movements.

"Tunnel Ratmen, level five!" shouted Jeni over the din, her goggles on. "The leader is level eight." She threw back her head and howled and charged towards the leader. When that fearsome cry filled the air, two of the ratmen in the rear took off back down the alley. A temporary effect, but it evened the odds for now.

"Jeni and I will concentrate on the leader!" I shouted, my left arm still bent uselessly in front of me. "Trick, send your minions at the other two."

Jeni reached the leader with three long strides and swiped a clawed paw into its face. The creature emitted a high-pitched wail of pain and circled behind, and I executed my cross-lash skill, lashing the whip four times. It ripped a large 'X' into its back, and thick red blood blossomed across its coarse robe.

I had no way of telling how much damage we were doing without my goggles, but fortunately Jeni seemed to read my mind. "He's at about seventy percent!" she shouted, as she swung repeatedly at the leader's face and torso.

Shorty had leaped on the back of one of the lower-level ratmen, digging in with her claws and biting repeatedly at any exposed part she could find. Dexi was a whirlwind of wings and flame, and the cloak of the other ratman smoldered. Both creatures emitted shrieks of anger and pain as they unsuccessfully stabbed and hacked at their attackers. The monkeys were firing their tail weapons at regular intervals, peppering whichever came closest with a barrage of energy bolts.

One of the ratmen spoke in a strange language and pointed to Trick, and the one being hounded by Dexi bolted towards Trick with surprising speed, its cloak still smoking. When the creature got within about two meters of Trick I lashed out with my whip, and the three blades skewered it right between the shoulder blades. I tried to yank it backwards, but the creature was too heavy. I did, however, stop it in its tracks, its frantically grabbing arms coming up with nothing but handfuls of air. Trick slipped his new dagger from under his robes, lunged at the beast and thrust upwards, burying it to the hilt in the soft part under the creature's chin, up into the brain. The ratman collapsed into a heap at Trick's feet, and he stepped on its head, giving me the leverage necessary to yank my whip free.

Jeni continued her onslaught on the leader, who was retaliating with a pair of short daggers. Both were bleeding freely, and Jeni appeared to be slowing down.

I lashed out, catching her attacker in the back of the head. It spun around and launched one of its daggers at me so fast I didn't have time to react. The blade embedded itself in my thigh.

Within the span of about five heartbeats, I knew something was wrong. My body felt sluggish, my skin cold and clammy, and my heart started pounding so hard my whole body reverberated. I looked at my wristband, still visible under the layer of frost that covered my useless arm, and saw the health orb less than half full, and dropping visibly. And the orb was no longer red. It was green.

"I think I've been poisoned," I said, and dropped to one knee, yanking the dagger out of my leg, growling in pain through clenched teeth.

The leader had turned its attention back to Jeni, while Trick's minions kept the other remaining ratman occupied.

"Yeah, I have too," Jeni said. "But I think you got a bigger dose. He just scratched me." She continued dancing around the leader, slashing whenever she saw an opening, but she was sweating and breathing heavy, and I was certain couldn't keep it up much longer.

"I've got you!" Trick shouted, and he threw open his cloak, revealing two holstered pistols on his hips. He drew the left one, adjusted a dial on the base, then drew the other and adjusted a dial there too. He raised them both and pointed one at each of us and each shot a thick stream of clear liquid. I took the majority of mine in the face, but unlike the healing potions, whatever this was absorbed into my skin instantly, leaving no trace. Right away I felt better, and a glance at my wrist showed my health orb had returned to red. I could also bend my arm again, and as I slowly straightened it, chunks of ice fell to the ground.

"Nice guns!" I called to Trick, returning my attention to the battle.

"Yeah, I like em. An engineer whipped them up for me. Squirting in style, now!"

Trick cast his *sloven* spell at the leader as Jeni continued her onslaught, and the creature's movements slowed to a crawl. The third ratman collapsed under the attacks of Trick's minions and lay in a heap on the ground, but the two that had fled earlier sprinted back out of the ally, and the minions engaged once again, assisted by a continued barrage of scorpion blasts from the monkeys.

"Twenty percent!" Jeni shouted. I lashed out with another cross lash, all four strokes ripping into the creature's back, adding to the mess of torn fabric and blood.

Jeni's eyes turned dark; finally, she had the creature where she wanted it. She struck out with both hands, her claws impaling it just below the sternum. With a wicked grin, she thrust her arms outwards, and the creature ripped open from neck to belly in an explosion of blood and innards. Intestines and flesh dangled from her claws as she breathed heavily, giving me a smile through blood-soaked fur.

"Holy..." Trick started, staring wide-eyed.

"I *like* this eviscerate thing," Jeni said.

The grin never left her face as she turned her attention to the final two enemies. Trick recalled his minions, which vanished with a pop, to let Jeni and I finish the job. The first was nearly dead already, its cloak smoking and deep scratch marks visible on its arms and snout. One crack in the face with my whip was all it took to finish the job.

Jeni rushed at the second one, but it cowered down, arms outstretched in a gesture of submission.

"Wait! Wait!" the creature pleaded in a squeaky, terrified voice.

Jeni pulled up short, and I went to stand at her left as Trick approached and took up position on her right. The three of us glared down at the pitiful creature, then took a second to look around us.

The sky was now in full twilight, streaks of orange clouds glowing against the western horizon, the twin moons now high over the mountains to the east. The ornate street lamps cast a comfortable orange glow, illuminating the nipnicks around us.

And there were a lot of them, dressed in their industrial finest, standing in a wide circle around us. Some of them were recording us on their phones. It struck me then how odd we must look—I remember how I felt when I had first seen Jameson flailing down the street

Wow, was that only four days ago?

I gave the crowd a little smile and a wave then turned my attention back to the rat-creature, which none of them could see.

"Give me one reason to keep you alive." I sneered at the creature.

"I know things, yes!" hissed the creature. "Yes! I can show you where the door is, yes! I can't open it, but I can show you." Its hood had fallen back, revealing a grotesque, vaguely human head—aside from the long, rat-like snout and teeth. Its goggles were plain circles of yellow metal with smoky black lenses, attached to a black strap.

"What door?" I asked, glaring at the thing.

"The door to the great underground, yes!" the creature said with a hopeful expression. "There is treasure! Treasure!"

"I highly doubt that there's just a pile of treasure lying around down there.".

"Oh, but there is, there is! Yes!" hissed the ratman. "But it is guarded, you see. But don't worry. I know the secrets, yes. I know how to deal with the troll!"

CHAPTER TWENTY-SEVEN: PERSUASION

The sun had fully set, the last hint of daylight receding from the west as we looted the corpses. I took the ice pistol—Jeni and Trick both told me to keep it, seeing as it took my left arm out of commission for most of the battle. I'd need to get a holster for it, so for now put it in my bag.

The leader also had a couple other interesting tidbits on him. We found a gem that Trick identified as a summoner's stone. It fit in the third socket on his gloves, the one that opened up at level eight, and we had no idea what it summoned. We also found a schematic for a 'mobile gadget base.' It looked like a tripod with its own power supply that could move contraptions around on its own. My thoughts immediately went to the sprinklers. I'd have to try to make a couple when I got back to the guild—the monkeys would certainly be grateful for it, especially in light of their new toys.

Jeni reverted to her human form, and thankfully the blood that had matted her fur disappeared.

I was still shocked by the brutality of her eviscerate spell. I'd seen my fair share of blood and guts in VR games, but seeing it in AR, on the streets of my city, hit me on a much deeper level. It had actually seemed like a living thing had *died*, ripped apart, right before my eyes.

Might need a bit of a break, once this quest was done.

The still living ratman was now tied up, Trick was leading him on a rope, like a dog on a leash. The rope was a product of the game, Trick explained, otherwise it wouldn't work on game-created creatures. I was glad to have him around—he had a better sense of what was possible and what wasn't in this augmented world.

After about ten minutes of listening to the creature whine, Trick also tore off part of his robe to use as a gag, and for this, we were all very grateful. The crowd around us had lost interest, most headed elsewhere after the sun had set anyway.

"Well lead on, ratman. Take us to this door," I said.

The cowering creature led us east, back the way we had come. He didn't appear to be in much of a hurry, but I didn't prod him. We were acutely aware that we might be being led into a trap, so cautiousness and a steady pace were just fine.

"Are we going to do this tonight?" Jeni asked.

"I just want to see where this door is," I said. "I think we're ahead of the game right now, at least until Hatman and the Witch get back to the alley and spread the word."

Jeni chuckled at the names I had spontaneously given the dastardly airship couple.

"I'd like to get at least one more level before we go in,

too," I said. "Those ratmen were hard, even for the three of us. Speaking of which…"

I turned around and saw Banjo walking with Lizzie, carrying on a muted conversation. Seemed to be warming up to one another. Jeni followed my gaze and gave one of those puckered-lip smiles reserved for babies and cute animals.

"Hey, Banjo!" I exclaimed, smiling. "Any chance of a level update?"

"Sure thing, Jakey," he said. "You're level five, of course. About three-quarters of the way to your next level. To be exact, you need 4,371 experience points."

Damn. The numbers sure are climbing.

Babiji and Lizzie reported in as well. Jeni had about 5,500 points to go while Trick had just over 7,000.

"How much XP did the ratmen get us, each?" I asked.

"The lackeys gave you each 450," Banjo said, "while the leader gave 825."

"Not bad, considering," Trick said. "I know a place where we can grind some level fives and sixes tomorrow. We should all have level six in time for lunch."

The ratman led us onward, then turned left down an alley between a tavern and a bookshop. A narrow staircase led to a basement-level door under the tavern. The ratman started making muffled sounds against the gag in his mouth, signaling that he wanted to speak. Trick, grimacing, reached into the creature's snout and removed the gag, holding it at arm's length before dropping it in a nearby dumpster.

"Here, in here!" it exclaimed in a rapid, squeaking voice. "This is the place you want to go! The entrance to the great underground is in here!"

I walked down the short flight of steps and examined the nondescript door. "This is the entrance?" I asked.

"No, this is a basement," the creature wheezed. "But the entrance, yes, is in here!"

I turned the knob, and the door opened, then looked over my shoulder back up the stairs. Nobody else in sight that I could see, but just to be safe, I had Trick order Babiji to perch on the corner of the tavern roof to act as lookout.

Blackness awaited us beyond the door, and we had no more night vision potions. Luckily Jeni still had her amulet of light, so she took the lead, and we proceeded inside. The glow from her amulet barely made it to the walls, which were nothing but featureless stone brick. The room smelled of dust and mold and had a few empty storage boxes in one corner. We walked once around the perimeter, finding nothing. No markings, no windows, and no doors of any kind aside from the one we walked in through. The hair on the back of my neck stood up.

I approached the pathetic creature on Trick's leash, drawing my new dagger as I did so. Grabbing him by the neck of his cloak, I pulled his face close to mine and pushed my blade to his throat. I accidentally pressed a little too hard, and a thin slit of blood welled up on the creature's neck.

"What is this?" I barked at the ratman. "Have you led us into a trap? If you've planned an ambush, we'll take care of them like we did your other friends, but I promise you, you'll be the first to die."

"No, no, good sir!" the creature pleaded. "There was a door here! A special door, a pretty door! But when I was here, there was no ground, no. Well, there was a ground, but not like this. The ground was low, down low, and the door," the creature pointed, "was right over there!"

I looked at where the creature pointed, then let him go with a shove. We approached the specified section of wall, and the top of stone arch could just be made out over the dirt. *A door?* I dug at the ground with my fingers, which was much looser than I expected it to be, confirming my suspicions.

Most basements with dirt floors were very hard packed; this was soft and loamy. The fact that I was standing on it also told me it was real dirt, leading me to believe that the creature had led us to the right place. I didn't want to let the beast know that, however.

I motioned for the crew to follow me out of the basement, and we climbed the stairs back into the alley, the ratman in tow.

"Trick, cut him free. His information is useless," I said.

Trick looked at me askance but did as I asked without questioning me. The creature bolted out of the alley without a word.

"Why'd you do that?" Jeni asked, folding her arms. "He said he knew how to get by the troll."

"The ground in there is new, and it's real. Bringing us

here is all I really wanted him for," I explained. "Plus, his voice was too annoying to handle anymore."

Jeni relaxed, and her arms dropped to her sides. "Can't argue with that."

"So, what's the plan now?" Trick asked.

"The entrance to the underground is in there, buried in the dirt," I said. "It's getting late, but tomorrow, we get an early start, go to that place you mentioned and grind to level six. Then we head back to the alley and hit the guilds—I want to see if I can incorporate this new schematic into the sprinklers, so the monkeys are a bit freer to act. Then we grab some lunch and come back here," I peeked at the doorway, "with shovels."

"Great," said Trick, rolling his eyes. "An RPG with thrilling menial labor action."

I chuckled. "Well, I'm the archaeologist. I can do it. You can sit on the side and bring me drinks if that's more your thing."

Trick held his hands out, waving passively. "No, I'll help, I'll help."

We began the trek back to the *Galileo,* exhausted from the day's exertion. Already I felt like I was starting to get into better shape, which was nice. Jeni offered me her water bottle, and I took a gulp from it, as I had left mine with my bag back in the car.

We reached the parking lot and Jeni logged out, Trick and I following her lead. I was getting reluctant to leave the game now, to replace the fantastical with the mundane. It was something I'd have to mention in my letter to Iggy. *Oh crap, the letter! I really have to write that tonight.*

I turned back to look at the avenue again, this time in reality. It was as it always had been: the string of shops now closed except for a couple of the taverns and restaurants. The vehicles were their normal selves again. Well, except for mine, of course. The doors of the shuttlecraft stood open, and we climbed inside, Banjo hopping on the dashboard.

"I'm going to have to look into getting a biosynth too," Jeni said. "I wonder if they'll be able to transfer Lizzie's personality over."

"I'm sure they'll be able to," I said. "Iggy told me that biosynths are easy enough to program."

At my command, the doors closed, the roof opened and retracted into the frame, and the *Galileo* rose into the air, banking south towards the nighttime city lights. Even without the turrets and airships, the skyline *was* still beautiful at night. I ordered the computer to set a course for Trick's apartment, where it arrived five minutes later. We said our goodbyes and Trick hopped out.

We ascended once again, but I hesitated before putting in the coordinates for Jeni's place. I stood up. My heart started to race, and I felt as if my throat were closing up.

"Hey, um, Jeni," I stammered. "You want to... come by my place and play some video games or something? We could play *Turtles in Time,* or *Smash Brothers*. I also have—"

I didn't get to finish the sentence. Jeni reached my side in one swift movement, threw her arms around me, and kissed me. Fiercely.

It wasn't a gentle kiss. It was a kiss of pent-up yearning,

and I responded in kind. Her tongue danced with mine, and I lost track of how much time passed before she finally pulled away, looking up at me with bright eyes and an affectionate smirk.

She wiped a finger at the edge of her lips, and looked at the ground, smiling with embarrassment, before looking up at me again through half-lidded eyes. "Sorry," she said, "but I've been wanting to—"

It was my turn to cut her off. The second kiss was every bit as wild as the first. I sat down on the side bench and pulled her with me, so she straddled my lap. The kiss continued until my hands started to roam, one hand under her shirt and up the smooth skin of her back.

She put a hand on my chest and pushed backwards.

"Jacob, I'm not ready... to go too much further," she said softly. "That's okay, isn't it? I just really wanted... to kiss you right then."

Gaaaaaaaaaaahhhhhh why, why, why. No, no, no. "I understand," I said aloud, and smiled. "It's no problem. You're... a good kisser."

She gave me a wide grin. "You're not so bad yourself," she said, then leaned in for another kiss, this time soft and lingering. I was just fine with that kind too. "But we have an early start tomorrow. I should probably get home."

I tried to think of something to say, but my brain felt like it had short-circuited, so I just nodded and set the course for her apartment. We rode the rest of the way hand in hand, my heart thumping like I was in junior high. I don't know how she could hold my hand, scarred as it was and covered in sweat, probably from all the adrenaline coursing through me.

"Jacob," she said softly. "What happened to your hand?" She stroked my burned thumb with hers.

More blood rushed to my face. I didn't want to tell her everything, yet. I was terrified of how she would react.

"A fire, a few years ago," was all I offered. Jeni read my expression and decided not to press further. Instead, she brought the hand to her lips and kissed it softly.

"There," she said. "All better." She gave me a warm smile that did nothing to lessen the guilt and fear that had welled up in me. By the time we got to her place, however, it had subsided, replaced with the feelings I had for this woman.

We landed on the roof of her apartment, and our goodbyes were brief but did include one more kiss for the road. I waited until she went inside to take off, and when I hit cruising altitude I stood up and bellowed a loud *"Woohooooooo!"* to help relieve the built-up anxiety. Banjo woke up and leaped about a meter into the air before giving me a dirty look and knuckle-walking to the rear of the cabin.

"Sorry, bud," I said and gave a soft chuckle.

I landed on the roof of my place, then rode the elevator down to my floor. The new security system recognized me and opened up, and Lexi greeted me from one of the living room televisions. All that battling, not to mention the kissing, had left me famished, so I went to the kitchenette, made a snack, and grabbed a soda to wash it down before proceeding to the gaming area.

After setting my goggles on the coffee table, I dimmed the lights and grabbed a copy of Dragon Quest XX for the Playstation Prime and popped it in, opting to play on the wide screen. This was one of the only Dragon Quests I hadn't completed, and I soon lost myself grinding slimes and drakees.

I didn't remember falling asleep, but when I awoke the room was nearly pitch black—I could barely make out some street lights casting light through the darkened windows, the ornate curl of the Edison light glowing within the steel cage outside my window.

I blinked and sat up. I had taken off my goggles. Why were there Edison lights?

"Hello, Jacob," a malevolent voice spat from behind me.

I had never in all my life, aside from movies, heard a voice I would describe as 'filled with hatred.' Until that moment.

I spun around as I stood up. There, standing in a spotlight in the dark room, was Jameson.

He paced slowly back and forth for a few seconds, seeming to revel in my uncertainty. The column of white light followed him as he walked, giving the act a theatrical flair, accentuated by the way he reflexively twirled one of the ends of his mustache as he studied me.

He must have logged me in as I slept. I reached up to power the goggles off and end his little stage show, but nothing was there. They weren't on my head. I was wearing my clothes, the real clothes I had put on that morning, and when I touched my head, I felt only hair—no bowler hat.

"Confused?" asked Jameson. "I would be. After all, I got kicked out of the game, right?"

The spotlight on him turned a deep red, giving him an even more sinister appearance. He cackled. "Oh, Jacob, my boy, you really don't have any idea what you've gotten yourself into, do you?"

"I know that you're spiteful, you seem to have a personal vendetta against Iggy, and you're one of the most insecure people I ever met," I growled at him. "Get out of here! Just—go find something else to do. I'm sure there's a small animal you'd rather be torturing." Despite my brave words, I had to fight to keep my hands from shaking, and a tremor from my voice. Inexplicable terror. A deep certainty that something was seriously *wrong* here, tried to overpower all my other senses. *Keep it together, Jacob.*

"Oh, no, Jacob, animals just won't do," he sneered. "I'll even do you a favor and fix that disgusting hand for you."

The next instant, it felt like lances of white-hot fire were shooting up my hand to my shoulder. I looked at my hand, horrified, as one by one the fingernails started to peel backward, exposing the bloody collagen underneath. And not dulled pain, but the real thing, far more agonizing than anything I'd ever felt.

A moment later, and I would have given anything to have that pain back. As I stared at my bloody hand, the thick, scarred skin started to peel back from the tips of my fingers and rolled down their lengths like a sock on an ankle. I collapsed to my knees between the sofa and coffee table, then fell over onto my side, curling into a fetal position as I clutched my destroyed hand in front of my face.

"Exit!" I screamed. "Log out! Computer!" I continued shrieking after that, no longer capable of words, my whole body trembling, unable to come to terms with the ruin inflicted on it.

From my spot on the ground, through my tears, I saw the red spotlight move around the sofa, then Jameson leaned down to examine me, slowly shaking his head.

"Ah, Jacob, how I hate to see you like this. Man up!" he shouted, and suddenly, blessedly, the pain stopped.

I blinked tears from my eyes and looked at my hand, flexing the fingers. They were whole and burn-scarred once more—everything where it was supposed to be. My heart still pounded in my ears, and I was breathing so fast I thought I might hyperventilate, but I somehow forced myself into a state of calm.

I got to my knees, used the sofa to pull myself up, then collapsed into the corner of it.

"Why... why are you doing this?" I panted.

"Well, Jacob," he said, his spotlight changing into a golden one. "I want your interests to mirror my interests. I want you to get that gear, and the next two, and I want you to be... receptive to my suggestions when you gain control of the alley."

"Go to hell," I spat.

"Wrong answer, Jake," Jameson said. "And I won't stop at you. I know about your parents in Massachusetts. Your poor sister."

I lunged towards him, but he crooked a finger at me,

and my body stopped listening to me, crumpling back to the floor.

The pain that followed was all-consuming and so intense I passed out within seconds.

When I awoke, the sun was up. Almost instantly everything that had happened came flooding back. Instinctively, I backed into the corner of my sofa, wildly swinging my head around, searching. No sign of Jameson anywhere. My vision still wasn't clear, but I could make out two figures sitting in my kitchenette.

"He's awake," I heard one of the figures say, a female. It wasn't Jeni.

The figures approached, and their outlines gradually formed into two recognizable characters.

Al and Alex.

"Where... where's Jameson?" I asked, still not fully aware of my surroundings. I glanced at the coffee table and saw my goggles sitting there, but not in the spot where I remembered putting them.

"He was gone by the time we got here," Al said. "We saw your sudden jump in your vitals and got here as soon as we could, but we were too late."

"But he's in the game again! He can..." I began but couldn't put into words exactly what I had seen or what he did to me.

"We've talked to Iggy. He's not in the game, but we think he's manipulating the game mechanics somehow. Iggy's got Quirk working on it, and he thinks she's found a lead," Alex explained.

This did little to relieve my fear and anger. "He... hurt me. He tortured me," I said softly. "The guy is a madman. And how the hell did he get in here? You told me this place was a fortress."

Al hung his head, the personal failure apparent on his face. "Jacob, I'm sorry you had to go through that. In a nutshell, he tricked the system into thinking he was you, and that you weren't here. We've fixed the vulnerability—it's not one that should have existed in the first place. Jameson is crafty, he has help, and he swings a mean stick."

I touched my temple, recalling all the pain this bastard had put me through.

Alex approached Al from behind and put her hand on his broad shoulder. "But don't worry, Jacob. Quirk has given us a bigger stick."

CHAPTER TWENTY-EIGHT: THE BIGGER STICK

The analog clock on the wall told me it was just after 7:30 in the morning. Al had taken the liberty of making coffee, and I couldn't find the words to express my appreciation. I grabbed a cup, and we all sat down at the table in the kitchenette. The day appeared cloudless, at least through my westward-facing windows, but I opted to keep my window opacity at about 75 percent. I wasn't ready for the sun.

I couldn't shake the memories of the torture from the night before, but at least there was no lingering pain or discomfort. Still, every time I looked at my hand, I expected to see the cartilage and muscle fiber exposed beneath peeling skin. Banjo kept looking at me with a worried expression on his face.

"How did he do that? What did he use?" I asked, my voice still gravelly from screaming. I took a sip of the hot black coffee.

"Our information is incomplete," said Al, running a hand over his bald head. "But from what we understand,

Blatman and Tardigrade Technologies have created another AI using the same adaptive neural circuitry that Quirk does, but at a much smaller scale. We think he managed to steal a bunch of the source code, either while he was there or through more nefarious means after his departure. The AI is small, an infant if you will, but even a baby AI is a force to be reckoned with. It will only get smarter as it matures."

"He's calling it 'Quark,' but I'm not sure what it stands for," offered Alex. "It gives him access to Panmachina, to an extent, but it doesn't give him access to the game mechanics. From what I understand, the Glitch doesn't have access to the raw computational power that brought Quirk to life—we think Quark is confined to just a handful of quantum processors, while Quirk draws from the power of more than five hundred, taking up the entire 87th floor."

"In other words," Al continued for her, "it's like a squirrel going up against a bear. Quark can't get in through brute force, but it's nimble enough where it can jump around and change in game parameters. Quirk has a whole world to maintain. All Quark has to do is throw a wrench into the gears where it can."

"So, Quark gave Jameson these... powers?" I asked.

"In a nutshell, yes," Alex answered. "Jameson logged you into *his* game while you were asleep. Then, he ran whatever program he was given. I don't think he's all-powerful, *per se,* but he can do certain things. Like locally manipulate what you see, as well as feel."

"You mentioned 'a bigger stick,'" I said. "What did you mean?"

Alex smiled, and she had a beautiful smile, one that naturally put me at ease, despite the events of last night. "Put on your goggles, and I'll show you," she said.

I looked across the room to where my goggles were sitting on the coffee table. "Are you sure it's safe?" I asked. "The program the Glitch wanted to install..."

Al shook his head. "Your goggles have been updated, remember? Any possible loopholes or backdoors have been contained and protecting the integrity of the goggles has become one of Quirk's top priorities."

A wave of anger swept over me, quickly replaced with a calm dread. "You said the security here was impenetrable as well," I said, my voice quiet, haunted. I stared at my hands, recalling the flayed flesh, the pain. This stuff was all way above my comprehension. "And how was he able to make me believe I was being tortured, if I wasn't wearing my goggles? You said he logged me into *his* game?"

"It was a projection. Think of Jameson and Quark as their own, portable game. If you're within a certain radius of him, probably around ten meters, he can make you see what he wants you to see and feel what he wants you to feel," Al said. "He probably attached a device to you, we're not sure. In essence, it was a hallucination."

"But Jameson was definitely here, in my unit?"

I stood up and retrieved my goggles. Then I put them on and logged in, seeing no change aside from Al and Alex's in-game clothing suddenly appearing.

"So, let's see what you got," I said.

"We got," said Al with a smirk, "what you need." He

waved his hand through the air, like Obi-Wan trying to convince me that those other droids are the ones I want.

A sudden roar and a cacophony of mechanical clanking made me spin around, my heart in my throat. There, stretching from floor to the ceiling nearly seven meters overhead, was a giant clockwork dragon. A thick membrane of green leather covered its belly and the internal workings beneath. Its elbows and knees joints were connected by accordion-sheathes, and a large, spiraling ivory horn jutting from its brass forehead. The rest of its body was encased in burnished brass, and its mouth was crammed with wicked-looking metal teeth as long as my index finger.

It swiveled its head to observe me, then brought it down slowly, nudging my chest with its nose. Hesitantly, I gave it a little pat on the snout.

Al laughed, and I turned to look at him. "He likes you," Al said, and with another wave of his hand, the dragon disappeared.

"My turn!" Alex exclaimed, then clapped her hands twice. The entire room morphed into a cave, including stalactites dripping water from the ceiling onto shorter stalagmites below. Even a pool of lava bubbled where my couch used to be. All the fixtures and furniture were gone, apparently masked by the program. I was sure, however, that if I tried to walk through the spot my coffee table was, I'd bang my leg on it.

Before I could examine any further, what sounded like hundreds of metal feet clattered on the stone floor. Then, from small openings in the cave walls emerged a torrent of tiny metal... robots? Hundreds of bipedal warriors, wielding small spears and shields. They almost looked like toys, except for their glowing red eyes and hateful scowls. More continued to pour out of the cracks, and soon a circle of them surrounded me, eight to ten deep, all pointing spears and muttering high-pitched orders in a language I didn't understand.

Alex clapped her hands again, and the tableau disappeared.

"Wow," I said, my voice flat. The wonders of AR had lost a little bit of their luster for me, after the events of last night. "So, you guys have what... creative access?"

"A bit, yes," Al said. "The thing is, the stuff we can create can only counter any manifestations that Jameson brings to the table, whether that be robot scorpions or the illusion of torture. If he forces himself into the game like that again, we can make *him* feel pain. And Quirk, well we're hoping she can trap him here, allowing us to have our way with him. Or lock him out permanently. She knows how he got in, she just has to figure out what she's going to do about it."

Alex nodded in agreement. "Outside of the game, though, we might need to take more... drastic measures." She opened her jacket, revealing a black pistol strapped to her chest. My eyebrows shot up.

"It fires rubber bullets. If you get shot with this, you're not getting up by yourself," she explained.

Part of me wished it was a real gun, just for a moment.

"Okay, so what's the plan?" I asked.

"You guys just play the game as normal, do whatever you were going to do today," said Al. "But we're going to tag along. We won't be part of your party, of course, but we'll have your back if anything unexpected happens."

Alex chuckled. "Just don't expect us to save your ass if you get jumped by a gang of clockwork zombies or something. Anything generated by the game itself is yours alone to deal with."

I nodded, then dialed Jeni and Trick to inform them about everything that had happened, and about our two new bodyguards. I left out the part about the torture—didn't want to terrify or worry them *too* much—but I did let them know that Jameson did have the power to affect the augmented reality around him.

Trick gave us the location to meet for our level grind, and, after a quick shower and breakfast, the Alexes and I were on our way to meet the rest of the crew at Lincoln Park, south of Alki.

Jeni and Trick were already there when we arrived, and it dawned on me neither had met the Alexes yet. I made the introductions, and we prepared for a morning of grinding. Both seemed relieved for the added security.

Ever since the fire, I had acquired the ability to seal away emotional trauma. I had gotten good at burying it. I was sure it would all spill to the surface one day, but for now, I couldn't let it. Jameson's attacks had made this personal, and if I sat at home reflecting on my torture, then he had won. He was *not* going to win. For my sake and the sake of my friends, I put on my happy face.

It was a sunny day in the park, and for good luck's sake, Jeni suggested we take a group photo. She had purchased a camera in the alley, and she said it could take pictures in game and send them to a real-world account. She pulled what looked like an antique out of her bag—a thick box of brass and wood, with accordion bellows with a screw-off lens at the end. It had a wireless shutter trigger, however, so she set it on a bench between the sun and our group. We squeezed together and lined up—the Alexes, Jeni, myself, and Trick, with Dexi and Biji hovering over the group and Shorty and the monkeys posing in front. On Jeni's signal, we all said some variant of the word 'cheese.' I said 'sneeze,' a habit I had since I was a kid.

She snapped the picture and sent us each a copy.

We spent the next three hours attacking steam demons and dodging dive-bombing clockwork owls, but I finally hit level six, followed shortly after by Jeni and Trick. I gained a point across all stats, and two to my stamina, in addition to an increase in my skewer skill, while Jeni picked up an extra point to her slash and Trick got an antidote spell. All in all, a profitable level-up.

The Alexes stood by, scanning the horizon, but didn't really have much to do aside from crossing their arms and looking mean. According to them, they could sense Jameson if he was accessing the game, but they hadn't had a blip on their radar all morning.

We were back at the alley before lunch, where I spent my point on upgrading the monkeys' scorpion augments and built two of the mobile bases for the squirters. I trained them both on me, and they followed me around like little spiders. Jeni put another point in her eviscerate skill, which allowed her to use it when her opponent was at eighteen percent or less. Trick said he had spent his guild point on the cover skill, allowing his minions to rush into his defense and pull aggro should he get attacked.

We hit that delightful satay stand to grab some lunch before heading out again. Tole had upped his game even further, and now had a full brass oven-slash-grill that rolled satay out on a little conveyor, while belching fragrant puffs of steam and smoke from the top. His umbrella spun slowly, and a sign reading 'Tole's Authentic Chicken Satay' adorned the front of the cart in nixie light lettering. A couple new buckles and gears adorned his top hat, and his mustache was waxed and curled. The cart had a constant line of customers about five long. *Good for him.*

Once I got to the front of the line, he greeted me. "Ah, hello, Mister! It is good to see you again."

"Hi, uh, Mister Tole," I said. "Can I get five orders of satay and fried rice please?"

"Sure thing, but please, no Mister, but my name is pronounced '*Toll-Ay.*'"

"Sorry, Tole," I said, trying to mimic the way he said it. "My name's Jacob." I figured I was going to be ordering from this guy enough where it might pay to be on a first-name basis.

He handed me five packets wrapped in brown paper, and we took them to the only open table and sat down to eat.

"So, are we ready?" asked Trick, between mouthfuls of

chicken.

"Well, we still need to get a couple of shovels," I said softly.

"A step ahead of you. Got them this morning at the hardware store by my apartment," said Jeni in a hushed tone.

Alex raised her eyebrows. "Why do you need shovels?"

I looked around at the crowd, then looked at Alex, subtly putting my finger to my lips and glaring at her. She seemed to get the message immediately and made a lip-zipping motion. I smirked.

"Well, it seems like we're ready unless you guys wanted one more level," said Jeni.

"Nah, I think we'll be okay," I said. "I have no idea what we're going to find down there, but we're about as prepared as we're going to get. Trick reloaded on potions, he's got an antidote spell now, and I have my two spider sprinklers. The monkeys are locked and loaded; you seem to like ripping things open. I even found a holster at the guild for my freeze ray."

"Freeze ray?" Jeni asked, cocking an eyebrow.

"Yeah, it sounds like bad sci-fi. But it was better than my alternative," I said.

They both looked at me silently.

"Nope. Not going to tell you. Just call it a freeze ray. It's a freeze ray. It freezes things," I said. Jeni laughed, and I chuckled despite myself.

"Tell us!" demanded Jeni. "What was it? Blast-o-cold? Snowjobber?"

I let my silence speak for me, and we finished the rest of the meal in good spirits. Soon, we were in the *Galileo,* heading back towards Gasworks Avenue.

I didn't feel pressured to hurry; we didn't think anybody had found out where this area was yet. The clue on the table had been incredibly easy to miss—I had just gotten lucky. But I could be wrong.

The day was beautiful and hot, and I had the top down as we coasted across Lake Union, the Alexes following us in their car—which had transformed into quite a lethal looking vehicle. A black cabin with chrome piping and fittings, suspended beneath a dark grey, oval canvas balloon. The words *"Alexecution"* were stenciled in military-style across the front of it. I wondered if they did that or if it was Quirk's attempt at humor.

The monkeys stood side by side on the dashboard. Shorty curled up and took a nap next to them. Dexi and Babiji darted in and out of the air currents, enjoying the moment as much as we were.

It seemed too nice a day to be going underground, digging a hole, and fighting unknown enemies under the watchful eye of two government-trained bodyguards, because someone might by hiding in the shadows to torture me. But, it was what it was. I wanted to find the gear, and take a good, long break from this game. At least a whole day. Maybe two.

I looked over at Jeni, who looked back at me affectionately. If she had any feelings of discomfort from the activities of the night before, she wasn't showing it. The word 'girlfriend' crossed my mind, but I shoved it aside—temporarily.

Trick sat quietly, looking out the window at the view. He hadn't spoken much all day, which was not like him.

Before landing, I wanted to get an unobstructed view of the park and the avenue, so we circled the area a couple of times just to see what we could see. I wanted to check if there were other players there—just in case. We circled the park once, my info-lens bringing up stats on every person down there. The majority were nipnicks, although I could make out a few NPCs. Most appeared to be vendors, including the one who had sold me the dagger.

On our second pass, however, I did see four players, fighting on the side of the central hill in Gasworks Park. After zooming in, I even recognized two of them— Mario and the beastmaster, the two guys we'd seen on the beach fighting crabs when we were just starting this whole business. It seemed like ages ago, but really it had only been four days. They were accompanied by a summoner and an Arborbound. The summoner also had a bobcat, but no other creature I could see. The Arborbound stood back from the others, peppering the creatures they fought with arrows whenever they appeared.

All four were cloaked in a red aura, but I wasn't about to take pot shots from an airship at them. Not if they didn't shoot at me first. My info-lens told me they were fighting something called 'diggerocks' - creatures which would apparently bury into the ground, then launch themselves at whoever got too close. The beastmaster still had his sapphire crab companion from the beach, although it looked bigger than I remembered it.

Were they just here grinding out XP, or had they learned about the area's secret?

We landed in the same lot we had the night before, but today the place was crowded. It was one of the first sweltering days we'd had all summer, and sunbathers mobbed the place, along with cyclists, mothers pushing babies, and people with kites and frisbees. Quirk, however, transformed every single one of them, and the area took on the air of a renaissance fair. Outfits of every kind, from dresses and simple suits, to elaborate contraptions of leather, straps, gears, embroidery—the place was a riot for the senses. I could have spent the whole day at the park just people watching.

We unloaded the shovels—they were the folding kind, perfect for the digging we would be doing. They fit into a small sack Trick flung over his shoulder, along with his backpack over the other. Jeni and I grabbed our packs as well, and I tied my rifle to the back of mine. We were encumbered, yes, but not overly so. I could still swing my whip efficiently, although I probably couldn't outrun much. My new Dagger of Bleeding was tucked into the right side of my belt, and my pistol holstered on my left hip.

Jeni wolfed out, then put on her dart gauntlet. We were ready.

We walked across the parking lot and crossed the street to the sidewalk fronting the row of shops. Nobody paid us much attention today, aside from the occasional glance or comment on our goggles. Just five weirdos on our way to a convention or something. We reached the mouth of the alley next to the tavern, and after looking around to make sure no one was watching, headed towards the basement door. Babiji flew up to a spot on the roof to act as a lookout. We descended the steps, opened the door and stepped inside.

We had come prepared this time, including a few vials of the night vision potion Trick had brought. Far more effective than Jeni's amulet.

After applying it, we stared around the room in disbelief. Trick dropped the bag of shovels he'd been lugging around. We wouldn't need it.

Someone had already dug out the door.

CHAPTER TWENTY-NINE: UNDERGROUND

I approached the hole that led down to the door, and planting my hands on the edge for support, hopped down inside. The hole was about a meter and a half deep, matching the door's height. The door was actually a double door, split down the middle and judging from the absence of hinges on the outside, it opened inward. I pushed, but to no effect. There was no doorknob.

Jeni hopped down beside me, a tight fit. I didn't mind.

"Do you think somebody already went inside?" she asked.

"No way of telling," I said. "but they would have had to figure out a way to open it. There's no knob, no latch, no nothing."

The door had an arched frame of dark stone and was carved with a frieze of airships floating over factories and houses, gears adorning the negative spaces. Something in one of the gears caught my eye. In the space between the spokes at the top, there was a letter 'A.' It was the same color as the rest of the carving, and very easy to miss. Score another point for my archaeological perception.

On a hunch, I grabbed the gear between thumb and forefinger and turned it. Some hidden mechanism inside clicked, and the 'A' turned into a 'B.' Jeni's eyebrows shot up, and she scratched her furry head. After examining the entire surface, I found more of the gears, each with its own letter.

"Well, it's obviously a code," Jeni said.

Trick and the Alexes were peering down into the hole, hands on their knees.

The first word I thought of was the reason we were trying to get in—'TROLL'. I turned each of the gears, from top to bottom, so that the appropriate letters appeared between the top spokes of each gear. Once the final 'L' clicked into place, I took a step back and pushed.

Nothing happened. I furrowed my brow in a mixture of disappointment, and looked again, concentrating.

"Try bottom to top," Trick suggested from the edge of the hole.

I followed his suggestion and pushed the door again, but it remained firmly shut.

Over the next thirty minutes, I tried every word I could think of. Gears. Steam. Alley. Nothing worked. I backed away from it for a breath, leaned back against the dirt in the edge of the hole.

"What about—" Trick began, then stopped, mumbling to himself. It was the first time I'd remembered hearing him speak that day.

Alex looked like she wanted to suggest something, but

bit her tongue, as she was not officially part of the group.

"*Bruse!*" exclaimed Jeni.

It sounded as good an idea as any other, so I tried it. Once the final 'E' clicked into place at the bottom of the door, a grinding of machinery sounded from inside the walls, and the door swung inward. Jeni clapped her hands together and let out a *whoop* of victory.

The space revealed beyond the door was so dark that, even with our night vision potions, I couldn't make out any features. I took a few tentative steps inside, Jeni right on my heels. Trick and the rest of the gang jumped down behind us. Babiji had returned from his perch on the roof with nothing to report.

Once we were all inside, the door closed behind us of its own accord.

"Damn," I swore.

"What?" asked Jeni

"The door shut. That means there might already be someone in here," I said.

I pulled the two spider sprinklers from my pack, both of them filled with Dwebble's goo. I set one to focus on Jeni, and the other on me, and then adjusted them to go off when either of us dropped below thirty percent health. They skittered off to either side of our party, falling a little bit behind, and matched our pace with silent precision. We also still had our rings, which would heal us when we got near death.

As our eyes adjusted to the darkness, the effect of the potions began to increase. We were in a tunnel, with featureless dirt walls held up by wooden rafters and beams. The tunnel was large. We had a good meter of clearance over our heads, and we could easily all walk side by side. It smelled earthy and moist, like a garden after a rain, but mixed with a chemical smell I couldn't identify. The shaft curved to the left out of sight. If it kept going that direction, it would reach the grassy strip separating the avenue from the lake. Right where I wanted to be.

"Can you send Babiji up ahead, do a little reconnaissance for us?" I asked Trick.

"You can ask me, you know," replied the bird, and took off from Trick's shoulder, down the tunnel and out of sight.

Even with my archaeologist's perception, nothing stood out in our current area, so we very slowly started to creep down the tunnel after the bird.

Ten minutes later, we'd progressed maybe a whole hundred meters into the tunnel, which had straightened out now, heading west. At least I thought it was west; nobody had brought a compass. Neither of the monkeys had spoken a word since we got in here, but they kept their hands on their trigger switches. The globes on their backs cast flickering white shadows against the dark dirt walls.

A metallic rustling sound further ahead drifted down the tunnel, and my hand instinctively went to my whip, but it was just Babiji returning from his scouting mission.

"I'd be careful," squawked the bird. "About fifty meters ahead, corpses start to appear. Robotic rodents of some kind, and their teeth are dangerously sharp. I didn't see any live ones. I counted thirty-five corpses before I gave up and headed back."

"Damn. Damn!" I swore. "Somebody else is down here. We should've pushed through last night."

I unclipped the whip from my belt and held it coiled loosely in my hand. Trick had Shorty and Dexi close by his side, and the fur on the back of Jeni's neck was standing up. The Alexes fell back maybe twenty meters— they wouldn't get involved in the game in any way. They were here for Jameson, or if we were really unlucky, for the Glitch.

We continued in silence, cautious, one tentative step placed after the other. About three minutes later we saw the first corpse. It despawned, disappearing in front of our eyes, as well as a couple more farther down the hall.

"Well that's the first time I've seen something despawning in this game," said Jeni. "Babiji saw these corpses about twenty minutes ago, so I'm going to guess about a thirty-minute despawn time."

"Sounds about right to me," I nodded. "It also means whoever's down here is about thirty minutes ahead of us."

The wooden beams and supports that had held the cave up until now were slowly being replaced with rusted beams of metal. They appeared to be girders—and I felt relief. These were the remains of the old bridge. I was sure if I took my goggles off, the beams would still be there. *But I wouldn't be able to see them,* I thought, frowning. *It would be pitch black without the augmentation.*

Ahead, jutting out of the right wall, I saw the twisted remains of a green road sign, reading '*Woodland Park Zoo, Next Exit.*'

We continued on, creeping like any other tunnel creature, cautious and quiet so we'd be able to hear any disturbances. If I had to guess, I would've estimated we were at least halfway to the base of the new Aurora Bridge, when we were presented with a sudden conundrum. For the first time, the tunnel forked.

Trick didn't have to be asked. "Babiji! Fly down the left tunnel and see what you can see."

Babiji took off once again, disappearing into the blackness. Jeni, Trick and I sat down for a quick rest, forming a close circle, while Al and Alex took up posts on opposite walls. We got some water and food from our packs. I peeled a banana and gave a bit to Banjo before taking a bite.

Babiji returned about five minutes later. He reported no creatures that he could see, and that the tunnel was just another jumble of girders and wreckage from the old bridge, strewn with glacial boulders and some antique construction equipment rotting away among it. He never reached the end but had flown in a good two hundred meters. Without prompting, the bird flew down the right tunnel and once again was quickly lost from sight.

Another five minutes and he returned, reporting a dead end, but with a hefty chest tucked against the last wall.

"Well that's convenient," said Trick. "Why would a chest be down here."

"Well, this is sort of a dungeon, I think. Dungeons have treasures, don't they?" Jeni offered.

"Well yeah, but this chest sounds just a little bit... too

conspicuous," Trick said.

Part of me didn't care if it was planted there, trapped, protected by a boss—it was a chest, damn it, and years of conditioning made the urge to go down there and open it nearly irresistible. But we had bigger things to worry about.

"Later," I said. "We have a quest to finish."

We packed our refreshments and started down the left fork. Trick handed us each a vial of white cream. I remembered it from the beach—Jerry's Gel, he'd called it, and it gave bonuses to stamina, strength, and resistances. It disappeared into my hands and arms as I rubbed it in, and I could feel the muscles throughout my body tighten.

The trusses were packed in thicker here, and sections of the cave floor were replaced by crumbling lengths of the old bridge road, the lane markings still visible in some places. The going was slow, as we had to duck and wind around old pieces of machinery discarded amongst the debris, their purposes long forgotten. Farther ahead, we could see one of the glacial boulders Babiji had mentioned.

As we approached, the boulder shifted, almost imperceptibly. If it wasn't for my heightened perception, I might not have noticed it at all. Reflexively, I slipped down my info-lens and confirmed my hunch.

'Glacial Erratic, Level Unknown'

"Guys! Stop!" I shouted, and everyone complied.

I pointed at the boulder. Jeni and Trick caught on instantly and looked at the creature through their info-lenses as well. Trick swore. The thing didn't have an HP bar.

"Maybe we can sneak by it," Jeni whispered, and I

agreed. No sense in fighting it if we didn't have to. But it wasn't happening. As we got closer, the creature revealed itself for what it was.

Two thick rock legs unfolded from the main boulder, and the thing stood up, towering nearly a meter over our heads. Two powerful stone arms, ending in fists that were boulders in their own right, extended from the top portion of the boulder, and two owl-like, dark grey eyes opened in the center of the mass, locking on to us.

Jeni craned her head back, emitting an eardrum-piercing howl, then charged.

She covered the ground between her and the creature in an instant and took a swing with her clawed fist. Unfortunately, her attack bounced off the creature's rocky skin, seemingly ineffective. She shook her hand, wincing, and the thing swung one of its boulder fists, which connected with Jeni's chest.

Usually, an attack from a being like this in VR would have launched the player back a good ten feet, but here in AR, there was no way to accomplish that. The strike did register an intense impact, however, and Jeni went to a knee, swearing.

The creature brought his other fist down on the back of her head, and Jeni crumpled to the floor.

Her spider sprinkler kicked into action, dousing her with a thick jet of Dwebble's potion. This seemed to reinvigorate her, and she rolled out of the way of a blow that thundered into the floor. She rolled into a crouch, panting and trembling from the adrenaline rush.

Seeing Jeni hurt enraged me, and my hand went to the freeze ray at my hip. In one swift motion I drew and pulled the trigger, sending a white orb of energy hurtling at the elemental. When it struck, the beast froze, his arm extended over his head for another blow, eyes stuck wide open. I lashed out with my whip and caught the creature in an eye, and three parallel slits appeared in the orb, followed by blood and white ichor dripping to the dirt floor.

"Aim for the eyes!" I shouted to the crew.

The monkeys launched twin bolts from their tail stingers, catching the beast in each eye simultaneously. The creature lumbered toward me, each step vibrating through my feet and dislodging showers of debris from the ceiling. The monkeys launched another volley, while Trick's *sloven* slowed the creature's advance to a crawl. I lashed out with my whip twice more, precision strikes catching the beast in each eye. It fell to its knees.

Jeni had gotten back up by this point, and circled around to the fallen creature, her chest heaving and her lupine face a mask of fury. She screamed, not the growl of a wolf, but the full-throated scream of a severely pissed-off woman, putting everything she had into a double-fisted jab. Both claws punctured the rock-beast eyes, her arms sinking into the ruined orbs up to the elbow. Blood and bits of white and pink eyeball followed when she ripped her claws back out, and the creature collapsed backward, dead.

Jeni stood over it, breathing heavily, her fur a mess of blood, eyeball and Dwebble's goop, but despite all this, she started to laugh—quietly at first but then with increasing energy. She thrust her hands in the air, shouting as her rage turned to glee.

Trick and I gave her a semi-enthusiastic round of applause—the girl could be *scary*. She turned back towards us, and for a second, I thought she was going to attack, before I realized it was just her big wolfy smile.

We took a moment to recoup before proceeding. I took a big swig from my water bottle, and Jeni tried to clean some of the goop from her fur. She wasn't very effective.

As we proceeded, we faced two more of the rock beasts and dispatched them both with relative ease, now that we knew how to do so. Banjo informed me that I was about halfway to level seven, and I thanked him for the information.

The passageway grew narrower, and we drew closer together as we negotiated the tangle of girders, cement, and earth as it curved towards the right. We had to duck at one point, even forced to crawl for a bit. Eventually the tunnel opened into a cavern.

Jeni, in the lead and still on hands and knees, waved us to stop, then she turned her head around, one clawed finger pressed against her lips. We all held completely still and listened.

Voices.

Quietly, we crawled into the chamber and shuffled behind a broken-down excavator to our right for cover. The Alexes stayed behind, crouching in the narrow tunnel.

Peeking around the excavator, we got an unobstructed view of the chamber for the first time. Edison-style lights hanging from ceiling cables kept the room well lit.

I dropped my zoom lens and focused on the far end where, surrounded by girders and debris, a massive cement troll loomed. Its right hand was splayed out in front of it on the hard-packed earth, while it's left curled around the remains of an ancient Volkswagen Beetle, covered with a layer of cement and dirt. Its right eye was hidden by a swath of what might have been hair. Its left eye, an antique hubcap ostensibly from the same Beetle, reflected the light from the hanging lamps.

Four silhouetted figures stood in front of the sculpture. Two of them I recognized from their outlines, and I swore. It was the man in the Cahill hat and his witch of a cohort. Jeni and Trick recognized them as well, and Jeni's expression grew grim. I couldn't tell what the other two were, so I grabbed my rifle and used the scope in tandem with my zoom. The figures jumped into view behind my targeting reticle.

"Well?" Jeni whispered.

"It looks like an engineer, and..." I shifted my aim, "I'm not sure. I'm guessing an alchemist, but I can't make out her face." I noticed something mechanical standing next to the engineer on a tripod, too big to be a squirter, but I couldn't make out what it was.

We could hear snippets of their voices echo across the cavern.

"... has to be something with the car. We need to get into it..."

"...maybe we can go around..."

"...go back to the chest..."

I looked at Jeni and Trick, then whispered, "Alchemist first, then the thaumaturge."

I looked at Trick. He nodded. I looked to Jeni, and she nodded too.

I raised my rifle, sighting the alchemist in the scope. I turned it clockwise, bringing him into sharper focus.

I took a deep breath, exhaled, and pulled the trigger.

JOSHUA MASON

CHAPTER THIRTY: THE TROLL

The surprise attack instantly caused a flurry of action. The projectile hit the alchemist in the back of his head and drained nearly half of his HP. Twin blasts from the monkeys brought the target's HP down another 10 percent, as did another burst from my rifle that caught the alchemist in the shoulder. By this time, Dexi and Shorty had joined the fray, the bobcat closing the distance and sinking his teeth and claws into the man's legs while the dragonkin flamed him from above, setting his robes on fire.

The alchemist's face was a mask of pain, but he calmly reached into his flaming robes and withdrew a flask of a golden-colored liquid, then smashed it on the ground at his feet. The flames snuffed out, and he immediately regained nearly half of the damage we'd caused.

The entire enemy group was now focused on the excavator we hid behind. Thankfully, it appeared none of them had purchased their familiars yet, which was odd—I'd first run into them in front of the pet store.

The thaumaturge started lobbing fireballs in high arcs,

which plummeted to the ground around us. Our cover prevented any direct hits, but the orange orbs exploded when they hit the ground or the excavator, peppering us with flame damage. And that mysterious tripod next to the engineer—a sentry gun. Any time we'd peek from behind our cover, the gun would focus on us and deliver a blast of green energy. One caught me in the shoulder as I was lining up for another shot, but the damage was negligible. Must've been a low-level creation. It was, however, effective against Trick's minions, twice knocking Dexi out of the air and forcing Trick to recall the animal while its HP regenerated.

The man in the Cahill hat—The Baron—was looking through the scope of his own rifle and caught Trick in the chest while he was administering a potion to Dexi.

Trick shouted a profanity and fell to the ground, covering the bloody wound with a hand. In his other hand he already had a squirt potion out, and administered it quickly, limiting the damage and keeping him in the battle.

"Keep on the alchemist!" I shouted, and everyone responded.

Jeni launched multiple dart volleys across the room, the majority of which embedded themselves in the potion maker's flesh. I fired three more shots in rapid succession, forming a tight grouping in his torso, while the monkeys launched another blast from their tail guns.

The alchemist reached into his robes for another vial, but before he could imbibe the potion a final headshot from my rifle sent him to zero, and his colors dimmed. Accepting his defeat, he walked across the room and sat against the wall, arms folded over his knees.

The bobcat had taken one too many energy bolts from the sentry gun and was now frantically limping across the room back to his master. But the sentry gun was locked on, and a final shot hit the cat in the side.

"No!" Trick yelled, as the cat tumbled to the ground, and remained still. Shorty's body turned into black ash, and blew away in a miniature whirlwind, leaving nothing remaining.

"Forget about the cat for now; concentrate on the thaumaturge!" I shouted.

Our cover still held, but the fireballs continued falling from the sky, and the engineer had lobbed a couple grenades much more potent than our shrappers. One exploded about three meters behind Jeni and me, peppering us with shrapnel and draining about a third of my HP and a quarter of hers. I was below fifty percent now, but our spider sprinklers whirred at the ready behind us.

I only had three of my own grenades remaining, and debated ordering Babiji out with them, but decided it was too dangerous and lobbed them myself in quick succession. They hit the ground and exploded, peppering the remaining adversaries with shrapnel and sending them into a frenzy of swearing and shouted orders.

I fired two quick shots at the thaumaturge, who didn't seem to have any other tricks up her robes except those fireballs. The bullets caught her in the right shoulder and were followed by a round of darts from Jeni, two more blasts from the monkeys, and a jet of flame from a newly reenergized Dexi, who'd returned to hover over their heads. Within seconds the thaumaturge went down too, then went to join the alchemist against the wall.

This made me pause for a second. Sure, they were out of the PVP fight, but it just seemed odd, them sitting against the wall like that. They were dead, but they weren't. I remembered what it was like to 'die'. The black and white screen, the counter. Couldn't really do or see much of anything. It's an oddity I never experienced in VR games.

I put the thought aside for later and ordered the crew to focus on the engineer. The sentry gun hit Dexi with a barrage of energy bolts, and the dragonkin turned to ash and blew away as Shorty had done. It didn't seem to affect Trick too much—the death wasn't permanent after all, but he did have to wait for the cooldown period to expire before summoning them back. I had no idea how long that was.

A thought struck me, and I grabbed my freeze ray, tossing it over to Trick, who caught it in mid-air.

At that moment a pair of grenades landed right between Jeni and me, exploding within a second of each other. Again, it was difficult to impart the illusion of force in AR—but if this had been VR or the real world, I'm sure the explosion would have thrown us back a good five meters. The shrapnel tore into our skin, and our HP plummeted, and we both let out throaty howls of pain. In an instant, the potion sprinklers kicked on, dousing us with streams of sticky green goo and washing away the pain from my wounds that spanned from my legs to my head.

The engineer already had another grenade in hand,

cocked back to throw, but Trick was quick. A blast from the freeze ray caught the man in the shoulder and his arm froze mid-through, causing the grenade to roll out of his now useless hand and fall to the ground at his feet. Before the engineer could even begin to run, it detonated. His HP dropped like a stone, and with the added blast from my rifle and the monkey guns, the poor guy didn't stand a chance. He too faded to nearly grey and went to join the ranks of the defeated against the cavern wall. His sentry gun powered down, and the barrel pointed at the floor.

The Baron didn't stand a chance. It was three against one, we had the cover, and in PVP he was fairly useless—all he had was his rifle.

"Jacob! Let's talk about this!" the Baron shouted. "Do you even know what Jameson and the Glitch are offering? We can beat Quirk at her own game, make this place into a profit-making machine! And that's just the beginning!"

"Go to hell, asshole!" I shouted. Even the mere mention of Jameson's name brought my blood to a boil.

"Invincibility, Jacob!" he shouted. "You can bend this game to your will if you join us. Riches, women, whatever you want, can be yours. Even..." the Baron paused for effect, then said, "immortality."

I went quiet for a second, not knowing what the Baron was talking about. I peeked around the corner of the excavator, watched him pace back and forth in front of the enormous troll statue.

"Ahhh, caught your interest, did I? Haven't heard about this bit, have you?" the Baron asked. "You see Jacob,

Iggy is dying, but you know that, don't you. But here, nobody has to die. Quark can give us," he paused, his voice growing quiet, "eternal life. We just need a place to live, and that place is here. In *Panmachina*."

I looked over at Jeni and Trick. Trick rolled his eyes, while Jeni pointed at her head, moving her fingers in small circles. Never thought I'd see a werewolf do that.

"So, what do you say, Jakey boy?" the Baron crooned, his face split by a wide, toothy grin. "Come join us."

I gave him my answer with my rifle, sighting the scope on his head, and pulled the trigger. The bullet caught him in the middle of the forehead, knocking his hat off. He dropped his rifle and clutched both hands to his bloody head, falling to his knees in pain.

"That was your one chance!" he spat through clenched teeth.

I could see his HP draining to zero. I stood up, abandoning the cover, followed by the rest of the party. Back at the entrance, Al and Alex stood watching the show. Al gave me a smile and a thumbs-up.

"I'm good, but thanks, Mr. Baron," I said.

"Yeah, thanks for the offer, but no," said Jeni, walking up to stand next to me.

Trick joined me on my right, silently, and held out his hands in front of him. His right hand made a cranking motion, and the middle finger of his left hand slowly stood up. He smiled.

The animals came over too, the monkeys squatting in front of us and Babiji perching on Trick's shoulder. Trick looked at his glove and pressed the two gemstones on his knuckles. Dexi and Shorty reappeared with a pop. Dexi perched on Trick's other shoulder and the cat wound itself around his legs.

The Baron's HP was sitting at about ten percent. He frantically rifled through his jacket pockets, apparently looking for a potion. We all raised our weapons, the monkeys included, and fired. The Baron died without ceremony.

His color washed out, but he continued to glare at us. "You guys think you're hot stuff, don't you?" he spat. "I'll show you who's the freaking boss around here!"

He reached into his jacket, pulled out a gun, and leveled it at my face. Not some antiquated yet futuristic gun like my rifle, but a real pistol.

"Now what, huh? Now—" His mouth stopped mid-word, making him look as if he was whistling.

We all stepped out of his line of fire, but he didn't move. Cautiously, I approached him, carefully removed the pistol from his hand, then took a few steps back. The Alexes, seeing the gun, rushed into the room. I handed the pistol to Alex without a word, and she ejected the clip and slid the remaining bullet from the chamber before tucking the gun into the back of her belt. Al slid behind the Baron, whose mouth was still in the 'O' shape, and wrenched his stiff arms behind his back, binding them together with a thick black zip-tie he produced from a pocket.

"What the hell just happened?" I asked.

Alex stood motionless for a second, her hand pressed

to the earpiece of her goggles. "Got it," she said. She turned to us.

"Taylor here," she said, motioning to the Baron, "has been kicked out of Panmachina."

As she said the words, the Baron's—Taylor's—body became animated again. His face twisted into an expression of shock and rage.

"What the hell do you think you're doing?" he shouted, struggling futilely against his bindings. "You can't do this! Let me go!"

"Oh, but we can do this," said Alex, with a cool smile. "We have video evidence of you pulling a gun against Jacob here, and Quirk has done a little research. You seem to have acquired a great deal of money from an offshore holding company."

Taylor's face went white, and the rage left him, replaced with cold fear, his whole body sagging. Alex turned to the others sitting against the wall, who'd been watching the drama unfold with slack jaws and wide eyes. "You three, get out of here," she said. "Al, be a doll and take him to the entrance." She gestured at Taylor with the clip in her hand. "Secure him there until Jacob and the crew are done here. I'll come out with them."

The three against the wall stood up and began walking hastily towards the exit, followed by Al with his captive in tow. Alex followed them to the cavern entrance, where she resumed her post, leaning against the tunnel wall.

"Well that was different," Banjo said.

"We had the benefit of cover, and they had no familiars,

so we outnumbered them, I suppose," said Jeni.

I nodded in agreement, but soon became lost in thought as I stared up at the troll. It sat silently under the dangling lights of the cave, its dingy hubcap eye reflecting the little light it picked up. I walked up to the base and examined the VW Beetle clutched in its hand. Banjo hopped on the hand, while Lizzie scampered to the top and sat on its enormous head. *Now what?*

"Do you think we have to say something to make it come alive?" Trick asked.

"I doubt it," I said. "If I'm right, this is the real troll. They can't animate real stationary things, not at this level." *Could they?* I decided to test my theory and powered down the goggles. I wasn't in battle, and the system offered no resistance. Resting them on my forehead, I looked around the cavern.

Nothing had changed, except for everyone's clothes. Jeni, of course, had reverted to her human form.

The troll, the lights, the cavern, the excavator—it was all real. I used the brief break to rub my eyes, then put the goggles back on, powering them up.

"Everything you can see in here is real," I explained to the group. "This is the real troll statue that was buried when they covered up the old bridge."

I walked around the statue, examining it from every side. The back appeared to be buried in the cavern wall, with no way around that I could see.

"Lizzie, can you see behind the head?" I asked. "We're looking for a way behind it, around it, anything. Anything that looks out of place."

"No," she replied. "The back of his head just disappears into the wall."

Looked like we might have to go get the shovels, but I didn't want to backtrack unless we absolutely had to. I walked back around to the Beetle.

The doors appeared to have been welded shut, but they were inaccessible anyway due to the splayed fingers of the statue's left hand. Cement had been used to fill the car's interior, with no seams or openings visible anywhere. The rear left tire of the vehicle was half buried in the dirt, the rubber disintegrating. I tried peering inside the rim at the center of the tire but saw nothing of interest. The engine compartment, where the trunk was on most road vehicles, was sealed as well.

The creature's right hand was spread on the ground, a large gap visible beneath it, but closer examination showed nothing their either. Jeni and Trick had been climbing over the thing, looking for anything out of the ordinary. Trick even crawled under the statue's long, bulbous nose and peered in its nostrils. No luck.

"Damn," I said, and sat down a few meters away from the sculpture. It mocked me, sitting there in silent reverie, remnants of decades-old graffiti still visible on its grey surface. I'd come so far in the past few days, but apparently not far enough. We hadn't even been the first ones to get here.

Jeni and Trick appeared to have exhausted their ideas as well and came over to stand by me.

That hubcap eye, a small dent in the middle for a pupil, looked down on me, taunting. But as I looked at the eye, I saw something. It didn't seem attached, like maybe it stuck out perhaps a half-centimeter from the cement surface.

A surge of adrenaline followed the discovery, and I stood up quickly, walked over to it, then climbed on top of the hand clutching the car and looked up.

Yes, there was definitely a gap. I climbed up the troll's arm and onto his left shoulder, so the hubcap was at eye level, and I could see behind it. I caught a glint of gold.

"Any of you have a real knife?" I asked.

"Yeah, hold on," said Trick, and walked over to where his bag sat on the floor. He rummaged through it and pulled out a ten-centimeter blade, then returned and handed it up to me. I stuck it in the gap behind the hubcap and twisted the blade. It came free, clattering to the ground.

In the troll's eye socket was a gold gear about the size of my hand, covered with intricate geometric designs, and shining as only gold can. I laughed and gasped at the same time, and my eyes went wide. I looked at Jeni, who stood there in stunned silence, a smile plastered on her face.

"Hell, yes!" Trick shouted, pumping his fist in the air. The monkeys locked elbows and danced in circles on the troll's head. Dexi and Babiji flapped around the room, excited from all the commotion. Shorty laid on the dirt a few meters away and gave an unimpressed yawn.

"Guys, wait," I said as I inspected the gear.

The celebrating stopped. The monkeys clambered back down to the ground, and the dragonkin and falcon returned to Trick's shoulders.

All the smiles faded, replaced by looks of confusion when they saw what I did.

The gear had started spinning.

CHAPTER THIRTY-ONE: JAMESON'S TRICK

We watched in silence as the gear spun, quickly gaining momentum. I had shouldered my rifle again and stood at the ready with my hand on my whip. Jeni wolfed out, tilting her head from side to side, making the bones in her neck pop. The monkeys went into scorpion stance, ready to fire on anything that may appear, and Trick's following went on the alert as well.

The gear spun so fast that it appeared to be nothing but a gold disc in the middle of the troll's eye. A thin beam of yellow light shot out of the center, striking a hole in the wall by the entrance, which I hadn't noticed before.

As the beam of light hit the wall, a sleek metal door dropped from the ceiling at the entrance, sealing it shut with Alex on the other side.

Every one of us jumped in alarm, then drew together in a tight circle, standing back to back, our necks on swivels to see where the next threat would come from.

At the same time, the ground in front of the door began to rise, swelling into a mound, dirt and debris rolling off it.

And all around the room, small holes began opening in the walls. I was instantly reminded of the spiders we'd faced a few days ago on the way to retrieve Jeni's amulet. If only.

A high-pitched mechanical whine, like that of a drone, echoed from one of the holes in front of me, making my ears ring. I put my info-lens down and saw the mob's stats before I could see the creature itself.

'*Optiraptor, Level 4*'

"What the hell's an optiraptor?" Jeni growled, seeing the same info I did. A second later we had our answer.

The optiraptor was a single, brass mechanical eyeball, supported by a swiftly whirling hacksaw. It hovered in place for a second, its baseball-sized eyeball scanning the room until it locked on me and blinked once with a brass eyelid. I went instantly for my whip and was beginning to lash out when a silver beam lanced from the pupil, catching me in the chest. It didn't hurt, but my movement slowed considerably, felt as if I was trying to crack the whip underwater, and the tip of the whip barely moved at all before falling at my feet. The flying eyeball charged at me, and three more emerged from other holes in the wall. Judging from Trick's reaction, a few more came out behind me as well.

The slow debuff didn't last for long—about five seconds later I was at full speed, but the original optiraptor was already on me, its whirling blades cutting into my shoulder with a spray of blood. I yelped and bit back a profanity.

Attacking me with its primary means of propulsion caused it to wobble unsteadily in the air, and I used the moment to lash out with my dagger. The strike took it for about a third of its hit points, and I managed to get in one another. Jeni swiped down with a mighty claw, sending the creature crashing to the ground in a shower of sparks.

More of the whirring devils started to fill the room. I glanced over at Trick—he was having remarkable success picking them off with the freeze ray, allowing Dexi to flame them while Shorty leaped into the air, swatting them out of the sky. Jeni was a tornado of purple fur and claws, apparently gone into her berserker rage, except when hampered by the creatures' slowness debuffs.

I swore as another blade cut into my back, and a second one sliced into my thigh. Jeni was also bleeding from several cuts. I ducked and spun around, stabbing upward at the one that hovered behind me. A ray of frost shot over my shoulder—good ole Trick—and the optiraptor immediately started to fall, and I slashed at the shaft that connected the rotor to the eyeball. The creature split into two, the eyeball crashing to the floor while the rotor whizzed across the room to *clang* harmlessly off the base of the troll.

The monkeys fired once every ten seconds like clockwork, their blasts apparently very effective against these beasts. More than one fell to their scorpion weapons, and they both wore looks of grim determination that I'd never seen on a monkey. I spotted Babiji on the top of the troll's head—without any shrappers, he had nothing he could really do. I'd look into this when I got back to my guild—*if* I got back.

Another rotor left a slash across the back of my knee,

and I fell to the ground involuntarily. I swung wildly at the two buzzing around my face and arms, but they were getting in licks too. A quick glance at my wrist showed my HP was getting dangerously low, but no sooner had I looked than the spider sprinkler kicked in, dousing me with another round of healing goop. Revitalized, I sprang to my feet, slashing at whichever creature strayed closet to me.

The mound by the cavern entrance had grown into a dome about three meters across and a meter high. I scowled but didn't have time to give it much thought with the battle raging around me.

Another mechanical creature swooped in front of me, this one with an asterisk next to its name. It looked a lot like the ones I'd been fighting, except for a grin tint in the whirring disk created by its rotating blades. I swung at it, but missed, and it caught me on the shoulder. About three seconds later, a cold clamminess spread from my chest, and a dull throbbing began to pound behind my temples.

"Jakey! You've been poisoned!" shouted Banjo.

I felt like I didn't even have the energy to swing a flyswatter, but Trick jumped in with a rescue. He held out his hand, palm open towards me, and shouted, *"Curuma!"*

Warmth spread from my stomach, replacing the cold in my chest and limbs, and ten seconds later I felt myself again, aside from the cuts crisscrossing my skin in eight separate places. My dapper new clothes were in shreds. I chuckled—silly, to worry about clothing at a time like this, but I'd just got them, and I thought they made me look good, damn it.

I lashed out with my dagger at the poison optiraptor

just as Trick hit it with a freeze blast. Jeni was still slashing at anything that moved, and a couple minutes later, she pounded the last one into submission.

We didn't have time to celebrate; the ground continued to rumble and the thing by the door was now maybe two meters out of the ground. I recognized it now, a mirror image of the troll statue on the far side of the room. The doppelganger's hubcap eye had already appeared, although this one was on the sculpture's left instead.

The holes in the wall had closed, at least, and we took the respite to tend to our wounds and clean ourselves up a bit. I used a towel I'd purchased earlier to wipe the blood and Dwebble's off my skin. Most of the wounds had already closed or were nearly there, and my HP was at 80 percent.

We sat together, cross-legged, sort of an odd little pow-wow as the new troll continued emerging from the ground. The deep rumble became almost soothing, and we sat in silence while we drank juice and ate some fruit to replenish our strength.

"So, what do you think? Is it going to attack us?" Trick asked.

"I'm going to assume it is," I said. "Doubt they'd go through the trouble of having it appear like this if they wanted it to just walk over and shake our hand."

The top of the Beetle breached the dirt floor. The ground continued to rumble, and we continued to sit there. I looked at my fingernails, breathed on them, and buffed them against my tattered jacket. Jeni was drawing pictures in the dirt with a claw.

"So, if we gain control of the alley, what are you guys going to do with the income?" Trick asked.

"I'm going to go back to school, I think," said Jeni. "Forensic anthropology."

Another silence swept over us.

"You, Jacob?" Trick asked.

"I'd like to open a museum, with every video game, system and computer ever made. All playable of course," I said. "What about you, Trick?"

"I've always wanted to own a chain of candy shops," he said, staring off into space and smiling. "Candies from around the world. I'm going to call it 'Trick's Treats.'"

"Catchy," I said. It was strange, though. I'd never seen him eat candy.

"Fine, nobody ask what the monkeys want," said Banjo.

"What do you want?" I asked, smiling over at the monkey.

Banjo looked at Lizzie, sitting beside him. "Pizza?" he asked, nodding. Lizzie nodded back, and Banjo looked at me. "Yeah, pizza. Pepperoni, sausage, but no pineapple. Who in their right mind would do such a thing?"

"Hey, I like pineapple," I said.

"Oh, do you? I hadn't noticed," said Banjo.

The troll had nearly fully emerged now, nearly as tall as the original, and we got to our feet. Trick handed us each another vial of Jerry's potion, and we rubbed it into our skin. Banjo confirmed the across-the-board stat increases, and I began to stretch.

"You're also getting pretty close to level seven, just so

you know," said Banjo. He walked over to stand between Jeni and me, Lizzie at his side. The last few centimeters of the troll emerged, and the rumbling of the last twenty minutes came to a stop. The room was silent. I looked behind me at the original troll and saw the gear had stopped spinning.

The hubcap eye of the new troll started to glow a dull yellow, then shifted to a light blue, then intensified into a blinding white. As quickly as it began, the light disappeared, leaving a black afterimage in my vision. With a voice like rocks bouncing on a snare drum, the troll opened his mouth and began to speak.

"You... have... found me..." it whispered, "but you... do not yet have... what you seek."

I looked at Jeni, then at Trick, who both shifted uneasily in anticipation.

"I cannot let... the gear... fall into the hands of the unworthy," the troll grated on.

I cleared my throat sympathetically, for the troll's sake, but it did nothing to help the rumbling voice.

"Prove yourselves to me..." the slow rumble continued, "and you can have my treasure."

The troll's left hand, splayed over the ground just like the other troll, lifted about a meter into the air, then barreled into the ground with incredible force. The whole room shook so violently I swore it had to have been real hydraulics under the ground or something similar causing it. We all lost our balance and fell to the ground, bracing ourselves on all fours while the quake continued. Finally, the tremors became still, but I was having trouble concentrating on anything.

"You've been disoriented, Jacob," Banjo reported. "So have I, for that matter," he said in a quieter voice as he shakily got to his feet.

I couldn't focus and felt as if I might throw up. The ground started to shake again, but not the thundering tremor we had just experienced. More of a vibration. I could see little patches of dirt rumbling all around us, as more objects started emerging from the soil.

My head was beginning to clear, and I watched in a sort of dazed fascination at the first new creature.

It pushed the last of itself through the soil, popped into the air and sprang open, revealing parallel rows of legs on each side, then fell back to the ground and skittered toward us. It looked all the world like a dog-sized pill bug or roly-poly, plated around its circumference with parallel bands of bone. I read the info over its head.

'Armored assassin, Level 7'

"These things aren't going to be easy!" I shouted to the group. I was getting sick of the fighting. My arms ached, and my head was pounding. But we were so close to our goal. I had to stick it out.

A small, circular indentation blinked open on the creature's front, and before I could react, a thick dart shot out and embedded itself in my ankle.

"Son of a..." I began, hopping on my good foot while holding my other one in my hand. I wrenched the stake out and dropped it to the floor, examined the bloody three-centimeter hole in my ankle as the woozy coldness of poison worked its way up my leg and into my chest.

"Jacob..., Banjo began.

"I've been poisoned, I know. Trick?" I asked, but he already had his hand out, casting his antidote spell.

"Thank you. Concentrate on slowing these buggers down with the freeze ray. Save your MP for... *Aaaargh!*" Another two bolts hit me in my other leg, and the first one hadn't even healed yet.

I counted eight of the giant bugs, forming a circle around us and we hadn't even got a lick in. I forced myself to remain standing as my HP dwindled below fifty percent, and I lashed out at the nearest with my whip. The tri-bladed tip struck true but bounced off the creature's shell with nothing to show for it but a couple of sparks. The thing's HP hadn't moved. The monkeys both blasted it as well, but again for no damage. A third spike hit me in the thigh, and my vision started blurring around the edges. Similar darts stuck out of Jeni and Trick.

"Banjo! A little help!" I panted, and the monkey scurried over and started yanking darts out. Trick hit me with another antidote spell, but his MP was draining rapidly. Hopefully he'd brought a couple mana potions.

"Screw this," Jeni spat, and rushed at the nearest one.

She slid her hands underneath the thing and with a strained grunt, flipped the creature onto its back. Its segmented legs waved frantically in the air, and when it failed to find purchase, it started to close into the ball shape it had formed as it emerged. Before it could shut completely,

Jeni thrust her clawed fist into the beast's soft underbelly, and, finally, the monster's HP dropped by nearly half. She seemed oblivious as two more darts struck her in her back, as well as the stream of green gel her sprinkler doused her with. With a roar, she plunged in her other fist, and the creature's HP plummeted to under ten percent. She stood up with the squirming beast impaled on both of her fists and thrust her arms apart, ripping it in half and sending a shower of bug guts in all directions.

Another spike hit me in the shoulder, and I received my own dousing of Dwebble's finest, but the poison began to spread up my neck. Trick shouted, "I'm out of MP. I have a potion, but it's in my bag by the excavator. Babiji, can you grab it?"

The bird swooped down from the original troll's head towards the machinery. My HP was nearly full but dropping fast from the multiple doses of poison, and I was so weak I could barely lift my arms. Jeni, meanwhile, had flipped another beast over and was going to town on its underside.

Babiji returned and dropped the bag at Trick's feet, where he retrieved a vial of blue liquid, and quaffed it in one gulp. In quick succession, he cured me, and then Jeni, before returning to blasting away at the approaching beasts.

I rushed the one closest to me and tried to tip it over as Jeni had, but only managed to lift one side slightly off the ground. I tried again but got nowhere. A little embarrassing. My real strength was waning after all the exertion.

"A little help here?" I squawked. Trick rushed in next to me, grabbed the creature under its armored shell beside me.

"Heave!"

With the two of us we managed to get the creature onto his back. "Monkeys! Finish this one!" I shouted.

Banjo and Lizzie obliged climbed on top of the old troll's Volkswagen and sent two shots into the writhing creature's underbelly. It only took about a quarter of its life, but the beast couldn't right itself, and ten seconds later they had the thing down to half.

Trick and I ran around flipping the remaining bugs onto their backs, joined by Jeni who had just finished off her third. Soon the remaining bugs were all writhing with their legs in the air, and from there it was just target practice. Dexi flamed the soft underside of one, causing it to emit a high-pitched squeal. The room filled with the scent of something like cooked lobster.

Two minutes later, the bugs were all dead, and the three of us stood there with our hands on our knees, panting. We were exhausted and covered in blood and bug innards.

"Good, good," the troll rumbled. "You have shown... that you can work... together. I will give you... five minutes... to gather your strength... and your wits."

"That was way harder than it should have been," said Jeni, her chest heaving as she gulped down air.

"It was those damn poison darts. When we get back, we need to look into getting some armor of some kind. I mean, I like the suit, but I like living more." I walked over to my bag and got out my water bottle, downing half of it and splashing some on my face. It felt cold and refreshing and helped to wash away some of the sweat and dirt. I almost felt human again. I grabbed a banana from the bottom of my bag and brushed my phone as I pulled it out. The screen came to life, and I noticed a ton of unchecked messages. *Curious.* I put the banana back and grabbed the phone.

There was no signal down here—either we were too far underground, or they had installed signal jammers like they used in classrooms these days. The phone showed four unchecked messages, and all of them from Trick, the time stamp showing the last message from about three hours ago, which would have been just as we were entering the underground tunnels.

14:48 *Guys, why aren't you answering? It's important.*

14:48 *Jameson found me this morning! He came into my apartment!*

14:49 *He knocked me out with a spray injection of some kind.*

14:50 *I just woke up two minutes ago. Please, call me as soon as you get this.*

I wrinkled my brow. "Trick," I asked, looking up from the phone. "Did you send me some text messages a while ago?"

"No, why?"

I walked over to Jeni and showed her my screen. She read the messages, not comprehending at first, then looked suspiciously at Trick.

"Trick, indulge me, would you?" I asked. "Where did we first meet?"

He laughed, but it seemed tinged with a hint of nervousness. "What are you playing at, Jacob? What's wrong?"

"Just tell me. Where did we meet?"

"At Steam Whistle Alley. Just before the mayor gave his big speech, wasn't it?"

My skin grew cold—almost felt like I'd been poisoned again. Slowly, I grabbed the rifle from my shoulder and leveled it at Trick.

Trick held out his hands and started to look like he was about to protest but seemed to change his mind and dropped them to his sides. He stared at the ground, face expressionless. Then he began to smile. Head still bowed, he raised his eyes to look directly at me, and in that instant, I knew. The hate I felt for this man immediately made my blood begin to boil, and the cold that had permeated my skin seconds earlier turned into a white-hot rage.

Trick's pudgy face began to morph, extending, pointed at the chin. His frame shrank inwards, and the robes, tattered from our recent battles, became baggy, hanging on the newly skinny frame like old curtains in an abandoned house. Facial hair began to grow, shaping itself into the handlebar mustache and pointed goatee that I had come to loathe. He raised his head.

"Hello, Jacob," hissed Jameson.

CHAPTER THIRTY-TWO: FIRST GEAR

My teeth clenched so hard I thought that they might crack. "What the... *hell*... are you doing here?" I demanded. I really wanted to say something more in tune with how I was feeling, but with the rage that was festering inside me, I was lucky to put two words together.

I knew I couldn't shoot him. But I sure as hell could punch him. I had never actually punched someone before, but at that moment, seeing his stupid goatee and contempt filled eyes, I didn't give a rat's ass. I crossed the distance between us and reared my arm back...

And I couldn't move.

Quirk's voice spoke inside my head. "Actual physical violence against other players is prohibited. You have been warned. Another violation will result in your immediate suspension from the game."

I couldn't even move my mouth to reply, so I tried answering in my head but got no response. Apparently, Quirk wasn't a mind reader, at least to that extent. I was frozen for all of five seconds before she released me, but it felt like an eternity.

When I could move again, I begrudgingly lowered my arms to my sides and stared at Jameson, no more than a meter in front of me. Not breaking eye contact with him, I tilted my head up slightly.

"Quirk!" I shouted. "Can you hear me? This isn't right! This is not Trick. This is Jameson, the guy you banned?"

I got no response. Jameson clapped his hands once and laughed at me—a spiteful, hate-filled laugh that nearly made me try to punch him again.

"Jacob, Jacob... the game won't help you. Iggy can't help you, and Quirk... well, Quirk thinks I'm Trick," Jameson said with a self-satisfied air. "You're stuck with me, buddy. We are going to defeat this thing, and *we* are going to get the gear. Then the next two as well. You can't defeat me, so you might as well just go along with it."

"What do you mean, they think you're Trick?" Jeni asked spitefully. Her upper lip looked like it kept threatening to curl, and her eyes were narrowed in a disgusted glare.

"It's all qubits, isn't it?" Jameson asked rhetorically. "The great thing about quantum computers is that once they have established something is verifiably true, they tend to roll with that result." He looked back to me. "They don't like admitting when they're wrong."

"But Quirk can hear us, right now. Why isn't she doing anything to stop this?" Jeni asked.

"Maybe she can't," I said, and Jameson laughed again.

"Oh, she can. She just has more... pressing problems to

worry about right now," Jameson sneered. "As we speak, she's..." he thought for a second. "Let's call it a chess match," he finished. "Against her big brother, Quark. But the thing is, Quark doesn't play by the rules."

Something was nagging at me, and out of nowhere, it hit me. "Wait. Wait. I took off my goggles earlier and looked right at you, and you... you were still Trick!" I exclaimed. But even as I did, I began to piece out what his reply would be.

"You haven't figured it out, Jakey boy?" Jameson sniggered. "I can control what you experience now." He clapped his hands theatrically, and his face morphed back into Trick's. His green robes returned and expanded, and once again my friend was standing in front of me.

Jameson chuckled quietly. "The same exact trick," he paused, raising his eyebrows and smiling at the unintentional joke, "that I got you with in your hidey-hole. You know what they say. 'Fool me once.'"

"So why are you here then? If you can control the game, why bother with the gear at all?" Jeni asked.

I looked at her. "Blatman's puny AI can't do a millionth of what Quirk is capable of. But he can generate illusions. Small-scale card tricks. If he can fool Quirk into thinking he's part of the game, and if he gets the deed to the alley—"

"Oh, Jakey boy, it's much more than that," Jameson interrupted me. "*Panmachina* is mine! I helped build this place, and so did the Glitch!" He was slowly morphing back into his true form, and within seconds the transformation was complete. "We will run this place, one way or the other.

But for now," he said, as he tapped an antique analog watch strapped to his wrist, "I don't think you have any choice but to work with me to get this gear."

The familiars had all parked themselves on top of the original troll's head, watching silently at the scene unfolding before them. I looked up at them—Banjo looked scared out of his wits and Lizzie didn't look any better. Babiji sat so still he might have been a shadow.

I turned towards Jeni, about to ask her what she wanted to do, when the troll made my decision for me.

"Your time..." it rumbled, "is at hand."

The creature's right hand opened, releasing the Volkswagen it had held captive, and its arm raised into the air. It lifted its other arm as well and curled both stone hands into enormous fists. With a bellowing roar it slammed them into the ground.

The earth shook, throwing us to the ground, and chunks of the ceiling tumbled down around us. One hit me square on the head, knocking off my bowler and draining my HP by nearly a quarter. I swore. I could tell it was an augmented blow—the falling rock had imparted no force, only pain, a pain that had already started to ebb. But blood was trickling into my eyes, and the headache was all too real. I looked over in time to see Jeni roll out of the way of another falling rock, and Jameson had taken a blow to the shoulder. My info-lens was still active, identifying him as Trick, and showing he had lost a good chunk of HP as well.

The troll went still, breathing in enormous, grating breaths as the dust cleared. His info line was no help.

'Gearkeeper Troll, Level unknown'

When this was done, I was going to seriously look into upgrading my lenses. Then, a new line of info popped up, over the cement-filled Volkswagen.

'Volkswagen Golem, Level 9'

I could tell by the way Jeni looked over at me that she had seen it too. Neither creature had an HP bar, which felt like the game telling us we were in over our heads.

As the rumbling died down, the Volkswagen... *unfolded.* Two legs sprouted from under the chassis, and its side doors and front wheels furled out into two arms. Instead of hands, it had what appeared to be energy weapons of some kind—circular hollows at the end of each arm glowed with green crackles of electricity. Chunks of cement mixed with dirt began falling from its exterior, revealing a banana-yellow paintjob underneath. A head folded up from the golem's chest, and two shiny gears adorned the face where eyes should be, lit up with brilliant green motes of energy the same color as the creature's arms.

I've seen this somewhere before. I didn't have time to worry about it, though. The creature's left arm powered up, emitting a sound similar to a hive of bees, and blasted a streak of green energy at my chest with such force the arm recoiled like a shotgun. I twisted out of the way, but not quick enough, and the bolt grazed my chest, burning through my clothes to the skin below. I glanced quickly at the troll. It hadn't moved.

"Attack!" I screamed, and the cavern became a whirlwind of activity.

The monkeys went into their stance and began alternating their shots. The golem fired off another blast at me, which flew over my left shoulder, then three seconds later it launched one at Jameson and caught him just above the knee.

Jeni released one of her fearsome howls, then the look of intense berserker rage washed over her lupine features. She tore into the Beetle, claws blurring and sparks flying from the creature's torso. The golem brought an arm around and fired a bolt point-blank into Jeni's head. Again, no force was imparted, but she stumbled backwards away from the beast, the look of rage replaced with a wide-eyed 'what the hell just happened' look. She fell to her knees, and the sprinkler hovering nearby doused her with a jet of goo.

"Jeni!" I shouted, not taking my eyes off the creature. It sent another bolt hurtling towards me, and I dove out of its path.

"I'm okay!" she said. "I think." She got back to her feet, wobbly, but didn't charge in again.

"Wait for your openings!" I shouted. "Get in and get out."

Jameson had entered the fray, casting Trick's slow spell at the beast, lengthening the time between the blasts of green energy. He sent all three of his animals at the golem—Shorty and Babiji couldn't do much but distract the beast, but the flapping, angry bird and persistent ankle biting cat proved useful. Dexi swooped in and flamed the creature each time she passed by its head. The monkeys continued to blast unopposed from the original troll's head.

My turn, I thought and rushed the beast, activating my cross lash. I slashed four times, then four more before the golem, encumbered by Trick's slow spell, managed to get his arm around to aim at me. A giant 'X' shape rended the metal of the beast's chest, revealing hints of machinery glowing from within.

"Guys! Focus your attacks on the chest!" I ordered, and the monkeys complied, aiming their scorpion tails at the target I'd created. I lashed out again, this time with a single stroke, landing it directly in the center of the 'X', and more pieces of stone and metal fell away, exposing more inner mechanisms of this mechanical monstrosity. It appeared to be lit from the inside, but by what I couldn't tell.

Jameson hit the golem with yet another slow spell, and Jeni rushed in and pummeled the creature with her left fist and then her right, before ducking away again. She probably could have gotten a couple more swings in, but she didn't want to risk getting blasted like last time.

I looked at her for a second as she withdrew, letting my guard down, and that was all it took. A blast from the golem caught me square in the chest, and I fell back from the sudden eruption of pain. My sprinkler emptied the last of its potion onto me, and I got back to my feet, the pain already a memory. I lashed out with my whip, again connecting in the chest, and a large slab dislodged and fell to the floor. The creature's chest cavity was exposed— a complex array of gears, cogs, pulleys, flywheels—all lit up by a pulsating green orb glowing at the center.

That looks like a target if I've ever seen one. I recalled so many of the classic games—*Secret of Mana, Chrono Trigger, Act Raiser*—they all featured bosses that had a glowing core of some kind you had to aim for. Iggy must've decided to go with what worked.

Before any of us could attack the pulsating heart, all hell broke loose. The troll awoke once again with a roar like an avalanche of boulders tumbling down a mountain. He brought both fists into the air again. The golem copied the troll's movement, lifting both arms over its head, glowing green with energy. Simultaneously, all four fists thundered into the ground, and the resulting tremor made the earlier quakes seem like mere vibrations.

Once again, we were all thrown to the floor. *This has to be hydraulics; there's no way the AI can achieve this level of realism.*

No time for guessing—chunks of rock rained from the ceiling—but this time the boulders were infused with the radiant green energy. When the first one hit, it exploded, sending green shrapnel in all directions. It peppered my forehead and legs, and my face contorted with pain. Jeni and Jameson got some as well, and as the rocks continued to fall, we scrambled for the cover of the original troll. It didn't provide much, but it gave us a moment to regroup. Dexi, Shorty, and Babiji all ran behind us and took cover in the shadows, their energy spent after constantly harassing the golem.

The ground stopped shaking, thankfully, and I checked my wrist—thirty percent, and no sprinkler left. Jeni had no more squirts either, and a glance at her wrist showed she was barely better off than me.

"Allow me," Jameson said, and put a hand on my shoulder. I shrank from his touch, revolted, but before I could break contact he whispered, *"Can you feel it,"* and tingling waves of cold enveloped my body.

I remembered when Trick had first told us about that spell. It had seemed funny then. Hearing Jameson whisper it made me want to knock his teeth out.

A look at my wrist told me I was nearly full. I jerked away from his touch. No way was I going to thank the bastard. He repeated the spell for Jeni, who looked as disgusted as I felt.

The golem took advantage of the pause to concentrate fire on the monkeys, who had been peppering him with energy bursts since the beginning of the battle. Lizzie took a bolt to the chest and went flying back against the cavern wall. Banjo ran back to help her, just as another bolt sailed over his head, crashing into the ceiling.

"That's it. Now you die!" Jeni shouted, and lunged from her cover towards the monster, reactivating her berserker rage.

Jameson fired off another slow spell, and I sprinted forward as well, waiting for Jeni to move out of the way before I attacked. She went right for the heart, slicing and swiping at it with her razor-sharp claws. Every time she hit it, it dimmed and flickered, and the machinery inside started making whining and clanking noises. Twice I noticed the golem bring an arm around, but a couple of well-placed whip cracks into the interior of the arm-

cannons stopped it from completing the attack. The rest of
the animals, aside from the monkeys, had joined in again as
well, and the creature had too many targets to be effective
against any one attacker.

Jeni finally pulled back, and the pulsating green heart
was in my sights. I flung my arm out and the tip of the whip
sliced across the room, its three blades skewering the
glowing heart. The golem screamed in agony, and for a
second, I thought we had finally beaten the thing. Instead,
green energy arced out of the heart and crawled up the
length of my whip, and in less than a second the energy
reached my hand. When it did it felt as if every centimeter
of my skin was pierced with white-hot needles. I nearly
threw up, the pain so intense I couldn't even bring myself to
scream. I let go of the whip, and the pain vanished instantly.
It reminded me of when Jameson attacked me in my
apartment. I fell on the ground and lay there on my side,
staring at the scene before me, unable to move—the pain
had gone, but my brain-to-body connection had not entirely
been restored. I felt a warm wetness in my pants.

The asshole made me piss myself.

Jeni spared me a glance, then turned back to the
creature. My whip was still lodged in the thing's heart, but
the energy that had electrified it had dissipated. Jeni looked
back to me, then at the handle of the whip, lying on the floor
less than a meter from her. Without a sound, she went to
the ground, scooped the handle of the whip off the floor
wrapped it around her wrist twice, and heaved with both
hands. The whip went taut.

And the golem started to spasm, limbs and head twitching violently, uncontrollably. The heart slowly began to slide out of the chest cavity, and springs and gears shot across the room. Once again, that terrible green energy started crawling up the length of the whip, but slowly this time, as if most of the golem's energy had been expended. Jeni cried out with exertion, with frustration, with anguish—and it wasn't the wolf's voice I heard. It was Jeni's.

The energy reached the end of the whip, and as it started to crawl over her hands, her eyes went wide, and her muzzle opened.

But she didn't let go.

She continued to pull, and sparks and pieces of metal shot out of its chest. Finally, with a pronounced pop, then a fizzle, the heart fell out the creature's chest, and the golem went limp. Jeni fell to the ground in front of me.

I finally had the energy to prop myself up, and I crawled over to her. I placed my hand underneath her head, and another on her stomach. Her wolf features began to retract, and her purple fur disappeared into her skin.

"Jeni! Jeni, talk to me!" I said. She wasn't breathing! This wasn't the game, was it? *What the hell is going on here?* I pressed my ear to her chest, but I could hear nothing... no heartbeat, no breath.

I panicked. "Jameson! Help her!" I demanded, but the bastard laughed at me. The asshole laughed.

"Sorry, Jakey boy, I'm all tapped out," he said, then strolled across the room to examine the corpse of the golem.

I turned my attention back to Jeni. Time to try CPR,

although I had no idea how. But before I could start, something on Jeni's hand began radiating yellow light.

The ring. The one we'd purchased at the beginning of this mess.

The glow intensified, then died out, and the ring crumbled to dust and fell to the floor.

Jeni took a breath. Then another.

"Oh, thank God." I gasped, then threw my arms around her. I squeezed, then pulled away and brushed the purple hair out of her eyes as she opened them. She smiled at me.

"Are you okay?" I asked. "I thought you were..."

"I feel fine," she said. "Great actually." She propped herself up on an elbow to turn around and look at the destroyed golem. "Hell yes!" she exclaimed, then lay flat on her back and emitted a loud scream of joy.

"She wasn't dead, idiot," sneered Jameson. "It's the game. Fooled you, didn't it? If someone really dies in the game, the whole thing shuts off. At least it does for now, that's how they programmed it. When it goes wide, it's bound to happen eventually, so I don't know if a complete shut off is a good idea. But for now, that's what we got."

I had stopped listening to him. Jeni and I got to our feet, brushing the dirt off what remained of our clothes. The rumbling troll voice broke the silence, and we spun around to face it. I hurriedly snagged my whip from the ground, but it was still wound around the darkened heart of the golem, so I let it drop. Banjo and a very dazed looking Lizzie crawled down from the troll behind us and stood between Jeni and me. Jameson leaned back against the original

Beetle, his arms folded across his chest.

"You have done... well," the troll rumbled. "Fear... not. The fight has... left me."

I reached out and took Jeni's hand.

"My gear... is yours now."

A deep grinding reverberation filled the room again, and my heart sped up and my muscles tensed, expecting another rain of boulders. Instead, the troll grabbed the remains of the Volkswagen golem, and slowly began his descent back into the earth.

At that same moment, the door to the cavern slid open. There, in the archway, stood Al and Alex, and a wide-eyed Trick between them. Jameson's face went rigid as he saw the expressions on their faces. It looked like they wanted Jameson's head on a plaque.

Al threw his hands in the air, and the dragon he'd summoned in my apartment appeared in the room with a pop.

"Neat trick," Jameson sneered, but it wasn't his usual cocky sneer, and he didn't seem as sure of himself as he was before. With a grin, he snapped his fingers. Nothing happened. The smile left his face. His eyes began frantically darting back and forth, as if he were reading an invisible book. "Where's... the program... I can't access anything!"

The dragon, nearly the size of the troll, charged at Jameson, its ivory horn lowered. Jameson screamed and cowered into a ball on the floor. The clockwork beast flew across the room, its meter-long horn aimed for the center of Jameson's chest. The bastard had nowhere to run, and the horn sunk into his flesh. A gurgling scream erupted from him as he coughed up droplets of blood. Al clapped his hands, and the dragon disappeared without a sound, as did Jameson's wound.

"What did you do?" Jameson demanded. "Where is Quark?!" He scrambled backward on his hands and knees, like a crab, against the wall of the cavern. "I can't log out! Quark! Let me out! Let me out!"

"Quark's not here," Alex said. "This is Quirk's game. Quirk's rules." Alex clapped her hands, and holes started opening once again on the cave walls.

Jameson's eyes stretched wide with terror as hundreds of the tiny, spear-toting humanoids began pouring out of them. Their voices were high pitched and spoke in a language none of us knew, but their intent was clear. They focused on Jameson with their red, scowling eyes, and swarmed on top of him, hundreds of tiny spears stabbing, voices loud and frantic. I could barely hear Jameson's screams over the din, but that made them no less pleasurable.

This went on for a good twenty seconds, before Alex clapped her hands. The miniature army disappeared, but Jameson continued shrieking cries of pain and terror.

Eventually, he collapsed against the wall, whimpering and drooling. "This... this isn't over," he gasped.

Alex crossed the room and kicked Jameson over to his back. He got out another zip-tie and roughly bound Jameson's hands behind him. Trick and Al walked over as well. Al smiled broadly, but Trick was expressionless. He stared at Jameson for a moment, then kicked him hard in the ribs.

"There," Trick said. "I feel better." Apparently Quirk finally recognized Jameson for who he was, so the rules against physical violence no longer applied. I walked over to his cowered form, lifted my leg above him, and brought my heel down hard in his gut.

"You're right, Trick, that does feel good."

Jeni gave Trick a huge hug, and I gave him a clap on the back.

"Welcome back, man. We missed you." I said.

Banjo sprinted across the floor and leaped onto the cement hand holding the real Volkswagen. "Hey, guys, I hate to interrupt the lovefest here, but aren't we forgetting something?" He pointed up at the golden gear in the troll's eye.

I smiled at Jeni, then walked over to the troll, pulling myself up on the hand next to my monkey. I climbed the stone arm to the shoulder and removed the gold gear from the troll's eye.

CHAPTER THIRTY-THREE: DEAR IGGY

I held the gear for a moment, tossing it in my hand to get a feel for its weight. It felt real, but I wasn't ready to log out just yet to verify. If it *was* real, we'd have to keep it in a safe somewhere, perhaps even a safety deposit box. If it were just a figment of the game—well I wasn't sure yet. It wasn't my decision to make alone anyway.

I handed the gear to Jeni, who studied it, turning it over in her hands before passing it off to Trick.

"Is it real?" Trick asked.

"Not sure," I said.

Banjo scampered up my arm and perched on my shoulder as Trick handed the gear back to me.

"Oh, it's real," Banjo said. "Just like the mansion at the alley. Keep that safe, Jakey. But I wouldn't talk about it now." Banjo gave Jameson a dirty look. He was just another nipnick now, but the contempt had never left his face.

Al got Jameson to his feet and gave him a push towards the exit. "You, sir, are not going to like what happens next. We've contacted the authorities, and we have enough dirt on you that you probably won't see daylight for a good long while." Al gave me a nod and a slight smile as he led Jameson past me and they disappeared through the cavern entrance.

"I am so done with that guy," said Jeni.

"Guys?" said Banjo.

"What's up?" I asked.

"Ding. Ding, and um, another ding," he said. I chuckled. It appeared he got his dings under control finally, although he still didn't seem too pleased about it. "You have gained two levels and are now level eight. Congratulations!"

He proceeded to give me a slew of stat updates, including a rather generous increase in my intelligence and dexterity, as well as an upgrade to my basic whip and cross lash techniques. I would pour through the numbers when I got home, but for now, I was exhausted. Trick and Jeni both got two levels as well—apparently Trick gained the same amount of experience we did—his character had been playing, even if he had not. Their familiars filled them in on their upgrades, and then we packed up our things.

We scavenged for a few minutes among the remains of the defeated creatures and turned up nothing major—a few mechanical bits and pieces I might be able to use later, a medium-sized ruby, and a few of those brass-coated eyeballs from the optiraptors. Those might come in handy for something.

Trick picked up the golem's heart and brought it over to me. It was the size of a soccer ball, and warm to the touch. A series of tubes surrounded the outside, attached to small metal fittings that encircled the device at regular intervals. A faint glow still emanated from within, much dimmer now.

Finally, there was no further reason to stay in the chamber, or in augmented reality for that matter. I powered down my goggles, removed them from my head entirely and put them in my bag. Compared to the last time I logged out, or more accurately when Jameson made me think I did, this felt right— relaxing, an inexplicable feeling of relief washing over me so hard that I shivered involuntarily.

The rest of the crew logged out as well, and soon it was just the four of us and Banjo, who gave a happy chitter from my shoulder.

Jeni gave Banjo an affectionate look. "There's a biosynthetic monkey in my future, I think," she said as she took my hand. Banjo jumped from my shoulder to hers and began picking through her purple hair. We took one last look around, then left the chamber and navigated our way to the entrance. The tunnels were lit now, and we were impressed to see that very little augmentation had been done to them on our way in.

The rest of the day was uneventful, and I was more than happy to have it stay that way for a good long while. We dropped everyone off at their homes, except for Alex, who wanted to meet Al at the police station downtown. The sun had set a while ago, and I had *Galileo's* top down, as usual, taking in the cool night air of the city.

"Alex," I said, "I'm still not sure what just happened, with Jameson and all. How could Quirk not know that he wasn't who he was supposed to be?"

"That's a good question, and one I can't answer. I'm not too well versed on the quantum aspect of the game. I just catch bad guys," she replied. "From what I understand, he used his AI to replicate Trick's brain patterns. I guess it takes an AI to fool an AI. You'd better save those questions for Iggy."

"I sent him a message, but he hasn't responded," I said.

The *Galileo* slowed down, and the computer informed us we had reached the downtown Seattle Police Department precinct. Alex turned around and smiled at me as she hopped down onto the roof.

"Take care, Jacob," she said.

I set a course back to the man cave, and the computer chimed its compliance. Banjo was asleep on the seat next to me, snoring contentedly and giving the occasional twitch. The moon was out, and so were the stars, so I decided to take the long route home, swinging west over the waterfront and buzzing the Ferris wheel, lit up in shades of green. I didn't get too close, but close enough to where I could see one guy give a thumbs-up for—almost certainly—my Trek-inspired paint job.

As the *Galileo* cruised over the water with the city skyline as the backdrop, I put the van into hover mode and reclined in my chair, looking up at the stars. I took out the gear from under my shirt, where I'd attached it to a leather cord. It caught the reflection of the gibbous moon and sparkled brightly. I traced a finger over it and smiled to myself before stuffing it back in my shirt. We'd done it.

As the van continued to hang over the still water of

Puget Sound, I ordered the computer to call Iggy. About five seconds later, an automated reply told me the person I was trying to reach was unavailable. I left yet another message, then disconnected the call.

"Computer, call Trick," I said. His wide-eyed, freckled face popped up on my viewscreen. His red hair was unkempt and stood out all over the place, but he didn't seem to care.

"Hi, Jacob!" he said. "Man, have you logged into the message boards yet? We're famous, man! We're all anyone can talk about. Well, all the 300 can talk about anyway. Everyone's been waiting on a statement from Iggy, but he's been MIA for the past couple of days it seems. I can't wait until we can tell other people about this—this game is going to be huge!"

It was good to see that the day's events hadn't affected him too much. Back in the cavern, he was sullen, pissed off—but now, he appeared to be his old self again.

"We're famous, huh? Cool," I said. "Personally, I think I'm going to take a little break from the game. Lie low, play some old RPGs. You're always welcome to come on over, whenever you want."

A voice rang out from somewhere off-screen. "Patrick? Patrick! Get your butt in here and finish cleaning the kitchen!"

His expression went from gleeful to annoyed in about a half a second. "I'm coming, Mom," he said over his shoulder. "I might take you up on that offer sooner than you expect, Jacob." He gave me a half-hearted salute and logged off.

I chuckled after he hung up. Didn't see that coming, but rent was prohibitively expensive these days. Lots of twenty-somethings still lived with their parents.

I pulled out my e-cig and took a puff, blowing the vapor into the air. There was very little breeze, so the cloud just hung there over the van, drifting over the edge and down toward the water. I watched fingers of the vapor create little eddies and swirls before fading out of sight. Time to call Jeni, but she beat me to the punch.

"Hey," she said as I answered the call.

"Hi," I said, with a sheepish smile. Why was I feeling so nervous? "I was about to call you."

"Jakey... do you think I can come..." she paused, looking a bit bashful herself. Good to know I wasn't the only one. "I mean... can we hang out tonight?"

I was at her apartment twelve minutes later.

I stood up as she entered the *Galileo* and gave her an awkward hug. I went to kiss her, but my mind shouted *'abort!'* at the last second, and I ended up kissing her just below her right eye.

Smooth, I thought. *I was doing good a day ago, now I'm back in tenth grade.* She just smiled and took my hand before sitting down on one of the side benches. I sat down next to her.

"Where to?" I asked.

"Can we get out of the city for a bit? I'd like to see the stars without the light pollution, you know?" I nodded, but part of me didn't want to. She looked terrific in the city lights.

"East or west?" I asked. "It's all mountains either way."

"Let's go east," she said. "I haven't seen Snoqualmie Falls since I was a girl."

"East it is," I said, then ordered the computer to set a course for the falls.

Once the lights of the city were behind us, Jeni looked over to me. She was beautiful in the moonlight, against the darkened silhouette of the pine tries with the stars sprinkled above. Her hand went to my head, and she started stroking the white streak, tucking behind my ear like I always did. I decided to tell her everything. The game, the fire, down to the last detail. She looked at me, silently. Her eyes held no judgement, just compassion, and a moment later, her arms were around me, her head resting on my shoulder.

Less than a half hour later, the cascading waters of the falls were below us, lit up with giant spotlights. She was right—the stars were an order of magnitude brighter out here. The sky looked like the cover of a sci-fi novel, minus the spaceships. I ordered the *Galileo* into a low hover beside the waterfall, perhaps 100 meters away, close enough to where we could feel the cool mist, even through the climate shields. A few lights twinkled in the resort hotel at the edge of the falls, but no other signs of civilization could be seen. Banjo snored away on the dashboard.

Jeni turned to. "Thank you for taking care of me back in the cavern, Jacob," she said. "I wasn't in any real danger, you know."

"Yeah, I know. I overreacted. It's just... I—"

She cut me off with a kiss. I once heard of a kiss described as 'toe-curling,' but I never understood what they meant. Not until that kiss. Aside from a few embarrassing moments in VR, my kissing experience was... limited. About a minute later—or five, my sense of time had been completely shot by the sensory overload—she pulled away.

"Jacob," she said, looking down at her feet before smiling up at me again, "what do I press to turn these benches into a bed?"

A couple hours later, I sat propped up on my pillows with Jeni's head on my chest, breathing the deep breaths of sleep. I kept on expecting her hair to smell like grapes, but she smelled herbal, perhaps a little sweet. It was intoxicating and heightened the star-watching experience. *I have to come out here more often.*

Jeni wasn't my first, but it had been a very, very long time, and I was slightly delirious from the rush of it all. I kissed her on the top of her head, then pulled out my phone. I had a letter to write.

Dear Iggy,

I hope you are doing well. We've heard of your condition, and if there's anything you ever need from us, let us know. I can't imagine how you must feel, but I think that if I were in your position, I wouldn't want anybody to treat me differently. I'd want to kick back and play a few more games. Speaking of which, you owe me a rematch.

Panmachina AR is an absolutely beautiful game, and the experiences of the last few days have been amazing. Quirk has done an incredible job graphically. I never once noticed any errors in the rendering of the augmentation. The buildings, people, outfits – they all blended in seamlessly and made the game nearly too immersive at times.

That being said, I didn't like everything about it. The PVP was a bit clunky. Maybe we can institute an arena combat system or something, to let the players work out those PVP needs, and we can leave the rest of the world to the story. Just a thought.

I recommend everyone start the game with their familiars or have it be one of the very first quests. Banjo has proven invaluable to me, and I think it helped a great deal with my enjoyment in the early levels. If you could work out a deal with the biosynth people—it's kind of nice having that in-game out-of-game dynamic with Banjo. He didn't seem to mind at all either way, and Jeni looked sad whenever her pet would leave when we logged out and mine wouldn't. Maybe I'm just imagining it—I dunno.

I'm going to take a little time off from the game. The whole deal with Jameson and the Glitch was very exhausting, to be honest, and I'd like to talk with you face to face before I log back in. The man tortured me, Iggy. I thought I was going to die. I know you're not at fault here, but he tortured me using loopholes in the game, as far as I can tell. Your game. I hope Quirk can find out what those loopholes are and close them because I don't want to deal *with that ever again, or have it happen to someone else. I don't want to see Jameson again. So please, get ahold of me as soon as you can. I am really into this game, but it's hard to concentrate on it when so much is going haywire. Oh – if you could let us adjust our own pain levels, that would be great. Your game freaking HURTS, and I think it might scare a lot of players away.*

Sincerely,
Jacob Tutor

I hit send on the email, and lay back on the bed, staring up at the endless stars and breathing in the scent of Jeni's shampoo. The viewscreen said it was twelve degrees outside, but it was a pleasant twenty-three within the confines of the van's climate forcefields. Within minutes, I was asleep.

When I awoke the next morning, it took me a couple seconds to remember where I was. I closed my eyes again against the brightness of the blue morning sky. I stretched before opening my eyes, then winced. My muscles were *sore*. Augmented reality had made me use muscle groups I didn't even know I had.

I rolled over to my side and opened my eyes to look at Jeni.

Except Jeni wasn't there.

I bolted upright in bed, scrambled to my feet. The *Galileo* was still hovering over the mountains near the falls, but Jeni was gone. My heart raced as the adrenaline pumped and panic set in.

Banjo... Banjo was gone too. I screamed both of their names, but of course it was pointless this high up. Then my hand went to my chest. The gear was missing as well.

I turned in circles a couple of times. The fog that came from just waking up had gone, replaced by gut-wrenching dread.

Then the viewscreen beeped, and the computer informed me I was receiving a call. I answered it.

There on my screen was the smiling, sweaty face of Chuck Blatman, contorted in a twisted mask of pleasure. The Glitch.

"Lose something?" he asked.

THE END of BOOK ONE
PRESS START TO CONTINUE

Thanks for taking the chance on a new author. For information on Second Gear: Steam Whistle Alley Book Two, as well as other projects I'm working on, please visit my website at joshuamason.net. Make sure to sign up for the mailing list as well. In addition to series news I'll be giving away some merch and signed copies.

One of the best things you can do for a new author is leave a review. I value all feedback, and every review helps me out, even if it's only two words. Even if you don't, thank you for making it to the end of this book. See you in book two.

www.joshuamason.net
www.steamwhistlealley.com
www.facebook.com/steamwhistlealley
www.twitter.com/whistlealley

ABOUT THE AUTHOR

Joshua Mason has done a little bit of a lot of things. He was a Nintendo game play counselor back in its pre-internet heyday. He got a degree in archaeology from the University of Washington, and has been on a few digs, from the round-the-clock daylight of a northern Alaska summer to the remote Spice Islands of Indonesia. He spent four years teaching English in Jakarta, where he met his wife. They now live in Seattle.

Made in United States
Troutdale, OR
07/26/2024

21531596R00289